Praise for *Toad Words*

"…a book of re-told fairy tales, all in the quirky, matter-of-fact-in-the-face-of-total-nonsense style that I've always loved. They're often dark, sometimes sad, but always endearing, even when they're disturbing."
　　—Pixelatedgeek.com

Praise for *The Seventh Bride*

"…[a] knack for creating colorful, instantly memorable characters, and inhuman creatures capable of inspiring awe and wonder."
　　—NPR Books

Praise for *Bryony & Roses*

"The writing. It is superb. Ursula Vernon/T. Kingfisher, where have you been all my life?"
　　—The Book Smugglers at Kirkus Reviews

Praise for *The Raven & The Reindeer*

"…an exquisitely written retelling of Hans Christian Andersen's *The Snow Queen*… I love this book with the blazing passion of a thousand suns. I'm sitting here almost crying at the thought that I had to wait until I was fifty-seven (almost fifty-eight!) years old before having a chance to read this book."
　　—Heather Rose Jones, *Daughter of Mystery*

Summer in Orcus

T. Kingfisher

This is a work of fiction. Nothing is true, except for the bits that are, and even those don't resemble anybody in particular.

SUMMER IN ORCUS

Published by Sofawolf Press, Inc.
St. Paul, Minnesota
www.sofawolf.com

ISBN 978-1-936689-59-0
Printed in the United States of America
Third trade paperback edition: January 2019

Cover and interior art by Lauren Henderson

For Cassie
Minion Extraordinaire

Chapter One

Once upon a time there was a girl named Summer, whose mother loved her very very *very* much.

Her mother loved her so much that she was not allowed to play outside where someone might grab her, nor go away on sleepovers where there might be an accident or suspicious food. She was not allowed to go away to camp, where she might be squashed by a horse or bitten by diseased mosquitoes, and she most certainly was not allowed to go on the Ferris Wheel at the carnival because (her mother said) the people who maintain the machinery are lazy and not very educated and might get drunk and forget to put a bolt back on and the entire thing could come loose at any moment and fall down and kill everyone inside, and they should probably leave the carnival immediately before it happened.

Occasionally, when Summer expressed a desire to do some of these very dangerous things, her mother would get quite upset. She would grab Summer's chin and stare deep into her eyes, as if she could see straight down to Summer's heart, and say, "I'm only saying this because I love you. You're all I've got, and I can't let anything happen to you. You understand that, right?"

And Summer would nod and say that she understood, because what else could she do?

Her mother went through weeks when she was worse than usual—barging into the bathroom to make sure Summer wasn't drowning in the bathtub (she was nearly TWELVE! And she could dog-paddle really well, the swim instructor said so!)—or walking through the house, calling her name frantically, and when Summer dropped whatever she was doing and came running to see what the problem was, her mother would only say, "I just wanted to know where you were," and go back to cooking or working on her computer. It was very difficult.

Summer had never had a father, and wasn't entirely sure what you did with one, and certainly her mother never had anything good to say about the one Summer didn't have. But she sometimes thought that it would be nice to have a brother or a sister, not because she particularly liked other children but because it would have been nice to have somebody to share the burden of her mother's love. If there had been two of them, maybe they could have taken turns. Surely her mother wouldn't have the energy to keep barging in on *both* of them in the bathtub.

Unfortunately, there was only Summer.

It is hardly surprising, given this sort of treatment, that Summer was very timid (at least at home) and soon learned to stop asking to ride the Ferris Wheel or go on sleepovers. But it is also not very surprising that in the secret depths of her heart, where her mother could not go, she had vowed to make her escape.

She didn't want to hurt her mother. During good times, her mother baked cookies and sang songs and showed her how to tie her shoes and helped her with her homework when it was hard (and sometimes when it wasn't, which was a little bit annoying.) She just wanted her mother to love her a little bit less, like a normal person, so that she could go to camp and not have to leave the carnival early.

Sometimes when her mother grabbed her chin and stared into her eyes, Summer wondered if she could see these traitorous feelings lurking down in the depths. It seemed as if she ought to be able to, because the feelings were so strong, as if they were big rebellious slogans wallpapered around the walls of her heart, saying I THINK I COULD PROBABLY RIDE A HORSE IF IT WAS NICE and I AM NOT AFRAID OF THE FERRIS WHEEL.

But her mother never said anything about it, and so Summer went on thinking these thoughts, and over time she thought them more and more.

～

One day in spring, when she was playing in the back garden, a house walked into the alley.

The house was very clearly walking, because the roof would go up when it took a step and then sink back down at the bottom of the step, then bob up again. Summer couldn't see its feet because there was a high wall around her back garden, but she could not think of any other explanation.

The roof of the house was small and sharply peaked, with a jutting gable over the front door. Summer stared at it open-mouthed, then ran to the gate in the wall that led to the alley.

It was a wooden gate, higher than Summer's head, and it had a big metal latch with a padlock through it. Summer's mother would have bricked up the gate entirely if she could have, so that criminals couldn't come through it, but she had to leave another exit in case the house burned down and they couldn't get out of the front door. She had compromised with the padlock, and had also told Summer seventeen times that she was never, ever to open the door, particularly not if anyone knocked and asked to be let in. Since Summer had no idea where the key was, she couldn't have done so anyway, and so was spared being told an eighteenth time.

But even if the gate didn't open, there was a large crack between the hinges and the wall, and Summer put her shoulder against the bricks and peered out through it at the house.

The house had gigantic scaly legs like a bird. They went up past Summer's shoulders and they ended in clawed feet as big as bathtubs. The round scales on the front of each leg were the size of automobile tires.

As she watched, the house took another step forward. The roof went up and came bobbing down. The house's foot came down on an old soda can in the alley and it went *crink!* and was crushed flat.

"Whoa," said Summer.

The house heard her. It stopped, and instead of taking another step forward it put its other foot down beside the first one and hunkered down on its heels.

The underside of the house was now about three feet from the ground. The bird legs didn't seem to attach to the house in any way that Summer could see. They vanished instead into a tangle of pipes, which were probably plumbing, but which looked suspiciously scaly, as if they had also been made out of chicken feet.

A little faucet, the sort you would attach a hose to, stuck out from the side of the house nearest Summer. Instead of a knob with spokes, it had a little skull on it, no bigger than Summer's palm. The skull's jaws were open in a huge grin, and it was turned sideways so that it looked rather silly as well as alarming.

It wasn't a very large house. It couldn't have more than two rooms in it, one upstairs and one down, and even those wouldn't be any larger than Summer's own bedroom. Even so, the sides of the house came very close to the walls on either side of the alley. If it walked by the gate, Summer would be able to fit her hand through the gap at the hinges and touch the faucet as it went past.

She twisted around so that she could look down the alley in the other direction. Surely someone was going to come along any moment—a delivery driver or one of the people who parked in the alley sometimes—and get out and complain about the house blocking the road?

But nobody did. Summer took a quick look behind her at the back porch to make sure that her mother hadn't come out.

One of the windows of the house flew open and the shutters banged back. "Not here!" said a woman's voice from inside the house. "The next yard over, fool house!"

The house stamped its feet and settled even lower to the ground.

"Gah!" The woman reached through the window and slapped the house's outer wall. She was wearing long black gloves with the fingers cut out of them. "The next one! I'll have you breaded and fried and made into colossal drumsticks!"

The bottom of the house hit the concrete of the alley with a thud.

"Saint Sunday's bones!" cried the woman, pulling her hand back, and then she said a great many other things, some of which were extremely rude. Summer paid careful attention to these and committed many of them to memory.

After a moment, the front door opened and the woman came out.

She was very old and very stout. Her black gloves went up to the elbow and the ends were frayed and unraveling. Her dress was gray and shapeless and she wore a tall purple hat like a top hat, with a live salamander on top of it. Summer could tell that the salamander was alive because its throat pulsed as it breathed, and it blinked its eyes very slowly in the sunlight.

She was leaning on a cane but could stand without it, because as soon as she stepped out of the door she turned around and whacked the house across the gutters with the cane.

The house rattled its pipes and slammed all its windows shut with a *hmmmph!* sound.

"Glorified chicken coop! I'll take you apart and sell you for scrap!" cried the old woman. "You're not my first house, you know! I had a marvelous cottage that padded about on leopard feet, and I had it shot and stuffed and turned into a storage shed for a much more minor infraction than this!"

Summer could not help but feel sorry for the leopard-footed house and made a small noise of dismay.

The old woman whipped around, scowling, and Summer did not pull back nearly quickly enough.

"Aha!" she cried, stomping toward the gate. Summer backed away hurriedly, but although she could not see the old woman, she could hear the click of her shoes and the tap of her cane. "I see you there! Spying on me, were you?"

"I was not!" said Summer, indignant. "I was just looking! I've never seen a house like that before!"

There was a long pause, during which Summer remembered that she was never ever *ever* in ten million years on pain of death supposed to talk to strangers, and the old woman went *hmmmph!* rather like the house.

"Well," said the old woman grudgingly, "I suppose that's true enough. There aren't any other houses like mine. What's your name?"

"I'm not supposed to talk to strangers," said Summer, and because that felt horribly rude, she added, "I'm sorry." She looked back over her shoulder, but her mother had not come out to demand to know who she was talking to.

"If you're waiting for someone to come and make introductions, you'll be waiting a long time," snapped the old woman. "Besides, it's not *strangers* you need to worry about—it's the ones you *know* that get you." She came closer and peered through the crack in the gate. Summer could see one bright black eye and the side of her nose. "I'm Baba Yaga."

"I'm Summer," said Summer.

"Hmm. Suits you. What do you think of my house?"

"It's a very interesting house," said Summer, "but I don't think you should hit it. It's not very nice."

The house rattled its pipes in a loud, satisfied manner, and Baba Yaga cackled. "Fair enough!" She turned away from the gate to say, over her shoulder, "I see why you stopped."

The house preened a little.

Baba Yaga put her eye back to the gap in the hinge. "Open the gate, will you?" she said. "Whispering through cracks is all very good for foolish lovers and eloping brides, but you're too young and I'm too old and have had far too many husbands besides."

"I can't," said Summer. "I mean, there's a padlock. It's only a little bike lock, but it's still locked. And my mother would never let me. And how many husbands have you had?"

"Plenty," said Baba Yaga. "Good and bad and most points in between, starting when I wasn't much older than you and had less sense than the gods gave geese. But never mind that. A padlock, eh?"

Summer heard the crack of her cane against the wooden gate, and Baba Yaga chanted, "Open, lock! Open, bar!"

The padlock twisted neatly open and fell off the latch. The gate swung silently open.

Summer took another step back. Baba Yaga was rather alarming (if quite interesting) and if her mother saw her talking to a strange old woman in the back garden, with the gate open, Summer was going to be in more trouble than anyone had ever been in in the history of the world.

Baba Yaga stood framed between the walls, with her house squatting behind her. The salamander on her hat fixed Summer with eyes like wet pebbles.

"Are you frightened?" asked the old woman. "You should be, you know. I am as old as sinning and twice as dangerous. I drink my beer from the skulls of heroes."

Summer did not know that women drank beer. Her mother never drank beer. She called it nasty, low stuff and said that she'd never allow it in the house.

Summer said as much to Baba Yaga.

The old woman's eyes narrowed. "You're dangerously ignorant, girl," she said. "It is not your fault at the moment, though if you grow much older, it will be."

Summer looked back toward the house.

"Hmmm," said Baba Yaga. "Stand, girl, and let me know you."

Baba Yaga took two steps forward, digging her cane into the ground. Summer knew that she should run away, run back to the house and get her mother and call the police immediately, but her feet seemed to be stuck to the ground. She tried to lift one up and it stayed stuck, as if the soles of her sneakers had turned to glue.

Baba Yaga came up right next to her, close enough that Summer could smell her. She didn't smell like an old woman, like cold cream and antiseptic, the way Summer's grandmother smelled in the home. She smelled like an animal, like a cat's fur, like sharp herbs and old books.

The salamander on her hat twitched its tail restlessly back and forth.

The old woman stared into Summer's eyes, down deep, deeper than her mother ever saw. Summer could feel Baba Yaga looking all the way down into her, into the chamber with her thoughts written on the walls.

"Well," said Baba Yaga, taking a step back, and Summer could move again.

She could have run, but she didn't. She felt dizzy. She blinked several times and rubbed her forehead. She could hear crows cawing behind her eyes.

"All right!" Baba Yaga called over her shoulder to the house. "You were right, you overgrown lump of yesterday's architecture!"

She turned back to Summer and poked her in the chest with the tip of her cane. "Tomorrow. You come to the house tomorrow, and I'll grant you your heart's desire, unless I'm in a bad mood, in which case I'll probably suck the marrow out of your bones. Either way. Tomorrow, you hear?"

And she turned and stumped out of the garden, leaning on her cane. The gate slammed shut behind her and the padlock clambered up the wooden crosspiece on the gate and swung itself out to the latch.

The bird-footed house stood up. It paced down the alley, two yards down, to the house with a FOR SALE sign out front. Then it rose up high on one leg and stepped daintily over the wall.

For a moment it stood there, very tall against the sky. An upstairs window sash rose an inch or two, and the house winked at Summer.

Then the house settled down on its heels, and that was that, at least until tomorrow.

Chapter Two

Summer spent most of that evening trying to decide on her heart's desire.

For a number of years—at least since she turned ten—she had wanted to be a shape-shifter, or if that wasn't possible, at least to understand the language of animals. But being a shape-shifter would be best. Imagine being able to turn into any animal that ever lived! She could go anywhere—fly like a bird, see with her ears like a bat, swim in the water like a fish. She could talk to the oozy newts along the foundation of the house and the alley cats that strolled along the top of the fence. It would be *incredible.*

When other girls at school were mean to her, she could turn into a wolf—a bear—a wooly mammoth!—and trample them to pieces, or at least pretend that she was going to, because if it came right down to it, Summer was not sure that she wanted to trample anybody.

(This may seem an unusual ambition, but Summer had read a great many books about magic and animals and changing your shape. Summer's mother believed that books were safe things that kept you inside, which only shows how little she knew about it, because books are one of the least safe things in the world.)

Summer had just about decided to ask Baba Yaga to make her a shape-shifter—surely someone with a walking house would not find that difficult!—when it occurred to her that while it was all very well to think about trampling the members of the fifth-grade class, if somebody saw her, there would undoubtedly be trouble. Turning into a woolly mammoth was bound to get you detention or suspended or even expelled.

If you were expelled, your parents had to teach you at home. Summer would never get to leave the house except with her mother. She would never get to be the person she was at school, when her mother wasn't looking, again. (Summer's mother, in addition to being wrong about books, would also have been quite surprised to learn that her daughter was a very different person at school than she was at home. This is a common problem among parents.)

Summer poked at her dinner with her fork, chasing bits of corn around the plate and teasing a few strays out of the mashed potatoes.

If somebody found out you could turn into animals, what would happen? It would be awesome if they asked you to talk to real animals and find out what was wrong with them—maybe tell endangered species what to do to not be so endangered any more, maybe warn them about cars and people with guns—but Summer had a gloomy notion that it wouldn't be like that. She had read enough books to know that she'd probably wind up in a government lab somewhere, with people poking her with needles and hooking her up to big monitors covered in jaggy lines.

This was definitely not her heart's desire.

"You're awfully quiet," said her mother. "What are you thinking about so hard?"

Summer looked up guiltily. "Nothing."

"Did something happen at school?"

"No." Summer took a hasty mouthful of mashed potatoes.

"So what were you thinking about?"

"Um…"

Summer knew when she'd taken too long to answer because her mother's smile got brittle around the edges and the skin under her eyes went funny and tight. "Fine. Don't tell your mother, then." She turned away from the table.

I wish I was an orphan, thought Summer, and was so immediately horrified at her own thoughts that she said out loud, "I was thinking about being a shape-shifter and whether people would want to poke you with needles and stuff to find out how you did it."

"Oh, Summer," her mother said, and laughed, and that was all right then.

Her mother cried after dinner. This happened sometimes. Summer looked up and saw that her mother had put her face in her hands and that meant that it would be one of those nights.

She knew her job by now. She put her arm around her mother's shoulders and said, "It'll be all right." Then her mother said, "No, it won't be," and Summer said, "What's wrong?" and her mother talked about how bad her job was and how she was probably going to lose it because no one appreciated her and one of her co-workers was talking about her behind her back.

It was all very normal. Both of them knew their role and performed it, like actors in a long-running play. As long as she could remember, Summer's role had never really changed. It was always a little frightening, but it was also always the same. She could perform her part with only half her attention, while the rest of her thought about her heart's desire.

"I know he's out to get me."

"That's not nice of him. Why are people like that?" *I could be a bat! I could finally find out if sonar's like hearing things or if it's like seeing things…*

"People are terrible, most of them. They never appreciate anything. And after I helped him with all those files!"

She cried a bit more. Summer patted her back and thought about sonar. Maybe she could be a dolphin after she was a bat, and compare the two?

"It's all right, Mom. It'll be okay."

"No, it won't…it's always like this…"

When the storm had passed, there was only the final bit of the ritual, where Summer said, "I love you" and her mother said, "At least someone does!" and made a kind of pained half-laugh. That meant it was nearly over. Every now and again it would all start up again, but those nights were rare. Summer hoped very much this wouldn't be one of them. She had other things to think about, important things, like echolocation and dolphins and bats.

～

Summer laid in bed that night, staring at the darkened ceiling, and wondered if she'd meant it when she'd thought, *I wish I was an orphan.* What if you didn't *need* to tell Baba Yaga what you wanted? What if she could look all the way down into your heart and pull it out without any help?

What if her heart's desire really *was* to be an orphan?

She didn't *think* it was. She loved her mother. She would have cried for ages if her mother died.

On the other hand, she was eleven years old and her mother still bought safety scissors and had childproof plastic caps on all the electric sockets. She didn't want her mother *not* to love her, she just would have liked things to be…different.

Thinking like this was like trying to walk down a hallway in the dark, feeling around with her foot for each step, except the hallway was inside her chest and she wasn't sure where she was going at all.

She fell asleep, still wondering what her heart's desire could be.

School dragged on forever, and Summer didn't raise her hand once. She was usually a pretty good student so the teacher didn't call on her or embarrass her in class, but Mrs. Selena did give her a rather thoughtful look when she ran out the door to recess.

She was not allowed to take the bus home because other kids on the bus might try to give her drugs, so she waited by the curb with her book bag until her mother pulled up with the car to drive her home. Summer spent the ride home staring out the window and not talking, but fortunately her mother was listening to a radio program and didn't notice.

Her mother went to work on her computer, and Summer went out to play in the garden. She looked immediately over the wall and saw the roof of the bird-footed house.

She waited ten minutes, to make sure that her mother wasn't going to get up from the computer, then went to the gate.

The padlock had locked itself again, and Summer wasn't sure what she should do. She didn't think she could climb over the gate, and if she tried to go back through the house, her mother would probably notice it.

Still, if it had worked for Baba Yaga yesterday, maybe there was still a little magic left on it…

"Open, lock," she whispered to the padlock, putting her lips right down next to it. "Open, bar! Oh please, please open!"

The lock made a cheerful little *click!* and slid open.

"Oh, thank you!" said Summer. "Good lock!" She put it into her pocket and looked around quickly. She was probably going to get in horrible trouble, but if Baba Yaga could grant her heart's desire—that was worth it, wasn't it?

She slipped the gate open and pulled it most of the way shut behind her, just enough so the latch wouldn't catch. Then she pelted down the alleyway to Baba Yaga's house.

The gate was open. Summer peered around the edge of the wall, then slipped into the yard.

The house was standing several feet above the ground, scratching idly at the grass. There were deep gouges in the lawn. When it saw Summer, it clapped all its windows and plopped down onto the ground.

Now that she had to actually walk up to the door, she felt so nervous that she was almost queasy, as if someone had dropped a brick into her stomach.

What if Baba Yaga *hadn't* been joking yesterday, and she was in a bad mood and sucked the marrow out of Summer's bones?

What if it turned out that Summer was a horrible person and her heart's desire was an awful thing that nobody should want?

She halted halfway to the door and pressed her hands to her chest.

She hadn't noticed yesterday that there was a skull on the front door, right in the middle, where a normal person might hang a wreath.

The house lifted its back end up and inched forward a little, like a dog wanting to play. This must have made the floors tilt inside, because Summer heard a banging and sliding of furniture and Baba Yaga yelled, "Fool house! I'll trade you in for one with turtle feet and a three-car garage!" The house sank back down, but wiggled forward a little more, until the front door was only a few feet away.

The skull on the door wasn't human, or at least it wasn't entirely human. It had big canine teeth like a dog and long antlers like a deer.

Was it a door knocker? Was she supposed to grab the dangling jawbone and rap it against the door?

Summer gulped and reached out her hand.

The skull opened its eyes.

Since it had empty eye sockets and no eyelids, Summer wasn't quite sure how its eyes had been closed in the first place, but something flipped in the eye sockets and the skull was very definitely looking back at her.

"I shouldn't go in if I were you," said the skull.

Summer squeaked and took a step back.

"I did," said the skull mournfully. "You can see where I wound up."

"Did she *kill* you?" asked Summer, ready to run away at once.

"Well," said the skull. "Well. Not *exactly*. Not as such. I was already dead. Sort of dead. Rather dead. I came in feet first, you might say. But I didn't ask to be made into a door knocker!"

"I can see how that would be bad," said Summer. She put a hand on her neck, in the spot where you could feel your pulse. Her heart was pounding furiously. "Um. Is she—is she in a bad mood?"

The skull clattered its jaw from side to side. "Not today. She's in a pretty good mood, I'd say. She's had breakfast and lunch and afternoon tea. I shouldn't go in if she were waiting on dinner. Baba Yaga gets very impatient if she hasn't been fed."

Summer exhaled. It didn't sound as if the marrow was going to be sucked out of her bones. Of course, there was the matter of the skull—but it had already been dead, and it was a little wicked to fool around with dead people's bones, but not nearly so wicked as making them dead in the first place.

"Did you always have antlers?" she asked. "When you were alive?"

"No," said the skull, glancing up at its antlers with obvious pride. "I wish I had. They're the best thing about being a door knocker. At Yuletide she turns them into reindeer antlers. Those would have been marvelous."

"They're very good," said Summer. "Can I go in? She said she'd give me my heart's desire."

"Oh, well then," said the skull. "If that's what she *said*. She doesn't go back on her word, you know, although she could teach the Devil a few things about loopholes."

The door swung open.

Summer stepped up into Baba Yaga's house and went inside.

Chapter Three

The inside of the house was dark and smelled strongly of bleach. That wasn't the smell that Summer would have expected inside a magical bird-footed house, but maybe even magic bathtubs needed scrubbing occasionally.

"There you are," said Baba Yaga. She was sitting in a rocking chair in front of the fire. There were a few coals in the fireplace, giving off a little red light.

"Is now a good time?" asked Summer. "Only I don't know if I can get away later, because of my mother—"

"Pick a candle," said the old woman, ignoring this speech.

"A c-candle?"

"One of the ones on the table, girl! Quick, quick! I may be immortal as makes no odds, but I'm still not getting any younger."

"Oh," said Summer. "Um. Okay." There was a little round table in the middle of the room, and on it stood a dozen candles. They were all colors and sizes. A few of them had been melted partway down. Several were shaped like animals. Summer's hand hovered over a silver unicorn, with the wick coming out of its horn, but then settled on a plain beeswax frog. The wick had been burned down a little way already and beads of honey-colored wax ran down its sides.

"This one," said Summer.

"Bring it here."

The frog candle felt surprisingly heavy in her hands. She walked towards Baba Yaga's chair but stopped a pace short, a little afraid.

"Scared?" asked the old woman, raising an eyebrow. Her hat with the salamander was sitting on the mantelpiece. The salamander looked to be asleep. Baba Yaga's hair was long and gray and fell over the back of her chair in a stringy curtain.

Summer nodded.

"Sensible of you. Hand me the candle." She stretched out one gloved hand and Summer dropped the frog into it. Baba Yaga's fingernails were short and blunt and it looked as if she bit them.

"The frog. Hmm. Plain beeswax. Interesting. Neither here nor there yet. You're not much more than a tadpole yourself, are you? Already burnt, though. Hmm. Well, that's something, anyway."

Summer wondered what Baba Yaga would have said if she'd picked the unicorn.

The old woman reached into a pocket—she was wearing a shapeless gray housecoat over her shapeless gray dress—and brought out a shiny silver lighter. She snapped it a few times and then lit the wick on the frog's back. When the flame had caught, she reached up and set it on the mantle next to her hat.

"There. *That's* done. Now then, about your heart's desire…"

Summer's stomach turned over again. Maybe she didn't want to know. She had a sudden mad urge to bolt from the room.

"What would you ask for, if you could ask for anything?" asked Baba Yaga.

"I don't know," Summer confessed. "I was going to ask you to make me a shape-shifter—so I could turn into animals and talk to them, maybe—but I don't know if that's my heart's desire and now I don't know if I even want that at all."

"Hmm," said Baba Yaga, nodding slowly. "A surprisingly good wish, all things considered. Not practical in this day and age perhaps, but I've heard a lot worse." She propped up her chin on her hand. Her wrinkles carved deep shadows around her mouth.

"You can tell a lot about people by the things they think they want," she said. "At least yours is interesting. I'm sick to death of young fools who want wealth and power and the hand of their true love. I started eating them a while ago, but it still doesn't keep them away. Everybody thinks they're special."

Summer did not feel at all special. She didn't think Baba Yaga was joking about eating people. She thought she was telling the exact truth.

For one thing, she didn't seem to be the type to make jokes.

For another, Summer had just this very moment noticed that her rocking chair was made out of bones.

She wondered if she could make it to the door.

"Noticed my chair, have you?" asked Baba Yaga, and cackled. She rocked back on the chair's runners, and the bones creaked and tapped against the wooden floor, like a dozen people cracking their knuckles all at once. "Relax, girl. I'm not hungry—not right at the moment—and anybody who has such interesting wishes is too good to waste on an afternoon snack."

She rocked again. Those heavy black eyes bored into her, down into the chamber of her heart again. Summer felt as if there was a small animal inside her guts, clawing her stomach and chewing on her nerves. It was hard to breathe.

"Y-e-e-s-s," said Baba Yaga after a moment. "Yes, I see. *Very* sensible. Even more so than being a shape-shifter, and less chance to get caught up in being a deer or a stoat or something and not wanting to turn back."

"W-what?"

"Very seductive minds, deer. You'd hate to be one otherwise."

Summer was having a hard time thinking about deer. Things were shifting around inside her. Baba Yaga was not just reading the words written on her heart, she was moving the furniture around and hammering on the walls.

She held out a hand as if to ward off the old woman's gaze. "W-what are you doing?"

"Giving you your heart's desire," said Baba Yaga. "Here, you'll probably need this." She looked away (Summer gasped for breath) and rummaged around in her housecoat. "Blast! I left it in my other coat. Be a love and pull it off the coatrack, will you?"

There was a coatrack by the door. Summer had a brief mad notion of trying to wrench the door open and run away, but the coatrack shuffled forward to meet her. It had carved wooden feet like a crocodile. Its claws clicked on the floor.

Summer would have liked to think that she was having a nightmare, but she couldn't bring herself to believe it. Everything was too crisp and clear, from the clicking claws to the smell of bleach and beeswax. She reached a hand out blindly and the coatrack turned so that a large gray coat was in front of her.

"Left front pocket," said Baba Yaga. "Pockets are important. Yours don't hold enough, but that's easily fixed." She waved a hand negligently in Summer's direction.

Summer dipped her hand in obediently and felt…fur.

She tugged. Something in the pocket let out a yawp and a sharp triangular little head poked over the top of the fabric.

She jumped back. Baba Yaga cackled.

"Go on, girl," she said, "go on. It's only a weasel."

"Does it bite?" asked Summer warily.

"Of course it bites. It's a weasel. They don't kill their prey with pretty words and poisoned sweetmeats."

The weasel rolled its eyes. It was less than a foot long and its eyes were tiny blood-black beads, but Summer actually saw the eye-roll. She felt obscurely comforted and put out her hand.

The weasel stepped gravely onto her palm and sat down.

"I'll need a weasel?" asked Summer.

"Possibly. It gets him out of my coat, anyway, and that's all to the good." Baba Yaga leaned back in her rocking chair and closed her eyes. "Close the door behind you on your way out."

The door swung open. The skull winked at her. Summer was only too glad to leave, but some perverse instinct made her pause on the threshold.

"But—er—Baba Yaga—ma'am—what about my heart's desire?"

The old woman on her chair of bones opened one eye. "What about it?"

"You said—I *thought* you said—"

"I said I'd give it to you," said Baba Yaga. "I never said I'd tell you what it was. That's another sort of gift. Be off with you! The candle won't burn forever, and I'd get back before the flame goes out, if I were you." She flapped a hand at Summer.

The door was under her hand, practically pulling her out of the odd little house. "Go, go!" whispered the skull. "Hurry now, while she's still in a good mood!"

Summer stepped out of the house, deeply confused. She'd asked for her heart's desire and gotten a weasel. What did that mean?

She looked up from her furry handful.

The yard was gone.

The wall and the gate and the alley were gone.

She was standing in a long hallway with a bare wooden floor, lined by empty suits of armor and cut with arching windows of purple glass.

Baba Yaga's house had vanished.

She looked down at the weasel. It looked back up at her and shrugged, a tiny shrug that rippled through its entire body.

"What do I do?" she whispered.

"I've no idea," the weasel whispered back, "but you might start by watching where you were going."

Summer was so startled to hear the weasel talking—although after the skull, she didn't know why she'd be surprised—that she nearly dropped it. It whipped between her fingers, as quick as a skink, and threw its front paws around her thumb.

"Sorry," whispered Summer. "You surprised me!"

She hadn't expected the weasel to talk. The skull had talked and the house had been pretty…err…expressive, but the weasel was something else again.

Then again, she hadn't expected to walk out of the door of the bird-footed house and find herself in a hallway either.

It was ironic—a word that grown-ups used a lot, and which Summer felt she was finally coming to understand—that after all that time wanting to be able to talk to animals, when she finally had a real honest-to-god talking animal in front of her, she could only think of a single question.

"Where are we?" she asked the weasel.

The weasel climbed up to her shoulder. It—he—peered both ways down the hall and said, "I haven't the foggiest idea. If it's a chicken coop, it's an awfully big one."

"I don't think it's a chicken coop," said Summer. "There's a lot of stained glass."

"Perhaps they're very religious chickens."

Summer thought that this was no help at all, but since talking to the weasel was keeping her from being scared of the fact that she was somewhere very strange, she didn't say so.

At the end of the hall, a long way away, she could see a door. Since there didn't seem to be anything else to do, she began to walk towards it.

The stained glass windows were interesting. They were extremely purple. There were saints and angels in them, clad in purple, with purple halos and wings. Only their faces and hands were a different color, and some of the angels even had purple hair.

Summer walked past three or four windows, full of saints smiling and solemn and stern. When she reached a window with an elderly saint with a long white beard, she had to stop and smile.

"He looks nice," she said.

"I suppose," said the weasel, who was licking his shoulder. "Humans are the best judge of other humans."

He did look nice. He was skinny and bony and his wrists stuck out of his robes. His beard fell down to his waist, but didn't quite disguise a grin. Two grim-faced angels flanked him, their enormous purple wings outstretched.

In one hand, the saint held a very large book.

Summer went on to the next window.

It was the same saint again. This time he seemed to be leaning forward, and he was pointing a finger toward the viewer.

She hurried on to the next one, and was delighted to see the same saint again. He was giving her a knowing grin and was pointing at his book.

"They're almost like a flipbook!" she said, walking more quickly. "Where each page has a drawing and if you flip the pages really fast they move!" She was aware that an actual flipbook made of stained glass would weigh thousands of pounds, and flipping it would probably be very difficult and involve a lot of screaming and crashing and breaking glass, so perhaps this was the best that the window-makers could manage.

In the next window, the saint was making a run for it. He was half out of the frame, his beard flapping behind him, and the two shocked angels were just starting to turn after him.

Summer broke into a run. The weasel clutched at her hair.

Even though he was made of stained glass, she couldn't escape the feeling that the saint was running alongside her. The next few windows flashed by, and in each one, the saint was running full-tilt, book clutched to his chest, with his robes flapping behind him and his bony ankles showing. He was wearing purple stained-glass sneakers with no socks. Summer giggled at the notion of a saint wearing sneakers.

Eventually the angels caught up to him. *Not very fair,* thought Summer. *They have wings!*

And indeed the wings were the first things you saw, a few feathers in the left side of the frame, followed by an outstretched hand. The angel had long fingernails, almost like claws.

"Do you think angels really have claws?" she asked the weasel, slowing down a bit.

"Wouldn't surprise me," said the weasel. "I have claws, and I eat eggs and mice and rabbits. Sins are probably a lot tougher than eggs or mice."

"What about rabbits?" asked Summer.

"Don't mess with rabbits."

Her side was starting to hurt from running, so she settled for walking quickly. The saint, still grinning, had turned to look over his shoulder at the pursuing angels. You could just see one's face now, mouth open as if the angel were shouting.

On the far side of the next suit of armor, the angels finally caught him. They grabbed the back of his robes and hauled. The saint's book went flying through the air.

In the last window but one, the angels hauled the saint away. Their purple wings seemed to quiver with outrage. The saint, still grinning, adjusted his halo with one hand, and with the other, tucked under the edge of his flapping robes, he pointed toward the book.

Summer reached the last window. All that remained of the saint and the angels was a stray feather on the far left and the tip of a purple sneaker. The book lay open at the bottom of the window. Words had been painted across the lavender pages in a bold, flowing script.

"You know," said Summer, "it almost looks like you can read it."

"Maybe you can," said the weasel. "I can't read."

"You can't?"

"It doesn't come up much when you're a weasel."

Getting close to the stained glass book meant stepping between two suits of armor. That was a little creepy. They were very definitely empty—the visors were up and you could see inside—but it was still all too easy to imagine them waking up, the visors clanking down and those big mailed fists reaching for you.

She was also just a little afraid that she'd knock into one by accident and it would fall over and clatter into dozens of little armored pieces and then she'd have to try and put it back together the right way before the owner of the hallway came back and found it.

Up close, the stained glass book was much bigger than any textbook Summer had ever had for school. When she stood on her tiptoes, she could read the words. She read each line out loud to the weasel.

1. Don't worry about things that you cannot fix.
2. Antelope women are not to be trusted.
3. You cannot change essential nature with magic.

"Hmm," said Summer. "I understand the first one. But what's an antelope woman? And what does the last one mean?"

"It means you can't change something into something else with magic, not really," said the weasel. "If you turned me into a human, I'd still be a weasel inside. If we turned you into a rabbit, you'd still be a little girl down deep, where it matters."

"I'm nearly twelve," said Summer, a bit indignant. "I'm not *that* little."

The weasel flipped his tail across her neck and said nothing.

She took a last long look at the book and read the three statements over again to herself. They seemed important. The saint had run away from the angels in order to show them to her—or to show them to someone, anyway. There was no telling how long the hallway had been here. Obviously the stained glass maker had had a very peculiar sense of humor.

She glanced back down the hallway. If she walked back down, the other direction, would she still see the running saint, or would the windows be full of the angels dragging him back to his original spot?

It was an unsettling thought. Summer found that she didn't really want to know, and instead went to the door. It stood slightly ajar, and she could smell cool air and leaves through the crack.

She pushed the door open and stepped outside.

Behind her, the stained glass saint stuck his head back in the final window. He picked up his book, grinning, tossed his beard over his shoulder, and danced a jig with a suddenly joyous angel.

Chapter Four

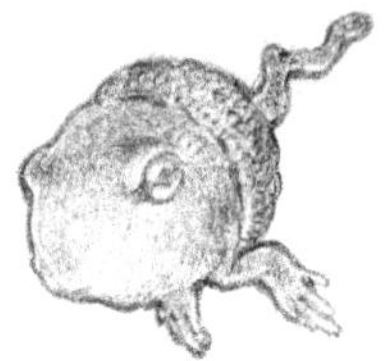

As it turned out, the hallway was sunken in the ground, and so the first thing she saw was a flight of broad stone steps leading upward. Leaves had collected in drifts at the bottom and on the edges of the stairs. They crunched as she walked upward.

It was a little cold. Summer was wearing a T-shirt with short sleeves. She rubbed her arms to warm them.

At the top of the steps was a forest. She turned to look behind her, and the hall was buried, up to the bottoms of the stained glass windows. Moss grew up the stone walls and ferns had sprouted in the cracks.

It was an odd forest.

The air was dry, much drier than it had been back home, and the nearby trees had gnarled, contorted trunks. Their leaves were shaped like the Ace of Spades on a deck of cards.

Farther away from the hall, the contorted trees gave way to tall pines. There were pine needles all over the ground, and not very many smaller plants. Summer felt as if she were walking through an enormous room with lots of pillars holding up the ceiling.

There was a particularly enormous tree off in the distance, with white bark that was scabbed and spotted, almost like a Holstein cow. Could you have a Holstein tree?

For lack of anything else to do, she walked toward it.

Leaves crunched under her feet, then the crunching became muffled as she reached the pine needles. In the distance, she could see other trees like the ones around the buried hall, crowding their trunks together and dusted with ferns. Between those trees were the tall, tall pines.

"I smell desert," said the weasel. He sat up on her shoulder, his small nose working furiously.

"We're in the woods," said Summer, not arguing, just stating a fact.

He gave a short, sharp nod. "I know. But I smell desert. We're at an edge place, I think. Those trees—those are cottonwoods. They're growing up wherever there's a seep of water."

"Does that mean anything?" asked Summer. "That we're in a desert, I mean, not about the trees."

The weasel shrugged a rolling weasel shrug. "It means the mice will be fast as fury."

"I thought deserts were hot," said Summer, wrapping her arms around herself.

"Not at night. Not in winter. Maybe not in this place, ever."

Summer shivered.

She hoped that she wouldn't have to spend the night here, wherever here was.

Summer wondered if this counted as being lost. She did not feel an immediate urge to begin weeping or running in circles or calling for a policeman or a park ranger or any of the usual things that children are supposed to do when they're lost.

Part of that was because Summer was a sensible girl and knew that weeping and running in circles, however satisfying it might be at the moment, was not going to help very much. And partly it was that Summer knew full well that an enormous sunken hall and a forest-that-might-be-a-desert would not fit anywhere in the alley behind her house. She had not gotten lost in a city park or someone's backyard, and therefore it was not a matter of finding the nearest cross-street and figuring out how to get back home before her mother noticed she was gone.

But Summer had read a lot of books, and among her very favorites were stories of children who opened doors and wandered into Narnia or Fairyland or some mysterious world on the other side of the hedge. It was patently obvious that this was what had happened to her. Baba Yaga had given her a weasel and kicked her out the door into…someplace else.

If she was indeed in another world, then two things would happen. Either time would go differently, and her mother would never notice she had been gone (and Summer hoped very devoutly that this was the case) or time would go on in its usual rollicking way, and by the time Summer managed to get home, it would be hours or days later.

And at that point, Summer said to herself, *I shall be in so much trouble that it will not actually be possible for me to get in any* more *trouble, so it doesn't really matter how long it takes.*

There is something very freeing about knowing that you are in the worst possible trouble that you can be in. No matter what you do, it cannot possibly get any worse. Summer would get home and be grounded until she was eighteen, and even if she dyed her hair pink and got her ears pierced while in Fairyland (somehow she didn't think they did that sort of thing in Narnia) she couldn't be grounded any longer than that.

As the saint's book had said, *Don't worry about things you cannot fix.*

She strode out with a light heart.

～

The spotted tree turned out to be farther away than it looked. By the time she got near it, she was starting to get thirsty, and she was no longer cold at all.

It was a very large tree. The branches went up as tall as a skyscraper, and the trunk was as big around as a house. Summer stopped many feet back from the trunk and craned her neck backwards, trying to see the whole tree at once.

"Do you think it's magic?" she asked the weasel.

"All really old trees are magic," he said, rummaging around in her pockets with his paws. "You've got a lock in your pocket. Did you know that?"

"It's from the gate," she said absently. "It was nice and opened up when I asked. Do you think this one is *more* magic, though?"

The weasel looked up at the tree, then back down into her pocket. "Probably not. These are excellent pockets, by the way. You don't usually get ones this size."

The pockets were, in fact, part of the reason that these were Summer's favorite jeans, but she had other things on her mind at the moment than tailoring. "It *could* be," she said. "The Vikings thought the world was built on a giant tree." (In addition to books about visiting other worlds, Summer had read a lot of mythology, which was almost as good.)

"Yggdrasil," said the weasel. Summer tried not to resent the fact that he could pronounce the name easily. He looked up at the tree, scampered over to her other shoulder and looked at it from that angle. "Yggdrasil's bigger," he said, and went back to digging around in her pockets.

"What are you looking for?" she asked, annoyed.

"I was hoping you might have an egg."

"I don't carry eggs around in my pockets!"

"Then there's not much point in having pockets, is there?"

As if their voices had woken it, the tree shook itself. Leaves tumbled from the highest branches and fell around them.

The nearest leaf struck the ground and stopped being a leaf. It became—or perhaps it always had been—a lizard, a flat-bodied, stubby-legged lizard like a horned toad. It scurried away through the pine needles.

Summer took a step back, surprised. She could hear the rustling as other leaf-lizards ran off through the forest.

"On the other hand," said the weasel, "it might be magic after all."

They walked around the tree, slowly. The leaves were broad and flat. One drifted down, just out of reach, and Summer jumped forward and caught it in her hand.

It was just a leaf. It had tight little veins, like a lizard's scales, and the stem was thick and curved like a tail, but it was definitely a leaf.

She dropped it.

It turned into a lizard when it hit the ground, then it scampered over her shoe and vanished into the leaves.

There was another spotted white tree beyond the first, not so far away. Summer walked toward it, delighted. She was ready to see marvels, and the tree did not disappoint.

Its leaves were long and pointed and slightly furry, the way lamb's-ear or mullein is furry. They tumbled to the ground and became mice, beautiful white mice with intelligent eyes, who squeaked and danced and ran in circles, chasing their own pink tails.

The weasel chattered his jaw, the way a cat will when it sees a bird, but stayed on Summer's shoulder. "Tempting," he said. "Verrrry tempting. But they're either leaves enchanted to look like mice or mice enchanted to look like leaves, and enchantment curdles in your stomach when you eat it."

There was a third white tree, forming a line with the first two. Summer walked toward it in a hurry, so that the weasel didn't get any ideas.

But there was something wrong with the third tree.

The leaves were green, green as glass bottles, small and blunt with hardly any stem at all. It was obvious even as they fell that they would be frogs.

Little green frogs, thought Summer, *like little emeralds.*

But they did not change. They touched the ground and they were only leaves.

The tree rustled its branches, harder, and more leaves showered down. She heard the trunk groan, the way trees groan and mutter in a storm.

These leaves hopped. Some of them changed, but there was something wrong with the frogs. They had no legs or too many legs or they plowed forward on their bellies. In a very few seconds they were all leaves again, and Summer was glad, because there was something horrible and piteous about the frogs. They had looked as if they were dying.

The white tree thrashed. Its limbs swayed in a gale that only it could feel. Behind them, the other two white trees moaned and swayed in sympathy.

Every leaf on the tree fell down, leaving the branches as bare as winter.

Many people have heard of a rain of frogs, but very few—far fewer than say they have—have ever seen one. Summer became one of those few. For a moment the air was full of tiny green frogs, transforming before they even hit the ground, all of them croaking like fingernails dragged over a comb.

They rushed into the leaves, hopping and dancing, croaking and cavorting, and Summer let out a breath she hadn't known she was holding. She had been terribly afraid that the tree would not be able to do it.

Indeed, the tree looked exhausted. Its branches drooped and it shivered. Summer took a step forward and put a hand on its bark.

"You did it," she said to the tree. "They're beautiful."

The tree muttered something in the language of trees and let out a long wooden sigh.

"It did," said a woman's voice behind her, "but it cost the tree dearly."

Summer spun around. The weasel squeaked and dove into her pocket.

A bear stood behind her—or not a bear. For a moment Summer could have sworn she saw the flash of teeth, the heavy jaw and small black eyes—and then the woman pushed back her hood, and it was only the skin of a bear. Her face bore the haggard remains of great beauty, and her voice was hoarse with disuse.

"What's wrong with the tree?" asked Summer, who felt sorry for it and proud of it for making the frogs, all at once.

"The same thing that is wrong with all of us," said the woman in the bear skin. She looked proud and angry and tired, and her eyes did not soften as they rested on Summer's face. "There is a cancer at the heart of the world."

In movies, when someone has just made a very dramatic statement, everyone gasps or recoils in horror, so you might think that when Summer heard the bear woman say, "There is a cancer at the heart of the world," she would have done something similar. In real life, though, a very dramatic statement is usually met with awkward silence, and then somebody makes a joke to try to break the silence, and somebody else decides they need a cup of tea.

Summer would have liked a cup of tea, but there didn't seem to be much chance of getting one in the middle of the forest, and she still wasn't entirely sure that the woman in the bearskin hadn't been an actual bear a minute ago. Jokes might not be a good idea.

She said, "Um."

The woman in the bearskin frowned, and another woman popped up next to her, wearing a bristly skin with a great tusked boar's head on top. "Are you on about that again, then?" she asked, and turned to Summer. "Never mind her."

"No one minds me," said the bear woman, a good deal less dramatically. She sniffed.

"I'm Boarskin," said the woman wearing the boar's head on top of her own. "This is Bearskin. Our sister Donkeyskin is around somewhere, but she has a hard time with strangers."

"I'm Summer," said Summer shyly. She wondered if she should introduce the weasel, but he didn't say anything, so she decided not to. She kept one hand on the bark of the Frog Tree. "Please—if you know—can you tell me what's wrong with the tree? Can we help it?"

Bearskin opened her mouth to say something, and Boarskin thumped her in the ribs with her elbow. They didn't look very much like sisters. Bearskin had long blonde hair streaked with gray, and Boarskin's hair was short and black and bristly.

"There's a great many things wrong," said Boarskin. "But one thing in particular, you understand, and not something I want to talk about in the open, where anybody might be listening." She nodded to the tree. "As for whether you can help it—well, I suppose you might. If you had great courage and great good luck."

"Oh," said Summer glumly. She knew that she didn't have great courage, but she did feel badly for the poor tree. "Maybe—maybe some fertilizer?"

"I'm afraid it's not that kind of tree," said Boarskin kindly.

"There used to be others," said Bearskin, in her angry, prophetic voice. "One with leaves like a weeping willow, that fell down and became snakes with cut glass eyes. One with striped brown nuts that turned into quail chicks. You can see their trunks rotting in the woods if you walk far enough."

"Oh *no,*" said Summer, feeling her eyes prickle with tears. Were they saying that the poor Frog Tree was doomed? What about the Mouse Tree and the Tree of Horned Toads?

"Leave off," said Boarskin to her sister. "You've said quite enough. It might not happen, or it might not happen just that way."

Bearskin folded her arms and turned her back on her sister.

"Come on," said Boarskin to Summer. "You don't look to have been here long, but traveling between worlds takes it out of a body. Come have some tea and we'll talk."

"Okay," said Summer. She looked up at the Frog Tree, at the bare branches. She could hear the rustling of the frogs hopping about in the leaves, and her heart clenched in her chest. It was one thing not to know that a tree with leaves that turned into frogs existed—quite another to know that it had existed once and now was dying.

She laid her cheek against the tree's beautiful spotted bark and whispered: "Your frogs were wonderful. Please don't die."

The tree sighed.

The bark did a strange thing under her cheek. She stepped back in a hurry, and saw it ripple like water, and then a hand came out and a shoulder and a head.

It was a person, although Summer couldn't tell if it was a boy or a girl or neither or both. Its skin and its hair and its eyes were the same white-mottled color as the bark, and it had an enormous number of rooty fingers.

It smiled at Summer, and held out its hand. When Summer held hers out in response, the bark-person dropped something into her palm. Then it stepped back into the tree, like a swimmer stepping in the water, and was gone.

"Dryad," said Boarskin. "Hmm." For a moment her gaze was as sharp as her sister's. "They don't come out often. Whatever it gave you, keep it safe. It might just be a souvenir, but...well."

Summer looked down at the object in her hand.

It was an acorn carved—or seeing where it had come from, perhaps not carved after all—into the shape of a tadpole. The stem was a thick paddle of tail, and the shell of the acorn had goggling eyes and tiny, tight-folded webbed feet.

She put it in her pocket next to the friendly padlock. The weasel moved against her fingers, the brush of his tail like a kiss on her knuckles.

"Come on, then," said Boarskin. Summer followed her, with several backward glances into the desert forest.

Chapter Five

The skin-wearing sisters had a little campsite by a little pond at the bottom of a little valley. Boarskin called out, "Donkeyskin! A visitor!" as they approached.

Donkeyskin was taller than either of the other sisters, and her face had a sweeping scar that ran from the corner of her left eye down to her chin. It pulled the corner of her mouth down into a permanent frown, and her eyes were like a dog that has been kicked too many times to be hopeful.

She started up when Boarskin and Bearskin arrived, and Boarskin said, "Easy, easy, dear heart. It's only a girl with a weasel in her pocket."

Donkeyskin settled back down onto her rock, watching Summer with her ravaged eyes.

There was a fire. Summer was glad for the heat, for the forest seemed to be getting colder, and the sky was definitely changing from bright hard blue to a softer, velvety color. Red light began to creep up from the western horizon.

It occurred to her that she was definitely going to be out after dark, and her mother had most certainly noticed that she was gone by now. The thought gave Summer a pang, because her mother would be very angry and very frightened. But she remembered what it had said in the saint's book, and she rubbed the acorn in her pocket and decided not to worry about it. Either time would pass differently or it wouldn't, and there was precious little she could do about it right now.

"Would you like tea?" asked Boarskin. "It's made with white sage and the hips of the desert rose. The tea leaves themselves are imported, of course."

Donkeyskin silently poured out cups of tea and handed them around. Summer's cup was made of bone china, with a lizard painted on the side. There was a white spiral through the center of its body, and another on the bottom of the bone china saucer.

The teacups and saucers seemed terribly out of place in the middle of the desert, and she looked from them, up to Boarskin, and back again.

"No need to look so surprised," said Boarskin, smiling.

"We do have *some* nice things," said Bearskin. "It's important to have beautiful things in exile."

Donkeyskin said nothing.

"*Are* you in exile?" asked Summer. She had always assumed that people in exile had to live in prisons or on distant islands.

"Most assuredly," said Boarskin. "We're princesses. Well, more or less."

"I was a chieftain's daughter," said Bearskin, as if announcing that she had some terrible disease.

"Close enough, close enough," said Boarskin. "Our fathers went quite mad, I'm afraid. Long and sordid tales all, and I won't trouble you with them, not on your first night in the world. But it's a hard thing when your father goes mad, particularly when he's the king. The only thing left to do then is to put on an animal skin and go out and try your fortune. So we did. Some of us, admittedly, with more difficulty than others."

Donkeyskin shifted restlessly on her rock. Her teacup clattered in its saucer.

Summer's father had died a long time ago, so long ago that Summer never remembered him. Occasionally grown-ups told her how sad it must be, to grow up without a father, and Summer always nodded politely, because you had to be polite, even to grown-ups who had no idea what they were talking about. It was entirely possible that some children who had lost their fathers felt very sad about it, but Summer was not among them.

She had tried, once or twice, to work up tears about it, when she was in the mood to feel small and sad and ill-used, but she couldn't really manage it. Her mother had made it abundantly clear that they were better off without him, and since there were other children at her school who had fathers that yelled and screamed, or vanished for years at a time, Summer thought it was not so bad. It could have been better, but it could have been worse, too.

Apparently it could have been a great deal worse, if these women had to put on animal skins and flee into the desert.

"You're leaving out a great deal," said Bearskin grimly.

"Yes I am," said Boarskin. "It's my story to tell or not tell if I choose, and I choose not to tell it tonight. If you want to tell yours, go ahead."

Bearskin said, "Hmmph!" but nothing more.

Donkeyskin got up from her rock and wandered a little way away. There were tumbled red rocks through the valley, and ferns grew in cracks near the pond. Farther away there were no ferns, only tough little scrubby bushes with a wild, clean smell. She stood beside one of the bushes, breaking off little bits of leaves with her fingers. The tail of the donkey skin hung down behind her.

"Now then, Summer," said Boarskin, pouring more tea into Summer's cup. "How did you get here? Did you ride in by fern-fish or step through a door in the hedge? Did you walk into a dragon's shadow?"

"She doesn't smell of dragon," said Bearskin.

"Well…" said Summer, wrapping her fingers around her teacup to keep them warm. "Baba Yaga told me she was giving me my heart's desire, and then I went out of her house and I was in the hallway with the stained glass windows."

"Baba Yaga sent you?" asked Boarskin and Bearskin at once, and drew together on their rock.

Donkeyskin drew the hood of her cloak up over her head. Its long donkey ears were tattered and it had white stones sewn into the eyes.

"Um," said Summer. "Yes?"

They looked at each other, then back at her.

"Baba Yaga, the cannibal?"

"Baba Yaga, the crone?"

"Baba Yaga, the witch, the wonder-worker, the teeth-that-bite-the-ground—" Boarskin pressed a hand to her lips. *"That* Baba Yaga?"

"Don't be a fool," said Bearskin sharply. "Do you think anyone else would dare claim that name? She'd feed them into her cauldron and take them out as a hundred spiny salamanders. She'd turn them into a drift of wildflowers and plant them in a sheep meadow. She'd make their bones into the root of a fig tree and sink them into their own children's graves."

Summer gulped.

"She—she didn't do any of that. She said she'd eat me if she was in a bad mood, but I didn't think she meant it. Well, she had a chair made of bones, so I wondered, but…" Summer twisted her fingers together. "Um. She gave me a weasel."

The weasel stuck his head out of her pocket and gave her a dirty look.

"Very useful animals, weasels," said Boarskin. This appeared to mollify the weasel. He gave Boarskin a tiny nod and then went back into Summer's pocket without giving any sign that he could talk.

"It was a student of Baba Yaga's that gave me my skin," said Donkeyskin.

Her voice was as hoarse as a grackle's call. The other two sisters looked at her.

"Well," said Boarskin. "Well. I did not know that. I thought—" She stopped and became very interested in her teacup.

"There's a debt owed, then," said Bearskin.

"You don't owe me," said Summer hurriedly. The notion of these three women—who were sort of interesting, but sort of frightening—owing her anything was a little scary. She wouldn't mind help, but she didn't want them to get resentful, the way that her mother did about the credit card companies.

"No, we don't," said Boarskin. "But our sister owes Baba Yaga, and that is another matter entirely." She sat up straighter. "Well. Where are you going, then, Summer-who-Baba-Yaga-sent, in search of your heart's desire?"

Summer took a swallow of tea, trying to buy time for an answer. She still couldn't think of one. "I don't know," she admitted. "She didn't tell me. I don't know what I'm supposed to do, or which way I'm supposed to go. If I'm even supposed to go somewhere."

In the stories that she had read, when you went to another world, you usually knew what you were doing, didn't you? You were met by fauns who told you about prophecies, or you landed in the middle of a war and it was immediately obvious whose side you were supposed to be on.

"I don't suppose you know any prophecies?" she asked, without much hope.

"Dozens," said Boarskin. "Hundreds. They're not much use."

"There's a beach at Nag-of-Head that has slips of paper instead of sand, with a prophecy written on each one," said Bearskin, "and the tide brings new ones in each day."

Well, it had been a long shot anyway.

So far she'd seen a stained glass saint and three odd sisters who might be princesses and a very strange forest…

Summer slipped her hand in her pocket, past the weasel, and ran her thumb over the carved acorn. "Is there—can you tell me—is there any way to help the poor Frog Tree?"

"Why do you care what happens to a tree?" asked Bearskin.

Summer gulped.

"It—well—" What could she say? That maybe if she hadn't been there, encouraging it, the tree wouldn't have tried so hard and lost all its leaves in the process? That the dryad had looked sad and weary and hopeful all at once?

Were those good enough reasons for someone like Bearskin?

She tried to think of reasons that the sisters might understand.

"When Baba Yaga spoke to me," she said finally, "she had me pick a candle. And I picked one shaped like a frog. And then I saw the tree, and it needed help…"

The sisters exchanged glances.

"We'll send you to the Waystation," said Boarskin firmly. "Finding ways is what they do best. If you've lost your way—or if you're not sure of your way to begin with—you can't go wrong with the Waystation."

"Okay," said Summer. "Is it very far?"

"A half-day's hike," said Boarskin. "It'll come out to meet you if you get lost, so you needn't worry too much."

She was glad to have a direction, even if she didn't know anything about it. It was better to have somewhere that you were trying to get to— even if it was very far away—than to simply wander around lost. "Do I have to go now?" It was full dark in the desert now.

"You'll need to set out when the sand-stars come out," said Bearskin. "Beginning a journey by their light brings luck, and you should never turn down an offer of luck."

"You have an hour or two," said Boarskin. "Try to take a nap, if you can. You may use my bedroll."

So Summer laid down on Boarskin's bedroll, which was a thick sheaf of blankets that smelled like Boarskin's hair. The weasel crept out of her pocket and curled up against her neck.

For a little while, she thought she wouldn't sleep. She was very tired and her legs were sore, but she was also wide awake and excited. The three sisters were moving around the campsite quietly, murmuring to each other and scrubbing up the dinner plates with sand. But then Donkeyskin sat down by the fire and began to sing a wordless, crooning song, and Summer's eyes closed and she slept.

In the middle of the night, Bearskin shook her shoulder. "Up, Summer," she said. "The stars are coming out."

Summer opened her eyes. Overhead, the stars were a fierce blaze like she had never seen, great clouds of stars like foam, laying in white twinkling drifts across the sky. There were no stars like that over Summer's back garden.

"They're already up," she mumbled, sitting up and wiping at her eyes. Her skin felt gritty.

"Not those stars," said Bearskin. "Sand-stars. *You* know."

She didn't know. She pushed her hair out of her eyes and wished for a toothbrush, not because she enjoyed brushing her teeth but because her mother had impressed on her that if you do not brush in the morning, your teeth will probably turn black and fall out by nightfall.

Boarskin pressed a cup of something hot into her hands. If it was tea, it was a different tea than any she had ever had. It went down her throat like warm smoke. She wasn't entirely sure that she liked it—it tasted of campfires and burning—but the air was very cold and it warmed her.

"There's one," said Boarskin, and pointed.

Summer looked, and saw a star on the ground.

It *looked* like a star. It was small and it glowed blue-green against the sand. She could see a hint of light reflected on the curve of a mesquite bush and the hummocks of sand around it.

Another sand-star appeared, a little behind it, and then another beyond that, and suddenly they all came out at once, a hundred thousand stars, until the desert was lit from below as well as above.

Summer let out a long, shuddering breath.

"They're beautiful," she said.

"Don't touch them," said Boarskin. "Watch your feet. They sting."

Something heavy landed on her shoulders. The weasel squeaked and scurried away into her pocket again.

She turned, startled, and saw Donkeyskin standing behind her. The woman had thrown a heavy blanket over her head, or something like a blanket with a hole in the middle. "The desert is cold at night," whispered Donkeyskin.

"I didn't know that the desert got so cold," Summer said. The blanket had dark, heavy lines across it, but she couldn't make out the colors by starlight. A design of lizards chased one another across the hem. "Thank you."

Donkeyskin crooked up one corner of her mouth and turned away.

Boarskin fastened a bottle of water to Summer's jeans, through the loop that held belts (if you wore belts, which Summer didn't.) It was made of leather and had a little stopper covered in wax. "Use this sparingly, but don't be afraid to drink it. Walk toward the horizon, toward the highest mountain. Can you see it?"

Summer nodded. She could see the mountain against the sky, a deeper darkness against the velvety stars.

Bearskin came close. The former chieftain's daughter studied Summer's face for a moment, her own face dark and serious. Then she leaned in and kissed Summer's forehead. "Go quickly or slowly, near or far, in fear or courage—but come back to us."

Summer had no idea what you said to that. "Um." She shifted from foot to foot. "Thank you. Um. Goodbye?"

Bearskin and Boarskin nodded. Donkeyskin was crouched in the shadows of a sage bush, and made no sound.

It seemed strange to walk into the desert alone, away from the campfire. She was not entirely sure that she wasn't still asleep and dreaming. The dark mountain seemed a long way off.

She half-expected one of the women to call after her, to tell her to stop, or to wait, that they'd come with her. They were grown-ups and she was a child, and grown-ups didn't simply let children walk off alone. What if she fell into a hole or was attacked or got lost or died of thirst?

But they did not call.

When she reached the top of the first ridge, she looked back, and saw the campfire, surprisingly small, behind her. One of the sisters—Boarskin, she thought—was watching her. Summer raised her hand, and Boarskin raised hers in return.

It occurred to her that perhaps the sisters thought that she was capable of walking into the dark by herself, without a grown-up with her.

On the far side of the ridge, the stars lay spread before her like lanterns. One was only a few feet away. She approached, placing her feet cautiously in the white-blue glow.

It was a scorpion.

Its body glowed fiercely white. Her eyes travelled over the blunt claws and the wickedly curved tail. If it had made a move—even the tiniest shift

  Summer in Orcus

of its legs on the sand—she would have shrieked and bolted back to the campfire.

It didn't move. Summer took a deep breath and let it out and thought *I'm being stupid. It was beautiful when I didn't know what it was.*

"It won't chase you," whispered the weasel in her ear. "They're slow creatures, and not very bright. It'll only sting you if you step on it, and that's not likely to happen when they're glowing like fox-fire."

Summer nodded.

The mountain wasn't getting any closer standing here. Perhaps it was better if the scorpions were glowing. Less chance of stepping on one by mistake.

The air was cold. Her breath frosted in front of her. Slowly, one foot in front of the other, she made her way across the desert by scorpion-light.

Chapter Six

It was a long, long night.

She walked for hours, or what felt like hours. The sand-stars lit her path. She blew her breath out in a white cloud and pretended to be a dragon.

There was not exactly a path, but if she kept the highest mountain in front of her, it was easier. She wandered off course once or twice, when the horizon vanished behind a ridge, but then she would come up to the top and correct herself.

They were in the desert now, though like no desert she had ever seen. Instead of great sweeping dunes, there were rocks and stones and low scrubby bushes. Ferns were a distant memory.

When she had walked for a few hours, she began to see cactus, great big saguaros like the ones in cartoons. They were twenty and thirty feet tall, with dozens of arms.

She was very tired. She had been walking forever. The stars overhead and the stars underfoot spun together, until she seemed to be walking across galaxies. Perhaps the stars in the sky were scorpions too. In Summer's world, they were giant flaming balls of gas, but who knew about this place? Maybe the sky was a great black desert, and when she reached the highest mountain, she would walk up into it.

"Sit down," said the weasel, "and have a drink of water. You're giggling a little too much and it's starting to worry me."

She sat down on a boulder and had a drink of water. Her head cleared a bit. She dripped a little into the bottle's cap and let the weasel drink it.

No one knows where I am, she thought, *except the weasel. No one is expecting me to be somewhere. No one is going to come looking for me if I don't arrive.*

She took another sip of water. She knew that she should be afraid—and she was, a little—but also she felt…free.

There was a sand-star a few yards away, under the curve of a prickly pear cactus. Its light gleamed off the flat pads and winked on the pale thorns.

Movement caught her eye. As she watched, an owl walked past her on long scaly legs. It walked right up to the sand-star. Summer held her breath. Did owls eat scorpions?

It spread its wings and bowed to the sand-star, very deeply. The sand-star flexed its tail and bowed back, fanning its claws out. The light bounced and shattered across the cactus thorns.

The owl walked away. She lost sight of its shape in the maze of mesquite shadows. The scorpion didn't move again.

"Come on," said the weasel softly. "Let's get moving again."

Eventually the sun came up.

Summer became aware of this because the stars started to go out—first the stars in the sky, then the ones on the ground. It made her nervous, because then she didn't know whether she was about to step on one or not.

But even after the last sand-star went out, there was a gritty gray light from the horizon. The highest mountain stood out sharp and clear.

"Dawn," said the weasel, standing on her shoulder. "It'll be an oven out here soon."

"You didn't say anything to the sisters," said Summer, who was tired of the vast silence of the desert.

"No, I didn't." The weasel stretched himself like a very small cat.

"Why not?"

He lifted one small shoulder in a shrug. "Oh, well. They seemed pleasant enough, but seeming isn't everything. And they smelled like shapechangers. Real animals and shapechangers don't always get along."

"They don't?" This was news to Summer. She had wanted to be a shapechanger specifically so that she could talk to animals. It hadn't occurred to her that the animals might mind.

"Some of them aren't bad. Knew a fellow who spent half his days as a hawk, and he was fine if he wasn't hungry. But some of them don't move right and they don't smell right and they don't wear their skin right. You want to watch out for people who don't wear their skin correctly." The weasel rubbed his face on her shoulder. "Some of 'em don't mean any harm, poor souls, but some of them will have you by the throat before you can say 'rabbit.'"

Summer kept walking. The sun was coming over the horizon now, although the air was still chilled. She was sweaty under the blanket, but her face and the tips of her ears were cold. It was a strange sensation. The cactus threw long, long shadows across the sand.

"Is it true what they said about Baba Yaga?" asked Summer.

"True?" asked the weasel. "True enough. They said less than they might have and a great deal less than they *could* have. It doesn't pay to talk about Baba Yaga behind her back."

"Oh." Summer thought about that. "How did you wind up in her house? Did she offer you your heart's desire?"

"Not *hardly*," said the weasel, sounding very annoyed.

"Then how?"

"The witch's house lays eggs sometimes," said the weasel. "I tried to eat one."

Summer wrinkled her forehead. "But it's a house. Wouldn't its eggs be—oh—enormous? Bigger than me?"

"So maybe I'm ambitious," said the weasel. "Nothing wrong with ambition, is there? 'Shoot for the moon,' everybody says, 'if you miss, you'll land among the stars.'" He spat, a motion almost too tiny for Summer's eyes to follow. "Feh! I suppose, 'if you miss, you'll be captured by a great bloody hag out of legend and stuffed into a coat pocket for a week' was too much of a mouthful."

Summer had no idea what to say to that. "Um. I'm sorry?"

"Not your fault," said the weasel. "Also, we're being followed. *No, don't look!*"

Summer froze. "What do we do?" she hissed at the weasel.

"You keep walking," said the weasel. "Making light conversation, if you please." He raised his voice. "Lovely day for a stroll in the desert, isn't it?"

"Um—I guess—sure?"

"Stop at that rock up ahead," he whispered. "Have a sip of water and look around, casual-like. You don't expect to see anything, you're just taking in the scenery, understand?"

Summer nodded. She stopped at the rock and fumbled for the water bottle.

"And you can pour me a little while you're at it."

She did. The weasel's tiny pink tongue flicked in and out of the water, and Summer scanned the desert, looking for someone or something.

"I don't see anyone," she whispered.

The weasel interrupted his drink long enough to say "The way we came. Higher up the mountain. By the three cactuses standing together."

She found the cactus. There was a rock—a shaggy rock? A rock with ears?

"It's a…I think it's a donkey!"

"Burro, out here," said the weasel. "Might be your friend from earlier. I thought she smelled like a shapechanger."

"Should I wave?" asked Summer.

"No. If it's her, she knows it's you, and if it's not, no sense letting on that you've seen it."

"Could a burro really do something bad to us?"

"It could kick you halfway to perdition if it felt like it, I expect." The weasel cleaned his shoulder with his tongue. "Rather like giant rabbits in that regard. Keep walking. This Waystation place has to be somewhere."

She kept walking.

"Two of them, now," said the weasel a few minutes later. "The other one's a javelina."

"A what?"

"Desert pig," said the weasel. "Like a wild boar. I'm guessing it's your other friend, which means we should have a bear after us shortly, and won't that be nice?"

But Bearskin did not appear. The boar and the donkey flanked them for an hour, then melted away into the desert as quietly as they had come.

Summer was a little sad when they left. She could have crossed the desert by herself—probably—she was eleven, after all, and had a weasel besides—but it was still nice to know that there were people around in case she fell off a cliff or stepped on a rattlesnake.

They came upon the Waystation with very little warning. There was a stand of cottonwood trees tucked in the next valley, and the sound of water. Summer hurried toward it and found that the trees grew along the banks of a stream. The stream rushed briskly over tiny pebbles, and on the far side was a little fence, and a large round house the color of butter.

On top of the house, in enormous letters, was a sign that said, "WHEYSTATION."

Summer was quite good at spelling. She knew that "Waystation" was spelled with an A and no H. "Whey," on the other hand, had to do with… cheese?

There was a small bridge over the stream. At each end of the handrail was a carving of a mouse wrapped around a piece of cheese.

"I think this is a pun," said Summer, scowling. She liked puns well enough in their place, but this struck her as the sort of pun that a grown-up would make, expecting a child to find it hysterically funny.

It is difficult to walk across an enchanted desert and then be thrust into someone else's sense of humor.

They crossed the bridge and approached the Wheystation. A road ran from the doorway out across the desert, as far as her eye could follow it.

"Is this even the right place?" asked Summer. The weasel shrugged and climbed back into her pocket.

The door of the Wheystation was made of wood. Inscribed over the lintel in elegant script were the words:

1800 Desert Whey
"All The Cheese That's Fit To Please"

Summer gritted her teeth and knocked.

The door swung open. She poked her head around the doorframe and saw an enormous glass counter full of cheeses. A fat man stood behind the counter, wiping it with a cloth.

"Hello!" he cried. "Hello, traveler, hello cheese-lover! I am the Wheymaster. Come in, come in, out of the heat!"

Summer stepped inside. A little bell went *jingle jingle* over her head.

It looked like a museum of cheese. There were great round wheels bigger than car tires and tiny little cubes in trays. There were wedges and slices and tubs and bricks. There was blue cheese and green cheese ("FRESH FROM THE SLOPES OF MARE IMBRIUM" said the sign) and red cheese and white cheese. There were cheeses made from cow milk and goat milk and sheep milk and unicorn milk.

"Unicorn milk?" asked Summer.

"Every kind of milk," said the man behind the counter. He was tall and broad and had enormous forearms and bright green hair. "Every kind you can imagine. Except platypus. We're out of platypus."

"You are?"

"There's a problem with our supplier. They're monotremes, they sweat milk through bare patches on their belly, so it's not so much milking as wringing the platypus out like a towel. Except the monotreme milker's union is on strike right now. But I can cut you a lovely wedge of Gouda. Same flavor, not as oily."

"Err—not right now," said Summer. "I'm actually looking for—"

"Oh, just try a bit. A free sample." He dove into a case and she heard the clicking of a knife. A moment later he held out a cube on a toothpick.

She didn't want to be rude—and she was very hungry—so she took it. She nibbled.

It was rich and creamy and she thought it would make spectacular mac and cheese. "It's delicious," she said.

"A good seller," said the Wheymaster. "One of my favorites. Now what did you come looking for?"

Summer shook herself. She hadn't come here for cheese. "Ah, I'm looking for the Waystation."

"And here we are," said the green-haired man. "The Wheystation. You've found it."

"No, not whey—*way*. With no H. Boarskin told me to find it—she said it would be this way—"

"This whey," agreed the man, "right here, yes. All the cheeses you want. Nothing else." He mopped at his forehead with the rag in his hand.

A day ago, Summer would have believed him. Even if she hadn't she wouldn't have said anything, because if you are a kid, you never ever argue with a grown-up. But a day ago she hadn't crossed a desert lit by scorpions.

She took a long, long look at him.

The Wheymaster was sweating.

"Are you sure—" she began.

"Very sure! Absolutely sure! Just cheese. *Only* cheese."

Summer folded her arms and tapped her foot, like her teacher Mrs. Selena did when somebody in class was acting stupid. "Boarskin said you'd help me find my way."

The Wheymaster's eyes flicked toward the door.

"I could get in real trouble," he whispered. "I don't do that anymore. I had to repaint the sign and everything."

"But I need your help," said Summer. "I don't know where I'm going, or what I'm supposed to do. I don't even know what this place is called."

The Wheymaster nodded wretchedly and blotted his forehead again. "I can't," he said. "I know I should, but I can't. They closed me down, you know? *He* did. Zultan. Her lieutenant. *You* know."

"I *don't* know," said Summer. "I'm lost. I mean, I crossed the desert, but I don't know what I'm doing, and I don't even know where I am. I don't think I'm from this world, and that's okay, but I'm looking for my heart's desire, and I need to know how to find it."

She almost stamped her foot, but she really wasn't that kind of girl.

"I can't help you," said the Wheymaster. "I can't. I won't. I shouldn't."

Summer gritted her teeth and said, "Baba Yaga sent me."

The Wheymaster's skin went the color of blue cheese. He put his elbows on the counter and dug both hands into his hair.

"Oh me," he said. "Oh me, oh my. Oh, I am the unluckiest man in the world. If I don't help you, the crone will get me, and if I do, Zultan will get me. Oh, what to do?"

"I don't want to get you in trouble," said Summer. "I really don't. I just need you to tell me where I'm supposed to go."

The Wheymaster took a deep breath. He reached into the case and pulled out another cheese and cut off a slice. He popped it into his mouth and then cut off another piece for Summer, and another very small piece for the weasel.

This one was not the sort of thing that you would put on mac and cheese, but delicious nonetheless. It tasted a little like cheddar and smelled like new mown grass. It crumbled on her tongue, and her stomach warmed and her skin prickled. Summer felt taller, suddenly, taller and stronger and braver.

She thought she might be able to walk across the desert again, if it came to that.

"Manticore cheese," said the Wheymaster. "Ripened on the grass where heroes have slept. There's nothing like it for courage." In Summer's pocket, the weasel fluffed himself and lashed his tail.

"Can I have another piece?" asked Summer.

"Not a good idea," said the Wheymaster. "Too much of it and you forget the taste of fear, and that's a dangerous place. Find yourself charging lions barehanded and nonsense like that." He straightened up and took a deep breath.

"Very well," he said. "My grandfathers would be ashamed of me, cringing like this. We've always found ways, you know. The cheese was just a side business. If I am going to be hanged, might as well be for something I did do as for something I didn't do."

"I don't want *anybody* to be hanged," said Summer, quite alarmed.

"Well, we can hope. You are, my dear, at the edge of the Sonorous Desert, in the land of Orcus, and we will see what other information you require as we go. Come behind the counter." He held a curtain aside for her and ushered her into a small room in back.

The room was stuffed with cheese. There were barrels of cheese and more of the tire-sized wheels. A block of Swiss took up half the room, with holes in it big enough for Summer to crawl into.

"Cauldron…" muttered the Wheymaster. "Where did I put that cauldron? I used to have it right here…" He opened a closet and most of him vanished into it. Summer winced at the sounds of crashing plates and banging crockery.

"A-hah!"

What he pulled out looked a bit like a cast iron frying pan, only much bigger. It had little metal lion feet on it, and reminded Summer of Baba Yaga's coatrack.

It was stuffed full of cobwebs and covered in rust, and there was a forlorn bit of old cheese in the bottom.

Summer and the Wheymaster gazed into the cauldron together.

"Is it supposed to do something?" asked Summer.

"Years ago," said the Wheymaster gloomily. "Time was, you so much as poked your head over it, and it would tell you your Way. Usually it was one of us by accident, and only so far as the outhouse or the bathtub, but you'd bring a traveler by and it would get very excited. Ways used to spill out all over." He thumped the cauldron with one finger. It went "clonk."

"Not a drop of magic left in it, now," he said sadly.

Summer opened her mouth to say something—"It's okay," or "I'm sorry" or "But what do I do now?" (She was never quite sure herself afterwards.) But anything she might have said was drowned out by a sudden savage pounding on the wooden door. It sounded like a battering ram, like an angry mule kicking in the boards.

The Wheymaster's head shot up so fast that he struck it on a cheese hanging from the rafters. Summer put both hands over her mouth to hide a squeak of terror.

"Open!" cried a harsh voice on the other side of the door. "Open for Zultan Houndbreaker! *Open in the name of the Queen-in-Chains!*"

Chapter Seven

Perhaps it was the taste of the manticore cheese, but the Wheymaster didn't hesitate for an instant. He turned to Summer, swept her up in his arms, and plunked her down inside the block of Swiss. "Down!" he hissed. "Crawl down! Hide!"

Summer retreated as far as the holes in the Swiss would let her, until there was only a thin light in the distance. She crawled on her hands and knees through a deep, creamy darkness, until she came to a larger chamber in the center of the block. It smelled very strongly like Swiss cheese, which is a pleasant smell in small quantities and a rather nasty one when you are buried in it.

The weasel slid out of her pocket and weaseled back the way Summer had come. "I'll watch," he whispered.

The hammering on the door started again.

"I'm coming, I'm coming," shouted the Wheymaster. "If you'd knock on the door like a normal person, it'd open right up, you know. It's only when people get angry that it gets nervous and sticks." Summer heard the creak of the door opening, and the angry jangle of the bell over the door.

"Making trouble again, cheesemonger?" asked the harsh voice.

"Oh, it's *you,* Grub," said the Wheymaster. "What do you want?"

"Yes, it's me," said the voice. "And my master's on his steed outside, reading a book. If he has to come inside, he'll lose his place, and Zultan very much does not like to lose his place. I shouldn't risk it if I were you."

"Tell him to bend a corner down, or use a bookmark like a sensible man," said the Wheymaster, sounding bored. "Does he want cheese? I've got quite a good Manchego, settles the bowels and leads to clockwork regularity—"

"Spare me the sales pitch," said Grub. "We're not here for cheese. We—he—wants to know if you've seen someone hereabouts."

"I see lots of people," said the Wheymaster. "Mostly they buy cheese."

"Don't be a fool, cheesemonger," said Grub. Summer couldn't see him, but she imagined a nasty, sly expression, and stringy hair. "The sniffers picked up a smell. Somebody got through last night. Somebody not-from-around-here."

"Good for the sniffers," said the Wheymaster, sounding unimpressed.

There was a clattering noise and a thump. Summer cringed. It had been a violent sound.

"Don't lie to my face, cheesemonger," hissed Grub. "The sniffers said she came this way. You're telling me someone came across the desert and didn't stop here? Try again."

"Fine," said the Wheymaster, in a shaky voice. "Fine, all right? No need to go hitting me. There was someone, yes. A human girl came through here."

"Looking for a Way, was she?" Summer could practically see Grub rubbing his hands together.

"Yes," said the Wheymaster.

Summer closed her eyes. Was he going to tell this awful person where she was? They would have a hard time getting her out of the cheese—but no, it was only cheese. They could just hack it to bits and pull her out.

"She was looking," said the Wheymaster, his voice rising. "And I wish to the great grim gods I'd given her one! But you've won, Grub, you and your master. I don't do Ways anymore. I played the fool and gave her some cheese and sent her back the way she'd come, told her to find whoever had sent her to me and ask for a better direction. Are you happy?"

"You sure you didn't give her a Way?" asked Grub suspiciously.

The Wheymaster's laugh could have etched glass. He stomped into the back room—Summer trembled—and she heard the clanking of iron. "Here! Here's the damn cauldron! Hand it off to a sniffer if you like, there's not a drop of magic left in it. Something must have gotten into it ages ago. Merlin himself couldn't find a Way with this thing. Nor your nasty queen, either."

"Don't be speaking like that about Her Majesty," muttered Grub, but his heart didn't seem to be in it. "How long ago?"

"I don't know. A few hours. Around dawn, I expect. I was up with the cheeses early."

"Fine," said Grub. "I don't say I believe you, but I don't say I don't—what in the name of her Majesty's chains is *that?*"

"Hmm? Oh. It's a weasel," said the Wheymaster.

Summer pressed her hands to her mouth. *Oh no!*

"Why've you got a weasel in your shop, cheesemonger?"

Oh no, oh no, he saw the weasel, what if he kicks him or something, what if he realizes I'm back here, oh I wish I were back home—

"To make weasel cheese, obviously," said the Wheymaster. "Milking the little things is the very devil, and you need about fifty of them to get even a small wheel, but you drizzle a little honey over a cracker and—"

"Oh gods, don't start," said Grub, sounding disgusted. "I don't need to know all the revolting details. Nasty business, cheesemaking."

"I hope to have enough weasel cheese to offer for sale by next spring," said the Wheymaster with dignity. "Of course, if your master would like a sneak preview, the first wheels should be ready next month."

"My master wants to catch this trespasser," said Grub. "This one's got a scent on her like old magic. We've been riding half the night, and we'll probably ride all day."

"I don't expect you want me to wish you luck," said the Wheymaster sulkily.

Summer heard Grub spit on the floor. "For what your wishes are worth. If you see her again, keep her here and send us word, you hear? If not for your Queen, then for the reward. For there'll be a reward, oh yes. Enough to keep you in filthy cheeses until you die."

The bell jangled. The door slammed. Summer heard the Wheymaster moving around out front, muttering to himself.

The weasel poked his head into the Swiss cheese a moment later. "They're gone. Wait a few minutes and make sure it's not a trick."

Time dragged intolerably inside the cheese. Summer was sure that she would go crazy if she couldn't breathe air that didn't reek of Swiss cheese.

Approximately a million years later, or so it seemed, the Wheymaster said "Come on out. It's as safe as it's going to get."

Summer lunged for the opening to the block of Swiss and hung her head out of it, gasping.

"Awfully close in there, isn't it?" said the Wheymaster. He glared at the door. "Sorry about that. The Queen's lackeys aren't everywhere these days, but they like to think they are."

There was a thin smear of blood at the corner of his lip. Part of his face was bright red, as if he'd been sunburned. Summer stared at him.

"He hit you," she said. "Grub *hit* you."

No one ever really hit Summer. Another girl had punched her in the stomach in third grade once and Summer had fallen down, as much in shock as pain, and had gone to the nurse for an hour. Her mom never spanked her. It would no more have occurred to Summer to hit someone than to turn cartwheels off the edge of a cliff.

A man had just hit another man for helping her.

"He'll do a lot worse than that if he catches you here," said the Wheymaster grimly. He dabbed at the corner of his mouth. "From another world, are you?"

"I think I must be," said Summer. "I've never heard of Orcus."

"Well, it happens." He narrowed his eyes. "You're not from Faerie, are you?"

"No."

"The Dreamlands?"

"No."

"That one world with all the nasty grabby tentacles?"

"N-no…?" Summer hadn't realized that there were so many worlds out there, or that some of them were so unpleasant.

"Well, then." The Wheymaster waved a hand. "We used to have a lot of coming and going. We don't discriminate against otherworlders. They're allowed to hold public office and everything. We're very progressive. "

"That Grub-person didn't sound very progressive," said Summer.

"Well, no. The Queen's people aren't like the rest of us." He sighed. "Come on, we haven't much time. Let's find you a Way."

"I thought your cauldron was broken," said Summer.

"It is," said the Wheymaster, "but when in doubt, there's always cheese." He reached up onto the shelf and pulled down a wheel wrapped in silver paper. He had to blow the dust off the top.

"Harpy cheese, aged in moonlight, washed in the pool of the Oracle," he said. "As close to a prophetic cheese as exists in the world. I stocked it a few years back, just in case."

He took her hand and set it atop the silver paper. "Now tell the cheese what it is you want to do."

Summer took a deep breath and addressed the cheese. "I want to help the poor Frog Tree. And find my heart's desire." She thought for a minute, then added, "And I should probably figure out how to go back home afterwards."

In the stories, a way home always turns up, even if the hero doesn't want to leave, but it probably won't hurt to mention it in advance.

The Wheymaster pulled a knife from a wooden block and handed it to her. "Now you cut it."

Summer gulped. It was a much bigger knife than any she had ever used before. It looked like a short sword.

The Wheymaster had to hold the cheese down while she sawed into it, but he didn't offer to help her. The second cut was easier. When she pulled the wedge out, it had a ragged side and a smooth side, marred with little slivers of silver.

"Do I eat it?" asked Summer.

"Not unless you want to start telling the future in rhyming couplets. No, give it a minute, it's a very old cheese now…"

The cheese seemed to quiver in her hands, like jelly, and then something fell out onto the floor.

Summer squeaked and jumped backwards. More of the small objects rattled from the wheel of cheese, clattering to the floor in a cascade of pale blue.

"Turquoise," said the Wheymaster. He picked up one of the objects. It was a blue stone that looked like chewed bubble gum, with little black lines in it. "Interesting."

"Is that—does that—is that how it works?" Summer clutched the cheese knife and the cut piece of prophetic cheese to her chest, while little blue stones pattered down around her. There seemed to be a lot more contained in the cheese than there could really have been space for.

"More or less," said the Wheymaster. "Your Way is marked in turquoise. Look for it, and it will not steer you wrong." He considered for a moment. "Well, mostly. If your Way involves being deceived, then—look, it's complicated." He took the slice of cheese away from her and pressed a stone into her hands. "Take one with you. I'll clean up the rest before I go."

"You're going?" asked Summer.

The Wheymaster nodded. "Grub and his Master will chase your scent through the hills awhile, thinking you doubled back on your own trail, but they'll figure it out eventually. Then they'll be back here, and I'd best be gone by then."

"Thank you," said Summer. "I'm sorry. I didn't mean to get you in trouble."

The Wheymaster shrugged. "It was bound to happen sooner or later. It may be the manticore cheese talking, but I'm tired of cringing here and waiting for the axe to fall. Now!" He dusted his hands off.

"Now?"

"One last cheese," said the Wheymaster. "Grace or luck? Pick one."

Summer thought that probably she was supposed to say luck—everybody talked about luck, luck would probably be very useful. But on the other hand…

She didn't like church. Church was boring, and she wasn't allowed to read any books except the ones on the back of the pews. Her mother said that they should go every Sunday, but she had headaches a lot, so they went every other Sunday at most.

But they had gone one Sunday a few weeks ago, and there had been a woman singing hymns at the front of the church, a huge woman in blue velvet with a voice like swan wings, and she sang a song called *Amazing*—

"Grace," said Summer firmly. "I'll take grace."

The Wheymaster nodded. He pulled down a cheese from under the counter, wrapped in a black wax rind, and cut off a piece.

"Nightmare milk," he said. "Aged in granite and mixed with honey from clockwork bees."

It was deep purple, the color of beets, and didn't look like cheese at all. She nibbled.

It was dark and bitter and she almost wanted to spit it out, but it melted away into sweetness. It left a taste on her tongue like cream. She licked the corner of her lips, trying to prolong the taste, but it vanished like a dream on waking, like something you wanted to hold on to and can no longer quite remember.

"*Oh,*" she said. "Oh…that was lovely…"

"A marvelous cheese," said the Wheymaster. "One of my favorites. Only recommended in the morning, of course, and never with grapes. Now go, go, hurry!"

Summer paused in the door. She was still holding the cheese knife, and he didn't seemed inclined to take it back. "But what will happen to you?" she asked.

"I'll find a Way," he said, and winked at her. "It's what we do. They can hammer on the door all they like, but I'll be well away, and the best cheeses with me. Now go!"

She went.

Chapter Eight

Summer was half-expecting the world to have changed outside the Wheystation, the way it had changed outside Baba Yaga's house, but it was the same landscape as before. Cottonwoods huddled closely around the stream. The road ran from the front door of the Wheystation off into the hills, following the path of the stream. There was a split-rail fence running along it on the left side. At some point the fence had been painted blue, but all that remained were cracked and faded stripes.

Your Way is marked in turquoise.

The paint was…not turquoise, maybe, but not far from it. Grub and his unseen master were nowhere to be seen. They had presumably gone over the hill and into the desert.

Summer started down the road.

It was hot. Dust puffed off the road under her feet, and stained her sneakers and socks a grayish-tannish-gritty color.

Carrying the cheese knife was difficult too. Holding a sharp object in one hand requires a little bit of attention all the time, so you don't cut yourself.

Summer's mother would never have let her carry it at all, for fear that she'd trip and cut her own head off. It was really almost the size of a sword, particularly for an eleven-year-old girl. The blade swept up in a curve and came to a double point at the end, like a fork.

She wouldn't have expected anyone to have a cheese knife that big, but then again, given the size of some of the cheeses at the Wheystation, you'd need a cheese-sword just to cut them.

There were words etched in the handle, in a language she didn't know.

"If this were like *The Hobbit*," Summer said, to herself or the knife or possibly the weasel, "you'd have elvish runes and glow when enemies were around."

"What, enemies of cheese?" The weasel clung to her shoulder and peered at the blade. "Like mice? That could be useful. I'm feeling a bit peckish. I could go for a nice juicy mouse."

"Yuck!"

"I'd catch you one, too," said the weasel.

Summer considered this. She did not want to eat a mouse, but it was nice of the weasel to offer. She wasn't sure if the weasel qualified as a grown-up—probably not—but…well… "Thank you very much," she said carefully. "But I don't eat mice."

"Suit yourself," said the weasel, and went to sleep in her hair. (Summer had very thick, dark, curly hair and it supported a weasel admirably.)

She kept walking.

The hand holding the cheese-sword sagged. It wasn't very heavy, but she had to hold it out away from her body and it was making her arm tired. If only she had a sheath or something. She didn't feel right just dropping it by the side of the road—what if she needed it? She was in a fantasy world, after all, having an adventure, and adventurers always seem to need swords.

Maybe she could tie it to her belt loop somehow…

It required the sacrifice of both shoelaces, but she managed to tie the cheese-sword to her belt loop so that the pointy bit pointed away from her and she didn't whack her arm on the hilt when she walked.

Of course, if I have to draw it out in a hurry, I'm going to be in trouble…

Still, she felt grown-up and resourceful for having worked it out. The tongues of her shoes flopped against her ankles as she walked.

She had walked for nearly an hour, stopping to drink from the stream once or twice, when a dragonfly landed on the split rail fence in front of her.

It was blue. It was bright, electric blue, blue like a neon sign. Its wings had tiny blue veins in them. Its eyes were huge and mossy green.

It perched on the fence, as immobile as a stone.

Summer looked at it. She dug a hand into her pocket, past the lock and the acorn, and pulled out the piece of stone that had fallen out of the cheese.

Blue. The same color as the dragonfly.

The dragonfly lifted off the fence and droned through the air a few feet, then landed again.

"Do you think it's part of my Way?" she asked the weasel.

"Hzzt?" said the weasel, and rolled over and went back to sleep.

Summer bit her lip. When she was nearly abreast of the dragonfly, it lifted off again, but this time it was going away from the fence, through the cottonwoods.

Following the dragonfly meant she'd have to leave the road. If she stayed on the road, she wouldn't get lost—but if she stayed on the road, what if Grub came up behind her and caught her?

She looked back the way she had come. There was no one there.

It occurred to her that if Grub did follow her trail back through the desert—with the "sniffers," whatever they were—then he might run into Boarskin and Bearskin and Donkeyskin. She hoped that they would be all right. They had seemed very tough, but Grub had been frightening and hit people, and Summer didn't know how someone like Donkeyskin would cope with being hit.

The dragonfly buzzed toward her again, zipped in a circle over her head, then flew back into the trees.

Well, I guess that's pretty obvious…

She put a foot over the split rail fence. It was hard to get over the top—it was nearly chest high and the cheese-sword banged against the post—but she managed. The weasel woke up and made grumbling noises behind her left ear.

When she stepped through the band of cottonwoods, she saw that the landscape had altered subtly from the desert. The shrubs grew in pockets of dirt wedged in between long bands of rock.

Because Summer had paid attention in class, she knew that the rock was the type called *sedimentary,* which lays down in long bands at the bottom of prehistoric lakebeds. But something odd had clearly happened here, because the bands were not flat but diagonal, as if some enormous force had picked the rock up and dropped it down off-kilter.

She stepped up onto the stone.

"Stone's good," offered the weasel. "Hard to track someone over stone. Doesn't leave footprints."

The stone ridge went on for twenty or thirty feet—the length of the driveway to Summer's house—and on the far side it fell away into nothing. When she peered over the edge, she saw the tops of pine trees far below.

"It's a cliff!" she said, startled.

She took a step back. If her mother had been there, she would have screamed at Summer to get away from the edge before she fell, and Summer would have been annoyed, because she knew perfectly well not to fall off very steep cliffs and wasn't going to start doing cartwheels on the edge or anything like that. You would have to be very stupid to fall off a cliff that was so obviously *there*.

But her mother wasn't there. She could stand as close to the edge as she wanted, and look down into the valley below. The pine trees were deep green and the cliff gave way to a long slope of shattery scattery stones. They looked sharp, like broken plates.

A cool breeze whispered up from the valley. It smelled like Christmas trees and cedar chests. A bird called somewhere in the forest, and another one answered it.

Summer took several more steps back, until she was a comfortable distance away from the edge. When she looked back toward the road, she couldn't see anything through the cottonwoods. Maybe that meant that no one could see her, either.

The dragonfly buzzed away over the stone, along the cliff's edge, and she followed.

~

The day got on and Summer got hungry.

Manticore cheese is very filling, but even it runs out eventually. Summer concentrated on plodding along the rock, one foot in front of the other, and tried to ignore the growling in her midsection.

She got in the habit of checking the dragonfly every minute or so, and it was always there, zipping along the cliff's edge, until suddenly it wasn't and she didn't know where it had gone.

She stopped in her tracks. "Weasel? Did you see where it went?"

The weasel had been making a perfect rat's nest of her hair, trying to find the most comfortable position. He stuck his head out and said "No."

Summer turned in a circle, looking for flashes of turquoise.

Nothing.

The sky was hard and blue, but it went on forever and even in this mad world she could hardly be expected to walk into the sky.

"Should I just keep walking?" asked Summer. "I mean—will something show up, do you think?"

                                    Summer in Orcus

"It occurs to me," said the weasel, going back to mussing around in her hair, "that you are laboring under the impression that I am some sort of magical familiar. I'm not. I'm really a very ordinary weasel—although quite good-looking, of course—and not magical at all."

Summer sighed. "You talk though."

"All weasels talk," said the weasel. "Most humans are just bad at listening."

Since standing on the edge of the cliff wasn't going to get her any closer to food, Summer started walking again.

She walked for about a dozen steps, and then a lizard shot across her path. It was black with narrow cream-colored racing stripes, and its tail was as pure and brilliant blue as the sky.

It came out of a crack in the ground and went over the edge of the cliff, clinging to the stone with all its tiny toes.

"Oh no," said Summer, stopping. "I am not jumping off a cliff! I don't care where my path is supposed to lead me! And not on an empty stomach!"

She might have continued in this vein for quite some time, but the weasel said, "Hsst! What's that?"

Summer stopped. For a moment, the only thing she could hear was the wind sighing through the trees below the cliff.

Then there was a thud and a jingle and another thud and a clip-clop-clip-clop and the distant throbbing that happens when somebody says something a long way off.

"Someone's on the road," whispered the weasel. "They're coming this way."

"Do you think it's Grub?" whispered Summer.

"I don't know, but I don't like it." He stared over her shoulder, the way they had come, and his tail lashed once-twice like a cat's. "The hoofbeats are wrong. The horse has too many legs."

Summer was perfectly willing to believe that in this world, there were horses with four legs, six legs, eight legs, maybe a hundred legs, like some kind of centi-horse, and maybe they were still very nice horses that would like to have somebody feed them apples, despite however many legs they might have.

Maybe.

On the other hand, when you knew that somebody was after you and probably behind you on the road, and suddenly you heard a lot of commotion and a horse that maybe wasn't quite a horse after all…

The lizard skittered over the cliff's edge and ran across her shoe. Summer watched it spin on top of her foot, blue tail flashing, then it scurried over the cliff's edge again.

"I think we should get out of here," said the weasel.

The lizard poked its head over the cliff again.

Summer gulped. The jingle-jangle-thud-thud-thud was coming closer. She knelt on the edge of the cliff and reached a hand over.

Her fingers touched metal. She traced a round outline—a ring? It was the size of the big rings that held towels in the bathroom back home.

There was another one beside it. The lizard skittered frantically back and forth.

Someone laughed from the road. How had they gotten so close? If they came through the cottonwood trees, they'd be sure to see her. She had to stick out like a sore thumb on the bare rock.

Could she really go over? Wouldn't she just fall? Was she supposed to hang by the rings?

She leaned farther out over the cliff. She could just see the rings now, under the stone lip, and there was a little bit of a ledge a few feet down. Enough to put her feet on, maybe.

"Go," whispered the weasel. "Oh, go, go, there's something bad behind us, I can smell it from here—"

"Hold on," whispered Summer, and grabbed one of the rings.

She truly didn't know how she was going to get down, and for a minute she didn't think she could bring herself to swing over the edge, but then she heard the worst sound of all.

The hoofbeats had stopped.

There were monkey bars at school. Summer hung on them all the time. It wasn't much different from that, surely?

She grabbed a ring and swung herself over the edge. The world lurched, or maybe it was just her stomach. She grabbed for the second ring, couldn't find it—*oh no, oh no, where is it no no—*

Cold metal under her fingers. She locked her hand around it. Her toes just reached the little ledge. She looked up.

She could see the edge clearly. If somebody looked over, they'd see her.

The lizard was practically under her nose. It scurried sideways, sticking to the rock as easily as if it were flat ground. Summer pressed her cheek against the stone. Her fingers burned.

The metal rings were cast in the shape of bees, a whole circle of little bees, nose to stinger, and the sockets holding them to the cliff were great

                                              Summer in Orcus

blooming roses. They were very pretty. More importantly, they seemed to be very solidly attached.

The rock sloped sharply inward under the overhang at the top of the cliff, forming a shallow cave. The ledge widened. Summer thought she could probably reach it, although there would be a bad second or two when she didn't quite have her feet in the cave and she didn't quite have her fingers on the metal rings.

The lizard skittered out of the cave, then back in.

"Somebody's coming this way," whispered the weasel. "I heard them climb the fence." His mouth was right next to her ear, he was speaking so quietly, and she could feel a tiny puff of breath on her cheek.

Summer nodded.

She moved both hands to the ring closest to the cave and slid her feet along. The scrape of her sneakers on rock sounded much too loud.

The last bit wasn't as bad as she feared. She stretched out as far as she possibly could, got one foot solidly inside the cave, and half-jumped, half-fell over it.

It was deeper than she'd thought. It was deep enough that she could sit down with her knees drawn up and not be in any danger of falling. She could probably have slept there, if she wasn't worried about rolling around in her sleep, and if her heart hadn't been hammering in her chest like a jackhammer.

"So you've lost her, then," said Grub. Summer jumped, but managed not to squeak. The weasel pressed against her neck. She could hear his tiny heart humming along, even faster than hers.

Grub was standing on top of the cliff, she thought, maybe ten feet back the way she'd come.

"Lost," said another voice. It was a man's, and it sounded older and deeper and much more tired than Grub's. "I don't know about *lost*. She might have come this way, or not. I'm a tracker, not a miracle-worker. I'd guess she's been walking along the ridge for a few hours now, and I haven't seen any signs to tell me she's left it. I thought I saw something flash through the trees here, but might have been a bird or something else. It's gone now."

"Lovely." Grub did not sound happy. She heard his footsteps crossing the rock. "Zultan will *not* be pleased."

"That's as may be," said the tracker. "But I can't call tracks out of thin air. She may still be ahead of us."

"A sniffer could find her," said Grub sulkily. "It was sniffers who knew she'd come through."

"Then go get a sniffer," said the tracker. "And while you're at it, get the wagons full of the water you'll need to keep it damp in this here desert, why don't you?"

Grub made a frustrated noise and scuffed at the ground. He had to be right over the top of the cave. Summer breathed through her mouth and tried to not even *think* loudly.

"You're supposed to be the best," he said.

"No, I'm not," said the tracker. "I'm supposed to be good, and flattery won't help. My great-grandfather *was* the best, and not even he could track someone across naked rock. That's the way it is. You like it or you don't, but you can't change it."

There was a brief silence. Someone—maybe Grub—hawked and spit. Summer winced. Her mother would be deeply horrified. Spitting in public was only slightly less grim than murder in her mom's world.

"What does he want with her, anyway?" asked the tracker. He was moving off now, farther up the canyon rim.

"She's a human," said Grub.

"So? Plenty of humans around, even now. You were one yourself, I hear, before you got into the wight-liquor—"

"Yes, *well*," said Grub, cutting off whatever else the tracker was going to say. "This one came through from somewhere outside. It's crone magic, they think, and you know how the Queen feels about crones…"

The tracker said something else, but Summer couldn't make out the words. They'd moved too far off. It was very frustrating. She wanted very much for the men to go away without finding her, but she also wanted to hear the rest of the conversation, which seemed like it might be important.

So they were after her because she was human and she'd come from somewhere else. That didn't seem very fair. She hadn't *done* anything.

Summer knew, of course, that a crone is a not-very-nice term for an old woman, and she could guess that they meant Baba Yaga, who was, after all, a not-very-nice old woman. Still, it wasn't her fault. She hadn't asked for Baba Yaga to send her somewhere…

…had she?

This must be my heart's desire. I didn't think that it was to wander around hungry in the desert and then have scary people try to catch me, though!

And what were sniffers, anyway? Or wight-liquor?

She was torn. She wanted her heart's desire—that was the point of having a heart's desire, after all!—but she didn't want to be chased through the desert by strange men who might or might not be human.

It's an adventure. I am on a grand adventure. It's like when the children went to Narnia, and they were chased by wolves. It was probably pretty scary to be chased by wolves, but they stayed anyway and there were centaurs and fauns and talking lions.

And this was all true and settled her nerves a bit, but it was a long time before she felt comfortable leaving the cave.

Chapter Nine

Getting out proved easier than getting in. There was a crack in the stone that was almost like a handhold, on the top of the canyon, and even though Summer scraped her knuckles hauling herself up, she didn't feel like she was in any danger of falling into the canyon.

Of Grub and the tracker and the mysterious Zultan Houndbreaker, there was no sign.

"We must be behind them now," she said. "That's better, right?"

"Probably," said the weasel. "As long as they're headed away from us, and there aren't more of them. Oh, for an egg, or a nice fat mouse!"

Summer was not much interested in a mouse, fat or otherwise, but an egg sounded really good, particularly a hard-boiled one. She liked peeling them and trying to get as big a piece of eggshell flaked off as possible.

As there were neither eggs nor mice, she made her way to the road and kept walking.

The desert ended gradually, not all at once. The stubby little bushes became stubby little clumps of grass and then the clumps of grass grew together and got taller, and in an hour (or maybe two), the road ran alongside fields of golden wheat and swaying stalks of rye.

"Half a minute," said the weasel, scurrying down her pant-leg. "If there's not a mouse in this bank, I'll eat my own tail."

Summer shoved her hands in her pockets and leaned against a fence post. The cheese-sword banged against the wood.

There were no people in the fields. Presumably there had to be farmers somewhere, but all she could see were the long swells of grain, rippling in the wind. Little birds would rise out of the field, by twos and threes, and then settle back down again.

She looked around for something turquoise, but there was only the sky.

Maybe I'm on the wrong road. No, but I didn't see anything…maybe I'm on the right road, and I'll only see something turquoise if I need to change it… Summer scowled down at the ground. Magic was complicated.

The weasel came back, licking his lips. "*That's* better," he said. "Are you sure you don't want one? I might be able to rustle up another."

"It's okay," said Summer, not wanting to think about how hungry she'd have to be to eat a mouse, or how soon she might get there. "If there's fields, maybe there's a farmhouse somewhere, and they'll give us some lunch."

"Unless that Grub-fellow got there first," said the weasel.

Summer didn't want to think about that.

They didn't see any farmhouses. The only sign of life was a bird, a big bird, far off in the next field. It was black-and-white, with a tan head, and it was dancing by itself.

The road curved around the edge of the field, so they passed quite close by the dancing bird. Summer saw that it had an enormous orangey-tan crest and scaly gray legs. It was wearing a black waistcoat around its midsection, with a scarlet handkerchief folded into the pocket.

It bounced and whirled, wings outstretched, and as they passed by, Summer heard:

"…and *one* and two and *dip* and turn…"

"It talks!" whispered Summer.

"I am giving you fair warning," said the weasel. "The next time you say that, I shall nip you."

"Sorry."

The bird finished a turn, bowed deeply to an imaginary partner—it was a very extravagant bow, and made much use of its striped black-and-white wings—and then approached the fence. In addition to the waistcoat, it had an elaborately knotted neckcloth and a pair of spats. "Yes?" it said. "May I help you?"

"Um," said Summer. "Sorry. I didn't mean to interrupt—"

"You're not interrupting," said the bird. "I finished the set. It's not good enough, but it'll do for now, since my brain's gone all to collywobbles and I shan't get any better at it today. Reginald Hoopoe, of the Almondgrove

Hoopoes, at your service." He stood on one foot and stuck his other foot out toward her.

Summer reached down—she had to reach rather far, since Reginald only came up to her waist—and shook the gray foot tentatively. He had large black claws and his toes felt like twigs.

"I'm Summer," she said.

"Not a bad name," said Reginald Hoopoe. "Full of seasonal significance. But rather short, don't you think? Have you considered adding a surname or five?"

"I don't have even one name," said the weasel, nodding down to Reginald. "You don't happen to have an egg about you, do you? No offense intended, it's just, you being a bird and all—"

"None taken," said Reginald. "But no, I don't, and if I had I wouldn't give it to you. No desire to be disaccommodating, but a fellow can't go handing his unborn children out to anyone that asks, now can he?"

The weasel sighed and looked put upon, even though Summer thought Reginald had a very good point.

"Please," said Summer, "do you know if there's a farmhouse, or—or a restaurant around here? I don't have any money, but maybe I could—um— wash dishes?" She had read in books that sometimes you could wash dishes and pay for a meal that way, although she didn't like washing dishes any more than the average eleven-year-old and they would probably have to find her a stepstool to stand on to reach all the way into the sink.

"There are no restaurants," said Reginald. "Nor are there farmhouses, dear me, no. This is hundred-year-wheat, and you check on it once a decade or so, as I understand it, though I might be wrong. I am a middling dancer and highly skilled with dice or cards, but as a farmer, I am strictly bottom-drawer."

"Hundred-year-wheat?" asked Summer.

"The primary ingredient in Croissant of Ages, which is sweetened with nectar from the century plant." He looked expectant. "You know it?"

"Um. No? I'm sure it's very good…" said Summer doubtfully, who didn't think that anything a hundred years old would taste nice at all.

"It's dreadful, actually," said Reginald cheerfully, hopping to the highest fencepost. This put him on eye-level with Summer. "Only good for the sort of parties where members of the finest families throw around the blunt."

Summer felt lost.

"Display the scratch."

"Err?"

"Money," said Reginald patiently. "They show off their money."

"Oh!" That didn't sound very nice to Summer. Her family wasn't poor—her mother was very clear about the fact that they were middle-class, thank you *very* much, and would have gotten very angry if anybody said differently—but they weren't rich either. You knew the rich kids at school, because they had better calculators and clothes with designer labels on them.

"But if you're hungry," said Reginald, "it might be, may be, could be that I've got a bit of tucker put away for just such an occasion."

"Oh, *do* you?" asked Summer gratefully. "I'm very hungry. It's been a long time since the cheese this morning, and—I suppose I could wash dishes—or—err—something?"

"Not at all," said Reginald gallantly. "Duty of a Hoopoe. Can't leave a young lass wandering about in distress, even one a bit short of feathers."

Summer knew that you were not supposed to take food from strangers, although mostly that was candy and she really would have preferred a sandwich to candy right now (strange as that was!), and anyway when people at school talked about "strangers" they almost certainly were not talking about two-foot-tall talking birds.

And she'd already had strange cheese and stew made by shapechangers.

"Hang on," said the weasel, arching his whiskers forward. "If there are no farmhouses and no restaurants and you're not interested in the wheat, what are you doing out here?"

"A capital question!" said Reginald. "Fair, absolutely fair. I am, in fact, a trifle cleaned out, and so I'm rusticating."

Summer and the weasel exchanged puzzled glances.

"I have outrun the bailiff, and now my pockets are to let."

"Um?" said Summer.

Reginald sighed. "I spent all my money and now my bills are due and I can't pay them, so I pawned my gold watch-spurs and went out in the country where they won't follow me."

He began walking along the top fence rail. Summer and the weasel followed.

"That sounds awful," said Summer.

Reginald shrugged his wings. "It's not so bad. Happens to all of us, sooner or later, unless we're as rich as Golden Egg. Hardly a season goes by that it's not low-water with me somewhere or other, but I always come about."

Reginald's "bit of tucker" was actually a rather large set of packs, dropped under a tree. The tree itself was about twenty feet from an old-fashioned pump with a handle that went up and down. Summer recognized it from pictures, and after sawing on the handle for a few minutes, she managed to coax some water out of it.

She thought it must be for watering the wheat, but Reginald shook his head. "There's pumps and waystations all over the empire. The dogs set them up, oh so many ages ago, and even though they're long gone, you still find the pumps along the major roads."

Summer wasn't sure what dogs he was talking about, but presumably if weasels talked and birds talked, dogs could also talk and set up pumps. She wondered if there were any creatures around that didn't talk, and whether that made it awkward at mealtimes.

"Come on, then," said Reginald cheerfully. "You must be fair gut-foundered." He opened his packs—he used his feet, she saw, and his beak, not his wings—and produced, as if by magic, a loaf of bread, a small pot of jam, several slabs of cheese in wax paper and a sausage.

"Oh, *thank you,*" said Summer, sinking down into the dust under the tree.

Between the three of them, they made a very good meal.

"Now, then..." said Reginald, leaning back and picking at his beak with a talon. "I know why I'm out here—dibs not in tune, as I said!—but what are you doing here?"

"Oh," said Summer. She glanced at the weasel. The weasel shrugged. This wasn't helpful. Still, Reginald seemed very nice, even if he spoke a little oddly. "I, uh, came here on accident." She hesitated. "Baba Yaga sent me."

Reginald sat bolt upright, his crest raising like a paper fan unfolding. "Baba Yaga? The prime article?"

"Yes?"

"Huh!" He lowered his crest again thoughtfully. "*Did* she, now? Kicking up some kind of lark with the powers that be, is she?" He eyed Summer thoughtfully. "Well, I'd say it was all a bag of moonshine, but...no, p'raps I *can* see it." He tapped his beak. "So what does she have you doing, if I may be so bold?"

"I don't know," said Summer gloomily. "She didn't tell me to do anything. Well, to take the weasel, but—"

"I don't know either," said the weasel hurriedly.

"—and my path is supposed to be marked in turquoise—at least, that's what the Wheymaster said—but I haven't seen anything turquoise for hours, so I don't know if I'm on the right path. I just wanted to help the Frog Tree, and maybe find my heart's desire, but I didn't expect all this walking. And this awful person named Grub and somebody named Zultan were trying to find me, and I had to hide—"

"*Zultan Houndbreaker!*" Reginald's crest went up and down like a bellows for a minute, and his pupils expanded until his eyes were a thin ring of gold around a well of black. "The Queen's general!?"

Summer wrapped her arms around herself and said, "I don't know." She felt a little like crying, despite having eaten, except that she thought the weasel might say something sarcastic if she did.

"Bad blood, those people," said the hoopoe. "Very bad. Whatever they want with you…" He fluffed up all his feathers, until he looked twice his size, then shook them all down again. "Brr!"

"I haven't done *anything*," said Summer, feeling a tear leaking out despite her best efforts. "I *haven't*. I don't know any of these people, and Grub hit the Wheymaster and he was only helping me and I don't know *why!*"

Another tear squeezed out. The weasel arched his back like a very small cat and rubbed against her cheek.

"Here now," said Reginald, clearly upset, "none of that, no need to turn on the waterworks! I'm not going to cry rope on you to any of the Queen's men. Word of a Hoopoe."

Summer scrubbed at her eyes with her wrist, feeling embarrassed.

"Let me think," said Reginald. He put his wings up to his head and bounced from foot to foot. "Let me think, let me think. Oh yes! I tell you what, Summer-who-needs-a-surname, why don't I take you to my father?"

"Your father?" asked Summer, sniffling.

"Yes! Just the chap we need!" Reginald bounced up and down. "Slap up to the echo, he is, up to all the tricks—err—that is, very smart, very *wise*. If you're in the suds, he's the best bird you could talk to." He beamed at her.

"Will he help me?" asked Summer.

"Oh, yes. Head of the household, you know, an Almondgrove Hoopoe down to his pinfeathers. Wouldn't dream of leaving a little lass to be chased about by Queen's men. Not a *Loyalist,* you know." Reginald gave her what was probably meant to be a reassuring pat, but since he could only reach as high as her knee, was more of a tap.

"Well, okay," said Summer, after a quick look around for any unusual turquoise insects or lizards. Reginald's plan seemed at least as good as just walking along the road until she ran into Grub or something worse.

"Right!" said the hoopoe. "We'll leave at once. When Father realizes why I've come back early, he'll probably help me raise the wind anyhow—"

He cast a brief look at Summer and amended it to "He'll give me some money to pay down my debts."

"That would be nice of him," said Summer politely.

Reginald clapped his beak together, making a hollow clacking noise, and a dozen small birds dropped out of the boughs of the tree. They were slightly larger than finches and each one wore a small round bowler hat on its head.

"My valet-flock," Reginald explained. "Lads, this is Summer."

The valet-birds lined up on the ground, and each one took the hat off the next bird in line with its beak. In unison, they all bowed to Summer.

"It's very nice to meet you," said Summer, who thought that she was probably supposed to curtsey but had never learned how. She bowed instead. The little birds put each other's hats back on.

"Do they talk?' asked Summer in a whisper. The weasel sighed.

"Talk! Lord, no. They're—uh—hang on, it'll come to me in a minute—flock-mind. You know?"

Summer shook her head.

"Ah. They're all smarter together than they are apart. Great chaps for taking care of a person's feathers and pressing his clothes and handling the luggage. Not *talking* smart, though—although if you pick the wrong color waistcoat, such looks! They've got ways of letting you know what they think, don't you doubt it!"

The valet-flock settled on Reginald's packs, grabbing multiple small straps in their claws. On some unspoken signal they all took off together, lifting the packs into the air.

"Right!" said Reginald cheerfully. "Let's go!"

<h1 style="text-align:center">Chapter Ten</h1>

Traveling with the hoopoe might not have been faster, but it felt like it.

He hopped along the road, from fence-post to fence-post, chatting to her. Occasionally, he would take to the air. "Nobody for miles," he reported cheerfully when he returned. "Not the shake of a cat's whisker. Zultan and his bully-boys have taken themselves off, I b'lieve."

Summer was glad for someone else to talk to.

The weasel…wasn't.

"He's a fop," muttered the weasel, as Reginald flew off on another scouting trip. "Look at that! Spats! Really? Who dresses like that?"

"You don't dress like *anything,*" Summer pointed out (quite reasonably, she thought).

"Yes, I do. I dress like a weasel. Weasel fur goes with everything." He sniffed.

"I like him," said Summer.

"Oh, he's likeable enough." The weasel flicked his tail. "Sure. But I don't trust him any farther than I could throw an ostrich egg."

Summer bit her lower lip, watching the distant speck of Reginald over the fields. "You don't think he'd sell us out, do you? Find Zultan and tell him where we are?"

"Well…I wouldn't go that far." The weasel studied his claws. "I don't think he's bad, per se. But if we get in a tight spot, he'll be up and away and never looking back, don't think he won't!"

"You think he'd do that?"

"Birds!" said the weasel. "Huh! Never trust birds."

"You're just mad because he didn't have any eggs."

~

They saw one strange thing, before they left the farmlands.

They smelled it before they saw it. It smelled like wet bread left in the bag to get moldy. Summer wrinkled her nose.

The source was obvious as soon as they reached it.

One of the fields of hundred-year-wheat had rotted where it stood. The stalks were black and wet-looking. The kernels had swollen into huge blisters, then burst with streaks of green and purple and clotted brown.

"Ewwwww," said Summer.

The weasel wiped his muzzle against her shoulder repeatedly, his mouth open in disgust.

"That shouldn't happen," said Reginald. "Not proper at all. Look at it—those stalks weren't high enough yet. Can't be more than eighty or ninety years old."

"Couldn't it have just gotten mucky?" asked Summer, covering her nose.

"Not hundred-year-wheat," said Reginald. "Never heard of anything that bothered a wheat field."

"It doesn't smell right," said the weasel. "It smells bad, but it smells bad like a termite mound, like something white and wiggly at the bottom. Not like plants. Not *just* like plants."

Reginald scratched his chin with a claw. "'Course, not a farmer, you understand. Maybe it does happen. Odd, though. Not proper. Cuts up my peace, I don't mind telling you."

He glanced at Summer and added, "Makes me uneasy, I mean," but she thought *cuts up my peace* described the situation very well.

Walking past the rotted field put Summer in mind of the poor Frog Tree. That hadn't been proper, either.

She put her hand in her pocket and rubbed her finger over the tadpole acorn. It was comfortable in her fingers, but the smell of rotting wheat hung in the air long after the field was out of sight.

It was a long day of walking, and Summer was already tired. She had walked for most of the night on a very few hours of sleep and then walked most of the day as well.

She had also been briefly frightened out of her wits. Unless you have ever been really truly terrified, you cannot know how exhausting that is. For a brief period, you are extremely awake and tense and terrified, but afterwards, when all the adrenaline wears off, you feel you could sleep for a week without stopping.

What kept Summer plodding along the dusty road after Reginald was hope that his father, Lord Almondgrove, would be a real honest-to-god grown-up.

Grown-ups are strange creatures, and many of them are useless, but even the worst of them has *authority*. Summer's second grade teacher had been a small fluttery woman with watery eyes, but when she cleared her throat and gave the class a stern look, everybody sat down in their desks and opened their books and stopped throwing spit wads. Summer's face had felt hot, even though she'd been sitting at her desk the whole time and hadn't done anything wrong.

Summer hoped that Lord Almondgrove would have that same authority. Maybe he could get things sorted out, like a teacher or a principal. If there were police in this world, maybe he could call them and explain about Grub and the tracker and that Summer hadn't done something wrong. A grown-up could explain things like that and have the police listen, whereas if you were a child, even if you tried very hard to speak slowly and clearly, grown-ups tended to steam-roll over the top of you. (Or worse, they smile and tell you what a *vivid imagination* you had. Summer did indeed have a vivid imagination, but she didn't know what bearing that had on anything.)

Reginald alighted on top of a fence post and shook out his wings. He proceeded in a series of short flights, darting this way and that, always coming back to Summer and the valet-flock.

Although Reginald clearly wasn't a child, he also wasn't quite a grown-up as Summer understood it. Summer was pretty sure that real grown-ups weren't supposed to run away into the country to hide instead of paying their bills.

It was awkward that the weasel didn't seem to like him, though. Summer felt embarrassed. She wanted both her new friends to get along, so she cringed a little when Reginald said something particularly foolish, and cringed again when the weasel muttered something cutting in reply.

She did like the bird, though, no matter what the weasel thought. It was hard not to like someone so cheerful and with such hopeful goals.

"Dancing," he said, hopping along beside her in the late afternoon. "I was practicing my dancing for the Grand Assembly. I shall take the claw of

Miss Merope, of the Lankyshire Bee-Eaters, and we shall stand up together for the country dance and the aerial waltz." He sighed and clacked his beak. "Not that I wouldn't dance the sarabande and the cotillion and the reel with her as well, but her chaperones will not let her stand up with a single gentlebird for more than two dances. It wouldn't be proper, not unless they were betrothed."

"You must like her," said Summer.

"Oh, I'm passionately in love with her, of course," said Reginald, as if commenting on the weather. "Everyone is. She goes everywhere in the best company and has fans made of sugar-spider silk. Her throat is as golden as the sun and her eyes are the color of pomegranates and her feathers are as green as—well, as a deuced green thing, I don't know, something very green anyway."

"Grass?" offered Summer.

"Oh, much greener than that. You wouldn't think much of grass after you'd seen Miss Merope."

"Peas?"

Reginald thought about this one. "Y-e-s," he said slowly, drawing out each syllable. "I suppose that's accurate. Not very *poetical*, though, is it? If you were writing an ode to her beauty, you wouldn't want to compare her to peas. She'd likely get offended." He considered. "Although it does rhyme with 'bees.' I tried to write her a poem where I compared her feathers to emeralds, but hardly anything rhymes with emeralds. Had to use 'them scalds' and then I had to figure out who was being scalded, and by the end I had an army storming the castle and having boiling oil dumped on them. Miss Merope said it wasn't romantic and threw it away." He sighed.

Summer, for no particular reason, was starting to dislike the absent Miss Merope.

The fields were giving way to forests, like the one that Summer had seen from the cliff. At first it was just a few copses of trees, and then the copses got larger and larger and joined together, and soon they were walking through the woods and it was getting dark under the trees. The road led across a number of small streams, and Summer's feet went *clomp clomp clomp* on the wooden boards of the bridges.

The valet birds called a halt by virtue of flying off the road and dropping the packs under a likely set of trees.

"Oh!" said Summer. "Will we be safe here?" She looked around. There might be wolves in the woods, or cougars. Summer was very well read and knew that wolves hardly ever attack humans, but cougars are another matter entirely.

"Sure," said Reginald. "The flock'll keep watch, turn and turnabout, and we'll have a nice fire. Nothing to worry about."

"What about Grub and the Houndbreaker?" asked the weasel, stirring out of Summer's pocket for the first time in hours. "They might come back this way looking for us."

"Oh," said Reginald, looking worried. "Hadn't thought of that." He looked to the valet-birds.

The flock twittered and conversed among themselves, then picked up the packs again. They led the way back down the road a few hundred yards, to the last small stream they had passed, and then flew out over the water.

"Ah," said the weasel, satisfied. "*They've* got some sense, anyhow. We're to break our trail so they can't track us."

Summer raised her eyebrows.

"Water won't hold a smell," the weasel explained. "If you take off your shoes and wade down it, they won't know where you've gone or how far."

So Summer stripped off her shoes and socks and stuck her feet in the water. It was surprisingly cold for being so near a desert, but her feet were hot and throbbing and the water felt good.

Her mother would never have let her walk on the rocks—they were so slimy with waterweed that she'd likely fall and break her neck, or catch some horrible disease—but Summer went slithering and slipping and sliding over the rocks and didn't break anything. (She supposed she'd simply have to wait and see on the diseases.)

When the bridge had vanished around a bend in the stream, the valet birds led her up the bank and into a mossy clearing in the woods. They dropped the pack and several of them began hopping about gathering sticks and bits of pine needle.

Summer flopped down and began massaging her abused toes. They looked red and they ached when she wiggled them, but she didn't seem to have any blisters. By the time it occurred to her to offer to help, the valet-birds had built a small, tidy fire in the middle of the clearing. Several of them helped Reginald out of his waistcoat and into another one, which had candy-red stripes.

One of the birds landed on her shoulder and looked at her very seriously out of one tiny black eye.

"Um?" said Summer.

"Aren't you going to dress for dinner?" asked Reginald.

"I haven't got anything else," said Summer, looking down at herself. Her jeans still looked okay—jeans tend not to show dirt unless you've been wallowing around in mud—but her t-shirt looked like she'd slept in it, then sweated in it, then climbed into a cheese in it, then walked down a very dusty road and sweated some more.

Reginald clapped a claw to his beak. "Of course! I'm a wretch. Forget I mentioned it. Not important at all."

The valet-bird turned its head so it could stare at her out of the other tiny black eye. Apparently it did not feel the same way.

"I could wear the blanket…" said Summer, picking at the blanket that the shapechanger sisters had given her. It did not show the dirt nearly so badly, perhaps because it came from the desert and was the color of dust already.

"They'd prefer it," said Reginald. "Sorry. Don't think anything of it. Many's the time I've sat down to dinner in all my dust, and nobody minding but Great-Aunt Murgatroyd, and she's a regular Tartar."

Three more valet-birds landed on Summer's head, and with tugs and chirps, pulled her behind a tree. She managed to get her t-shirt over her head and the blanket back on, despite their help.

Two of the birds grabbed the shirt and flew toward the stream, joined by another with a scrub brush the size of a pack of gum. The third settled on Summer's shoulder and began futilely trying to groom down her hair.

Summer giggled. The tiny beak against her scalp didn't hurt, but it certainly tickled. (Her hair tended to eat hairbrushes, even on days when a weasel hadn't been nesting in it. "Just like your father's," her mother had said once, so Summer hadn't asked about it again.)

Any dismay she'd felt at being dusty and dirty rapidly vanished when she stepped out from behind the tree to see the dinner set out for them. Apparently bread and cheese was fine for lunch, but the valet-birds felt that dinner was a special occasion. There was a white linen tablecloth laid over a stone, thin metal goblets full of spring water, and little bone china plates. There was even a little saucer for the weasel.

"Cat-lap," muttered Reginald, hooking his beak over the goblet and taking a sip. "Can't offer you much better—didn't pack any ratafia or negus, not thinking, you understand, that I'd be encountering a little chit fresh out of the nursery here in the wilds—not that I'm not glad of your company! Not at all!" He took another sip. "But it's a shockingly mean drink for a proper dinner."

"I don't mind at all," said Summer. "I've never had—err—ratafia?"

"You won't like it," said Reginald. "Shocking stuff. All the ladies drink it, but I'm sure I don't know why."

The valet-birds brought out a little tin of ham and another little tin of some kind of meat paste, and little squares of bread and cheese. One roasted slices of apples on a stick over the fire. Two birds flew in from the woods with blackberries in their claws—only a few, but enough to make a lovely dessert.

This was the sort of adventuring that Summer could get behind whole-heartedly.

"We'll have a proper feast at Almondgrove Manor," said Reginald. "Roasted fish and Beef Arvington and potatoes as big as your head and a hundred sauces and lobsters and stuffed eggs—"

"You eat eggs?" asked Summer, a bit shocked.

"Not from anyone we know," said Reginald. "Chicken eggs, same as anybody. Chickens aren't much for conversation, you understand, and the eggs wouldn't hatch anyway. Not like going into somebody's nest and stealing a proper egg. They'll have you up on charges for that, or someone'll call you out before the Dawn Chorus, and heaven help you."

The weasel muttered something into his tinned ham.

After dinner, alas, things were not quite so pleasant. While the valet-birds had stocked Reginald's pack with many good things to eat (and a spare waistcoat) they had not included any bedding. Reginald simply hopped to a low branch and put a wing over his head.

Summer was left to curl up between the roots of a tree (which despite the moss was not very pleasant) and pull the blanket around herself. She had to take off the cheese-sword so it didn't dig into her ribs. The valet-birds twittered and hopped around her, apparently quite upset that they could not make her any more comfortable.

Eventually, after much discussion, four of them picked up the corners of the linen tablecloth and dropped it across her shoulders.

Summer smiled a little, touched, and was asleep before the birds had finished twittering.

Chapter Eleven

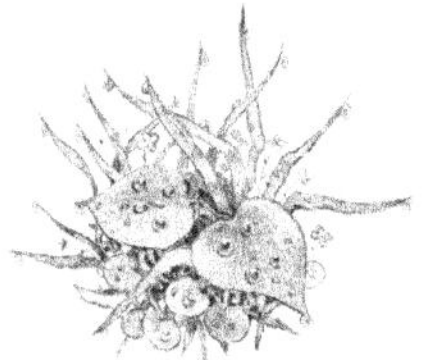

Poets and even ordinary people make much of dew. They point to it on grass and sing its praises on spiderwebs. Words like "silver" and "gossamer" and "a thousand glittering diamonds" are thrown about whenever dew comes up, often by people who should know better.

Occasionally, they will even go so far as to speak of "nymph tears sparkling on the grass" or some such. When it has gotten to this stage, they generally need to be sat down and given a stern talking-to, and perhaps a settling cup of tea.

What these people forget, or never knew, is that dew is real and solid and if you are sleeping out of doors, you can go to bed warm and dry and wake up cold and soaking wet and not at all inclined to admire the sparkling of a thousand dewy diamonds.

The only good thing about waking up cold and soaking wet is that you don't much feel like going back to sleep.

Summer sat up. Her neck hurt where it had been wedged on the tree root and her feet hurt and her calves hurt and the heavy muscles on top of her thighs hurt from nearly two days of walking.

If she had been at home, she would have tried to convince her mother that she was feeling much too miserable to go to school. But she wasn't at home, and two of the little valet-birds were pressing a mug of hot tea into her hands.

"I'm cold," she grumbled. "And my feet hurt."

"Can't say I'm surprised," said Reginald cheerfully. "You go walking about on them instead of flying."

She tried again. "I may die."

"Oh, I shouldn't think so. Nowhere near sticking your spoon in the wall just yet."

When you are looking to have a good whine, this sort of response is unsatisfactory. She tried the weasel instead, but he gave her a weaselly look and said, "What do you expect *me* to do about it?" so she stopped and drank the tea instead.

She thought, down in her very private heart of hearts, that she wanted to go home.

She felt immediately guilty for thinking it. In books, nobody who found themselves in a fantasy world ever wanted to go home. (Well, nobody but Eustace Clarence Scrubb in Narnia, and you weren't supposed to agree with him.)

She was definitely not feeling grateful enough for being on a superb magical adventure. She told herself this sternly several times and then wanted to cry, because it doesn't help to yell at people who are cold and wet, even when the person yelling at you is you.

But the fire was warm, and the valet-birds built it up until it was warmer yet, and Summer crouched down next to it and felt the heat on her face.

There were scones. They were rather hard, but they tasted good. Summer began to feel a bit better. Her shirt was dry and clean (if smelling a little of campfires) and putting it on made her feel better still, and then the valet-birds began ferrying more blackberries in from a distant bush, and she started to think that perhaps she didn't want to go home quite yet after all.

After all, when you go home in the books, sometimes they make you forget. And I don't want to forget this.

She made sure to say, "Thank you," to each valet-bird, as it perched on her finger and dropped a berry into the palm of her hand. She felt very grown-up saying it, and each bird dipped its beak in acknowledgement and chirped before it flew away.

The forest was different this morning. Fog puddled in the hollows and lay like milk across the road. Moisture dripped off the trees, onto the pine needles and the tree roots and the back of Summer's neck.

They walked for most of the morning. After an hour, Summer took off the blanket and looped it over her arm. The air was cool and tingly, but walking had warmed her up, and even her sore feet didn't feel quite so sore anymore.

The valet-birds had spent part of the night redesigning her shoelace scabbard for the cheese-sword. The knots were much neater now and it didn't bang into her thigh when she walked.

It was getting on time to stop for lunch when the valet-birds suddenly halted and the weasel said, "Hsst!"

Summer tensed. Was it Grub again?

"Eh?" said Reginald, who had been practicing his aerial waltz.

"Something up there, to the left," said the weasel. "Big. And jangling like metal."

"Elk?" asked Reginald. "We do get 'em up here."

The weasel shook his head. "Not stomping. *Padding.* But not very far."

Reginald and Summer looked at each other helplessly. Summer put her hand on the hilt of the cheese-sword.

"Well," said Reginald. "No sense being pudding-hearted!" He took to the air and flew forward determinedly.

Summer took a deep breath. It made sense for Reginald to go ahead—he could fly, after all—but he also barely came up to her waist and he wasn't terribly sensible. She hurried after him.

Reginald fluttered down to the ground. He stopped with his beak open and his wings half-extended in surprise.

It was a wolf.

When Summer had been nine years old, her mother took her to the zoo. It was a very good zoo, and the animals were behind deep moats and high fences, so there was no chance that they would escape and rampage through the crowd. Summer had been enchanted by the spotted skunk and the clowning of the otters and the comical faces of the puffins—but the wolves and lions and bears had disappointed her.

The problem was that they were so *small.*

The black bears weren't much bigger than humans. The lions looked nothing like Aslan. Their hips and shoulders were so narrow that you couldn't imagine riding one anyway.

And pictures in books always showed wolves as huge, but the wolves in their enclosure looked like rather large dogs, no bigger than Buddy the chocolate Lab down the street. When you looked at these wolves, sleeping contentedly on their rocks, you could believe the signs that said that wolves were shy and avoided people.

Summer had gone home, very thoughtful, and put her book with Little Red Riding Hood in it behind some others on the shelf. She felt embarrassed for the story.

And now here she was, in a fairy tale world. If she made it home, Summer thought that perhaps she would pull the book out again, because here was a wolf worthy of the name.

It was enormous. It was easily the size of a pony, with paws like dinner plates and a skull as broad as a frying pan. It met her eyes with icy green ones, and it did not look shy or evasive at all.

The only reason that Summer did not turn around and run immediately was because the wolf was in a cage.

The cage had shining metal bars and an enormous ring at the top with a rope through it. It looked as if the wolf had been walking between two trees and the cage had dropped down over it. There was a bit of a gap at the bottom where a tree root lifted it, and the ground had been clawed and scrabbled into dirt around it.

"Have mercy," said the wolf, staring into Summer's eyes. "Let me out."

"Oh!" said Summer.

It was not that the wolf talked. The weasel had made it very clear that she could expect all sorts of creatures to talk. But she had never heard a voice like that, so deep and growling and wild, threaded through with a howling music.

She wanted to help him. Creatures with voices like that did not belong in cages. Still—

"Have mercy," said the wolf again. "If it was not you who put me here, then help me."

Reginald hopped closer. "Steady now," he said. "I don't like to see a dirty trick like this played on anyone—for that's a trap you're in, sure enough—but how do we know you won't come after us when you're free?"

"I give you the word of a wolf," said the wolf.

"Is that good?" asked Summer timidly.

"Not really," said the weasel. "Wolves make no promises, except to each other."

The wolf grinned. His teeth were as long as Summer's fingers. "That is true," he admitted.

"Well, we can't leave him here," said Summer. "He'll starve!"

"He doesn't look like he's missed any meals lately," said Reginald, eyeing the width of the wolf's shoulders.

"I am not so worried about starving," said the wolf. "But if I am still in this cage by nightfall, it will shatter my windows and burn my doors."

None of this made any sense to Summer, but Reginald hopped a bit closer and examined the bars speculatively. "Hmm. Silver wash over iron, are they?" He tapped a bar with one claw.

He was standing in reach of the wolf's jaws, if the beast sprang. Summer wanted to dart forward and grab him and pull him back, saying, "It's not safe!"

She had opened her mouth and taken a half-step forward—

—and then she stopped as if she had run into an iron bar herself, because it was exactly what her mother would have done.

For one horrible moment, Summer felt as if she had gone down to the secret chamber of her heart and found her mother writing on its walls.

The wolf met her eyes with his own fierce, impossibly green ones, and Summer thought, *I have to get him out. It doesn't matter if he eats me. If I leave him here, I won't feel like* me *any more.*

The weasel stirred.

"You could flip that cage over if you wanted," he said to the wolf. "One paw in that gap, and I don't think it would stand for a moment. But you haven't and you aren't touching it, and the bars are made of silver…"

The wolf looked at the sky.

"You're a were-wolf, aren't you?" said Summer.

"No," said the wolf. "I am a wolf and was born a wolf and will be a wolf until I die. I am a were-house."

"A warehouse?"

The wolf sighed. "No. A were-*house*. I am a wolf by day, and by night I turn into a rather pleasant cottage with white curtains."

A great deal of Summer's fear evaporated and she folded her arms and said, very grimly, "This is a *pun*, isn't it?"

"Only by accident, I assure you," said the wolf. "We wolves are prone to such maladies. A cousin of mine is a were-library, and another turns into a very large skylark on solstices." He scuffed at the ground with his paw. "I believe the hunter meant to trap me and put a silver chain through my tongue, and when I change tonight, I will be trapped in that form forever and can be sold on the real estate market."

"Well, we can't have that," said Reginald. "Wouldn't turn a rat over to the house-hunters." He looked at Summer. "What do you think?"

Summer took a deep breath, and let it out. "If you promise you won't eat us," she said. "Promise as if we were wolves."

The wolf stepped up to the bars and looked at her thoughtfully. "Yes," he said. "I promise by tooth and marrow and bone. Show mercy to me and I will show it to you in return. There's too little courage in the world to go eating it up."

It seemed to be the best that they were going to get. Summer turned her thoughts to getting the wolf out of the cage.

"Do you think the valet-birds could lift it?" she asked.

Reginald shook his head. "Only one who could possibly lift that thing is him, and he can't touch the silver, worse luck."

"What if we had something to put between him and the silver?" asked Summer.

In the end they sacrificed the linen tablecloth, which made the valet birds very unhappy. They wrapped it around the lowest bar, by the gap, with many grumpy twitters, while Reginald shouted encouraging things like, "There's a lad!" and, "Rightly done!" and the weasel kept an eye out in case the hunter should return.

When the bar was wrapped, Summer took a branch and wedged one end under the cage to use as a lever. She and Reginald threw their full weight against it, and the wolf got the linen-wrapped bar in his teeth.

"One," said Reginald. "Two. Heave!"

They heaved.

The wolf's neck muscles pulsed and the cage flipped over with a great crash. Bracken and rotten wood flew in all directions.

"Free!" cried the wolf. He shook himself and gasped air untainted by silver. "Free!"

Summer had bright spots in front of her eyes from pulling so hard on the lever. Bark had scraped across her palms. She sat down on a tree root.

When she looked up, the wolf was six inches away.

She swallowed hard.

"Mercy for mercy," said the wolf, leaning forward. He touched his nose to her forehead. "My name is Glorious."

"Summer," said Summer, through a mouth gone dry.

"Summer. We would call a cub that, before it grew into its paws and its name." He lolled his tongue out between teeth as long and white as stalagmites. "Now let us go from here, and tell me, human child, what brings you wandering in the woods with a bird and a weasel and the scent of crones about you?"

They left the cage. The wolf walked beside them. His shoulder came halfway up Summer's ribcage, and his tail was longer than her arm.

It was unsettling to walk beside a wolf. She tried to watch the road, but she kept getting little glimpses of him out of the corner of her eye, and then her heart would hammer and her spine would tingle.

Summer tried to think of him as a were-house. She didn't think anybody could be unsettled by a were-house.

It was *very* hard to look at Glorious and think of a cottage with white curtains.

"Is Glorious—um—a usual sort of name for wolves?" asked Summer timidly.

"Yes," said the wolf. "My sister is Strong and my brother is Splendid. We call ourselves what we are, or wish to be, or could be again." He shook his head, and his fur stood out in a ragged corona. "Now. Speak to me of crones, Summer-cub."

So she told him the whole story, about the saints and the sad Frog Tree and the Wheymaster and Grub. At the end he asked her only one question: "How did Baba Yaga smell?"

"A little like you," she whispered. "And a little like an herb garden, and a little like bleach."

The weasel came out on her shoulder and said, "Like—" and chittered a long, chattering passage in the language of weasels.

The wolf listened gravely. Then he nodded.

"That is a true story," he said. "My people know her well."

They had gone on for quite some time, and neither Summer nor Reginald quite wanted to ask if Glorious planned to accompany them until night-fall.

Finally the weasel did it for them. "Well?" he asked, standing on Summer's shoulder and looking down at the wolf (but only a little way down). "You are walking along with us instead of tearing off into the woods, and you've heard our story. What do you mean to do about it?"

Glorious grinned. "I mean to walk with you until I am out of these woods with the house-hunters about. I am quite helpless at night, but a hunter will not take a house with people already in it. And in return—well. If we should encounter this 'Grub' person, or this 'Houndbreaker'—" he pronounced the name with exaggerated care "—he will find, I think, that wolves are not broken so easily as hounds."

Chapter Twelve

When they stopped that night, Summer was more than ready. There was
a blister on the back of her heel, and when she took her shoe off, it was one
of the big squashy ones. She poked it with her finger and it turned bright
white, then red.

"Ow," she mumbled.

The valet-birds flittered around her, trying to bandage it up with nap-
kins, but there was only so much they could do.

It was getting late. The sky was turning purple. The valet-birds hopped
about gathering sticks, but Glorious yawned. "Don't bother," he told them.

He sat back on his haunches, threw his head back, and howled.

Summer let out a squeak and jumped a little. She can be forgiven for
this, because the howl of a real wolf sitting right next to you is shockingly
loud and shockingly strange. It starts deep and works its way up to a high
pure note, and it shivers along your spine and down your arms and makes
your fingers tremble.

The sound seemed to say to Summer that the world was divided into
predators and prey, and Summer herself was most definitely prey.

But it was also very beautiful. It made her heart ache with its wildness
and its sorrow and she loved Glorious for being exactly what he was.

The howl lasted for a long time. Even after it died away, Summer
thought that she could still hear it, hanging in the air around them like
smoke.

The first star came out and balanced on the point of a pine tree.

"That's that, then," said Glorious. He yawned again and laid down on his side. "Don't be alarmed," he added, as an afterthought. "It doesn't hurt—" and then he turned into a house.

From Summer's perspective, it looked as if Glorious just…unrolled. There weren't any unpleasant inside-out bits. (She had been rather nervous that it would involve guts and bones and things.) He simply unrolled as if he had been a carpet, into a wooden floor. Planks slid under Summer's feet as politely as bedroom slippers. Walls shot up around them, formed a ceiling, and then, in less time than it takes to tell it, she and Reginald and the valet-birds and the weasel were standing inside a neat little cottage with a roaring fire in the fireplace and white curtains blowing in the evening breeze.

"Well!" said Reginald, turning around several times. "Well! You don't see that every day, indeed you don't! If you'd told me about it, I'd say you were trying to sell me a bag of moonshine."

Summer turned around in place, her mouth open. The door and the cupboards were painted blue, and the stones of the fireplace were the color of wolf-fur. The trim around the windows was painted the pale green of Glorious's eyes.

It was not a very big cottage. There was one large room with the fire-place and a low table, and the roof peaked overhead. There was one small room with a bed in it and a pink comforter the color of a wolf's tongue. The rafters were carved with running wolves and the chairs had cut-out pawprints on their backs.

"Oh, Glorious!" said Summer. "This is lovely!" She wanted to hug the wolf, but it is rather hard to hug a house, so she ran a hand over the back of the chairs. "Oh, how wonderful!"

They went outside to admire the cottage, and Summer's heart turned over and gave a funny little squeeze.

The outside of the front door was painted turquoise.

She stared at it for a little while and didn't think at all, and then finally she thought: *So that's all right, then. I am on the right path. And I was meant to meet Glorious and help free him from the cage. It's all right.*

It is a great relief, when one has thrown away normal life in search of their heart's desire, to know that one is doing it right and isn't going to get yelled at for going the wrong way.

It was a very pleasant evening. They toasted cheese and bread in the fireplace and Summer slept in the bed while Reginald perched on a chair back.

She thought that if she did have to go home—and probably she would eventually—she would do everything possible not to forget this.

"Do you think it's safe?" she asked. "When he wakes up, we won't all be—be squished up inside him somehow, will we?"

"Shouldn't think so," said Reginald. "He'd have said something, surely."

And indeed, when Summer woke up in the morning, after a long and luxurious sleep—for there is nothing better than a real bed when you have been sleeping on sand and tree roots—she was very warm and not at all squished, and curled up with her head pillowed on Glorious's side.

The wolf grinned lazily at her as she sat up.

"You are a very nice house," said Summer shyly.

"Indeed," said Glorious. "But I am a much better wolf."

He rose and stretched from nose to tailtip. "Start on without me. I shall catch up to you when I have eaten—small brother, would you care to join me?"

The weasel hopped out of Summer's pocket and swarmed up one of the wolf's legs. "Very much so," he said.

They loped off into the woods. Summer watched them go, feeling a little left out.

"Thank goodness," said Reginald. "He's a marvelous chap and very sound in the architecture, but I was dreading having to feed him. He could eat us both up in two bites and probably have room for a bit of trifle afterwards."

"Will they come back?" asked Summer.

"Once they've eaten," said Reginald firmly. "And we should do the same."

They did indeed come back, licking their lips. Summer would have been more bothered by that, but her blister was much worse this morning and she was limping badly and biting her lip.

She wanted to cry, but it is very hard to cry when you are travelling with a wolf. There is something about them that is so much larger and braver that you feel determined to try and look large and brave as well, even if you are rather small.

   Summer in Orcus

Glorious trotted along beside her for perhaps ten minutes, then sank down into a crouch.

"Up on my back, "he said. "There is no running on torn paws, and we will make better time without it."

"Are you sure?" asked Summer. "I mean—um—you're a *wolf*—"

"And you a human," said Glorious, "and that is a weasel and that fluttering fellow dancing up ahead is a hoopoe. But here we all are nonetheless. A slow rabbit is a dead rabbit, Summer-cub."

Summer rubbed her suddenly sweaty hands on her jeans and put a leg over the wolf's back.

It was not like riding a horse. Summer had never actually ridden a horse, it must be said, but she had read every book in the library about girls and horses and all the *Black Stallion* books, even the ones toward the end that got very strange and had aliens in them. Riding a wolf was not anything like those books.

For one thing, wolves are not nearly so broad as horses, even very large ones, and for another their bones are arranged differently, and there is nothing that resembles reins. (There is no real reason you *couldn't* put a halter on a wolf, provided you don't mind ending with fewer fingers than when you started.) Summer sank her hands into Glorious's mane. She could feel his ribcage expand as he breathed.

He stood up, shook himself a little, and moved into a quick trot and from there into a ground-eating lope. It rattled Summer's bones until she got into the rhythm of it and flattened herself down across his back.

I'm riding a wolf. I've never ridden anything scarier than the carousel and now I'm riding a real wolf.

Overhead Reginald, who had been holding his speed down in deference to his companions, let out a whoop and went across the sky like a streak of lightning in a tastefully pinstriped waistcoat.

Such a pace cannot be kept forever, of course. Soon enough, Glorious slowed to a trot, with his tongue hanging out, and Reginald landed and strolled alongside them, hopping to low branches and practicing the occasional dance-step.

Meanwhile, Summer was doing her best to engage Glorious in conversation. She loved the way she could feel his voice rumbling down in his chest when he spoke.

"But how did you come to be a were-house, anyway?" she asked.

"Indeed!" said Reginald. "Were you bitten by a hinge or cursed by a hearth-witch?"

"Oh, that." Glorious stretched hugely and yawned, showing a vast pink gullet. "I went down to the stream where the houses drink, and drank there under the full moon. You could probably do so without taking harm, but wolves are prone to metamorphic instability, and so what with one thing and another…" He shrugged. "It's not so bad. Houses aren't hungry, and most of the necessary business of life can be accomplished during the day."

"I didn't know houses had to drink," said Summer.

"They get thirsty on the long migrations," said Glorious.

"It's a magnificent sight from overhead," added Reginald. "A hundred houses in a herd, stampeding across the savannah, the big bulls slashing at each other with their rain-gutters…"

Summer was very suspicious that they were making fun of her, but then she thought of Baba Yaga's house, walking about on enormous bird feet. Perhaps the house had come from this world initially.

"Are all houses wild here?" she asked. "Do people ever build them?"

"Oh, well," said Reginald. "You *can* build them. It's a bit shabby, but of course there isn't always a well-grown warehouse—begging your pardon, Glorious—about when you need a place to store the potatoes." He flitted his wings. "And the big manor houses are almost all gone, from overhunting. You can only get them from house-herders now, and they're never as good as the wild ones."

He took to the air and did a brief pirouette, then landed before Summer and walked backwards. "You'll see, when we get to Almondgrove. The old family seat there is a real manor, one of the big wild ones. Fifty point cornices! My great-great-great-great-hatchfather hunted it across the—"

Without any warning, without so much as a sound, Glorious leapt off the path and into the woods.

Summer had let go of his mane with one hand to scratch her nose, and nearly fell off. She threw herself forward, clinging with her legs and managed to get a grip just as Glorious vaulted over a fallen log. Her stomach lurched and she nearly fell off.

"Eh?" said Reginald. "What's—"

Then he too stopped and lifted his head. The valet-birds twittered and murmured, dropping the pack and flying up into the trees.

Glorious turned, nose-over-tail, like a dog lying down, and curled himself into a fern-encrusted hollow at the base of a tree. Only the very top of his head poked out, watching the road through a screen of branches.

With a clank and a jangle and the thudding of hooves, a group of riders came around the bend in the road.

Chapter Thirteen

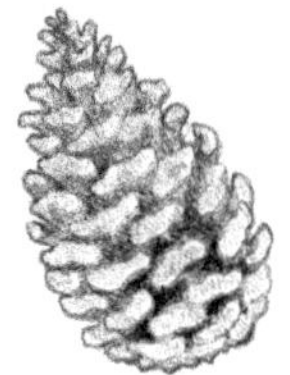

Summer laid herself flat against Glorious's fur and stared between his ears. Reginald, who had obviously been spotted, did not try to escape. He was a tiny figure in the road, staring up at the oncoming riders.

The weasel scurried up beside Summer, and laid his tail across her mouth like a bar for silence.

He needn't have bothered. Summer knew, as soon as the riders came into view, that they were bad.

It was the horses.

From a distance, if you weren't looking too closely, they might have passed as real horses. From thirty feet, even viewed through ferns and bracken, they were clearly something else.

Each one of them had eight legs, in two sets, front and back. She could not see their hooves. They had no tails or manes, and the faces—oh, there was something badly wrong with the faces.

Summer felt queasy. She had doodled a lot of horses in her notebooks over the years and she had a folder with an Arabian running across the cover. Each of the eight-legged horses had a large round eye, like a black stone set into a little cup of bone, and then under it, another cup of bone and another smaller black stone, and another—

They've got four eyes, she thought. *Or eight, since there's four on this side. The horse is really a spider, or part spider, or something spidery, and if I'm sick they'll hear me, so I can't be sick, but those are* nasty…

There were a dozen of the spider-horses. Ten of the riders wore leather, with helms that shadowed their faces. They were dusty and had shields slung over their packs. Summer could see dark, pitted metal, crossed with iron chains.

The eleventh rider had a very strange helmet. It looked to be metal as well, but it was shaped like a dog's head, with its lips rolled back in a savage snarl. From the back were dozens of thin metal chains, hanging down like hair. If the rider had any hair of his own, she couldn't see it.

He was sitting on the back of the spider-horse, holding a book in one hand, and appeared to be reading it. Occasionally he would reach out a gauntleted hand and turn the page.

The twelfth rider was out in front of the column, and held up a hand. The entire group came to a halt in the middle of the road, facing Reginald.

When the twelfth rider spoke, Summer recognized his voice immediately.

"Well," said Grub. "What have we here?"

Summer craned her neck. She didn't want to make any noise, but she desperately wanted to see what Grub looked like. Being chased is bad enough, but it's much worse if you don't know what they look like.

Unfortunately there was a particularly dense hemlock branch in the way, and when he stopped, all Summer could see were his legs.

"Can I help you gentlemen?" asked Reginald. "Fine day for a ride or a fly, isn't it?"

Fly away! Summer thought frantically. *Fly away! They're bad, Reginald, can't you see it?*

"You're a bird," said Grub.

"I can tell you're the clever sort," said Reginald, tapping a claw to his beak. "Spotted it right off. 'Now that fellow, there, he's a clever one,' I said to myself—"

"It is a hoopoe," said the rider with the book. His voice was very deep and seemed to come from a long way away. "A noble, by the look of him." He turned a page. "Ask him, Grub, and let us not waste time."

Grub swung down off his horse. Summer felt her lips curl back. Her mouth tasted sour.

There was something not-right about Grub in the same way that something was not-right with the spider-horses. He was enormous. His skin was wet white with gray shadows. He had no real neck, but his flesh puckered in at regular seams, like the segments of a soft-bodied insect.

Reginald hopped backward on the road.

"Now listen up, bird," said Grub. "We're looking for a girl. A human. Have you seen her?"

Summer's heart rose into her throat and stuck there.

"A human?" said Reginald. "I see lots of humans. All the time. Thick as flies. Not out *here*, of course." He waved a wing. "Nothing out here."

"Then what are you doing out here?"

"Eh?" Reginald cocked his head. "P-practicing my dance moves for the—for the Assembly, dontcha know?" He did a half-hearted pirouette. "For the lovely Miss—Miss—well, dash it, all the lovely misses."

"You sound nervous, bird," said Grub. "Something you're not telling us?"

Summer clenched her fists in Glorious's fur. *Oh Reginald, be careful, Grub hits people…*

"Be nervous too," muttered Reginald. "Dozen horses like that staring at you and thinking of drinking your vital juices."

"Indeed," said Grub. "But I am sure it will not come to that, if you answer our questions. I'm sure you *want* to answer our questions, being a loyal subject of the Queen-In-Chains."

"Oh, well, queens," said Reginald. "Very important people. Don't stand up at Assemblies though, do they?"

"I'm going to ask you the question again," said Grub. "And this time, I want you to think very hard about what might happen if you don't answer it."

There was a soft *snick* sound. One of the other riders was aiming a crossbow at Reginald.

Summer clenched her fists in Glorious's fur. What would she do if Grub tried to hurt Reginald? Should she get up and turn herself in? Whatever they were going to do to her, surely she couldn't stand aside and let them shoot her friend!

What if I'm too afraid? What if I just sit here and can't move?

"Have you seen a human girl on this road?" asked Grub.

Reginald shook his head violently. "I haven't seen anyone!"

There was a second snick sound as another crossbow was pointed at him.

"Why are you on this road?" asked Grub. "Don't give me some nonsense about dancing."

"Th-there's an inn," said Reginald. "Isn't there? I was rusticating, but I'm out of clean waistcoats and the valet-flock's getting cheeky about it.

So I thought I'd go to the inn, you know, see what they had in the way of laundry and interesting cheeses?"

Grub dropped down to a crouch. Perhaps he meant it to be friendly, but Reginald took another two hops backward. "And you haven't seen a human girl on this road? Smells of shapeshifters and crone magic?"

Reginald shook his head.

Grub looked as if he wanted to ask more questions, but the rider with the book said, "Most birds have very little sense of smell, Grub, as you would know if you read more."

Grub hunched his shoulders. He looked like a giant pillbug trying to roll into a ball.

"Not much for the old sniff-box," said Reginald apologetically, taking another hop backward. "Not a *seabird*, you understand. One of the Gracepetrels, now, they could tell you what you had for breakfast."

"I wonder how bird would taste for breakfast," said Grub. He rose to his feet and turned back to his horse.

"Errr…could ask a vulture, perhaps? Fine sniffers on those fellows. Not much for talking, though, not like civilized birds…"

The crossbows never wavered.

I should go. I should go now. They're going to shoot at him. I have to stop this.

I'm scared!

Whether or not she would have moved to save Reginald, Summer never learned, because the valet-birds got there first.

The whole flock erupted from the trees, chattering and swooping around the guards. The men with crossbows looked away from Reginald, only for an instant, but that was long enough for the hoopoe to launch himself off the roadway and into the trees.

THWACK. THWACK.

Bolts slammed into the trunk. Summer made a tiny noise of terror and the weasel slapped his tail across her cheek for silence.

"Grub…" said the rider with the book, sounding bored. The valet-flock vanished into the trees.

"We could shoot him out of the tree, Master Zultan," said Grub. "He knows more than he says, I'll bet."

"We do not shoot loyal subjects of the Queen," said Zultan Houndbreaker, turning back to his book. "And I am sure that he is *very* loyal. Are you not, hoopoe?"

"Err. Yes. Very, um, loyal," called Reginald, from the other side of a tree trunk. "Long live her Majesty, wot?" Pinecones rained down as he flew for deeper cover.

"Indeed," said Zultan, looking back down at the page. "Indeed. We are wasting time, Grub—time we would *not* have wasted if your precious tracker had not run off in the night."

Grub swung onto his horse, and the whole company started off again.

"I wouldn't expect too much of the inn, if I were you—" Grub called over his shoulder, and the whole troop went clopping down the road and out of sight.

Summer let out a long, shuddering breath and buried her face in Glorious's fur.

What felt like a long time passed. Reginald did not come looking for them. He stood in the road and muttered to himself and hopped and fluttered about, then set out down the road by himself.

"Waiting to make sure they're not watching," whispered the weasel. "We'll catch up to him."

And indeed, after the hoopoe was long out of sight, Glorious rose to his feet and padded through the woods, as quiet as a cat.

"*You* said he'd fly away at the first sign of trouble," said Summer to the weasel.

The little animal had the decency to look embarrassed. "Fine. I misjudged him, okay? He's still a fop."

When they came out onto the road, Reginald was soaring overhead, and came down for a landing at the wolf's feet.

"You were so brave!" Summer cried, and swept him up in a hug. He weighed hardly anything.

"Here now!" squawked the hoope. "Careful, Summer, you'll bruise my feathers—oh, well. Suppose I did rather a good job at that." He looked guiltily pleased. "Not that I could very well turn you in. Wouldn't have. Word of a hoopoe."

"I never thought you would," Summer assured him, "but you were so brave! I thought you'd run away!"

"If he'd run, they would have chased," said Glorious. "And on those mounts, they might have caught him, or gotten close enough to put an arrow into him at least."

"Sleipnirians," said Reginald grimly. "Breed 'em out of horses and giant spiders, and don't ask me how, but there's no way it can't be a bad business." He ruffled all his feathers and settled them back down again.

The valet-flock came out of the trees and gathered on the road. Four of them set something down at Reginald's feet.

Summer looked over at them, and her heart turned over, because one of the birds was lying silently in the dust.

"Oh *no…* "

The flock silently took off their hats and held them over their breasts.

"Nicked with an arrow," said Reginald. "Poor little blighter's stuck his spoon in the wall." He sighed and dipped his wings, bowing very low to the fallen bird.

Summer bit her lower lip to keep back the tears. She bowed as well, feeling clumsy and useless and huge. "What do we do?" she asked. "Do we bury him?"

Reginald shook his head. "The flock will handle it," he said. "He's one of theirs. They won't thank us for sticking our beaks in."

The valet-flock put their hats back on and lifted the body of their comrade. They flew into the forest in a small, swirling knot.

"They'll catch up to us," said Reginald. "We'll keep going."

Summer pinched the bridge of her nose. She still wanted to cry, but it seemed like there were other things to do first. "Where do we go, though?"

"We keep to our original plan," said Glorious. "When we reach Fen-town, the smell of humans will confuse your trail beyond all following." He nodded to Reginald. "And you are certain that your sire will welcome us?"

Summer noticed the *us* and was warmed by it.

Reginald nodded vigorously. "Sure of it. M'father's up to all the tricks, and if he hears you've got the Houndbreaker after you—well, nobody in all of Orcus I'd rather have at my back. And Almondsgrove's only a short flap from Fen-town."

"Do they let wolves in Fen-town?" asked Summer timidly, imagining the uproar if she had tried to walk into the middle of her home town, riding a wolf the size of a pony.

Glorious's teeth gleamed. "I don't see that they have any way to keep us out. Do you?"

Chapter Fourteen

They reached the inn—or what was left of it—at midday.

"I smell burning," said Glorious, when they were still a little way off.

Reginald took to the air, and when he returned, the little patch of skin at the bridge of his beak was pale.

"Bad business," he said. "Bad. The Queen's men—well. You'll see."

There was a large clearing in the woods, ringed with tree stumps. In the center stood the inn, or what was left of it.

The fire had been set quite a while ago, Summer thought. Maybe even the night before. The beams were charred black and most of the walls had fallen down.

She could see the outline of the building in blackened beams, and one standing wall.

Along each standing beam, their wings riding above their heads, hunched great black vultures. Summer counted fifteen of them. More drifted in circles overhead.

By the road stood a signpost. The sign had been torn down and lay in the dust—a golden pig with a comical expression.

A piece of metal—tin or something like it—had been nailed to the signpost. Words were stamped into the metal.

TREASON IS PUNISHED
IN THE NAME OF
THE QUEEN-IN-CHAINS

"They've started the burnings again," said Reginald distantly. "M'father told me about it. Before I was even an egg—when the Queen first came—they would ride and burn buildings if they suspected you of being an informer or just in their way." He shook himself. "But they haven't—not for years—not since the Queen pulled down the Tower of Dogs. It's why Zultan's called 'Houndbreaker,' you know."

"I didn't," said Summer, watching the vultures circle.

"Sorry. Forget you're not from here." He shifted from foot to foot. "The dogs built things. M'father says you could trust a dog, even if you didn't know him. But taking down the Tower took a lot out of them, and nobody's seen the Queen in ages, so…" He trailed off.

"Can we do something about the vultures?" asked Summer. Her fingers were clenched very tightly in Glorious's mane. She felt as if she were watching everything from a long way away.

Reginald shook his head. "They do their job. It's what they're for." He scuffed at the dust. "The bargain, you know, in the old story—oh, maybe you don't know. Can't tell it too well m'self. But they promised they'd always show up at the end. It's the world's last little kindness."

They show up at the end.

Vultures don't show up for ruined buildings.

There's dead people in that building. Real people.

The vultures are going to eat them.

It did not seem like a kindness to Summer.

Grub and Zultan Houndbreaker killed them.

And Grub is out here because—

"They burned the building looking for me, didn't they?"

Glorious began trotting rapidly down the road, away from the building. His ears flicked backward toward her voice.

"Oh, surely not," said Reginald, flapping along the side of the road. "They—surely not! Treason, they said. Probably a nest of smugglers or—or—"

"It is likely that they did, Summer-cub," said Glorious, ignoring Reginald.

She took a deep breath. She thought she might be sick or fall off the wolf's back, or both.

"Then it's my fault."

"No," said Glorious. "You did not hold the knife or strike the match. They had never met you nor you them. Grub is responsible, and Zultan Houndbreaker. They are no pack of yours. We do not hold ourselves responsible for the acts of others."

"But if I'd never come—" wailed Summer.

"If I kill you," said Glorious. "I can claim that the moon made me do it, or the sun, or a man in another land whom I have never met. But it is my teeth that have blood on them." He turned his head so that Summer had to meet his eyes. "Do you understand?"

"Yes," said Summer. The smell of bodies were all mixed together in her head with the image of the fallen valet-bird. Her voice sounded very high in her own ears, and then she put her face down in Glorious's ruff and sobbed.

The lock and the acorn and the turquoise stone clicked together in her pocket as the wolf walked very carefully down the road, away from the burnt-out inn.

Dinner that night was subdued. Glorious's fire crackled in the hearth and the valet-birds fluttered from chairback to rafters, but no one felt like talking.

When Summer went to bed that night, Reginald hopped into the room after her and scuffed awkwardly at the floorboards.

"Look," he said. "Wanted to say—look. Not your fault. Really not. Glorious was right. They're mad—bad—shockingly loose in the haft. Been doing this sort of thing since before I chipped the egg."

"But I came here looking for my heart's desire," said Summer miserably. "It wasn't that anybody *die.*"

"Yes, but Baba Yaga sent you," said Reginald. "Shouldn't wonder if she had some reason. It's got all the Queen's nasty little termites squirming around in an uproar, hasn't it?" He perched on her bedpost and managed a grin. "Wonder what it is they think you're going to do?"

Summer blinked.

Under her left ear, the weasel snickered.

"Now *that,*" he said, "is a good question. And a much better one than asking who's fault something is."

"But I can't *do* anything," said Summer. "I'm—I'm not a hero. I'm scared of a lot of things. I almost didn't want to help Glorious out of the cage. I've hidden every time Grub is around. I just want to help the poor Frog Tree and maybe find my heart's desire, but I don't know if I'm getting any closer to either of those things!"

Reginald considered this. "You know," he said. "Just occurred to me. You could talk to a Forester. They know trees. One might know your tree."

"Okay," said Summer. It wasn't much of a direction, but it was better than nothing. She couldn't shake the feeling that she was *supposed* to help the Frog Tree—why else would Baba Yaga have sent her to that exact place, and why else would she have selected the frog-shaped candle. "Does your father know one?"

"Probably knows a dozen, but it doesn't signify." The hoopoe preened. "*I* know one. Marvelous old girl. Fierce as a dragon, but I can always turn her up sweet. Don't know why I didn't think of her before."

"How do we find her, then?" asked Summer.

"We'll pass near enough on the way to Almondsgrove. Just a quick flap off the road." He considered. "Well, maybe a half-day's flap, for you wingless folk."

Summer rubbed her finger over the surface of the acorn, feeling the carved eyes of the tadpole. She felt a little better. Maybe she couldn't do anything about Grub or Zultan, but at least she was still trying to help the Frog Tree.

That had to count for something.

Still, she thought, *that's twice now I've hidden while Grub threatened someone who was helping me. The next time, I'll have to do something.*

I hope it's not already too late.

Summer was surprised when they reached the marsh.

You could not exactly accuse geography of sneaking up on you, but it felt like an ambush. One minute Glorious was trotting through dense trees, which were, if anything, getting denser—and then the trees stopped and the road was lined with short bushes and the horizon was many miles away.

The wolf stopped for a moment. Summer blinked, dazzled by the sunlight.

It was a desolate landscape. Grass rippled in the wind, cut by channels of gray-green water. It was hard to tell where grass stopped and water began. Little clumps of bushes, like the ones along the road, stood out from the marsh. They seemed to huddle together for support. The air smelled like salt and rotting vegetation.

A bird cried once, thin and sharp and a long way away. Then there was only the wind.

"Killdeer," said Reginald, spiraling down for a landing. "They can talk, after a fashion, but it's not worth listening to. All they ever say is, 'Help, help, my wing is broken, don't eat me.'"

"Are their wings broken?" asked Summer.

"Not a bit of it. They just do it to get people away from their nests. You tell them a hundred times that you're not the slightest bit interested in their nests, that there's nothing more tedious than having to look after other people's children, but they never listen." Reginald shrugged.

"This seems like a lonely place," said Summer, after they had been walking for a few minutes.

"Yes," said Glorious. "Lonely and treacherous. There is little solid land."

"The road seems solid enough," said Summer.

"Dog-built," said Reginald. "There'll be wide spots for camping. They were always good about that. But I wouldn't stray off it."

Far across the marsh, a clump of trees stood up. They appeared to be rooted in the back of a giant turtle. The turtle lumbered to another channel of water and plopped itself down. The killdeer cried again. Other than that, nobody seemed to take any notice.

"There's so many different landscapes," said Summer, looking back over her shoulder at the forest. "All packed together so closely. I started in the woods and then it was desert and then it was farmland and a different kind of woods and now it's a marsh. Things in my world aren't so close together."

Glorious stretched, and Summer had to grab for his ruff to keep from being dislodged. "Perhaps your world is larger. Orcus runs from the icewalls to the north down to the great sea. There is a continent to the south—the dragonfly riders go there—and the plains where the houses run stretch a long way to the east. North is many weeks of mountains, until you reach the ice. But here, we are very near the sea."

"What's on the other side of the sea?" asked Summer.

"There is no other side," said Glorious.

"Are you sure?" Summer scratched the back of her neck. "In my world there's two big oceans, but if you cross them, you get to other continents. And eventually back to where you started."

"Really?" Reginald cocked his head. "You don't get into the sun's shadow?"

"Our sun doesn't have a shadow," said Summer.

"Everything has a shadow," said Glorious. "Perhaps your sun simply keeps it somewhere else."

"Here, if you go far across the sea, past the islands, you come under the sun's shadow," Reginald said. "The whale-speakers—odd chaps, to be sure—say that the water out there gets cold and dark and deep. There's giant squid and worse things. You can't go past that or you get eaten." He scowled. "They say Zultan came from out that way, but I think that's a load of foolishness. He was born in Orcus, same as the rest of us, he's just trying to pass himself off as something scarier."

"The great gray albatrosses talk to my people sometimes," said Glorious. "They say that if you fly far enough, you come to a hole in the sky. It leads to another world."

"Oh, well, *albatrosses.*" Reginald flipped his wing. "Prophets and poets, the lot of them. Not bad-hearted, but you ask one the time of day and he tells you time is an illusion, and how is *that* getting anything done?"

Glorious huffed with laughter.

Chapter Fifteen

Fen-town was a city built on stilts.

They saw it coming from a long way away. It was the only thing that stuck out of the waving marsh-grass. The road ran right through the middle of it, and at first Summer thought that the stilts would mean the city would be above their heads, but the road rose to meet it. The packed earth turned to great blocks of stone with bits of moss growing in the cracks, and by the time they reached Fen-town, they were ten or fifteen feet above the level of the water.

The city didn't have a gate, but it did have two tall pillars along the road. A guard leaned against one pillar. She looked mostly human, but her skin was mottled green and she had webbed toes and a pleasant expression.

"New to Fen-town?" she asked. When Summer nodded, she pointed to a building. A wooden bridge led to the front door. "First-time travelers need to go and talk to the Clerk of Records."

The building smelled like damp paper inside. There was a broad desk covered in folders and binders and papers and booklets and diaries and notes and blotters and a great many pens.

The person behind the desk was also green with webbed feet, but his expression was far less pleasant. His nose was beaky and he had thinning, spiky hair. Summer had never met someone who could look like both a frog and a heron at the same time.

"Name?" asked the Clerk of Records, grabbing a sheet of paper apparently at random.

"Reginald Hoopoe, of the Almondsgrove Hoopoes."

"Glorious."

"Summer," said Summer. If Glorious could have just one name, so could she.

"Hmmph!" The Clerk scribbled furiously. No ink came out of his pen, and he tossed it aside and grabbed another one. "Business in Fen-town?"

"Just passing through, dontcha know, on the way to the jolly old family seat," said Reginald.

The Clerk's eyebrows drew together like angry caterpillars. "Do you have any fruit?"

The travelers exchanged glances. "Err," said Reginald. "No. We could go and get some if you like?"

"No fruit!" barked the Clerk, discarding another pen. "No dangerous animals?"

Glorious grinned. "One," he said.

The weasel muttered something in Summer's pocket.

The Clerk stared over his desk at Glorious for a moment, then made a note. "Rules!" he said. "No entering the city after dark! No panhandling! No accordion music without a permit!" He leveled a finger. "And pets must be on leashes, do you hear me?"

"He's not my pet," said Summer hurriedly.

"Wasn't talking to *you,*" said the Clerk. He jerked his head at Glorious. "If your human causes trouble, you'll be up on charges, you understand?"

Summer's jaw dropped.

"I'll try to keep her under control," said the wolf drily. "Now tell me, is there a small village green or a lot? I require some space for the evening to transform."

"Transform?" The Clerk threw aside his pen, grabbed yet another, and began writing notes in a frenzy.

"But don't worry, he doesn't turn into fruit," said Reginald helpfully.

"What does he turn into?" The Clerk's voice rose hysterically.

"Just a house!" said Summer hurriedly. "A nice house! A cottage! Nothing dangerous—"

The Clerk's face turned an ugly mottled gray. "You're bringing in outside real estate?!"

Summer wondered if this was better or worse than fruit.

"I don't intend to stay," said Glorious. "Just for the night."

"It's like pitching a tent," said Reginald. "Only more civilized."

"Am I to understand that this is *your* house, Mister…Hoopoe?" asked the Clerk nastily.

"If we're being technical," said Reginald, "it's *Viscount* Hoopoe. And no, he isn't mine."

The Clerk swung his gaze on Summer. "Is he *yours?*"

"Uh—"

"Yes," said Glorious. "Legally. Not an abandoned house, not available to house-hunters, not on the real estate market." He nudged Summer.

Summer gulped. She could take a hint. "Um. Yes. That's right. He's mine."

"Do you have a title on file at the Registrar of Deeds?"

You were definitely not supposed to lie to grown-ups. But she remembered Glorious's fear of house-hunters, and if it meant protecting the were-house—

"Yes," she said. "Only not here. Back home. He's—um—mobile. But we're on file in my home town."

The Clerk scowled. "Do you have papers for him *here,* then?"

"We weren't told we'd need them," said Summer staunchly. She had gone to the DMV with her mother last month. She'd finished her book early and spent two hours watching people talk to the clerks there, and they all seemed to say the same things.

"How am I supposed to work under these conditions!?" he shouted at her, which the clerks at the DMV didn't do. "Outside real estate! Do you want to crash the housing market? It's all snails, you understand, snails and hammocks! And we had a woman come through last month on a stone salmon and not a license in sight!"

He flung down his papers and put his face in his hands.

Summer felt on suddenly firmer ground.

She stepped forward and patted his arm. "It will be all right," she said. And then, cautiously, "It wasn't very nice of her to come through on a stone salmon like that." (Privately she wondered what a salmon had to do with it, but never mind.)

The Clerk sighed and dropped his hands. "No, it wasn't. It did terrible damage around the foundations. And she didn't pay for any of it!" Amazingly, his color seemed to be settling.

Summer made a polite noise of horror and nudged Reginald, who said "Oh—err—I say—that's not right at all!"

"I'm sorry we're making more work for you," said Summer. "We didn't mean to."

"Well," said the Clerk. "You were *supposed* to bring papers, but if you haven't got any, we can fill out a temporary house license for you. But it's only good for thirty days, and you have to keep it in the window at all times."

"Thank you for your help," said Summer. She'd noticed that the people who got out of the DMV the quickest usually said that.

"Mmm," said the Clerk, but the storm had clearly passed. Normally at this point she'd tell her mother that she loved her and it would be all right, but this did not seem quite appropriate. Instead she said, "We're sorry to be so much trouble."

"Hmmph!" said the Clerk, but his heart wasn't in it. He dug a form out of a stack and filled in a few blanks. "Now sign here."

Glorious nudged her. Summer took the leaky pen and signed her name in her best cursive writing.

"There's that, then. In the window at all times, you hear? And we'll keep this other copy on file."

Summer presented the paper to Glorious, who swallowed it in one gulp.

"Thank you again," she said. Reginald bowed to the clerk. All three of them hurried out of the building.

"Wow!" said Reginald, as soon as they were clear. "What a load of whoppers that was!" He slapped Summer on the shoulder with his wing and laughed. "I didn't know you had it in you! 'We're on file in my home town' indeed!"

Summer giggled. You weren't supposed to feel proud of yourself for lying, but she couldn't help it.

They made their way across the stone causeway into Fen-town.

Everything was on poles and stilts and pilings. The village appeared to be made of at least a dozen layers. Birds the size of Reginald flew back and forth overhead between birdhouses on tall poles.

There were shops above the level of the road, accessible through folding staircases. There were also fruit-vendors and little carts, like the kind that sold hot dogs on the street in Summer's world. (Her mother had never let her buy one of the hot dogs, because she said the carts were unsanitary and crawling with germs, but they always smelled delicious.)

It was odd, though—unlike the carts back home, these didn't have wheels. In fact, they seemed to be built on the backs of glistening carpets.

Summer was trying to figure out why the carpets looked so familiar, when one *moved.*

It stretched and rippled. Summer let out a squeak.

"Hmmm?" Glorious rolled an eye up at his rider.

"Oh," said Reginald. "Snail-cart. Don't they have them where you're from?"

"We don't have snails that big where I'm from!"

The carts were indeed built on the backs of snails. The counters were fitted around the spiral shells and boxes of produce were set out atop them. Awnings overhead shaded the fruit-sellers. Some of the snails were pulled all the way into their shells, but others had their necks stretched out and were sunning themselves. Each one was the size of a small car.

"Aren't they *slow?*" whispered Summer.

"Well, sure," said Reginald. "But they go under the city at night—upside down, you know—and you sling a perch or a hammock between the awnings and sleep dry all night." He shrugged. "If you fly under the road, you'll see 'em."

"Good eating on a snail," said the weasel. "Easy to catch, too." He eyed the nearest cart hungrily.

"I don't think they'd appreciate it if you ate their snail," said Summer.

"Don't think a snail wouldn't eat you if it got the chance!"

The valet-birds dug into the packs and produced a few coins, then flew to the nearest fruit seller and began a round of vigorous chirping.

"I thought you didn't have any money," said Summer.

"I don't have *real* money," said Reginald. "Debts up to the ceiling!" He sounded almost proud of the fact. "But a few bits tucked away here or there, for an inn or a pint or a bit of a bite—of course I've got that."

Summer had eleven cents in her pocket. She didn't think that it would be worth much in this world.

The fruit-seller apparently came to an arrangement with the valet-birds. She was a tall black woman who would have looked perfectly at home in Summer's world, except for the fact that she was wearing clothes made entirely of matchsticks and string. She took one of the coins and the valet-birds began ferrying a bunch of grapes—one grape per bird—back to the packs.

They proceeded through Fen-town. The valet-birds stopped at three other snail-carts, buying biscuits and a number of small tins. Summer found the vendors that they didn't visit much more fascinating—there was a creature like a haystack selling wind-chimes, and a hooded person with glowing green eyes whose cart was covered in dozens of hands.

"Are those *real* hands?" whispered Summer. Many of them were dried and curled up, like dead spiders.

"Hand-smith," said Reginald. "Yes, of course they're real. He'd soon be up on charges if they weren't."

In the center of town, the road split into an enormous circular platform. In the center of the platform was a turtle.

It was gigantic, as big as a parking lot. Its eyes were at least ten feet tall. Summer was glad they were closed. Its pupils might be bigger than she was.

From its shell rose a grove of trees and a neatly manicured lawn. There were several park benches and picnic tables. A sign said, "Chelonia Park."

"Should be as good a place as any to spend the night," said Glorious. "I don't relish trying to balance my foundations on these poles, or having the tide come in through my windows."

"The sign says, 'No fires,'" said Summer.

"Good thing we've got an indoor fireplace, then, eh?" said Reginald.

Summer had been worried that someone would come and yell at them for putting a house in the park—even a very well-behaved house—but nobody did. Perhaps the fact that Glorious's temporary license was posted prominently in the window helped, or perhaps the people of Fen-town were simply used to such things. But they couldn't build a fire on the back of the turtle—Summer had a feeling that Chelonia Park would not have liked that at all—and so there was no hot tea in the morning for anyone. Eventually they just decided to leave and sort breakfast out later.

She felt very out of sorts as they left Fen-town. Her eyes were full of grit and the morning air was cold and smelled like rotten fish.

The stone causeway continued across the marsh, toward a dark line of trees on the other side.

Halfway to the trees, Summer could make out a large, oddly shaped lump.

"What's *that* supposed to be?" she grumbled.

Glorious said nothing. Reginald, who was incurably cheerful at this hour, said "I'll go check it out, shall I? Nothing like a dawn flight to get the old heart pumping, is there?"

"Morning people should be shot," said the weasel, although he waited until Reginald was in the air.

The wolf and his rider paced down the causeway for several minutes.

"Reginald's coming back," said Summer.

"Flying fast too," said Glorious.

"Probably forgot his waistcoat," muttered the weasel.

The hoopoe landed on the road. "Turtle," he said. "Like last night. The skeleton only. You can see the shell from miles off, though."

Summer wound her fingers tightly in Glorious's ruff.

Slowly, slowly, the skeleton came into focus. It was vast, bigger than Chelonia Park had been, with a shell as big as all of Fen-town. There were trees growing on its back, with trunks so wide that Summer could not have reached even halfway around them.

The trees were green, but it was a pale, sickly green. The leaves had yellow veins that stood out in sharp relief, like the tendons on the back of an old man's hands.

The turtle shell was half-buried in mud, and a skull protruded from it. It was broad and flat, striped with moss. The eye-sockets hung deep and empty.

Summer swallowed a few times. "It's so big…" she said finally. All the analogies she could think of were things from her own world—dumptrucks, bulldozers, earthmoving equipment. The skull alone was broad enough to park a dozen cars on.

It did not seem right that something so large could be allowed to die.

The weasel stood atop Glorious's skull and made small sounds of distress.

"I smell it too," said Glorious.

Summer wiped at her nose. She knew that she couldn't smell as well as the wolf and the weasel, but still, there was something in the air…something strange and moldy and foul…

"Like the wheat field," said the weasel. "And the Frog Tree."

Glorious nodded. "I have smelled it before."

"But what *is* it?" asked Summer. Her eyes were prickling. She did not mind bones, generally, but there was something breathtakingly sad about the turtle skeleton, with the lonely marsh behind it and the killdeer's cry echoing over its bones.

"Perhaps we shouldn't discuss it here, eh?" said Reginald. "Don't know what sort of chaps might be listening." He looked nervous, which was so unusual for the hoopoe that it made Summer want to look over her shoulder. (She did. There was nothing but the road, and, far in the distance, Fen-town.)

Glorious shook his head. "This is safer than the forest," he said. "We will see anything coming for a long way. But let us move a little from these bones. The smell burns my nostrils."

They went down the causeway. Moss grew up the sides and over the edges of the stones. The moldy smell went away and was replaced with more of the rotten fish smell.

At last, Glorious halted. He sat down and Summer slid off, though she kept her hand on his ruff, unwilling to let go entirely.

"So you, too, have smelled this before," said Glorious, not to Summer but to the weasel.

The weasel flicked his ears and nodded. "Several times since we came to this world," he said.

"I, too," said Glorious. "And I have heard of more. My people speak of it sometimes. Always great things, great magics, collapsed and rotting in on themselves. Always a smell, like a burning anthill. Always immense and irreplaceable things that no hunter would have touched."

"The cancer at the heart of the world," said Summer, almost inaudibly, remembering what Boarskin had said. The words tasted strange on her tongue.

"Yes," said Glorious. "Yes. Exactly. Whoever said that knew, Summer-cub. Something is doing this deliberately."

"But why?" asked Summer, anguished. "Who would want to hurt the Frog Tree, or that poor turtle, or—or—a field of *wheat?*" She could just barely imagine a giant turtle stepping on something important, but it was hard to imagine anything less offensive than a wheat field.

"There are those who need no reasons."

"Could it be Zultan?" asked Summer.

"Huh!" said Reginald. "The Tower of Dogs, maybe, an inn here and there, but he'll cut his coat to fit his cloth in the conquest department. And that was all before I was born. Doubt he could muster an army now."

"His power may be weakened," said Glorious slowly, "but even my people know the name of the Queen-in-Chains."

"It's been years," said Reginald. "She's probably dead."

Glorious ignored him, looking over his shoulder at the turtle skeleton. Summer could feel his breath going in and out, long and slow, his shoulder-blades moving as he breathed.

"This is why she sent you, Summer-cub," he said.

"Baba Yaga?"

"I believe it to be so," said Glorious. "I am sometimes wrong, but not often."

"But what can I do?' asked Summer. "I can't bring any of them back! I can't even stand up to Grub! This wasn't my heart's desire!"

Glorious shook his head. "I do not know," he said. "But I smell her even under this. Like clean stone under rotten meat."

He stood. Summer put a leg over his back and they began to walk again, while the turtle dwindled, becoming only another faded hillock in the marsh grass.

"What do we do?" asked Summer. The killdeer called and she felt the sound of it echo inside her chest, as if she were as hollowed out as the turtle's shell.

"Let us find this Forester of the hoopoe's," said Glorious. "Perhaps she will know a little more."

Chapter Sixteen

"What are you thinking?" asked Summer, when they had walked what seemed like a long way. They had already stopped for lunch, and Summer was tired and feeling groggy. Reginald was in the air and the weasel was asleep in her pocket.

"My own thoughts," said Glorious.

He said nothing more, and Summer felt a squirming unease in her stomach. Why wouldn't he tell her? Was he thinking something bad? Was he thinking of leaving them? She wasn't sure why he was staying anyway, and if they kept finding things like the giant turtle and the rotted wheat—if that was the path she was going down—maybe he would want to leave. Who would want to see more things like that?

She fisted her hands in his mane and stared down at them.

He flicked an ear back at her. "You're wound tight as a hare's hind leg, Summer-cub."

"Why won't you tell me?" she whispered, although by now she didn't want to know.

He snorted. "Because what I think is of no concern to anyone but me, unless I choose to tell them. And my thoughts are not ready yet to be shared, so I will not share them. Is that all?"

Put that way, she felt foolish. She thought of her mother saying, "Fine. Don't tell your mother what you're thinking," and felt the edge of some emotion so vast and complicated that she did not know what to call it.

"The thoughts of others are dangerous," said Glorious. "But it is not a danger that we can protect ourselves from." He shook himself, but cautiously, so that she did not fall off. "Be at ease. A friend will not think unkindly of you, and an unfriend will not tell you the truth of their thoughts, so what purpose is there to worry?"

"It's not as easy as that," said Summer sadly. "I can't stop myself from worrying."

"You're human," said Glorious. "Humans hoard up their fears as if the world might run out." He huffed a laugh. "Still, you build cities with them—and towers and artworks and families and faiths. It seems to work for your people, even if it would not work for mine."

"I wish I was a wolf," said Summer.

"That is a very sensible wish," said Glorious. "But even Baba Yaga cannot grant you that. So you will simply have to be a brave human."

Reginald landed on the causeway before them. "Turn off at the end of the causeway," he said. He waved a wing at the line of trees that had appeared on the horizon. "The Forester holds all the woods on the left side." Glorious nodded.

Summer was glad to leave the fens. There was something about their emptiness that made her feel empty, too.

If I had more fears, like Glorious says, maybe I'd want to feel empty. Maybe it would be easier.

She wondered what her mother would think of the fens. *Probably that the mud was dirty and full of broken glass and you'd cut yourself and get tetanus.* She sighed. Her mother's fears were too vast for a mere landscape to heal.

The trees on this side of the marshes were not like the pine forest on the other side. The trunks were spaced like pillars in a cathedral. The leaves rustled in every breath of wind, so that it was like walking through a constant murmuring *wshhhht wshhhht*. Great thickets of blackberries tangled around some of the trees, throwing up whips higher than Summer's head.

They went a little way into the woods and Reginald stopped them. "Here," he said, pointing to an opening in the trees that looked just the same as every other opening in the trees.

"How can you tell?" asked the weasel.

Reginald laughed. "No fear," he said. "I can't, and probably neither can anyone else. But if we go into the woods, the Forester's birds will pick us up, and then there'll be a guide."

"A guide for *birds,*" said the weasel, but did not protest as Glorious padded off the road and into the forest.

Summer was fairly sure that the weasel wasn't really bothered, and was just snipping at Reginald on general principle. She petted his tiny furry back. He grumbled.

It was not more than half an hour before the valet-flock set up a startled twittering. Glorious halted.

Summer looked around to see what had upset the birds. She couldn't see anything at first, and then suddenly she did see it, and wondered how she'd missed it before.

An owl sat on a low branch, directly in front of them. It was the biggest owl that Summer had ever seen. Its chest was as big around as hers was. It had mottled brown feathers and two enormous ear-tufts.

There was a thin gold chain wrapped around its left foot. The talons, where they gripped the branch, were as long as Summer's fingers.

"Settle down, you lot," said Reginald to the valet-flock. "He's the Forester's bird. He won't eat you."

"It wouldn't take him two bites if he did," breathed the weasel, pressing up against Summer's leg.

The valet-flock settled, but it was clear that they didn't like it.

The owl tilted its head sideways, which would have been comical if it were not so gigantic.

"Hello…?" said Summer carefully. Did the owl talk? She didn't want to hurt its feelings by asking.

Apparently it did not talk, or it chose not to. It spread its wings instead and launched itself off the branch, passing so close to Summer's head that she could feel a wash of air from its wings.

"Don't mind them," said Reginald, as she ducked. "Not a talkative bunch. He'll lead us right in a trice, though."

"I thought owls didn't like the daytime," said Summer, as Glorious followed the owl.

"They don't," said Reginald cheerfully. "But they know their duty, and if we go blundering around at night—with a cottage in tow, begging your pardon, Glorious—we won't get far, will we?"

Glorious grinned briefly. "If we do not reach your Forester by nightfall, you may have to."

"No, no," said Reginald. "Once we've got an owl leading us, won't be half a heartbeat. You'll see."

Summer wished she felt as confident as the hoopoe. The owl landed on a branch a hundred feet away and waited. It did not look patient or impatient. It did not look like anything but a truly enormous owl.

As long as it doesn't look hungry…

The owl watched them approach. The valet-flock swirled, and then landed, all at once, on Summer's shoulders and head.

They startled a laugh from Summer. The owl turned to look at her. Its eyes were vast and golden and looked nearly as large as her palm.

The weasel muttered something unkind as the valet flock twittered, but Summer noticed that he stayed close against her knee, where the owl might not see him.

When they had passed underneath the branch, the owl flew again. This time it landed on a small hummock on the ground and turned its head to watch them.

Glorious paced past it, close enough that Summer could have reached out her hands and touched the owl's feathers. She knotted them in the wolf's mane and did nothing of the sort.

On the ground, the owl seemed even larger. The weasel lay flat as a rag and the valet-flock did not even peep. Summer could feel their tiny claws prickling in her hair.

If it jumped for me, it could knock me off with one wing.

The owl did not fly after them. Instead, Glorious pricked up his ears and went forward. Reginald flew from tree to tree ahead, and at long last, Summer's human ears picked up the sound as well—*hoo-hoo-koo-hu-yu?*

She peered around, and saw a smaller owl, feathers striped with black, in a tree off to the left.

"It's over there," she said quietly.

Glorious nodded. "Humans have better eyes," he rumbled. "Owls don't smell very strong themselves, though their leavings stink to heaven. There's at least two more."

Summer craned her neck. The valet-birds on her head adjusted their grip.

The big owl was still on the ground behind them. Summer picked out another, much smaller owl in the crook of a branch, then another, then another.

The woods were full of owls. All of them wore golden chains on their claws. Sometimes one would hoot, but mostly they stared in silence.

It was more than little bit creepy.

Glorious paused and Reginald landed next to them.

"It is easy to follow one guide," observed the wolf. "Harder to follow a hundred. Which way do we go to find this Forester?"

Soft laughter came from behind him. "You have already found her," said the Forester, stepping into the open. "And I see that you have brought trouble with you."

Chapter Seventeen

The Forester was the largest woman that Summer had ever seen—not just tall, but enormously broad across the shoulders, with heavy hips and breasts and thighs like tree trunks. For a moment, Summer wondered if she was a regular human at all, or some kind of giantess.

Her skin was the color of fallen oak leaves, and her black hair lay tightly curled against her scalp. She walked toward them, and her footsteps were as silent as the wings of the owls.

"Reginald," she said, sounding amused. She held out her arm, and Reginald flew to it. Even though he was much larger than any normal bird, the Forester's wrist did not tremble under his weight.

"Ma'am," said the hoopoe, dipping his wings. "Begging your pardon for troubling you, but I happened on this chit of a human dragging a destiny along behind her, all about trees and Baba Yaga and of course I thought, 'Who'd know about trees? The Forester, that's who,' and so here we are."

"Indeed," said the Forester. "And did you happen on the wolf and the weasel as well?"

"Eh?" Reginald glanced over at them. "Oh, right. The weasely chap came along with Summer here, and we helped Glorious here out of a tight spot."

"And we will be in another tight spot in a moment, if I do not get clear of these trees," said Glorious dryly. "Forester, is there a clear place where I may transform? It is nearly sunset."

"Do you wish to transform?" asked the Forester.

"Wishes have little to do with it. I have no choice in the matter." Summer felt his skin ripple and she slid hurriedly off him. The valet-birds swirled and landed along her arms. The weasel climbed into her pocket.

Glorious shivered again and looked around for an opening in the trees.

The Forester stepped forward and laid her hand on Glorious's skull.

"Be at peace," she said.

The wolf inhaled sharply.

After a moment, he said, "You have stopped the change. I thank you, Forester."

"Not permanently," said the Forester. "But I know what it is to be in a body where you do not belong. In the bounds of my power, you need not fear the change."

The Forester tossed her arm in the air, launching Reginald. He flapped down beside Summer, settling his neckcloth. "Told you she was amazing," he whispered. "She'll fix us right up."

Dusk spread out from under the trees. Glorious's fur shone like a star.

The Forester knelt down and cupped her hands together. Warm golden light flared up between her fingers.

When she took her hands away, there was a tiny animal curled up in the leaves. It had quills like a porcupine, and every quill burned like a candle-flame.

"Phoenix Hedgehog," said the weasel. "You don't see many of those any more."

The hedgehog stretched and yawned. The light grew brighter.

The Forester patted a log next to her. "Come and sit, child. Tell me about your journey, and start a little before the beginning, because we are usually wrong about where things begin."

Summer sat down. The hedgehog fire was as warm as a real fire, but without smoke. Glorious's eyes reflected flat green discs back at her.

"I *think* it started when Baba Yaga's house walked into the alley," she said slowly, "but if I start before that…I was in school, and then I went home. I live with my mom…"

"Tell me about her."

So Summer tried, starting with how tall she was, and what she looked like, and what she did, and how she cried at night.

The Forester watched her, her eyes in shadow. She was listening. She listened like Glorious did, with her whole body, with her head cocked and her elbows on her knees, and Summer began to feel as if no one had ever listened to her so intently in her entire life.

Without quite knowing how, Summer began to talk about how her mother worried and that spilled over into how Summer wasn't allowed to ride horses and—"I know she loves me!" said Summer, and her voice startled her, because it sounded like she was going to cry. "But she won't let me do things and it's like they're all the same thing, like riding a horse and crossing the street and playing with matches, except they aren't the same at all and I never know what they're going to be until she won't let me do them!"

The Forester nodded. "Now we are starting to learn things," she said. Summer rubbed her eyes and felt grateful and resentful all at the same time. *I won't cry. I won't.*

"And into this, Baba Yaga's house came walking," said the Forester. "Yes. That would have called her, I think. If you want a mouse, look in mouseholes. And then what happened?"

Summer told her.

It was a long story, and the weasel put in a few words about Grub, and then Reginald talked about meeting Summer, and Glorious did too. "And she won my license by means of words," said the wolf, which warmed Summer as much as the hedgehog-fire did.

"And then we went into the woods here," said Summer finally, "because Reginald said you could help. And then there were owls, and I guess you know the rest."

The Forester nodded.

The silence stretched out. Summer began to feel uncomfortable, as if there was something more she should have said. "Does that help?" she asked. "I mean, do you know what we should do?"

"Yes," said the Forester. "And no. There are, perhaps, things I may tell you, but you will decide what to do with them. But first, Summer, I have a question for you."

"Okay," said Summer, sitting up straighter.

"You are not a hero," said the Forester. "That is no insult to you. You might become one, I suppose, but I would not wish it on you."

Summer did not quite know how to feel about this statement. It still sounded vaguely like an insult.

"And yet you are here," said the Forester. "Why? What is it that you are hoping to do?" She smiled. "You may take time to think, if you like. I believe that your friends are eager to have dinner."

     Summer in Orcus

The valet-flock was, indeed, twittering around Summer's ears. They took flight at this, and went to the packs. They kept very low, watching the owls, but they nevertheless laid out meat and cheese and grapes for everyone.

Summer ate without tasting it, trying to think of the answer to the Forester's question.

What did she want? She had wanted an adventure, and her heart's desire, but then they found the burned inn, and it had no longer been an adventure. Her heart's desire was nice, but it wasn't worth having people die.

So why had she not given up and tried to go home?

Because it wasn't just about her heart's desire.

Because something else was relying on her.

"I just wanted to help the Frog Tree," said Summer. "I mean—you must think it's stupid—people are dead, and Zultan is awful and maybe it's stupid to worry about a tree, but it was so—it was trying so *hard*, and it was doing something *wonderful* and it wasn't hurting *anything* and—and—"

She dissolved into tears.

Half of Summer was shocked, because she hadn't expected to cry—she hadn't even known how much she cared until right this minute—and the other half of Summer was sobbing her heart out on the Forester's shoulder.

I thought I'd cry about my mother, and I didn't want to, but I didn't know I'd cry for the Frog Tree!

She was embarrassed for a moment about crying in front of her friends—but they had already seen her cry, over the burned out inn. What was once more?

The Forester gathered Summer up in her large arms. "There it is," she said. "There. All may yet be well."

"It was only a tree," whispered Summer, feeling as if she were stabbing herself in the stomach with the words. *Only a tree.*

"And you are only a girl," said the Forester, "and Reginald is only a bird and I am only…what I am. We are all still worth saving."

Summer let out her breath in a long sigh. It caught a little at the bottom, but only a little.

"Now," said the Forester. "Saving a single wondrous thing is better than saving the world. For one thing, it's more achievable. The world is never content to stay saved."

Summer laughed a little at that. The Forester set her down on the log and she wiped her face on her sleeve.

"As to the saving…well." The Forester closed her eyes for a moment, and then—"Look," she said, turning her face toward the light.

Summer looked.

The Forester's eyes were not human. In the shadows, they had looked normal enough, but when the light struck them, the pupils contracted into slits instead of circles.

Lizard eyes.

"What—" said Summer, startling back. "How—"

The log was not wide enough. She overbalanced and fell over on her back in the leaves.

The Forester laughed softly and held out her hand.

Summer took it. "I'm sorry," she said. It had been very rude to jerk away, she knew that, as if the Forester had something wrong with her. "I'm sorry."

The Forester smiled. "It's all right," she said, pulling Summer back up to her seat. "The first time I saw myself in a mirror, I did the same—though not, I think, for the same reasons."

She tilted her head so the fire caught in her eyes, and they were brilliantly blue, the color of a turquoise stone or a lizard's tail.

I couldn't have missed that. She did something. Or stopped doing something. Her eyes weren't like that before.

"Are you human?" asked Summer timidly.

Wanting to say: *It's not like you have to be. Glorious isn't and Reginald isn't and the weasel isn't and I love them all.*

Wanting to say: *I don't think being human is any better than anything else, really I don't. Only I don't quite know how to say it without sounding like I'm saying the opposite.*

"The answer to that," said the Forester, "is not quite no, and not quite yes." She shook her head and one of the barn owls raised its wings and made a soft, creaking call.

"I am half a dragon," said the Forester.

Summer considered this. "You mean your mom was a dragon, or your dad?"

The Forester shook her head. "No. Then I would be a dragon or a human. Being a dragon is like being alive or being dead. It is a thing you are or a thing you are not."

"Like being a wolf," rumbled Glorious.

"Very much like being a wolf," said the Forester, nodding to him. There was a smile in her voice, if not in her slitted eyes. "Well. I was a dragon. I had a dragon's body and a dragon's heart. And then someone got hold of a great and terrible magic, and wished to be a dragon."

She shook her head, and there was no smile in her voice now. "You cannot turn your heart into a dragon's heart. Hearts can only be changed from within, and there is no magic in the world that can change them from without. But a dragon's body can be stolen, and I imagine that I was the nearest."

"They took your body?" whispered Summer.

"And left me this one in trade," said the Forester. She ran her hands over her heavy brown forearms. "Poor thing. It did not know what to do, having a dragon's soul slammed inside it. Like trying to catch a bonfire with a candlewick. But it was a child's body, then—yes, this was long ago, longer than you know—and it still had a little give to it, so it wrapped itself around me as best it could."

Glorious made a sound that Summer had never heard him make before—a whimper, almost, of sympathy.

"I woke in the middle of my hoard, in a cavern full of rings and crowns and shadows, and I was freezing cold and smaller than the egg I hatched from."

"I'm sorry," said Summer, who had sometimes dreamed of being a dragon, and could not imagine having it taken away from you.

"It was long ago," said the Forester. "And whoever did it—poor stupid fool—found themselves with a human heart in a dragon's body, and it was likely worse for them."

At Summer's expression, she laughed a little. "Think, child! There was too much dragon heart to fit in a human body—there must have been too little human heart to fit into my body. To be alone, inside a great mansion of dragonflesh, listening to the echoes in the empty places where more of *you* should be…" She shook her head. "I hated her at first. Now I think, perhaps, she has done more to punish herself than I ever could. The best a dragon can do is burn you alive, and while that is a very short eternity while it is happening, it ends. She has trapped herself in a prison that will never grow old."

"She?" asked Summer. "*Her?*"

"Her. For this must have been her body, so it must have been a human girl. One like you, perhaps." The Forester bared her teeth, not quite a smile, and Summer caught a hint of dragon fangs in her expression.

Summer sat up very straight. Her cheeks felt hot. She felt ashamed, even knowing that someone *like* her had done such a thing.

"I'm sorry," she whispered.

"It is all right," said the woman who was only half a dragon. "It is an old story. This body has lived for a long time, for its takes its cues from the heart inside it. And it has done its best." She patted her own arm affectionately, like a rider with a good-natured horse.

"Is there any way to put you back?" asked Summer.

The Forester shook her head. "That's a task for someone else," she said kindly. "A god, perhaps, or the ghost of a bird, or a hero born of moonbeams. Not a human task. Yours is large enough already, and will lead you far and fell."

"It is? Then—then you know what's wrong with the Frog Tree?"

The Forester nodded. "You've encountered others, haven't you? Other things dead or dying. Great creatures struck down."

Summer nodded. Glorious growled softly.

"They are being poisoned," said the Forester. "By the wasps of the Queen-in-Chains."

Chapter Eighteen

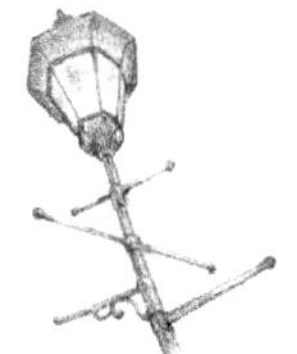

Summer was never quite certain, afterwards, how they left the Forester. She thought that they talked for some time, but she could not remember what was said. She had been gazing into the hedgehog flames, hadn't she? And the Forester said something to her—something that might have been *courage* or perhaps *Mother*.

All that she knew was that she came to herself sitting on Glorious's back, and the wolf was walking through the mist of early morning. She did not feel tired or hungry, although she could not remember having slept.

Summer tried to remember having mounted, or having said goodbye to the Forester, but she could not. The weasel was asleep in her pocket.

"Is…is anyone else having trouble remembering?" she asked carefully.

"Comes of talking to dragons," said Reginald. "Though I didn't know the old girl was a dragon! What a facer!" He did a little sarabande in midair. "And me making free with her forest, too, and strolling in like she was my old maiden aunt. Ha!"

He seemed to be pleased as much as abashed.

Glorious flicked an ear back at her. "It is not entirely clear," he admitted. "Though like a dream, not like magic."

"Dragons aren't magic," said Reginald. "Dragons are *dragons.*"

"I thought they were magic," said Summer.

"Magic is like rain," said Glorious. "Dragons are like mountains. Or wolves. Magic may happen to a dragon, but mountains are not made of rain."

Summer digested this. It sounded very simple, but it would probably have made more sense if she knew more about dragons.

Or about magic, for that matter. She sighed.

"Never fear," said Reginald. "She's given us a direction, hasn't she?"

"Certainly," said Glorious dryly. "Find the Queen-in-Chains, whom no one has seen since the fall of the Tower of Dogs. That will be no easy task, hoopoe."

"I don't know why not," said the weasel, waking up with a yawn. "She's sending out wasps, isn't she? Why don't we just find a wasp, then?"

There was a thoughtful silence.

"If we could find one of these wasps," said Summer, feeling a slow excitement building in her stomach, "then we could follow it back to the Queen!"

"Thought they died when they stung a chap," said Reginald doubtfully.

"That's bees," said Summer confidently. She had done a report on honeybees for school last year. "Bees sting you and the stinger pulls their guts out. It's kind of awful. But wasps can sting you over and over again and it doesn't hurt them."

"Huh!" said the hoopoe. "Well. Never too late to get an education. So we find a wasp and follow it back. But how do we find a wasp?"

"That should be easy," said Glorious, in his deep, somber voice. "We need only look for a great and wondrous thing. Before long, as things are going, a wasp will come to poison it."

"Where will we find one, though?" asked Summer.

The wolf laughed, but kindly. "The great joy of the world, Summer-cub, is that it is full of wondrous things."

He shook himself and his muscles tensed. It was the only warning Summer had before he broke into a run.

"We're only two days out from Almondgrove," said Reginald, when Glorious finally slowed. "Had a notion we'd stop and get some provender. Introduce you to the old pater and all. M'father'll know where to find something wondrous." He laughed. "He's nearly a wondrous thing himself, come to that."

"Great," muttered the weasel. "A whole house full of twittering twits."

Reginald heard this, but he didn't look particularly upset. "Oh, quite! But there's no need to rustle up the whole clan. We'll stock up on supplies, though, and the valet-flock will be wanting to pick up a few more members."

The flock chirped agreement. Summer wondered if they missed the dead valet-bird.

Is he really gone, though? They're a sort of mind all together, like a beehive. Was there something that was specific to that bird that's gone, or do they just move the same mind around between them?

It was mid-afternoon on the second day when the road began to change. It was still narrow, but it turned to cobblestones instead of dirt. The trees became taller and more widely spaced.

Side roads branched off the main thoroughfare, reminding Summer of driveways, but the sort of driveways you got in an expensive neighborhood where the houses were not in sight of the street. The branching roads were framed with lantern posts, but each post had a dozen perches sticking off it and the ground beneath the posts was white with droppings.

The first bird they saw was some kind of partridge, sitting low on a perch with her eyes closed. She had a little leather helmet on, and a collar with a badge.

"Heyo, copper!" said Reginald cheerfully.

"Eh? Eh!" The partridge shook herself away, fluffing up all her feathers. "Eh? Oh, it's you, young Almondgrove. You'd best not be up to any tricks." She looked over Glorious and Summer and her round eyes went even rounder. "Friends of yours?"

"They're all with me," said Reginald. "Best friends a chap could have, wot? Companions in adversity, one and all."

The partridge snorted and settled back down on her perch. "Shouldn't think you know a thing about adversity, you young jackanapes. But go on, and give your father my best."

"Will do," said Reginald.

They went on. More and more birds appeared, flying overhead, filling the trees, chatting to one another. Ripples of silence spread as the wolf walked by, and then conversation rushed in to fill the void—"Did you *see?* A wolf!" "A wolf and a human on it!" "It's a small human…" "Yes, but it's a quite a large wolf!" "And was that *Reginald?*"

Reginald did not seem bothered at all. He called out greetings to birds as he passed, and did little aerial jigs and bounces of delight.

"I suspect that we are no longer travelling in secret," said Glorious wryly.

"They'll have word from here to the far ends of Orcus," grumped the weasel.

Summer said nothing. Surely Zultan and Grub wouldn't do anything with all these birds watching, would they? They had burned an isolated inn, but there were hundreds of birds here, and they could all fly away.

Reginald isn't worried. She sat up straight and remembered the saint's book again—*Don't worry about things that you cannot fix.* And overhead, the birds chirped and chattered and sang to each other about the wolf and the human girl on his back, and Summer felt as if she were in a parade.

They reached the branching road of Almondsgrove Manor just as the sky was beginning to show traces of pink. Two brick pillars framed the road, hung with lanterns, and in front of the lanterns stood two geese.

The geese were as tall as Summer. They had white heads and black throats and their bodies were sooty gray. Their orange legs were as thick around as Summer's calves.

"Heyo!" said Reginald happily. "It's me."

"Indeed," said the goose on the left.

"Welcome home, Master Reginald," said the goose on the right.

They turned their small black eyes on Glorious.

"You seem to have a wolf," said the left goose.

"We were not informed there would be a carnivore visiting," said the right goose.

Glorious grinned. "I would not pick a fight with such brave warriors," he said. Summer, listening, thought that there was a faint emphasis on "I," as if he had almost said "*Even* I" and then thought better of it.

The geese and the wolf studied each other for a very long moment.

"Indeed," said the goose on the left.

"Then we shall pick no fight with you," said the goose on the right. "Follow me."

Glorious dipped his head an inch and they passed between the brick pillars, following the goose.

"Would you really not pick a fight with them?" asked Summer in an undertone.

"Geese are perilous creatures," said Glorious. "A flock of geese can kill a foolish wolf." She felt a soft rumble through his chest. "Though I am not foolish, and two is not a flock. But we have other concerns for now."

Summer had always been a little frightened of the large flocks of geese that sometimes gathered on the school lawn. They hissed like angry cats and did not seem at all wary of humans. But she had also thought that her fear was just because she was afraid of everything. Hearing Glorious describe them as perilous made her think that perhaps she wasn't just a coward after all.

The goose ahead of them turned its long neck and winked at Summer. *And apparently they have good hearing, too…*

The goose led them down the road. It was narrow by human standards, more like a paved footpath than a street. Broad green lawns rolled out around them, studded with trees, fountains, perches, and something that looked like a giant wicker gazebo.

The house itself was shadowed in the dusk, but there were lights in many of the windows. The doors were flanked with lamps. There were three sets of doors, one per story, but only the bottom one had steps. The upper two were ringed with perches. A bird stood at attention besides each set of doors.

A footman, thought Summer, and then, *No, a footbird,* and then *…a wingbird? Maybe?*

The goose dipped its head to the footbird or whatever it was, and the bird hurried to open the doors.

Glorious paused at the foot of the steps. "It is getting late," he said. "And I would rather not change inside your home, however grand, Reginald."

"No, no," said Reginald. "Not the thing at all. Houses inside houses! Terrible damage to the millwork. Here, stay out here with him, will you? He'll turn into a very nice cottage in a few minutes."

This last was to the guard goose. The goose tilted its head for a moment, gazing at Reginald in bafflement, then said, "Very well, Master Reginald." To the footbird, it said, "Please take the master and his guests to quarters. Lord Almondgrove will wish to see them, but not in all their dust."

"Quite right," said Reginald cheerfully. "Wouldn't want to pester the *pater* in a crumpled waistcoat. Glorious, give a howl if you need anything at all."

Glorious shook his head, looking amused. "I shall need a very large breakfast in the morning," he said simply. "There is too much prey about, and I would be a poor guest to hunt any of it."

"Right!" said Reginald. "Huge breakfast! Sausage and kippers and eggs and ham."

"Sure," muttered the weasel, "give *him* eggs…"

Summer slid off the wolf's back and he trotted off beside the goose guard. The two of them went side-by-side, and Summer heard the goose say something too low to hear, but which made Glorious growl with laughter.

The foot-bird gestured. Reginald and Summer followed him through the door.

The door opened into a grand entrance hall, the sort of extraordinary tiled room that was designed to make an impression on a visitor. It looked like the sort of room Summer had seen in mansions in movies.

Unlike those rooms, however, there were no stairs. The upper level was lined with perches and immense windows, but where a human mansion would have had a giant staircase with gilt banisters, this hall had only empty space.

Well, of course. They've got wings.

"Now, then," said Reginald to the foot-bird, "this is my friend, Miss Summer. She's from a different world. Tough as a nut, game as a pebble, but probably wing-sore by now." He paused. "Err—foot-sore?"

Summer stifled a laugh. *He'd probably call foot-men wing-birds. We're all trying our best, though…*

"Certainly," said the foot-bird. He stamped a foot on the ground and his claws made a hollow knocking sound.

Servant-birds appeared. One plump bird, a mourning dove with a white lace cap, approached Summer. "If you'll follow me, miss…"

"Go on," said Reginald. "You'll be so clean and well-fed when I see you next that I'll hardly know you. And I'll have a clean waistcoat."

The valet-birds twittered in what sounded like relief.

Summer followed the dove.

They went through a large door on the side of the hall, and then a smaller door, and then a corridor lined with quite small doors indeed. The doors were set high in the wall, nearly six inches off the ground.

The dove opened the door. Summer stepped carefully over the threshold.

It was a small room, or perhaps it only seemed small because there was so much furniture in it. The bed was very large and completely circular. There was a wooden screen in one corner and a basin on a stand in another, a door in the far wall, and a wardrobe so large that you could have fit most of Narnia inside it.

Though I hope not, thought Summer, a bit wearily. *Orcus is quite enough excitement for me at the moment…*

Summer in Orcus

The servant-bird smiled at her, mostly around the eyes. "Just you take off those dirty clothes, mistress, and we'll get them washed for you"

Summer was thrilled at the thought of getting her clothes washed—the valet-birds tried very hard, but her t-shirt was still showing a great deal of wear, and her underwear didn't bear thinking about—but she was worried about the blanket Donkeyskin had given her. It looked so grubby and travelstained, surely they'd want to throw it away?

"It's very important I get this back," she said. "I know it doesn't look like much…"

"Cultural dress of your people," said the servant-bird. "I quite understand, mistress. We'll treat it very carefully. In the meantime, we've some clothes for non-birds here…"

She gestured to a screen. Summer went behind it and took her clothes off.

The clothes for humans, or at least human-shaped people, came in several varieties. One was rather like a sari and the other was rather like a bathrobe—shapeless, but belted in the middle. The sleeves had gigantic openings. The armholes went down nearly to Summer's hips.

I suppose they're used to fitting wings through them. They probably think these are quite tight!

She tied the sari-like fabric around herself, then pulled the bathrobe on over it. She had to roll up the cuffs on the sleeves several times and they still dangled past her wrists. She felt like a very small child playing dress-up.

She took the lock and the acorn and the turquoise stone out of her jeans and put them in a pocket in the robe. There didn't seem to be any place to tie the cheese-sword.

"There you are!" said the servant-bird cheerfully. "Would you like a dust bath or oil or water?"

"Um," said Summer. "Water?" She was rather curious about the dust bath, actually, but water seemed easier.

"Right this way, mistress."

The water bath was oddly shaped. It was very shallow and very wide, a tiled pool six feet wide but barely four inches deep. Summer had to scrub herself and crouch down to rinse.

Like a birdbath, she thought. And then, *Well, of course it is!*

She was just starting on her hair when the servant-bird came back. Summer yelped, but the bird bustled in with such cheerful professionalism that it was hard to feel embarrassed. "Fresh towels and oil for your fur if you need it."

Summer had no idea what to do with the oil, if anything. She used regular soap on her hair. There weren't any combs, so she raked her fingers through it and heard it squeak.

She dried herself off with a towel and then climbed into the robes again.

The servant-bird clicked her tongue at Summer and helped her tie the sari rather more securely. Apparently there was a trick to it. The over-robe was easier. The weasel, who had been napping, grumbled inside her pocket.

"I'm afraid we have no footwear for you," said the bird. "Human feet are very complicated, are they not? But now, if you are ready, Lord Almondgrove will see you before dinner."

Chapter Nineteen

Summer followed the servant-bird to the hallway, where she was handed off to a butler-bird, who took her through the halls and up a staircase. "Forgive me," said the bird, as they climbed. "The library is on the second floor, and the approach for the non-flighted is…less elegant."

It looked plenty elegant to Summer. The stairs were shallow, if narrow, and the wooden paneling on the walls was so dark that it was nearly black. Sconces in the shape of fantastic beasts coiled up the panels, shooting oil-lamp flames from their mouths.

The butler-bird turned right at the top of the stairs and led her to a set of doors. They were open at the top, like French doors, and the butler-bird had to open the bottom for Summer to step through.

It was a library, and it was incredible.

For one thing, it was completely vertical. The room itself was only about the size of the dining room in Summer's house back home, but it went up and up for stories on stories. Each wall was lined with bookcases, and perches ringed the room at intervals so that a bird could stand anywhere they chose and reach a book easily with beak or talons.

There were hundreds of books, probably thousands. At least as many as there were in the school library. They smelled like leather and expensive words.

"Miss Summer," announced the butler-bird, "of another world."

"Heyo, Summer," said Reginald, who was lounging on a low couch. "Quite the thing, isn't it? Didn't I tell you?"

The other bird in the room turned toward her.

He was also a hoopoe, wearing a black waistcoat. He was larger than Reginald and heavier, but his feathers were still bright. There was a faint milkiness to his eyes, as if he were in the very early stages of going blind.

He could still see her, though, because he smiled and dipped his crest. "Miss Summer. My son has told me much about you. You honor us with your presence."

"Oh," said Summer faintly. She stumbled through a bow, thought at the last minute that it was probably supposed to be a curtsey, realized she didn't know how to do one, and wound up bowing twice. "Are you Lord Almondgrove? I mean—of course you are. Sir. Thank you. Everything's lovely here. The bath was very nice."

She closed her mouth, feeling embarrassed. She'd never met a Lord before. Well, there was Reginald, but he didn't really seem to count.

Fortunately, the elder hoopoe did not seem offended. He smiled again. "Come in, come in. Reginald tells me that you are seeking to end the menace to our world…and that you are a delightful travelling companion and staunch in defense of your friends, and that the Forester likes you. Which are all most excellent qualifications, but I would like to ask a few questions, if I may."

"Uh," said Summer. "I mean, yes, sir." She looked around for a place to sit and eventually settled on something that looked like a footstool. Lord Almondgrove was on a perch at a reading stand, rather like a lectern, so she had to look up to meet his eyes.

"Is it true that Baba Yaga sent you?" he asked.

"Yes," said Summer. "She had a house with chicken feet and a skull on the door. Everybody says it was Baba Yaga. There can't be very many women with houses with chicken feet around, can there?"

"Not many, certainly," said Lord Almondgrove. "Not in this world, at least."

Summer cast about for something else to say. "She gave me a talking weasel. She said she was sending me to find my heart's desire. I don't think that's a weasel, though. Err, no offense."

"Feh," muttered the weasel. He poked his head out of her pocket and looked up at Lord Almondgrove. "It was Baba Yaga for sure. She sat in a chair made of bones, and she smelled like the wasting death of dreams."

"Told you," said Reginald. "The prime article herself!"

"Mmm," said Lord Almondgrove. "I would not be quite convinced—not that I believe that you are lying, Miss Summer, but because all the worlds are full of charlatans, and someone might be foolish enough to impersonate Baba Yaga herself. But I am told that Zultan Houndbreaker has pursued you, and that he has begun the burnings again, which means at least that *he* believes you have been sent to change things."

He fluffed up his feathers. "To pull Zultan's feathers, I'd dare a great deal, I confess."

Summer gulped. "Isn't that dangerous?"

The elderly hoopoe held out a clawed foot and turned it—*maybe yes, maybe no.* "Not so dangerous as it used to be. I do not know how much Reginald has told you…"

"Hardly anything!" said Reginald proudly. "Wouldn't cut a wheedle and pretend I knew more than I did."

"I wish you wouldn't use that dreadful cant," said Lord Almondgrove. "It makes you sound like a common criminal in a hedgerow."

Reginald grinned and winked at Summer. "Doing it up too brown, pater!"

The senior Almondgrove rolled his eyes. "Yes, yes, whatever that means. I could wish you'd paid more attention—what if you have to inherit someday?"

"Perish the thought! My sister'll be twice the Almondgrove I am."

Lord Almondgrove shook his head. Summer got the impression that this was a conversation they'd had many times before. "At any rate," he said, turning back to Summer, "the matter of Zultan. He had an army once, long ago, when he took down the Tower of Dogs. In those days, we lived in fear of him, and no one dared defy him too openly. But the Tower did not fall easily. He broke his army against it, and it was only the Queen that brought it down in the end." He tapped a claw on his beak. "He has no army now. He raised the first one with promises and wight-liquor, and people have learned to be wary of both now. So now he has only his little warband, a dozen strong. Dangerous enough in their way, but not enough to make war against members of the Dawn Chorus."

"But what *is* Zultan?" asked Summer. This question had been gnawing at her for days now. "Is he a—a—" She stopped herself short of saying *person.* "—a human?"

I'm learning. I hope.

Lord Almondgrove shuffled on his perch. "Hard to say," he said finally. "But no, I don't think so. Not unless humans live much longer than I think.

The Tower of Dogs fell long, long ago, before I was born, but Zultan still goes on."

"What were the dogs?" asked Summer. Here at last was someone who seemed able to answer questions, and to answer them clearly, without wandering off into strange cant, like Reginald, or into wild philosophies she didn't quite understand, like Glorious. "I mean—we've got dogs in my world, or things we call dogs, but they don't build towers or roads." (It occurred to her that she had not seen a dog anywhere in this world.)

Lord Almondgrove leaned forward, his crest flattening down a little with interest. "Really! Can you describe them for me?"

"Uh." Summer found herself making a few aimless hand gestures. How do you describe a dog to someone who's never seen one? "Like a wolf," she said, thinking of Glorious. "But smaller. And they don't talk. And they walk on all fours, and people keep them as pets."

Almondgrove let out a loud *chck-ck-ck* laugh. "No, no! Not the same as ours at all, then."

"Fancy keeping a dog as a pet!" said Reginald. "They'd have you up on charges, assuming you could find one."

Lord Almondgrove smiled tolerantly. He considered for a moment, then raised a claw. "Easier shown than described, I think. Wait a moment."

He flew upward, into the higher reaches of the library. The railings around the edges of the bookcase served as perches. Lord Almondgrove landed on one and ran a wing along the edge of the books. "Ah, there we are." He pulled a book from the shelf and flew back down to the main perch, setting the book on the podium.

The book was leatherbound and opened the opposite way from books Summer was used to. There were notches along the sides where bird claws could fit easily.

He opened the book up. Summer couldn't read the writing; it looked like bird tracks going in different directions, or like the runes that she had seen in school when her class did a unit on Norse mythology.

But there were also pictures, and Lord Almondgrove found one in short order. He turned the book toward her.

The dog in the picture stood on his hind legs, like Summer, though he seemed to be walking on his toes. He was very tall and thin, with enormous upstanding ears. He looked rather like a greyhound, or like the African wild dogs that she had seen in nature documentaries. His tail was short and curved, with a plumed tip.

"No," said Summer. "I'm afraid our dogs don't look anything like that."

Lord Almondgrove nodded. He turned the pages, showing her other pictures—more dogs, laboring together. They wore various clothes—tunics, armor, strapped sandal-like footwear. Often there was a tower in the background.

Near the end of the book, there was a final picture. Lord Almondgrove closed the book, sighing, before Summer could see it. "And then the Tower of Dogs fell, to Zultan and the Queen. And there may be no more dogs in Orcus. I have not seen one since…well, since I was younger than this young scapegrace here."

"You *saw* one?" said Reginald, looking up. "You're not that old, pater. Thought they all died with the Tower."

"Most of them did," said Lord Almondgrove. "And Zultan saw to the rest, in time. But there were a few travelling, far flung, who could not get back to the Tower in time. I met one. We travelled together for a little time ourselves."

Reginald sat up straight. "You never told me about this."

Lord Almondgrove sighed and rubbed at his beak with his foot. "It's an old tale, and a sad one. He was very old himself, and his fur had gone white. He was looking for a way back to his world."

He looked up at Summer and managed a smile. "It was why I asked about the dogs in your world. These dogs were not from Orcus. They came from some other place, a long time ago—centuries, if not longer. Their stories said that they came through corridors of stone, a long, long way, and when they emerged, they were in Orcus. The dog I knew was trying to find a way back. He thought he was probably the last one in this world." He shook his head. "All the writings say that they were good and decent folk, that they were as honorable as anyone alive. And my friend Stone Ear—he was *good*. He radiated goodness like heat from a stove. I can't explain any better than that."

"Stone Ear?" said Reginald. "Odd name for a chap, even a dog."

"It wasn't his real name. He was deaf in one ear, so I called him that. He said his name was in his own speech, and it was too painful to hear the language any longer, when he was the last." Lord Almondgrove shook his head. "He's long dead now, I suppose. But I hope he found his way back before he died."

Summer bowed her head. There were too many sorrows in the world. She thought that if she felt any one too deeply, she might drown in it.

"It was Zultan Houndbreaker who tore down the Tower," said Lord Almondgrove. "It was Zultan who called the Queen-in-Chains, and Zultan who left my old friend rootless and packless and alone in the world. And so, my dear Summer, if Zultan wants you, by the egg of the Mother of Dawn, I will do everything in my power to keep you from his grasp."

Summer went back to her bedroom in a pensive mood. Lord Almondgrove had promised them 'provender,' whatever that was—money, maybe?—and to pore over his maps until he found a wondrous thing they could stake out to look for wasps.

It was all very helpful, and good, but Summer was a little disappointed. On some level, she'd been hoping that Reginald's father would take over the whole project. It would be nice to have a real grown-up in charge of everything again. She didn't want to have to make any more decisions—not when people were getting killed and there seemed to be a whole *world* at stake!

But the elder Almondgrove had shown no inclination to do so. In fact, he was talking about having them leave again in a day or two, "When you've rested."

She felt a bit odd about that.

It didn't help that she had finally asked "But who is the Queen-in-Chains?" and found out that apparently nobody else knew either.

"The people who saw her are dead," said Lord Almondgrove. "Dead when the Tower fell. She leaves no witnesses behind her. Now only Zultan knows for sure." He sighed. "For all I know, there is no Queen-in-Chains, and he made the name up to frighten the rest of us. But the Tower was shattered, stone from stone, and Zultan could not do that alone."

This was not encouraging.

Summer cheered up a great deal, though, when she saw the tray in the room. "Begging your pardon," said the servant-bird, "but Reginald said you'd probably prefer a meal in your room and a rest, rather than going down for a formal dinner."

"Yes!" said Summer gratefully. The tray had toast on it, and butter and jam and some kind of little seedcake and a bunch of red-violet grapes and even two hard-boiled eggs, peeled and sitting in little cups. The weasel crowed with delight and went after one of the eggs, which was almost as big as he was.

She got through most of the meal and suddenly found herself so exhausted that she could hardly chew.

The servant-bird had turned down the bed. It was very high and Summer had to climb up it. "My apologies, miss," said the bird. "I'll get a little set of stairs for you immediately."

"It's fine," said Summer, or tried to say it, but her head was hitting the pillow and her body was sinking into a mattress like a cloud, and what came out may simply have been, "Izzzzz…"

Chapter Twenty

When she woke in the morning, her clothes were folded neatly on top of a chest. They were sparkling clean, even the blanket. The cheese-sword had been unknotted from its shoelace and slipped into a leather sheath attached to a narrow belt.

"It's a little loose in the sheath," said the servant-bird apologetically, bustling in. "The shape's a bit unusual."

"It's for cheese," said Summer.

The bird paused for an instant. "Are the cheeses very fierce in your world?"

Summer started laughing. "No. It's…it's a long story."

The bird smiled. "That's good to know. Master Reginald is down at breakfast still, if you'd like to join him."

Summer put on her clothes, and then the servant-bird draped a new robe around her and helped her tie it with a sash. It looked rather odd in the mirror, but the bird assured her that no human would dream of sharing a meal with the Almondgrove family in anything less formal.

The Almondgrove dining room was a long, low table with a sideboard and many perches. It was so low to the ground that a chair would have towered over it, but the birds had provided a cushion for Summer to sit on. Reginald waved cheerfully as she came in.

"Grab a plate," he said. "Help yourself. We're not formal in the morning."

It all looked rather formal to Summer, compared to eating in the kitchen at home, particularly when the butler-bird came out and poured juice for her. But she took a plate and went to the sideboard, which had jam and bread and cold cuts, as well as other things that looked rather more troubling. (Were those mealworms in jelly?)

She sat on her cushion and ate her breakfast. The weasel gorged himself on cold cuts.

"So!" said Reginald. "Sleep well?"

Summer nodded. She didn't know why she'd been so tired. "Very well," she said.

"Good, good. Wolf-chap went off to m'father's hunting preserve, says he'll be back later."

"Are we not leaving today, then?" asked Summer. She didn't have any great desire to leave, but she wasn't sure what she would do with herself all day. It is always a little awkward to be a guest in someone else's home when you have no way to occupy yourself.

"Thought we'd stay a day or two," said Reginald. "No great rush, is there? Father's tracking down something wonderful for us to go stake out for wasps." He took a sip of juice. "And there's a ball tonight in any event, so we can't possibly leave before then. Miss Merope will be there!"

Summer had nearly forgotten Miss Merope. "Ah," she said. "Um. Isn't that dangerous?"

"Far more dangerous to miss it! Reputation in tatters, what?"

"Well, suppose someone tells Zultan where we are?" Summer was not entirely sure if they were still on the run, exactly, but people with other people chasing them didn't stop and go to balls, did they?

"Oh!" The hoopoe waved a wing at her. "No fear! No self-respecting bird'll give Grub the time of day! That'd be the worst sort of *ton*! And everyone brings their guards, of course, in case of a duel."

"There are duels?"

"Only if we're lucky," Reginald assured her. "And it'd be over a matter of honor. Nobody'll duel a human, never you fear. It'd be lowering."

"I...see." Summer started in on the toast, to buy time.

"You'll come, won't you?" asked Reginald anxiously. "Not to dance— not much for the aerial waltz, of course!—but meet Miss Merope and the crowd? Great good guns they are, slap up to the echo—but you'll see that, of course!"

Summer followed less than half of that, but gathered that she was being invited. She was touched, but it sounded a little nerve-wracking. She hated school dances. Everybody stood around and looked awkward at each other.

"What do I wear?"

"Oh, it hardly matters," said Reginald. "You're a human, you can wear anything. No one cares. Um." He coughed, catching himself. "That is, sure you'll look smashing in anything, of course."

The weasel rolled his eyes and muttered something around a mouthful of ham.

"Sure," said Summer, grinning. His unconcern was very reassuring somehow. What did birds care what a human wore, after all?

In the end, she wore a tunic with an elaborately patterned waistcoat over it. The waistcoat was for a bird, she thought, so it was rather strangely cut and seized the bottom of her ribs whenever she took a deep breath. But she found that she quite liked the look in the mirror, particularly with the cheese-sword. She looked strange and almost dangerous and quite astonishingly tanned, and when you are twelve, this is quite an accomplishment.

To her mild surprise, they walked. "Only a quick flit of the wings," explained Reginald. "Even for a walker. M'father won't get the carriage out for anything short of a visit to the Chorus, says we'll get lazy. Some of the birds from farther out will drive, though."

The dance hall was only about a twenty-minute walk, down the well-lit roads. The goose-guards went alongside them, carrying their spears in strange horizontal holsters under their wings. It looked very strange, but Summer supposed that if you had to draw a weapon with your feet, it made sense.

Glorious and the weasel had gone off to hunt during the day, so it was a party of only four: hoopoe and geese and human. They were rapidly joined by other birds, though, most flying overhead but a few walking like the geese. Reginald called greetings and friendly insults but stayed politely on the ground beside her.

A small knot of quail with dozens of ribbons in their topknots fell in alongside them. "Marm," said Reginald, dipping his head. The largest of the group nodded to him. "Master Almondgrove." The rest of the quail lifted their fans almost simultaneously and gave breathless chirping giggles.

Summer was close enough to one of the guards to hear the goose snort. She caught the big bird's eyes and they exchanged glances. Summer felt suddenly very much older and very grown-up, and not just because the quail only came up to her knees.

When they arrived at the dancehall itself, she felt smaller again. The building was immense, the size of a barn—two or three barns, maybe—and there were carriages being pulled up in front of it. At first Summer could make no sense of the carriages, and then she realized that they were pulled by ostriches standing ten feet high, their plumed headdresses rising even higher.

As she watched, one of the ostriches turned in the harness and used his long, snake-like neck to reach the carriage door. "Madam," he intoned, in a voice like gravel.

He's the coachman and the horse all at once! That's certainly efficient!

Three orange birds got out of the carriage, their heads bizarrely rounded. Summer couldn't tell if it was a mass of feathers or a peculiar hair-style… *feather-style…oh dear…I wonder…*

"Reginald, do some birds wear wigs?"

The hoopoe let out a loud bray of laughter, tried to stifle it, and nearly choked. One of the geese pounded him on the back. "Dash it, Summer, what a time to ask that! Yes, but it's not done. You pretend not to notice and then talk behind their backs, that's the polite way."

"Sorry?"

"No, no. Human you know, ma'am, very different where they're from, no offense intended—"

This last was to the quail matron, who had turned a round-eyed glare onto Summer.

"Qwerrrrmk!" she said, and turned away. She gestured with her fan and all the quail ran forward, dipping their heads as they passed Reginald, and vanished through the open doorway. It was also the size of a barn door, but shaped like a keyhole, much larger at the top than the bottom. There were no steps, only a long ramp up to it.

"I didn't mean to offend them," said Summer sheepishly.

"Oh, bah, don't trouble yourself a bit. Some birds live to be offended. She'd be more offended if you didn't provide something to be offended about, in a manner of speaking. Ho, Thrasher! Is that you?"

A yellow-eyed bird dropped down beside them. "Reggie! Thought you were still rusticating!"

"Oh, I am," said Reginald happily. "This is just—ah—rusticus interruptus, you know? Had to come back home for a bit. Thrasher, this is Summer. She's a human."

"No doubt," said Thrasher. "Thank heavens you told me, Reggie, I'd have been completely at sea otherwise." He winked at Summer.

"We flocked together when we were barely out of the egg!" said Reginald. "Up and down and back around, one yolk in two shells—oh, I say, it's Banner!"

They had reached the doorway of the dance-hall, and Reginald darted into the air, calling after another bird. Thrasher gave Summer an amused look.

"Best bird in the world," he said, "but no attention span at all. May I get you some punch, Miss Summer?"

"Sure," said Summer. "Thank you?"

Thrasher vanished into the crowd. The geese gently shepherded her out of the way of the doorway.

The crowd was both overhead and underfoot. There were dozens of balconies and perches, the rafters lined with chatting birds, while more grounded fowl scurried back and forth on the floor. A band played in one corner, consisting of an enormous quantity of guineafowl, sometimes two or three to an instrument.

Some of the birds were dancing in mid-air, spinning and flapping and bounding in intricate figures. Far more, however, were milling about talking to one another, sparing only occasional glances to the dancers.

"It's a sad crush," said Thrasher, reappearing with a glass of punch. He handed it up to her. "Far too many people here to see anyone or have a conversation at all. Dreadful, really dreadful."

He sounded quite cheerful about this. Summer grinned into her punch.

The crowd on the floor was about knee height, but a few birds stood as tall or taller than Summer: another goose, far more elaborately dressed than the guards; an emu with strings of crystals braided into her feathers so that she sparkled like a galaxy; two black and white birds that stalked like dinosaurs on heavy gray legs.

She was the only human, but not, she thought, the only non-bird. There was someone in the corner who looked like a gigantic snail with an iridescent shell, although Summer wasn't sure if they were a guest or the refreshments.

Should I go talk to them? But what if I'm talking to food? Err…

Thrasher had stepped away to talk to another bird nearby. She didn't quite feel comfortable interrupting him. She looked for Reginald in the crowd, hoping she could ask him, but didn't see him.

In the end, she stepped back against the wall, near the goose guards, and tried to look as if she was having a good time. Which was like every

   Summer in Orcus

school dance she'd ever been to, honestly, except that the birds were far more interesting to watch than middle-schoolers.

The musicians struck up a fast number and conversation stilled as birds swung overhead. It looked as if they must surely crash into each other, flying wingtip to wingtip as they were, but somehow they all threaded the measures of the dance. It was quite extraordinary to watch, like a three-dimensional square dance.

Would that be a cube-dance? They had only just gotten to squares and cubes and powers in math. Summer was still rather proud of the idea and wished she had someone to tell it to. Did they do algebra in Orcus?

When the dance ended there was another one, and another after that. Summer's eyes were dazzled with feathers and jewelry and swirling fabrics, until the dances began to turn into long swoops and swirls of color. She had to stop and rub her forehead before her eyes unfocused completely.

When she opened them again, Reginald was in front of her with another bird in tow.

"Want you to meet someone, Merope, love," said Reginald cheerfully. "This is Summer. Summer, Miss Merope Bee-eater."

So this was the bird that Reginald was quite desperately in love with, thought Summer. She bowed.

Miss Merope was tiny, barely half the size of Reginald. She was magnificently sea-green, with a blazing yellow throat and dark red eyes. A black band of feathers ran from her bill over her eyes, like striking mascara.

She wore a white gown, with a fan on a chain around her throat. As Summer watched, she stood on one foot and caught up the fan in her claws, hiding her face behind it.

"A human!" she said, in a high, buzzy voice. "Reginald, darling! Is it your new bodyguard? Does it talk?"

"She's a she, not an it," said Reginald, casting an apologetic look at Summer. "She talks very well, for all that she's not that far out of the egg. Don't you, Summer?"

"I try," said Summer, who had just discovered that when someone asks if you talk, you have a sudden desire *not* to talk. At least, not to *them*. She made a mental note to apologize to the weasel.

"Summer's a brick," said Reginald cheerfully. "Been up and down the countryside with her, riding a wolf, no less. Such adventures we've had! You won't half believe them."

"I'm sure I won't," said Miss Merope. She gave Summer another long look over her fan.

Summer disliked her enormously.

"Reginald, dear," Merope said (not taking her eyes off Summer), "is that where you've been? Gadding about with a—a human?"

"And a wolf and a weasel!" said Reginald happily. "Went to rusticate, and fell headfirst into an adventure."

Merope shuddered delicately. Her gray-green tailfeathers trembled. "How dreadful!"

"It's been brilliant," said Reginald.

"Reginald has been very brave," said Summer. It didn't matter if she didn't like Merope, Reginald did, and that was the important thing. *She* wasn't going to have to marry the red-eyed bird, after all. "We would have been in a lot of trouble without him."

Merope shuddered again. "But you're home now," she said to Reginald. "And you'll be coming to my house party next Sunday, of course."

"Oh, ah," said Reginald. "Sorry, Merope, love. Adventure's not over yet. Just swung by the old family homestead for a bit of a nosh and some advice, don't you know?"

Merope deployed the fan aggressively. "But *Reginald…!*"

Reginald cast another look at Summer, this time pleading.

"I shan't like you at all if you don't come," said Merope, holding her bill up. "It shall be a sad crush and I shall be wearing my red crepe and you'll be off sleeping in a hedge like a bandit."

Summer had a brief fantasy of taking the fan away and beating Merope over the head with it. Unfortunately Merope was less than a quarter of her size, and it would have been incredibly unfair.

"You don't have to come," she said, feeling more hurt than she expected. "I mean, I hope you will, I'd miss you a lot, but it's not *your* problem. Baba Yaga didn't tell *you* to do anything. And you've gotten me all this way, and that's more than—I mean, we'd just met—"

It occurred to her, rather shockingly, that she might cry. Not from the hurt, although that was part of it, but from the sudden realization that Reginald had picked her up in the middle of the fields and shepherded her all this way, without asking for anything, simply because he was…well… *Reginald.*

At some point she'd gotten used to it and forgotten how grateful she was. It all came crashing back and she had to stare downward and pretend to be very interested in her drink.

"See, Reginald," said Merope. "Listen to the human. You want to stay, don't you?"

"Nope!" said Reginald, surprising both of them. "Nope. Can't let a chit like Summer go running off on her own. Word of a hoopoe." He patted Summer's foot with his claw. "There'll be other parties, Merope, love, and if I went back on my word, I shouldn't be fit company for any of them."

"Hmmph!" said Merope, and flew away. Other birds descended on her as she left.

"Isn't she lovely?" said Reginald, sighing.

"Err," said Summer. "She…um. She's very…brightly colored?"

"Oh, yes."

"She wasn't very nice to you, though," said Summer. With the gratitude had come indignation that anybody would treat sweet, noble, silly Reginald like that.

Reginald shrugged. "Certified beauties," he said philosophically. "They're used to having you hop when they tip their beak to you. Show signs of not hopping, and they turn into termagants."

Summer had no idea what a *termagant* was. "I thought you were in love with her," she said cautiously.

"Oh, of course," said Reginald. "All the rage, isn't she? Positively unfashionable not to be in love with her. 'Scuse me, Summer, I see Marcus! Ho, Marcus!"

He flew away, toward a heavy-bodied black bird with a spectacular ruff of feathers. "Marcus!"

Summer exhaled. To no one in particular, she said, "I don't think he's in love with her at all…"

There was a gentle laugh beside her. Summer turned and saw a lovely chestnut bird, with a long green gown and a spotted white breast.

Except for the gown and the fact that she was nearly two feet tall, she strongly resembled the hermit thrushes that lived in the park near Summer's home.

"Confused?" asked the thrush. Her voice was a long liquid trill.

"Very," said Summer. "Um. I'm Summer?"

"And I am Sophia," said the thrush. "It is a pleasure to meet you." She dipped her wings, and Summer bowed, more deeply than she had to Miss Merope.

"Now, then," said Sophia. "If you will bring me a glass of punch, my dear, I will answer the question that you are not quite sure how to ask."

Summer went to the punchbowl and brought back a glass as well as refilling her own. Sophia took hers and dipped her beak into it. "Thank you," she said.

Summer sipped her punch, more slowly. "So…Reginald…" she said.

Sophia shook her head fondly. "Young birds," she said. "So ridiculous, and so dear. We are not like your people, my dear. Most of us do not mate for life. The hoopoes don't, nor the bee-eaters, nor the thrushes. We fall in love for a season, mostly according to the dictates of fashion, and then we move on."

"But she's not being nice to him," said Summer angrily. "And he's my friend, and I don't want people to be mean to him."

Sophia smiled. "That does you credit," she said. "Friendships last a long time among birds, even if love doesn't. But you needn't worry about Reginald. He'll fall in love a dozen times in the next few years. Some of those—the kind ones—he may stay friends with. The ones, like Miss Merope, that are lovely and unkind, he'll forget in a season."

Summer frowned into her punch. "Don't birds get married?"

Sophia nodded. "Certainly we do!" she said. "But—correct me if I'm wrong—don't humans marry for a long time?"

"Well, yes…" said Summer. "You're supposed to get married forever, unless you get divorced."

"Ah," said Sophia cheerfully. "There's the difference. We birds marry for a season. The nest is built, the eggs are laid, compensation is given, inheritance decided, and then we go back to our own wintering homes." She finished her punch. "Very tidy. Very *short*. You aren't stuck with someone for years if it turns out you can't stand each other."

Summer realized with a shock that Sophia actually felt sorry for her.

No, not for me—for humans!

"Uh," she said. She took a gulp of punch because she couldn't think of what to say. "Oh. Don't you…err…ever…for longer…?"

"Oh, it happens," said Sophia. "Mostly when you're older, and get tired of bothering with romance. And some of the birds do it all the time—the swans and the falcons and whatnot. But really, it's nice to go home to your own roost and not having to worry about dealing with someone else about."

It sounded very lonely to Summer. Then again, if you lived in a huge manor house, like Reginald, with all your family around you, would you be lonely?

"I'm sure your way works for you," said Sophia. "Our way works for us." She patted Summer's shin. "It was very nice to meet you, Miss Summer."

"And you, Miss Sophia," said Summer, remembering her manners.

Sophia laughed again. "Miss! No, dear, it's Matron Sophia."

"Oh! I'm sorry—"

"Not at all, not at all." Sophia trilled softly. "Miss! Thank you, my dear. No one's called me that in a long time."

She swept away, her gown trailing behind her.

Summer mulled over the conversation, staring into her punch. It occurred to her that she had no real idea what Sophia had thought of the whole thing, while Sophia had clearly been able to read her expressions very well indeed.

"Zounds!" said Reginald, coming over. "In high company, there! I leave you alone for the shake of a cat's whisker and you're climbing the ranks like a trooper."

"High company?" Summer glanced after the thrush.

"I should say so! That was Matron Sophia, you know."

"She was very nice…?"

"Nice!" Reginald hooted. "Nice! Blimey, Summer, that was the leader of the Dawn Chorus." And when Summer looked blankly at him, he said "*You* know? The Prime Minister of Birds!"

Chapter Twenty-One

I'm sorry if I got you in trouble with Miss Merope," said Summer. (This was at least mostly true. She had been careful to phrase it that way, because in fact, she did not care in the least what Miss Merope thought, except insomuch as Reginald did.)

"Ah, not to worry." Reginald seemed distracted, looking upward across the trees. "I'll come around somehow…"

Summer followed his gaze and frowned. Birds were milling about in the air and there was a strange glow to the sky that she didn't like.

"What's going on?"

"I don't know," said Reginald. He fidgeted.

"Stay here, Master Reginald," warned one of the goose-guards. "If there's mischief afoot, you're safer with us."

"I smell smoke," said Summer.

The geese glanced at her then away, not as if they were offended but as if they had nothing to add. Summer suddenly remembered Zultan on his eight-legged horse, saying to Grub that most birds had no sense of smell.

She shivered at the memory.

They came through the trees and were brought up short.

There was orange light blazing from the Almondgrove manor. Smoke filled the sky in dark billows, blotting out the stars.

"Devil's yolk," said Reginald. "The manor's on fire!"

They ran toward the flames. Summer's mind was a gibbering panic—*it was Zultan it must have been Zultan it's because of me I got Reginald's house burned down—*

And then a much worse thought occurred to her. Glorious was somewhere on the grounds, and Glorious was a house now and couldn't run away *and houses burn.*

"Glorious!" she cried.

Reginald swore. "I'll find him," he said, and was away in the air in a moment. One of the geese honked a curse and followed.

Then it was only Summer and the goose-guard. The goose was waddling at high speed toward the house, and Summer ran after. "What can we do?" she said.

"Water from the lake," said the goose shortly. "There'll be a bucket brigade. We'll see how bad it is."

He spread his wings and flew. Summer ran with her head down, sneakers pounding on the grass, wishing she herself had wings.

Birds milled over the burning manor, the light flashing orange on their wings. One circled over Summer's head. "Lord Almondgrove says to come!"

Summer breathed a sigh of relief. Lord Almondgrove was all right.

She ran after the bird, who flew low over the ground. She could make out nothing about the bird's features, except that their outfit had gleaming buttons. The goose-guard spread their wings and followed in short hops, staying close.

They circled around the edges of the fire and reached a huddled knot of birds. Lord Almondgrove looked up from the center of the group. "Miss Summer!"

"I'm so sorry," gasped Summer, holding her aching side. It felt like someone was stabbing her in the ribs. She dropped to her knees, partly from pain, partly because of a desperate desire to make Lord Almondgrove understand how sorry she was. "I'm sorry. It was Zultan—it must have been Zultan—"

"It was Zultan," said Lord Almondgrove. He stretched out a wing around her shoulders. "And Zultan's band of villains. They lit the fires, not you."

"But they wouldn't have come here if it wasn't for me! And now your house is burning down!"

The old hoopoe snorted. "It's doing nothing of the sort. The servants caught them before they'd done much more than set the straw in the outbuildings ablaze. You cannot sneak up on a house this size, even under cover of darkness. We've lost two barns and blackened some of the millwork, but Almondgrove Manor has stood through worse. It will take more than a man who styles himself a Houndbreaker to break *us*."

He turned to the goose-guard. "You two will go with them. Protect my son, but use your own judgment. You are under my orders, not his. Be away as soon as the wolf-house can travel. Make for the Great Pipes. The wasps are striking there, I have no doubt, but I believe it still stands. Do you know the way?"

The goose nodded. "I will find it, Lord."

"Ask in Arrowroot if the way is unclear." He turned back to Summer. "Miss Summer, it has been an honor to meet you. If you pass this way again, Almondgrove Manor will always be open to you."

Summer wanted to cringe with the guilt of it all. Zultan had come and burned down their barns, and it certainly looked like a lot more than blackened millwork to her. And now Lord Almondgrove was telling her to come back and visit?

"But—"

"My son is a bit of an idiot," he said, cutting her off. "But travelling with you has done him no end of good. When I travelled with Stone Ear, I was no smarter, and it was the making of me." He shifted from foot to foot, then leaned in so that his beak was near her cheek.

"Take care of him, if you can," he whispered, too low for anyone else to hear him, and preened her hair back with his beak in an avian kiss.

Then he stepped back and a bird came up to say that the bucket brigade was starting on the north wing and the goose-guard was hustling her away.

Summer took a deep breath. The air smelled of burning, and she was the only one who could smell it. And Lord Almondgrove had asked her to take care of his son, as if she were a grown-up, or a wolf.

She straightened her back and followed the guard away, into the darkness, to find her friends.

It took them too long, working their way through the dark trees, to reach the cottage. Summer began to fret again—what if there had been a stray ember? What if Glorious was burning?

And then they came through the trees to a little pond and on the shore stood the cottage.

The door was open. Summer ran toward it.

She barely made a half dozen steps when the weasel came shooting out and leapt onto her pant leg. He climbed her as if she were a tree and burrowed himself under her chin. She could feel his small, hot body shaking.

"There was fire," he said. "There was so much smoke. I thought it might come here and I couldn't stop it. I didn't know what to do. I couldn't have put it out."

"I smelled the smoke too," said Summer. It seemed important. She had never felt quite so isolated among the birds as when none of them smelled the smoke.

The weasel's sides heaved. "Yes. *Yes.* I didn't know how far away it was."

She rubbed his ears hesitantly, as if he were a very small cat. After a moment he quieted and moved to her shoulder. "Anyway," he said gruffly. "I didn't know if I could make it to the manor house and warn someone. But I didn't need to, in the end."

"They didn't come here, then?" asked the goose-guard.

The weasel gave a small, hard laugh. "Oh, they came. Not that Grub fellow, but some of his flunkies. But *they* got here first."

He jerked his head toward the roof, and for the first time, Summer looked up.

There were three shapes on the roof. One of them was Reginald. At either end of the peak of the roof, great black shadows turned their heads and blinked yellow eyes at Summer.

"Oof," muttered the goose-guard. "*Owls.*"

"They stood the fellows off," said the weasel. "One had some kind of hooded lantern—I saw it when he put it down, I thought I'd have to bite him, I didn't know what else to do—but then an owl hit him. Talons like knives. Took his scalp all to pieces. He ran off yelling and they took the lantern away and dropped it in the lake."

The geese glanced at each other, then up at the owls. They spread their wings and bowed.

The owls blinked down at them in silence. One nodded its head almost imperceptibly.

"Not chatty fellows," said Reginald, landing, "but they like to be appreciated. Forester sent them, I'm guessing. Good woman."

"You have seen the Forester?" asked the goose on the left.

"Oh, yes. We were just…I think we were just there…Summer, do you remember?"

"I think so," said Summer. "There were owls and a dragon—no, not a dragon." She remembered the Forester's eyes, but it seemed like something in a dream, and when she tried to put words on the memory, it retreated just out of reach. "But we were somewhere in the woods, weren't we? And she's very tall."

"That's her, yes." Reginald nodded. "Always a bit fuzzy, you know, when you leave. But the best sort of person. Not the least bit missish."

The geese glanced at each other again.

"I suppose the advantage," said the rightmost goose, "of not knowing when something is dreadfully dangerous is that you do it anyway."

"Oh, bah," said Reginald. "Lovely woman. Told m'father about her. He said to stay in her good graces, he didn't say anything about *danger.*"

One of the geese said something under his breath that sounded like "*Hoopoes.*"

"Pardon me," said Summer, "but are you going with us? Did I hear right?"

"Indeed," said the rightmost goose.

"To the very end, if we must," said the leftmost goose.

"Then what should I call you?" asked Summer.

The geese honked.

"…errr," said Summer. "Can you repeat that?"

They chuckled. "It's all right," said the one on the left. "Humans have a hard time. I am *Ankh.*"

"And I am *Ounk.*"

When they said their names very slowly, Summer could just about hear the difference.

"It's kind of you to come with us," she said.

"Kindness has nothing to do with it," said Ankh.

"Lord Almondgrove set us to guard you," said Ounk. "We are Imperial Geese."

"We are sword-sisters sworn to his service."

"Sisters?" said Summer, startled. Both geese were baritones and she had assumed—well, apparently she had been wrong.

"Our eggs were side-by-side in the nest," said Ankh.

"Mind you, so were a half-dozen others," admitted Ounk. "But Ankh is the only one I could stand."

"It's mutual."

"Quite."

"Oh, joy. They'll be finishing each other's sentences next," muttered the weasel in Summer's ear.

Ankh smiled. "And you are Miss Summer, and this cottage, in the morning, will be Master Glorious. Ah…I'm not sure I know your name, sir."

She inclined her head to the weasel. The weasel grunted.

"Don't have one. Though I'm going to have to get one, at this rate."

"…Master Weasel, then."

He dragged a paw down over his eyes.

"You should try to get some sleep," said Ounk. "We will stand guard."

"Sleep?" said Summer blankly. *Sleep? Now? After—after everything— with the fires still burning somewhere in the woods?*

"Sleep," said Ounk gently.

Summer opened her mouth to say that she couldn't imagine sleeping, and suddenly it turned into a jaw-cracking yawn. She had forgotten somehow that it was the middle of the night, and that she had been to an assembly, and then run through woods and grass, and now that she was standing around talking and didn't have to panic right this minute…

She staggered through the open doorway into the cottage and collapsed into the bed without even taking off her shoes.

She woke in the morning with her head pillowed on Glorious's flank and the weasel curled in a tight, unhappy ball under her chin. She picked the little carnivore up and put him on her shoulder.

"It's all right," she said to him. "It came out all right."

He said nothing, but she felt two quick licks on her skin, there and gone.

The geese were still awake. They rousted Reginald and then they were on the way, the valet-flock twittering and grumbling and flying mouthfuls of food to them as they walked.

The valet-flock seemed bigger. Summer tried to count them—unsuccessfully—and finally gave up and asked Reginald.

"Oh, yes, added some fellows," he said cheerfully. "Flock-minds get nervous when there's too few, and of course we're a much bigger group now."

Two of the valet-birds brought a hard-boiled egg nearly as big as they were to Glorious. The wolf opened his mouth gravely and they set it inside. He did not close his jaws again until they were well away, and then gave a single chomp and swallowed.

"Trusting little beasts," muttered the weasel.

"They know that they're no more than a mouthful," said the wolf, "and brave companions for all that. I would not eat one, except by mistake."

Glorious had listened to the weasel's tale of the arsonists and the owls who had saved him. He did not blink, and when the weasel had finished, he nodded once, sharply.

"I owe the forest a favor, then," he said.

"The Forester, you mean?" asked Reginald, as the valet-flock packed away the remains of breakfast.

"They are the same," said Glorious, and that seemed to be the end of that.

The lands around Almondgrove were highly civilized, according to Reginald, and that seemed to mean that it was a great deal of lawn and pasture and deep old woods. Perches lined the roads and they passed the entrances to numerous estates. The hoopoe called out the names as they passed—"Herringpelt! Nestfarthing! Achingroost!"—none of which meant anything to Summer, although she did enjoy the names.

After they left the lands controlled by the noble-birds, the scenery grew wilder. There were small cottages built on stilts for shepherd-birds, often side by side with houses that could have held humans. The trees grew shorter and scruffier. Ankh and Ounk looked down the road behind them often.

"You have drummed your fingers on my neck for the last hour," said Glorious without turning his head. "Your thoughts are your own, Summer-cub, but if you need to speak them, I will listen."

Summer heaved a sigh. "I'm confused," she admitted. "I was thinking about Zultan, but he doesn't make any *sense.*"

Glorious cocked an ear back at her. "Things act according to their natures," he said. "But sometimes our natures are complicated."

"Maybe." Summer scowled. She didn't know if the problem was that Zultan was strange, or if she just didn't understand. She'd never been very good at knowing how people would act. It was as if she'd spent so much energy learning to predict her mother that she had very little left to spend on other people.

"I guess…" She trailed off, then started again. "What I don't understand is why, if he's got the Queen-in-Chains, who can smash a whole tower down and kill all the poor dogs…why is he just riding around the country with Grub and a couple of other people? Why isn't he in *charge?*"

"It's a fair question," said Ankh, dropping back to waddle alongside Glorious. "If you have a weapon that powerful and you've already defeated the only enemy to stand against you, why do so little with it? Why isn't he ruling us all now?"

Summer felt a vague relief that it hadn't been a stupid question after all.

"Some of us cannot be ruled," said Glorious. He glanced at Ankh. "I say that not to brag. Orcus would be a difficult pack to unite behind one leader, no matter how large your fangs."

Ankh honked a laugh. "Actually, Lord Almondgrove agrees with you. The problem with an immense weapon is that you may take a place with it, but not hold it. Zultan is a man with a handful of troops and one single enormous power. If he wants—oh, food, say, or money—he can descend on a town and threaten to raze it, but that is a hostage system, not governance. And Orcus would be difficult to govern even if he had an army."

She gestured with one wing at Ounk and Reginald. "There are simply too many people in Orcus, and we want too many things. Even the Dawn Chorus rules only the Upper Ten Thousand flocks of birdkind, and that only works because it is useful for everyone to have someone to handle trade regulations and to find a place to meet mates."

Summer rubbed her forehead. "I wouldn't want to be in charge of everyone," she said. "Maybe Zultan doesn't, either."

"Sensible of you," said Glorious. "And perhaps of Zultan as well."

Ankh shook her head. "You hate to think of evil being sensible," she admitted, "but Zultan's not a stupid man. What he likely wants is to be feared and to be given what he wants. And he has that, more or less. I suppose the Tower of Dogs seemed the most likely thing to stand in the way of that."

Summer rubbed her fingers through Glorious's ruff, wondering if that was all that there was to it.

"The other problem," said Ankh, "is that he dare not bring forth the Queen-in-Chains every time someone opposes him. No one is quite sure what she is, or what she does, but only because no one escaped the Tower. He cannot trust that he'll be that lucky twice, or three times, or ten. Sooner or later someone will see the Queen and see a weakness, and then he is a man with a handful of troops who used to have a great weapon."

Summer sighed. "So that's all he wants now? To be feared?"

"Perhaps," said Glorious. "Or perhaps he has simply been doing this for so long that he no longer knows any other way."

Chapter Twenty-Two

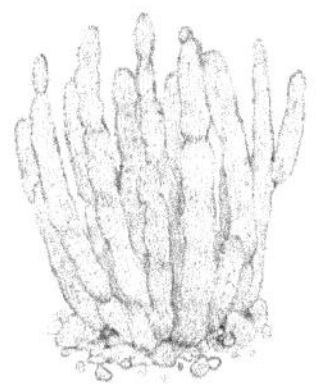

It took them five days to reach the Great Pipes. The land changed around them, the trees growing thin and tall again, reminding Summer of the desert. It was colder, though. Pine needles lay dry and crackling under Glorious's paws.

Ankh and Ounk waddled when Glorious walked and flew when he ran. Summer stopped thinking they looked absurd and began to admire the alert arch of their necks and the way they handled their weapons.

It was strange to feel safer because one was guarded by geese, but among so many strange things, it hardly registered at all.

At night, they took shifts. One stood guard outside the cottage while the other slept. They did not make any great fuss out of it, they simply did it.

"It is what we do," said Ankh, when Summer asked.

"Since the very beginning," said Ounk. "When the moon-fox killed the first earth and our ancestors were hatched to guard the second one."

"When were hoopoes hatched?" asked Summer.

Ankh glanced over at Reginald, who was practicing his dance steps. "When the gods were feeling particularly mischievous," she said.

"I heard that!" said Reginald, while the weasel snickered in Summer's hair.

Summer didn't recognize the Pipes when she saw them at first. At first they looked like odd mountains, and then like lumpy skyscrapers, and then like a rock formation. It was not until they had come over a ridge and begun their descent into a narrow valley that she realized what she was looking at.

"Is that a *cactus?*"

"It is," said Ankh.

"An organpipe cactus," said Ounk. "The largest in all the world, so far as we know."

It was larger than Summer had realized. The roots were down in the valley and the top stood well above the ridgeline. The many arms of the cactus filled the valley completely in both directions, a wall of knobbly green.

The Great Pipes were deeply grooved up and down, studded with spines as thick as a fence post. Holes riddled the cactus, edged with gray. Summer feared that it might be wasp damage, until she saw birds going in and out—not little birds, like the valet flock, but enormous woodpeckers the size of Reginald.

The hoopoe took to the air and flew ahead, calling out. Several woodpeckers looked out of their holes and flew out to meet him. They had pale bellies and wings striped black and white like a tweed suit. Each had a spot of red on top of their heads, far more vivid than blood.

They circled in the air, then Reginald perched on a cactus spine and the woodpeckers gripped onto the cactus and turned their heads to face him. Summer couldn't hear what they were saying to each other.

"Do you think it's dangerous to live there, with all those spines?" asked Summer.

Glorious made a *hrrrmmm* noise. Ounk shook her head. "It would be, but they clip the ends off," she said. "And down at the base, most of the spines are ground away, for land-walkers."

Land-walkers, thought Summer. *Does that include human-type people?*

Apparently it did, because a few minutes later, someone came out to meet them.

He was not exactly the same as the humans in Summer's world, but he was quite close. His skin was the same buff color as the woodpeckers' feathers and his hair was the same blinding red shade as their crests. Otherwise he looked perfectly ordinary. He wore a moss-green tunic and his arms were tattooed in swirls of red and violet.

"May I help you, travelers?" he asked. His eyes lingered on Glorious.

Summer took a deep breath. "Lord Almondgrove sent us," she said. (It was easier to say that than *Baba Yaga sent me*, and she suspected that people would be more likely to believe her.) "May we speak to someone in charge, please?"

She half-expected him to laugh at her or say something about how young she was, but he did not. Perhaps the wolf and the goose-guards made her seem like someone worth listening to.

Instead he said, "Is the matter spiritual or political?"

"…uh," said Summer. "It's…err…magical. Which is that?"

He screwed up his face in thought. "Good question. Well, I will take you to the Temple, and then if we've chosen wrong, they'll send you to the Mayor."

"That should work," said Summer gratefully.

"Then follow me."

The Temple was built deep inside the cactus. Their guide led them into a door in the base of one of the arms. A short flight of stone steps led up to it. The cactus had actually grown into the steps, the green flesh scarred but clearly alive.

"This must have been here a long time," said Summer.

"Centuries," said their guide. "The Great Pipes are at least ten thousand years old. Organpipes rarely flower until their first century, but in spring, there are so many flowers that the pollen falls like golden snow."

Reginald landed beside them. "Capital fellows here," he said cheerfully. "Always a little hard to talk to woodpeckers. All rat-a-tat-tat, too fast to follow! But decent folk. They say the Temple's where we want to be."

"Excellent," said the guide, and vanished into the cactus.

Summer went first, with Glorious beside her, then Reginald, then the goose-guard. It was large enough for two to walk abreast. The inside was cool and dim. She could not figure out what the walls were made of—something like wood, but like no wood she'd ever seen, full of polished hollows.

"Cactus ribs," said the guide. "Almost like bones. The most marvelous stuff in the world, but we only harvest a small amount, to keep the Pipes healthy. You can touch it if you like."

Everyone unobtrusively found a piece of wall to touch. The guide laughed.

The ribs had a strange texture under Summer's fingertips, like a hard sponge. It reminded her of coral branches.

The guide led them through several oddly shaped doorways. The openings were normal enough at ground height, but rose high in the air in irregular shapes, no two alike. One looked like an elongated heart and the next was a lattice of holes.

"The doors are where two of the trunks grow together," the red-headed man explained. "If they lie together too closely, they can begin to rot, and so we must cut away the damaged ribs. But we cut only so much as we must."

A flight of steps led down and then the walls belled out around them, into a chamber nearly as large as the hall where the noble-birds had danced. It was full of people, most of them the same buff-and-scarlet as their guide, and it appeared to be a market. There were people behind tables and even more people swirling between the tables, shopping and haggling. Summer saw woodpeckers perched on vertical stands behind tables, selling carvings and fruits and jars of things that looked rather like pickles. She glanced at one as they passed, saw that the pickles had legs, and looked away hurriedly.

In among the others were a few more exotic persons—green-skinned humanoids and copper-scaled lizards that walked upright, and one family that wouldn't have been out of place on a street in Summer's world.

Ripples of interest went out as their group threaded their way through the hall—"A wolf! Look at that!" and "Is that a dog?" and, "No, the dogs are gone. It's a wolf, I think."

Glorious's tongue lolled in amusement.

"I'm sorry," said the guide, "it's the fastest route, please forgive them, Master Wolf, we don't usually see your people here—"

"Let them look," said Glorious. "My hide is not so raw that another's eyes can scar it."

It was rather nice, Summer thought, to see someone else briefly baffled by Glorious's cryptic statements.

"Oh," said their guide. "Um, all right. This way, please…"

They came to more steps. The walls here looked less like bone and more like a fine tangle of roots and earth.

"The marketplace is underground," explained the guide, "as are most of the largest rooms. The cactus roots are not so sensitive as the ribs. The Temple is the largest room within the Pipes themselves."

The reason for this became obvious as soon as they reached the Temple. Here one of the vast arms of the cactus lay on its side. The grooved walls curved and twisted slightly. Summer felt as if she were standing inside some kind of giant sea creature.

It was here that they encountered the first actual door they had seen, rather than a doorway. The door was about eight feet high, round, and made of some pale, translucent substance, like pearl.

Or fingernails.

…I wish I hadn't thought that.

"If you will wait here, please," said the guide.

He slipped through the door.

A wave of incense came through the door as he closed it. It was so thick that the weasel coughed in her pocket and Summer had to wipe her eyes.

"Guh," muttered the weasel, sticking his head out. "What is that?"

"Even I can smell that," said Reginald, "and I'm not much for the old sniff box."

"Burning sage," said Glorious, lifting his head. "But there is another smell beneath it. Someone is hiding something."

Summer stared at the door, but it had no answers. She found herself trying to figure out where one would get a pearl that size, or for that matter, a fingernail.

"Do they have giant oysters in Orcus?" she asked.

"They say the island of Shellip is built on a giant oyster," said Reginald doubtfully, "but it looks like a perfectly ordinary island to me. I don't know how you'd tell. Why?"

"I was wondering what the door was made of."

"The lower carapace of a mammoth tortoise," said Ankh. "They are no longer hunted, for they are too rare. I suspect that this one is very old."

"Nearly a thousand years," said the guide cheerfully, stepping back through. "Come, travelers, the priestess will see you now."

He pushed the door open wide, and they stepped into a very long room. The floor was tiled in marble and the polished ribs of the cactus formed a starburst at the far end.

The smoke was pouring from braziers on either side of the room. It hung thickly over the ceiling, forming a cloud that one could hardly see through. A series of sneezes came from inside Summer's pocket.

A woman stood in front of the starburst. She was tall and stately, clad in long violet robes edged with silver. Her fingers shone with rings and she had vestments made from polished cactus ribs, linked together like chainmail.

She also looked almost exactly like Summer's fourth-grade teacher, Miss Hardert, except taller and with slightly different colored skin.

"The priestess Cereus, Voice of the Great Pipes," said the guide to them, and then, in a ringing voice, "Your Holiness, pilgrims sent by Lord Almondgrove to see you on a matter most..."

He paused and glanced at them.

"Urgent," said Summer firmly.

"A matter most urgent!"

What would he say if I'd said, "Oh, it's no big deal, really," I wonder? "A matter most casual?"

Priestess Cereus wore a headdress with a pair of serpents on it. They coiled down over her shoulders, turning their heads and flicking their tongues. It was impossible to see if she had Miss Hardert's salt-and-pepper hair under the serpents, but it seemed likely.

"Welcome to the Great Pipes, pilgrims," said the priestess. If she had followed with, "Please hand your homework to the front of the class," it would not have surprised Summer in the least. Still, her voice was deeper than Miss Hardert's, a voice for uttering prophecy and commandments, not a voice for handing in homework.

The priestess beckoned them forward.

It was a long way. Glorious's claws clicked on the stone floor. The valet-flock halted at the doorway, making tiny chirps of dismay at the smoke.

"It's all right, chaps," said Reginald. "Can't imagine I'll need a new neck-cloth in the next five minutes. Go back outside, will you?"

The valet-birds took off with glad chirps. Reginald shook his head fondly.

"Why have you come?" asked the priestess. The serpents on her shoulders watched with lidless golden eyes.

"Snakes," muttered the weasel. "Never liked snakes."

Summer licked her lips. She hadn't prepared a speech. She hadn't realized that she was going to have to make one.

"We came here looking for a wondrous thing," she said. "Um."

"The Great Pipes are wondrous," said the priestess impassively. "Is that all?"

"Errr. No. We're looking for—uh—that is, there's something attacking wondrous things. Wasps. We're trying to catch one. Has there been any damage? To the pipes? Like rotting or something eating away a chunk?"

She rubbed her hands on her jeans. Her palms were sweaty and the incense was making her a little light-headed.

"I will speak to the human girl alone," said Priestess Cereus.

Summer blinked. Ankh and Ounk bristled.

"We cannot allow that."

"She is in our care."

The guide frowned. "Do you question the goodwill of the Voice of the Great Pipes? Your charge could stab our priestess with that sword of hers, too."

The Priestess raised her hand. "Peace, Arlight. They mean no disrespect. Good birds, will you allow this? There are two entrances to this chamber, the one you have entered and one behind the altar, to my private quarters. If you will station yourself at each door, no one may enter or leave without your knowledge. Will that be acceptable?"

Ankh and Ounk glanced at each other.

"Summer?" asked Ankh.

"It's okay," said Summer. She wasn't sure what was going on, but surely this was only the next step in this adventure. She unbuckled the cheese-sword. "Can you hold this for me, Reginald?"

Reginald took the sword, tucking it awkwardly under his wing. The weasel climbed out of her pocket and onto Glorious's shoulder.

"Sorr—*achoo!*—I can't—not with the smoke—ah—ach-choo!" He sneezed and chittered simultaneously and had to cling to the wolf's fur to keep from falling off.

"May we inspect the room?" asked Ounk.

"You may."

Summer stood awkwardly beside the priestess as the geese waddled the length of the temple. Their guide, Arlight, rocked on his feet, looking slightly embarrassed. Priestess Cereus herself folded her arms inside her sleeves, as composed as the serpents on her shoulders.

The geese nodded to each other. Ankh went to the back and Summer heard the click of a door closing as she took her post outside it.

Glorious curled his lips. "Something is rotting," he said.

"More than you know, wolf," said the priestess, so quietly that Summer thought perhaps only she had heard.

"You sure about this, Summer?" asked Reginald.

Summer nodded. They'd come here to find rot. It would be silly to leave because they'd found it.

Perhaps it looked like courage or foolishness. Perhaps she was placing far too much hope on the resemblance. But Summer simply could not believe ill of someone who looked so much like Miss Hardert. Miss Hardert had told her that she had a gift for writing and suggested she enter a contest. Summer's story had come in third out of over two hundred entries, and there had been a certificate and the principal had congratulated her over the loudspeaker.

Her ears got hot at the memory, but it was a pleasant sort of embarrassment.

Glorious and Reginald followed Arlight out the main door. Reginald looked back. Glorious did not.

The door closed. The smoke roiled. And Summer was alone with the Priestess of the Pipes.

Chapter Twenty-Three

Right," said Priestess Cereus, and then, to Summer's surprise, she took off her headdress and flopped down next to the altar with her legs out in front of her.

"Have a seat," she suggested. Summer sat down next to her, wondering what would happen next.

"Sorry for the informality," said the priestess, "but the snakes get very heavy. Someone large sent you, didn't they? Not just the hoopoe lord. Someone with destiny held in their teeth."

"Baba Yaga," said Summer faintly.

"That'd do it." Cereus leaned her head back against the altar, rubbing her neck. "I won't lie, I was hoping for someone a little…ah…less volatile to get involved."

Summer raised her eyebrows. "Like who?"

Cereus shrugged. Her voice was changing as she talked, becoming more conversational and less like she was uttering deep wisdom. It also made her sound even more like Summer's former teacher. "Oh, no one in specific. One of the other great players in the game. Archangel Michael, perhaps, or the Blacksmith or the Wanderer with the Flute. Even the Bone Woman, though she rarely trifles with anything so large. But she loves the desert and we are in a city built of bones, so I thought perhaps…" She shook her head and gave a short, humorless laugh. "But Baba Yaga gives you what you deserve. What an alarming prospect!"

"But you were expecting *someone?*" asked Summer.

"I asked for help," said Cereus simply. "I am very small, but the Pipes are very large. Something would come from them, if only to stand witness as they died."

She put a hand over her face. "And someone came," she said wearily.

Summer sagged. The wasps must have gotten here already, if the priestess was so sad. "How bad is it?" she whispered.

The priestess made a wobbling gesture with her hands. "It is slow," she said. "We could still recover, if it would simply *stop*. But nothing has stopped it, not prayers, not magic, not poison sprays or cement. Believe me, I've tried. I even cut a section out, to clean flesh, and the next day the edges were rotting away…"

She sounded as if she might cry.

"It'll be okay," said Summer. She was on firmer ground now. "It'll be okay. Do you want to tell me about it?"

The priestess let out a long breath that caught a few times. "No, it won't be okay," she said, almost to herself. "But I had to do something."

The serpent headdress fell off the altar with a thump. It began to slither along the floor toward the two humans.

"Are they alive?" asked Summer, round-eyed.

"The snakes?" The priestess leaned back. "More or less. They're part of the hat, but they act alive. I call them Right and Left. Right's a bit more friendly, Left's a bit smarter. Give them a pat if you like, they don't bite. They can't, actually, the mouths don't open at all."

Summer cautiously stroked Right. It felt like the snakes she'd petted at the zoo, delicate skin overlaying hard muscle. It twisted around, rested its chin (did snakes have chins?) on the back of her hand, and appeared to go to sleep.

Priestess Cereus watched Summer petting the snake, then said abruptly, "Wait, I'm assuming things and I should know better. This *is* about the Pipes rotting, isn't it? You didn't come because, oh, Baba Yaga wants a citizen's skull for her fence, or is looking for the horse the color of dawn or something, right?"

"I think it is," said Summer. "I mean, the Queen-in-Chains is sending wasps and they're doing something—poisoning big things, huge things, things that matter—and we need to catch a wasp so we can follow it back to her. And Lord Almondgrove said that the Great Pipes were a wondrous thing, so we came to see if there were any wasps here."

"Wasps…well, it might be wasps. It might be anything. Here, I'll show you."

Cereus rose to her feet and helped Summer up. Her grip was strong and warm. She tucked the snakes under her arm and Right curled around her wrist. Left gazed off into the distance with a faintly contemptuous expression.

Behind the altar was a second, smaller door. Cereus tapped on it, and Ankh opened it.

"You may accompany us," said Cereus to the goose, "but I must ask you not to speak of what you see to any citizen of the Pipes. If they knew, there would be a panic and we cannot afford panic."

The smell of the sage was fainter here, but there was another, stronger odor, sweet and rotten.

Glorious was right. The incense is to hide something.

The corridor narrowed as they went through it. It grew dimmer, and then there was another door.

"Please guard this door," said the priestess to Ankh. "There is no way to the outside from here. If Arlight or anyone else comes, come and fetch me, but do not let them through the door."

The goose-guard turned her head. Her dark eyes flickered in her white face, but she dipped her beak in acknowledgement.

Summer was beginning to feel frightened. They'd come to find damage, but how bad was it?

The priestess opened the door only a few inches. She slipped through, then held it just wide enough for Summer to enter.

It was dark inside. The smell was so thick that she had to pull her t-shirt up over her nose and mouth.

She could hear Cereus moving about, and then a light flared up, and Summer saw what it looked like when a wondrous thing began to die.

The chamber was draped with rotting cactus flesh. It hung down in greasy cream colored strands, like pale seaweed. The great ribs were discolored and shone with oily reflections.

It was impossible to see how far back the room went. It did not so much darken as vanish behind layers of gauzy decay. The floor was marked with deep black holes, and Summer realized that they were footprints where the priestess had walked.

There was a bed, or something that had been a bed, against a wall nearby. It looked as if spiders had draped it in webs. Great sheets of decaying flesh had fallen down over it. In places it was thick and knotted like ropes while in others it had thinned nearly to transparency.

"The private chambers of the priestess of the Pipes," said Cereus. She did not sound like Miss Hardert now, but high and hard and frightened. Miss Hardert had never sounded frightened, not even during fire drills. "No one comes here, so I've been able to hide it. It doesn't break through the outer skin, you see. Cactus rot from the inside, like people…"

She put her hands over her face and gave a single dry sob.

How long did she sleep in that bed, with the room—no, the city—rotting around her?

It seemed, as the priestess's shoulders shook, that it had been too long.

Summer could not tell her that it would be okay. She could not say anything at all. She wanted to turn away and run.

It was monstrous. It stank.

This is what we came here to find, but I didn't…I thought it would be small…just a little gray hole, maybe, something we could put a jar over and catch a wasp…

The space inside her chest was a jumble of fear and revulsion, but a thought came clear nonetheless: if her heart's desire lay on the other side of this, she would be willing to go her whole life without finding it.

Summer hunched her shoulders. Her only thought was to make herself as small as possible, to keep her hands from touching those soft, rotten sheets of flesh. But when she shoved her hands into her pockets, her right hand touched three hard objects.

One was the lock from her own back gate. One was the turquoise stone. The last was the acorn from the Frog Tree.

Her fingers closed over the acorn, and she thought of the dryad who had given it to her.

The dryad lived inside the tree.

The inside of the tree must have looked like this.

The cancer at the heart of the world, Boarskin had said.

And she remembered another voice then, a woman with the eyes of a dragon, and though the edges of the memory of the Forester were fuzzy, she remembered weeping on that woman's shoulder for the plight of the Frog Tree.

If I can catch a wasp, perhaps I can stop this. If not for the Great Pipes, then for all the other wondrous things. For the giant turtles and the Frog Tree and the fields of wheat and all the other things in Orcus that I don't even know about yet.

She had to lift her foot up as if it belonged to someone else, as if her shoes were made of lead, but she did, and put it down again, and so took a step forward into the cathedral of decay.

The sheets of rotten cactus flesh swayed as she went through them. She did not want to touch them, but the thought of having them touch her face was even worse. She ducked low to avoid them.

Her feet seemed to bruise the ground as she walked.

"It started at the far end," said Cereus behind her. "Just a little gray spot like mold."

"That must be where the wasps started," said Summer. If she focused on the mechanics, she was not thinking about what it would be like if those pale seaweed tendrils brushed across her face. "If they're still there, maybe we can catch one."

"I'll try anything," said Cereus. Her voice was muffled, as if by tears. "Anything at all."

Summer saw a bright blaze of light ahead. Fire? No, it was golden and the curtains of rot moved slightly in a breeze. A doorway?

She said there wasn't a way out…maybe this is new?

"There's a hole up here." Summer moved forward. Had the wasp damage gotten so bad that it'd eaten through the tough cactus skin?

"Is it large?" asked Cereus. Her voice was rough with panic. "Look at it, tell me how big it is!"

The hole was on the underside. It was easily big enough for Summer's shoulders. *How did she not know this was here? Of course, maybe she didn't want to go this far in…I certainly wouldn't…*

Summer gingerly set her hands on the edge of the hole. This part was gray and dead and hard, not slimy and rotten. That made it easier. She leaned forward, looking out, and saw—

Feet?

"There's someone here!" she said, startled, and then the priestess of the Pipes shoved her, hard.

She tumbled forward through the hole and landed on her side. The fall was only about three feet down, but it knocked the wind out of her. The slope of the canyon wall was very steep there and she rolled down, unable to stop herself, until something stopped her.

"About time," said a familiar voice.

Summer blinked upward, still half-stunned by the fall, and at last came face-to-face with Grub.

Her mind seemed to move impossibly slowly. This was not happening. This could not be happening. Surely she was still back inside the cactus city, not lying here on the ground at Grub's feet. Surely she was not alone.

"Ankh!" she screamed. Her voice sounded pathetically thin in her own ears. She wanted to yell, not croak. She tried again. *"Ankh!"*

Someone grabbed her collar and hauled her up to her knees. She had a brief glimpse of Grub's soft white face, the lines of fleshy dots down his neck, and then everything went black and hot and hard to breathe. Was someone squeezing her throat?

"Don't strangle her," said Grub. "Zultan wants her alive."

The squeezing eased. The darkness and the heat did not.

I think there's a bag. On my head. Is that possible? Do people do that?

For some reason all she could think of was how they'd put the guinea pig in a sack in *Alice in Wonderland* and how it had been sort of a joke in the book and it wasn't a joke at all. It was horrible, the bag was mashed against her mouth and she couldn't get enough air; and when she tried to breathe in, the fabric got sucked in and she felt like she was breathing burlap.

"Ankh!" she tried to yell again, and then a more immediate thought struck her. *"Cereus! Run!"*

The priestess was right there, and Grub was out here, and he could just reach in and grab her and—

The world stuttered. There was a bright flash. Summer had been up on her knees and then she was falling and she realized this just as she landed on her side in the dirt. Her head, previously full of panic, seemed suddenly blank.

"Don't hit her!" cried Cereus.

…someone…hit me…?

Her thoughts, when they came, were slow and sloggy. It hadn't hurt the way she understood hurting. Maybe the pain had all happened when the world had seemed to skip, and she'd missed it. Her left ear felt very hot.

…I fell out of the hole…is this the same fall…was that before…?

There was a rock under her ribs that was jabbing her, and that was a normal kind of pain. She focused on that. What had the light been?

People were talking. She had a vague feeling that it was important to listen to what they were saying. It was hard to think around the pain of the rock and the slowness in her head. The heat in her ear was getting worse and it was starting to pulse. She could only pick up snatches of the conversation.

"…done what you asked…leaving…"

"Where…wolf?"

"Inside…god help me…" Was that Miss Hardert?

"Then we'll be gone. Get her on a horse, boys."

The world swung around. Summer thought she might throw up, but some small voice of self-preservation said that if she threw up in the bag, she was going to be stuck in the bag with it and that would be impossibly horrible. She gulped. Her eyes and nose streamed and made it no easier to breathe, but she didn't throw up.

"Wait! You said…you promised…"

"I don't know why you'd think that. We said we wouldn't burn this wretched city around your ears," said Grub. It had to be Grub. "Not that we'd fix whatever's wrong with it." He was standing very close.

"But…you…rotting…"

That was not Miss Hardert. Miss Hardert was in another world and she wouldn't be talking to Grub.

"Call a priest," said Grub, annoyed. "I don't know why your damned plant is stinking to heaven. It's caught whatever nasty rot's gotten everything else."

"…but…not going to hurt her…"

"Not my call," said Grub. "Zultan wants her. He's not known for sweet mercy."

A cry of despair.

It took a very long time to penetrate Summer's slow thoughts, and then the magnitude of the betrayal seemed to overwhelm her.

She pushed me out of the hole.

She was planning to give me to Grub the whole time.

And they'd walked in, as trusting as lambs, even Glorious and the goose-guards, and straight into Grub's clutches.

"Hurry," said Grub. Summer's breath went out of her as she got thrown over something, something hot and alive. "I don't trust that fool of a priest-ess to keep the wolf busy for long."

This was all to separate me from Glorious. They're scared of him.

Someone said something to Grub, but Summer lost track of it as her arms were wrenched behind her. Coarse rope slid along her skin. It hurt. Moreover it itched, and that was almost worst.

She was on her stomach. Her wrists hurt. And then somebody climbed up behind her on the…horse? Was it a horse?

Sleipnerians. They breed them out of spiders, Reginald said.

Ten minutes ago, the thought of touching one of the awful horse-mon-sters would have made her skin crawl. Ten minutes ago, she had been standing inside the Great Pipes with the priestess and the goose-guards right outside the door. Had Ankh even heard her scream?

This isn't really happening, is it?

It was too fast. Huge irrevocable things should not be allowed to happen so fast! It didn't make any sense that people were allowed to betray you and tie you up and throw you over a horse-monster before you had time to think.

Summer began to cry. The tears slid down the end of her nose and itched horribly and the fabric tried to get into her mouth with every sob. She wanted Glorious and her friends to rescue her. She wanted to have never needed rescue. More than anything, she wanted to go *home.*

The sky did not open. Baba Yaga did not whisk her back to her own backyard. Grub did not untie her and tell her that there had been a mistake. Instead the horse began to move and the rider dragged her sideways a bit so that she did not fall off.

She had to stop crying because she could hardly breathe. Something—a saddle or the bones in the horse's back, assuming horse-spiders even had bones—was ramming into her chest. The sack was strangling her.

Her vision grew bright and sparkled in time to her pulse.

The rider made a guttural sound and shouted something to Grub. Grub shouted something back.

Summer felt her throat get even tighter as the rider dug his fingers under the sack at her neck—and then he pulled it free.

She sucked air in so hard that it made her cough. The rider slapped her back as if she were choking. It was hot in the high desert, but the air felt blissfully chilly after the fabric.

When she thought that she might not die just yet, she looked at the rider.

He was human, or close to it. He had a hawk-like face, but only in the figure of speech, with a sharp nose and angled cheekbones. He glared down at her as if she had made a mess and he was going to have to clean it up.

That's not fair… thought Summer. *I didn't mean to…* She had a strong urge to apologize, which made no sense at all.

She turned her head a little and looked at the horse. Then she wished she hadn't.

The horse's muzzle was studded with round black eyes, set in little cups of bone. Its mouth bisected neatly down from the nose, strangely hairy, and *those are folded up mandibles like a spider what does it eat no let's not think about that that would be a* very bad *thing to think…*

She dropped her head, exhausted. Her skull was pounding. The legs stretching out in front of her looked like horse legs, more or less, except that there were too many of them. But they were segmented in strange places and there were tufts of bristly black hairs along the backs, stiff as wire. The hooves were neatly split into three heavy toes, and there was a heavy black hook on the back, in about the same place where Glorious had a dewclaw.

Summer closed her eyes. Possibly her head was going to kill her before the dreadful horse-spider could do it. It would probably just be one extra-hard throb and then everything would go dark and there would be a light at the end of the tunnel. That seemed infinitely preferable to what the Sleipnerian might do with its folded mandibles and those wicked bone hooks.

She wondered if she'd see Baba Yaga again as she was dying. It seemed likely, somehow. If Baba Yaga sent you somewhere, she'd show up again, if only to shake her head and tell you that next time she was going to get a competent little girl, maybe one with leopard feet or who knew judo, something like that, someone smart enough to ask for luck instead of grace, what good was grace when you were slung over the back of a nightmare anyway…

Without quite knowing it (or perhaps knowing how to stop it) Summer drifted off, half-dream and half-hallucination, Baba Yaga mixed up with the Forester and the Sleipnerian mixed up with Glorious, all of them talking at her, until the only real left thing in the world was the pounding pain in her skull, and then not even that.

Chapter Twenty-Four

Summer swam up out of unconsciousness. The spider-horse had stopped. The inside of her head still seemed to be moving.

The rider slung her down off the spider-horse. Her knees buckled and she dangled from his hand like a kitten in the mouth of a dog.

They were in some kind of little camp. There were a few tents, and a few tarps held up by poles to cast shade. The canyon wall rose sandy and unclimbable behind them.

Grub came up. Even through her pounding headache, Summer could smell a strange wet odor coming off him. His skin was so white in the desert sun that it was almost translucent in places, with strange blue-green shadows. She could see something moving at the base of his throat.

There were a half-dozen men behind him. She recognized the rider of the spider-horse among them.

"Search her," said Grub.

One of the riders moved forward, hands outstretched. Summer gulped.

"Back with your great groping hands," said a dry, amused voice, and someone stepped into Summer's field of view.

The woman was only little taller than Summer, but she had massive curved horns and an equally massive neck to hold them. Her ankles and wrists were as thin and fragile-looking as blades of grass. She wore no clothing, only dark brown fur over a body that was almost human.

She put her hand under Summer's chin and Summer felt thick, blunt nails and slick-furred hide.

Is she an antelope? thought Summer. The word seemed important somehow, but she couldn't seem to remember why.

The woman slid her hooved hands over Summer, patting her impersonally. One hand dipped into the pocket with the lock and the acorn and the turquoise stone, and Summer cringed, waiting for them to be pulled out.

Not the acorn! The lock—I don't know why I've still got the lock—but the acorn—

The antelope woman's eyes met hers. They were huge and dark brown, with red glints at the bottom. Her muzzle had long white stripes down it, angled over the eyes, giving her a permanently fierce expression.

She took her hand out of Summer's pocket and turned and said "She's got nothing. Tie her wrists and her ankles together and she'll be as helpless as a newborn fawn."

Grub nodded. One of the guards came with rope and the antelope woman took it. She bound Summer's hands in front of her, then her ankles with a short length between them.

"Tie it tighter," Grub ordered.

"And have her fingers turn black and fall off? No one's complained of my knots yet."

Grub muttered something, but did not argue. Whoever the antelope woman was, she had some kind of authority that Summer couldn't begin to guess at.

She watched the antelope woman walk away. Her hips swayed. She had a long, rope-like tail that moved like a pendulum behind her.

Why didn't she tell them about the acorn? Is she helping me?

Grub's hand closed on her shoulder. His fingers were so soft and swollen that they seemed to have no bones.

"Come on," he said. "Zultan wants to see the girl that's given him so much trouble."

Zultan had a tent as large as the living room of Summer's house. It was large and hung with tapestries, as if it had once been a riot of color, but the wind and rain had beat down on it and now it was shades of tattered blue and gray.

Grub swept the flap open and said, "Here she is, sir."

There were metal lamps on chains lighting the room. The air was hot and stifling. Zultan himself was lying on his side in a nest of blankets, with books piled up around him. The great metal mask, muzzle frozen in an eternal snarl, gazed at her sideways.

Summer had expected…oh, something else. A throne perhaps, or at least a desk, something that the Houndbreaker could glare at her over. She didn't expect to find him curled up like a sleeping child.

The stacks of books reminded her of her own bedroom. She found that this did not make her any less afraid.

"Kneel," said Grub, and shoved her down. Summer didn't mind. If she was kneeling, her trembling legs didn't bother her so much.

Zultan sat up slowly. He was very thin without the layers of cloaks over him. The mask was the largest thing about him.

"A human child," said Zultan. His voice was deep and hollow and unaccountably weary. "With the stink of crone-magic upon you, for all you've tried to mask it with wolf. Why are you here?"

"Because Grub shoved me in a sack!" said Summer angrily. "Why else?"

Grub sputtered and his hand on her shoulder squeezed tighter, like a fleshy mitten.

Zultan made a coughing noise. It took a moment for her to realize that was laughter, echoing through the steel mask.

"Why have you come to Orcus, human child?"

Summer licked her lips.

Crone magic. He must *know. I don't want to make him angry.*

"I don't know," she said finally.

Zultan tilted his head. The eyesockets of the steel mask stared at her, and even though the face snarled, the eyes seemed deep and sad.

"You are not lying," he said, "but you are also not telling the truth, are you?"

"But I don't know!" cried Summer. "Nobody tells me anything! I was supposed to find my heart's desire—" (Was that safe to tell him? Surely it must be. He couldn't know just by looking at her what her heart's desire would be.) "—but I don't know what it is or where to find it and then Grub was chasing me and I don't know *why!*"

Grub made a wet, sticky noise behind her, as if he were coughing up phlegm. Zultan laughed again.

"We could torture her," said Grub hopefully. "Give me ten minutes, lord—"

"Peace, Grub. That was truth." He tilted his mask back the other way, thoughtfully. "Was it Baba Yaga, then?"

Summer said nothing and tried very hard to keep her face still. *If he can smell a lie, how do I change my smell? What do I do?*

"It was," he said, satisfied, sitting back. "She who litters shadows, and nurses them at her dugs."

Summer suspected that this was not a terribly complimentary thing to say about someone, but said nothing.

He drummed his gloved fingers on his knee. His legs were very long, but so were his wrists.

Then: "Leave us, Grub."

"But sir!"

Zultan sighed. "She is very small, Grub, and I am very old, but not quite dead yet. I do not think she will tear out my throat."

"The crone sent her," said Grub.

"And I may yet send her back. Now go."

Summer didn't dare look at Grub, because that would mean looking away from Zultan. She felt the pale man shifting from foot to foot behind her, and then he turned and the tent flap rose and fell, and she was alone with Zultan Houndbreaker.

"Can you read?" he asked.

Summer blinked. Of all the questions she was expecting, this wasn't it.

"Yes, of course," she said.

The mask could not smile, but there was a hint of a smile in Zultan's voice. "There is no 'of course' with reading in Orcus. Books are rare here. Perhaps yours is a happier land, or at least a more literate one."

Summer did not know how to answer this. At the moment, home seemed a great deal happier than kneeling in the tent of a madman who burned down people's homes on a whim.

"I read a lot at home," she said finally.

"Ah," said Zultan. "I, too. I keep many books at my home." He gestured to the books in the tent. "These are only a few. Those I think might need on this trip, and those I have yet to read and might want, and those old friends that I cannot bear to leave behind."

Summer recognized a great deal of her own love of books in that, and bit her lower lip. She did not want to recognize anything of herself in Zultan.

"What sort of books do you like?" he asked.

"Oh…err…" Summer wondered if it was exhaustion from the ride on the Sleipneirian that was making this all seem extremely surreal. It was so hot in the tent and she was disoriented and a man who had chased her across the world wanted to talk about books. "Fantasy, mostly. Fairy tales."

"Fairy tales," said Zultan. "Yes. Fairy tales hold wisdom and foolishness in equal measure. Then you may understand how someone in a tale, when he tries to defend himself from his doom, often brings it closer. If you build a wall to keep out the enemy, you will find yourself walled inside with him instead, will you not?"

Summer nodded.

"So it is with you," said the Houndbreaker. "Some, smelling a crone upon you, would kill you at once. Grub would do it gleefully if I told him, but Grub is driven by a master crueler than I am, and it will devour him before long." He folded his legs neatly, crossing them at the ankles. "But Baba Yaga is subtle and older than I am by far. And if I sent a child alone into my enemy's jaws, I would make sure that she carried poison with her."

It was very hot. Summer lifted her bound hands and wiped the sweat out of her eyes.

"If I bite down, will I regret it?" asked Zultan.

Summer shook her head, baffled. "I don't know what you mean," she said.

"No," said Zultan. "You wouldn't, I suppose. And perhaps I am like the fool in a tale, trying to defend myself from my doom and embracing it instead. But I think I will not bite down just yet."

Summer sighed. It seemed pointless to argue, pointless to talk, but—"I didn't know anything about you until you came after me," she said. "I don't want to do anything to you. I just want you to leave me alone."

She was amazed at how clear and calm that sounded, when her thoughts were running in such useless little circles. *Does he know does he know about the wasps does he know about the Queen does he know I'm trying to stop the wasps…*

"Ahhh…and so perhaps I have already brought my doom a little closer by pursuing you." The mask shook from side to side. "Perhaps if I had ignored you, you would have seen a few sights and then gone back to your world again with a head full of stories and ended your days in a madhouse." He laughed. "Perhaps you still might, eh?"

This was far too close to Summer's secret fears. Her stomach turned over and she blurted out, "At least I won't end my days in a stupid dog mask!"

Immediately she regretted it. She thought she might throw up again.

"Ah…" said Zultan again. "You do not like my mask?"

He reached up and touched clasps at the bottom and the sides, then lifted the mask.

Most of his skull seemed to come with it. Summer had a brief, horrible thought that he was simply going to pick his entire head off his neck and sit there like the Headless Horseman in that story with Ichabod Crane.

But he did not. Instead the mask came up and the metallic braids with it. They seemed to belong to the mask rather than Zultan himself. And then Summer looked at last on the face of the one who had brought down the Tower of Dogs.

He was very old. The bones of his muzzle were long and fine and the skin over them looked like parchment. Where the mask had rubbed, his skin was raw and pink, and in places it had peeled away entirely and there was only bloodless bone.

One of his ears was gone. The other was only half there, crumpled at the tip. His fur, where he had fur, was white with age.

"I don't understand," whispered Summer. "You brought down the Tower of Dogs. Everyone says so. But…you look like…"

"I am the last of the dogs of Orcus," said Zultan. "You are quite privileged, my young doom. Very few people have ever seen my face. I am not so handsome as I was."

His lips curled up in a smile. He still had fangs, she could see, but there were gaps in the line of his teeth and they were blunted and yellow.

When he turned his head for a moment, shadows fell across his face and hid the sores, and Summer could see why so many people had loved the dogs. If you saw only the long bones and the white fur, he looked like an ancient herding dog, old and wise and dutiful. *They were good,* people said.

This one was not good. Something had gone hard and twisted inside him.

"You destroyed your own people," said Summer.

"Oh, yes." His eyes, now that she could see them clearly, were filmed with white, but he seemed perfectly able to see.

"It is very tiring to belong to a people of such relentless virtue," said Zultan. "I would not expect a human to understand, but then again, you read many books, so perhaps you can. I could not bear to be so noxiously valiant." He waved one long hand—paw? Suddenly the odd shape of his fingers seemed to make more sense.

"So you *killed* all of them?" Summer couldn't quite wrap her mind around it.

"And it was no easy task, let me tell you. I hunted stragglers for nearly forty years. One of the ones who fled was heavy with pups. Her grand-daughter was the second-to-last dog in Orcus."

"But *why?*"

"Because they would have forgiven me," said Zultan. "Unbearable thought, isn't it?"

He lifted the mask back onto his shoulders and blinked out at her through the eyesockets.

"But if they're all dead now, why are you still going around burning people?" asked Summer.

"One gets in the habit," said Zultan. "And I still have far too many books to read to allow myself to die. Grub! Please come and take my doom away. I don't think I will kill her yet. I want to think a little longer."

Chapter Twenty-Five

Summer sat on a rock.

It wasn't terribly comfortable, as rocks tend not to be, but at least she wasn't inside that terrible hot tent with Zultan Houndbreaker. She sat a little way outside of camp, in the minimal shade provided by the canyon wall, and stared at the rope around her wrists.

Because they would have forgiven me.

She did not understand, but she wasn't sure if it was a grown-up thing, and she would understand when she was older, or if it was an evil thing, and she would never be able to wrap her head around it.

She wanted to go home so badly that she could nearly taste it. It gave her something to focus on beside her dry, parched throat. She was incredibly thirsty.

If she were at home, she would wake up in bed. She would lie there and stare at the popcorn ceiling, the little hills and valleys of an all-white landscape, and then push off the covers. She would go out into the kitchen and get a glass of water and say, "I had a bad dream," and her mother would put down her coffee and say, "Oh, honey," and put her arms around Summer's shoulders.

If her mother was having a bad day, she would cry a little and say, "I wish I could have the dream for you, sweetie, you know I'd do anything for you." It would end with Summer having to reassure her mother that it

wasn't that bad, that her mother did a good job, and that was never fun, but at least it would be *familiar.*

Her wrists were sweaty under the ropes, and when she tried to wiggle the rope around to cool the sweaty patches, they were red and sore.

The antelope woman came wandering through camp, saw her, and walked toward her, and suddenly Summer remembered.

Don't worry about things you cannot fix. Antelope women are not to be trusted. You cannot change essential nature by magic.

The stained glass saint's book had warned her about this woman.

But she didn't take away my acorn…

"Do you want to escape, then?" asked the antelope woman without preamble. She sat down on the rock next to Summer. It was hard to tell, but Summer thought she was amused.

Summer licked her lips. Her mouth was so very dry and she would have done nearly anything for a drink of water—but somehow she didn't want to tell this to the strange woman.

"Ah?" said the woman. "I'm offering you an escape, human child. Is this language strange to you?"

"I was told," croaked Summer, "that antelope women were not to be trusted."

The antelope woman threw her head back and laughed. She had a deep, throaty laugh, like a movie star. Her fingers moved on her collarbone as she laughed, tapping the delicate bones as if they were musical instruments.

"Who told you that, human child?"

"A—" Summer had to stop and lick her lips again. "A stained glass saint."

"Very wise," said the antelope woman. "Very wise. We are not to be trusted. We are daughters of chaos and mothers of mischief. The best of us are wicked and the worst of us would break mountains just to see them dance. Let me get you something to drink."

She rose. Summer sat on the ground in an agony of indecision. Should she refuse the drink? What if it was something horrible, like the wight-liquor? How would she know?

What would Glorious do?

This was not as useful a question as it could have been. Glorious would have torn Zultan's throat out, pinned Grub under one paw, run into the darkness swifter than the Sleipnerians. She could do none of these things, so she sat on the rocky hillside and wished she were a wolf.

The antelope woman came back, carrying a waterskin. She offered it to Summer.

Summer stared at it, then at the woman's strange, alien face, then back at the water.

"I shan't poison you," said the antelope woman. "Here." She opened her mouth and squeezed a thin stream of water into it.

"I thought it might be wight-liquor," said Summer.

"No one would leave such a thing unguarded," said the antelope woman, passing over the waterskin. "Not in this camp. Grub would be on it in an instant. He wouldn't be able to help himself. And he's too close to the edge already—a good sharp shock will knock him right over." She grinned. It was a strange expression, her sly eyes and her herbivore's teeth. "That's true, incidentally. Not everything I say is, but that was."

Summer fumbled with the waterskin and managed to direct the water into her mouth. It was delicious, but it tasted like water, not like anything else.

"Besides," said the antelope woman, when Summer had finished drinking, "you'd have noticed. Wight-liquor pretends to taste good, at least until it's got its hooks in you. Then it doesn't bother any longer."

"Why does Grub drink it, then?" asked Summer.

"He needs it. The more you drink, the more you want. He hates it, but he loves it slightly more than he hates it, so he must keep drinking." She yawned. "He should have died of it long ago, but Zultan keeps giving it to him. When the change comes at last, it'll be quite grotesque, I expect." She sounded rather pleased by the prospect.

Summer huddled into herself, not sure how to respond to this.

"So, do you want to escape?" asked the antelope woman.

"Yes," said Summer, then, rather doubtfully, "but I shouldn't trust you. But…I suppose I don't have anything to lose, do I? If you help me, then I escape, and if you don't, then I'm not any worse off, am I? And why would you pretend to help me escape if you've already caught me?"

The antelope woman laughed. "Goodness, you are an innocent, aren't you? I could pretend to help you with the intent of being seen stopping your escape, so as to curry favor with Zultan. Or I could let you escape and then you could lead us back to your little friends—the hoopoe, wasn't it?— and we'd catch you all. And as for being worse off, once you try to escape, you might be killed, or we might decide to weigh you down with chains to keep you escaping again. Or cut off your foot. Grub would enjoy that, I expect. Perhaps you would have had an opportunity to escape otherwise, but because you trusted me, you'll lose that chance. And that is all off the top of my head, you understand. There are deeper games that I could play."

Summer stared at the antelope with her mouth hanging open.

She had a feeling she hadn't followed quite all of that, but she understood more than enough. More importantly, she understood that the antelope was actually arguing against herself, and that was…well, who *did* that?

"Why are you telling me all this?" she asked finally.

"Because I'm an antelope woman," came the answer. "Because I enjoy it. I suppose you're not from Orcus, are you? Do you not know the story, then?"

Summer shook her head.

"Ah!" The antelope woman tapped her blunt clawed finger on her collarbone again. "Well, mythology is a truth that isn't true, and that's as delightfully twisty as a lie in its own way. Very well."

She sat down, cross-legged, and drew her back straight. There was an odd sing-song note to her voice, as if she were reciting poetry.

"I tell you this as it was told to me," she said, "and if it is a lie, the gods told it first. Before the world of Orcus was another world, and in it were the animals and the birds and among them were hunters with the blood of the gods in them."

Summer shifted, trying to get comfortable on the stones. The antelope woman's eyes flickered to follow her, but her voice did not change.

"There was a hunter, the greatest of his tribe, and he had slain everything that walked or flew beneath the sky. The blood of gods was as thick in his veins as it is thin in the veins of mortals now.

"Came a time, in that other world, when the wise ones learned that the world was doomed. Great beasts had come, with teeth of stone, and they ate the world, grinding their teeth through the land and sky and water, taking away a little more with each bite. The stonetooth beasts could not be slain and they could not be turned and they could not be reasoned with. Their only purpose was to devour worlds that had outlived their usefulness, and they were determined to devour this one."

Summer shivered. "What were they?" she asked. She wasn't sure if she was allowed to interrupt, but it seemed important.

The antelope woman paused in her recitation. "No one knows," she said, in a more normal voice. "I always pictured them like jackals, scavenging on the bones of dead worlds. But the story doesn't say."

Summer nodded.

The antelope woman picked up the thread again. "The wise ones knew that there was no more hope for their world, so they made a hole in the earth and their people went through it. And the great hunter vowed that he would bring through the beasts and the birds of the world, so that the people would not be lonely."

"Was he an antelope?" asked Summer.

"He was not. No one knows what his people were. First, the bird that hunted with him went to all the tribes of birds and told them of the death of the world, and they came together in all their numbers and went through the hole in the earth. And because they were the first to follow the hunter's call, the gods of Orcus gave to them the gift of speech, and they are the bird clans of Orcus today.

"Next came the wolves, for they had seen the stonetooth beasts devouring the world, and they had sung to one another that the world was doomed. They went into the hole in the earth and the gods gave them no gift, but vowed to leave them alone, as wolves have always wished to be left alone."

That sounds like Glorious, thought Summer.

"The serpents went next, for the world was growing cold, and the gods gave to them the gift of prophecy, that they might see the future without blinking. And the elephants went through the hole in the earth, single-file, and the gods of Orcus gave them gifts, though the elephants will not tell anyone what those might have been."

She paused then, and took the waterskin back from Summer, drinking. Summer wondered if every single species in the world was going to be listed, and if so, how long it was going to take.

But the antelope woman's story changed then. "Those were the last of the ones who went willingly. All the rest had to be captured by the hunter. He caught as many beasts as he could, one by one, and took them to the hole in the earth, that they might be saved from the world's devouring."

She began to smile. It was not at all a nice smile. "And so he labored as the stonetooth beasts ate away at the land, until at last the only animal he had not yet caught was the antelope. For we were the swiftest beasts in all the world, and though we could be killed, we could not easily be caught. The hunter's tribe went through the hole in the earth themselves, begging him to follow, but he would not come until he had captured at least one antelope for the new world of Orcus. And the stonetooth beasts ate and ate and ate, and at last the only thing left of the world was a sliver of land and the hole in the earth and the hunter and the hunted."

Her voice dropped back into a normal cadence for a moment. "I imagine that he could look up and see the stonetooth beasts hanging over the world," she said. "Like mountains or clouds, something huge and hungry. But the story doesn't say for certain."

Summer shivered.

"At the very last, when there was but one bite left of the world remaining, the hunter captured an antelope. She was female and pregnant with twins, and the fawns in her belly slowed her down. He caught her and flung her through the hole in the earth, and then the stonetooth beasts devoured him and all of the world that remained.

"So she came to Orcus and gave birth to twin daughters. And the gods of Orcus cursed them all, naming them daughters of Chaos, in punishment for the death of the hunter."

"That doesn't seem very fair," said Summer. "She was just running away, wasn't she? Why would they curse her because antelope run away from hunters?"

The antelope woman laughed. "Because, my innocent, the gods are arbitrary and cruel and it is in their nature to turn mortals as cruel as they are. With my people, they succeeded admirably." She arched her neck and looked as proud as a warhorse. "You need not pity us. We have taken our curse and made a weapon from it. We sow madness wherever we go. We were the last to come from our dying world and we will be the last to walk this world, when all other things have passed away. Even the gods who cursed us will fall at last, and we will grind them beneath our hooves and dance together, and from our dance, who knows what new worlds may be born?"

Chapter Twenty-Six

The antelope woman's story left Summer cold inside. There was some-thing so strange and twisted about what she was saying, and yet…and yet…

They were cursed for something that wasn't their fault. That wasn't right.

It seemed as if the antelope women were saying, "Curse us, will you? We'll show you!"

"You're thinking very hard, my innocent," said the antelope woman. She stretched, arching her back and drawing one hand gracefully down her other arm. She was very beautiful, and Summer had a sudden vision of a dark world, empty even of grass, and antelope women dancing together in the darkness.

It was frightening, and yet she thought that she would like to watch that dance, for a little while at least. As if it might reveal something to her that she did not understand and that grown-ups had never been able to explain.

She did not know how to say this out loud. She was not entirely sure that she wanted to.

"Could you find another world?" she asked instead. "One where the gods didn't hate you?"

The antelope woman shrugged. "Perhaps. It is not always so easy. Some worlds lie together like the feathers on the breast of a dying bird, and some are as far apart as mountains. But why should we? If the gods punish us, let us stay here forever and remind them of what they could not tame."

"Do antelope women ever try to be good?" asked Summer. "Not wicked?"

"Oh, certainly," said the antelope. She flipped her hand in a dismissive fashion, wrinkling her broad nostrils. "They fall in love with dogs or saints or shapechangers. Someone with broad shoulders, who is so good that it makes your teeth ache, and then they wind up using their skills to save him from himself. They never live very long after that, but it makes a good doomed love story." She seemed unimpressed by this prospect. "There's a very nice shrine on the coast to the Stag Maiden, which is both historically and biologically inaccurate, but the marble work is lovely. She fell in love with the Sea Dragon's Daughter, and they had a marvelously tragic romance. I'd take you there so that I could make sarcastic comments about the tour guides, but Zultan would probably object. Are we going to escape or not?"

"I don't know!" said Summer helplessly. "How do I know if you're telling the truth?"

"You don't. You won't. Even I'm not sure." The antelope woman grinned again. Her eyes were as dark as a skull's eye sockets, and gave away even less. "I suspect, however, that if I were planning on betraying you right away, that I'd be more persuasive. But I am not quite certain, right now, whether it will be more fun to betray Zultan first, then turn on you, or perhaps the other way around."

She turned her head back toward the camp. Her ears swept up to catch the sounds.

Summer looked around desperately for turquoise, for any sign that this was the road to take. There was nothing.

I have to decide. I have to decide myself. *I know this is bad, and the saint warned me, but I have to decide what the warning means.*

Sometimes all the choices are bad.

She, too, looked back toward the camp. Grub was walking toward them. The eight-legged horses pawed at the ground, their muzzles studded with unblinking eyes.

"Let's escape," she said quietly.

The antelope woman laughed. "Clever innocent. Or foolish. I haven't decided yet. Wait for a signal, then."

⁓

Summer sat on a rock and waited for a signal and wondered what one would even look like.

A fire? A stampede? What could I even do? I can't run…

The sun tracked its way across the sky. A bird chirped somewhere in the canyon, or a bug that sounded like a bird. Guards came and went in the camp. Grub huddled under a tarp, looking pale and ill, although Summer had no idea if that was normal or not.

The landscape looked like that around the Great Pipes, but with even less vegetation. Large rocks littered the landscape. The campsite was set on a level place amid loose scree slopes.

Even if her feet were free, she would have had a hard time walking across the scree with any speed. The Sleipnerians had gone across it with spidery agility.

If I run…I can't run very far.

The antelope woman strolled through the camp, her tail swishing. She exchanged a few words with Grub and then laughed. Grub huddled deeper into his clothes and glared.

Maybe she's not going to help me at all. Maybe it was all a lie to amuse herself.

Zultan was nowhere to be seen.

She felt hot and exhausted and sore. She was no longer quite so thirsty.

The bird chirped again, closer. Then she actually saw it, a little dark shape hopping across the broken ground.

It was wearing a tiny bowler hat.

Summer wanted to cheer or scream or yell, but she didn't dare. She sat very quietly, watching the valet-bird hop around the ground.

It seemed confused, but it came closer and closer.

Could it get her out of here? Then she wouldn't need the antelope woman's help.

The valet-bird cocked its head and looked at her. It was hard to read the expression on its tiny face, but Summer thought that it looked…baffled.

She glanced around for the rest of the flock, but couldn't see any of them.

It hopped closer to her, settling at last on one of her shoes, and began picking at her shoelace.

"Are you here to help?" whispered Summer.

It glanced up at her, then back down. There was a burr stuck in her shoelace. The valet-bird worked it loose, chirping grumpily to itself.

Summer's heart sank.

Flock-mind, Reginald said. Smarter when they're together. Did they split up to try and find me? And now it's not quite smart enough to know what to do?

The bird looked up at her again, then scuffled at the ground. It seemed to be thinking hard.

"Can you tell the others where I am?" whispered Summer. "Or lead them back here?"

It began picking at her other shoelace.

Maybe it will remember when it gets back to the others. Maybe it'll be able to tell them then. Or maybe others will come, and then they'll be smart enough…

Summer scanned the air for other valet-birds, but saw only the hard blue sky, already softening towards evening.

Gravel crunched as someone walked toward her, and the valet-bird flew away.

It was one of the guards. His face didn't change when he looked at her. He set a thin metal plate on the rock beside her and walked away without speaking.

Summer stared at the plate, which had some kind of glop on it. It looked like very wet rice with some kind of sauce. There were chunks of something in it. It did not look terribly appetizing. Even goulash day at the school cafeteria was better than that.

She thought of wight-liquor and it became much easier to set the food aside.

Time passed with agonizing slowness. Summer watched the guards wander around the camp. No one seemed to care that she was sitting out here.

Well, where am I going to go? I can't run with my legs tied up, and the spider-horses can catch me in five minutes on these slopes…

She wondered if there were other guards posted out of sight, or if this was all of Zultan's army. Was it really just—she counted—eight guards and Grub and the antelope woman? How could such a tiny handful of people cause such misery?

I guess in the Old West, all those outlaw gangs were pretty small. And they robbed trains and shot people.

She'd gone with her mother to historic Tombstone once, and actors had done the shoot-out at the OK Corral. She couldn't remember how many there had been. Mostly she remembered her mother whispering, "It's okay. They're not *really* shooting at each other," and being annoyed because she knew perfectly well that it was a show. She wasn't a *baby.*

She wished she'd paid more attention to the number of people at the OK Corral, or that her school hadn't wasted so much time on vocabulary words when teaching history and had spent a little more time on important things, like how many people you needed to keep a land terrorized for a hundred years.

And then she remembered Zultan's face under the mask and her skin crawled again.

More gravel crunching. Summer realized that she had been staring at the ground and looked up.

Grub smirked down at her. "Not hungry?"

"Not really," she said.

"Oh, but you'll need to keep your strength up," he said, voice dripping with fake concern. "Who knows what might happen out here in the—"

"Don't be an ass, Grub," said the antelope woman, elbowing him out of the way. "Just because Zultan doesn't posture like a two-bit actor doesn't mean you need to fill in the gap."

She handed Summer another waterskin. Summer drank thirstily.

"Up on your feet," said Grub, giving the antelope an irritated glance. "I'm keeping an eye on you tonight."

The antelope woman rolled her eyes. "Give the child a chance to pee first, unless you want her wetting your tent."

Grub scowled. His strange translucent skin pulled tight over…something. Summer stared up into his face, trying to figure out if Grub had cheekbones in the wrong places.

The antelope woman picked her up by the rope around her wrists. "Come on, child. And turn your back, Grub."

She winked at Summer.

Wait for a signal…was that it? Are we running now, with Grub right there?

Is there anything that I can do to buy us more time?

She did not know much about being captured by enemies, but Summer was a veteran of the public school system, and she knew that there are things that even the cruelest disciplinarian was forced to accept.

"I…I think I might have to do more than pee…" said Summer.

Grub made a disgusted noise and turned his back.

"Then we'll go around downwind," said the antelope cheerfully. "Zultan'll be in a fine mood if he's smelling human crap all night."

She pushed Summer in front of her, with a hand between the shoulderblades. Summer made her slow, shuffling way across the slope.

"That's good," murmured the antelope woman. "A bit slower. He has to be sure you can't run."

This was easy to do. Summer stumbled repeatedly and the antelope woman took her arm.

"Humans are so *slow,*" she said loudly. "One of my sisters would be there and back again twice already."

"Your sisters don't have their feet tied together!" retorted Summer, and felt the antelope's breath stir against her ear as the woman laughed.

They made their slow way around the edge of a miniature canyon, out of sight of the camp. Summer cast a last glance behind her and saw Grub standing with his arms folded and his back turned.

They took two more steps and then the antelope woman crouched down at Summer's feet. "Hoof up," she ordered, patting her knee.

Summer obediently put one foot on the woman's knee. The antelope woman bent her long neck down, gripped the knot in her teeth, and made one rolling, chewing motion.

The hemp parted neatly in two halves.

"How did you *do* that?" asked Summer, amazed.

"It's easy when you're the one who tied the knots," said the antelope woman dryly. "Looks impressive, but there was only one strand holding it together. It was already starting to come loose. Now come on. There's a cut through in the back of the canyon here, and we can go up. Stupid thing to leave unguarded if you ask me."

She stood up, dusting off her knees, and began walking swiftly toward the back of the stone defile. The footing here was better,

"Does Grub know about it?" asked Summer, hurrying after her.

"I've no idea. I never told him. If he doesn't find it himself, he can wonder where we went. It'll do him good."

"What I don't understand," said Summer, scrambling to keep up while the ends of the rope flopped along the ground behind her, "is why you were helping him in the first place."

"I still might be," said the antelope woman cheerfully. "You don't know, do you? Even I'm not entirely sure. Trust an antelope and you get what you deserve. Everyone knows that."

Summer shook her head, baffled. The antelope woman was like the opposite of Glorious. You know what she meant, but you weren't sure if it was true, whereas Summer never doubted the truth of what Glorious said, she just had no idea what it was supposed to mean.

"But if everybody knows that, why did Zultan trust you in the first place?"

"Oh, *Zultan.*" There was no mistaking the contempt in the woman's voice. "He thinks he's a great deal smarter than he is. Assumes that just because he's angry at the world, he could understand my anger." She tossed her head and her horns hissed through the air like swords. "He wants the world to burn and I want to dance on the ashes, so he thinks that we are alike. But hate and chaos aren't the same thing. Occasionally, I see fit to remind him of that."

"I still don't understand him," said Summer wearily.

"Pfff." The antelope woman waved her hand. "Nothing worth understanding. His people are as good as mine are wicked. The better you are, the farther you can fall. Come from a race of angels and about the only thing you can be is a devil." She glanced over her shoulder. "Goes the other way too, of course. I could have been a saint. I thought about it very seriously when I was young."

"Did you really?" asked Summer suspiciously.

"No. That was a lie."

"Unless this is also a lie," said Summer, who felt that she was beginning to get the hang of things.

"Oh, very good."

The cut in the back of the canyon was easy to overlook, and Summer wasn't entirely sure that it counted as a way up for anyone less than an antelope. She could make three or four steps up the slope and then she would get stuck and her rescuer would grab her wrist and haul her up to the next little ledge.

She didn't look down.

It's not as bad as where I hid from Grub in the little cave with the lizard. It's not like that. If I fall, I'll roll down, not fall to my death.

She told herself that repeatedly and she didn't fall down and then they were standing on the canyon rim above the camp. Summer could see the glow of the campfire below, and wondered how soon she would be missed. Could they see her, if they looked up?

She stepped back from the edge, thinking they must look like two black cut-outs along the canyon rim. The antelope woman came with her, her tail swishing.

"Will they come after us on the spider-horses?"

"They can try. The beasts haven't fed for two days, though, and unless Grub cuts some poor sod up for blood and grain, they won't be happy about moving at night. And once they do, they won't get far with their saddle girths cut."

Summer stared at her back, honestly amazed.

"Do you have a name?" she whispered, when they had walked for a little way.

"Yes."

She did not elaborate on this. Summer tried again: "Will you tell me?"

"No. It's dangerous to lie too much about your name."

There were any number of things that Summer could have said to this, but she had a feeling that none of them would end with her learning the antelope woman's name.

When they had gone far enough that she could no longer see any light but the stars, Summer asked "Will Zultan be angry when he finds that you've gone?"

"Perhaps," said the antelope, shrugging. "His anger's no concern of mine. Where are your friends, do you think?"

"I don't know," said Summer. "Still back at the Great Pipes, maybe. Which way is that?"

"A little south of the setting moon," said the antelope woman. "As good a direction as any. Follow me."

Chapter Twenty-Seven

It took them the rest of the night and half a day. They had no food. The antelope ate grass and the tips of pine needles. Summer ate nothing. But they shared water from the same bottle and when they slept that night, the antelope woman sang a lullaby in a strange, rich voice. Summer wanted to stay awake, to watch for Grub, but she was exhausted. Instead, she slept and dreamed of horned women dancing in the dark.

She woke feeling strange and oddly glad to be a girl. It was not a thing that she thought about often, or at all.

They walked until nearly noon. Summer had no idea how to find the others, and perhaps it would have been impossible, but then a valet-bird dropped out of the sky and landed on her shoulder.

She wasn't sure if it was the same one she had seen in camp, but the prickle of tiny claws filled her with intense relief. The antelope woman was not comfortable company.

"Are you smart again?" she asked the valet-bird. "Is your flock nearby?"

The bird groomed a strand of hair down over her ear and made a small, gruff chirp. Summer didn't know if that was an answer or not.

Then it took off flying, not in the direction they had been going, but toward the road, which they had been avoiding for fear of encountering Grub again.

"We should follow him," said Summer.

"Should we?" asked the antelope woman. "I don't know that sort of bird. Are you sure they aren't in the habit of leading travelers to their deaths?"

The valet-bird made an angry chatter from the bushes.

"No, no," said Summer hastily. "They're friends. They belong—they *work* for a friend of mine."

"Chrrrk," said the valet-bird, mollified.

They followed the bird through the trees for perhaps twenty minutes, and then another bird joined him, then two more. Soon there was a bowler-hatted bird on each of Summer's shoulders and more chirping from the trees.

One tried to land on the antelope woman's long horns, but she shook her head and it flew away, disgruntled.

"Nothing personal," she said. "We have a deal with the chief of the Oxpecker Clan, and it's more than my life is worth to break it."

The snubbed bird blew something that sounded remarkably like a raspberry, but did not try to land on her again.

It was less than an hour before there was a gap in the trees and Summer saw the flash of burnt orange feathers.

Reginald! And—

"Glorious!" She ran forward and flung her arms around the wolf's neck.

His fur was coarse and hot against her cheek. She buried her face in it and smelled wildness and a single dry sob cracked out of her throat.

There might have been more, but a growl rose in the wolf's chest, so loud and grating that it rattled her teeth.

"Glorious…?" Summer lifted her head. "It's me…"

The wolf was looking past her, through the trees. Summer followed his gaze to the antelope woman.

"One of *them*," growled the wolf. "One of the daughters of chaos."

"Oh, very bad *ton*," said Reginald, almost to himself.

"A pleasure to meet you as well," said the antelope woman, sketching a small, ironic bow.

"She helped me escape," said Summer, feeling guilty, as if she'd been caught in some kind of wrongdoing.

"For her own reasons," said Glorious. "And those reasons will be ill ones."

"Very much so," said the antelope. "But I never made any secret of that."

"She didn't," whispered Summer. "She told me she was a liar—she told me she might be lying—but we got away anyway—"

The antelope grinned down at Glorious, her blunt teeth a strange mirror to the wolf's snarling fangs. "What will you do now, wolf?" she asked. "You can hardly blame me for bringing your little friend back to you, and not even under false pretenses."

Glorious twitched his shoulder and Summer stepped back, a little frightened. But he was not looking at her. Instead, his cold green eyes bored into the antelope woman's dark, amused ones.

"What game are you playing?" he asked.

She laughed. "Does it matter what I say? Would you believe it?"

Glorious lunged.

Summer had seen flashes of the wolf's astonishing speed before, but she had never seen him simply *uncoil* like this. He moved like a striking snake, leaping for the antelope woman's throat.

"No!" cried Summer. Even if the antelope woman couldn't be trusted, she had saved Summer, gotten her away from Zultan, been punished unfairly by the gods of Orcus. She'd been kind, in her own twisty way.

She was never sure afterward if her cry made Glorious lose a fraction of his speed, or if it gave the antelope woman a heartbeat worth of warning. Perhaps it wouldn't have mattered either way. But Glorious's teeth snapped on empty air and the antelope woman was gone, gone, bounding away down on the road on her spun-glass ankles, faster than a wolf could run.

She vanished into the scrubby trees. Glorious stood with his feet planted wide and his teeth bared.

"I could follow," he said aloud, almost to himself. "And she would doubtless lead me into a trap, and that would be the end of a wolf."

Feathers flashed overhead as Reginald went in pursuit.

"I'm sorry!" said Summer. "I didn't mean—I—she really *did* help me escape—"

Glorious sighed, and slowly the growl went out of him and his lips dropped back over his teeth.

"Yes," he said. "Or you were always meant to escape, and now you have led her to the rest of us. No, I don't blame you! You did the only thing you could do, Summer-cub, and our small winged friends found you and lost you and found you again, so of course they led you to us. They are not complicated enough creatures to put up against an antelope, and you are from another world and could not know."

"We don't have them there," said the weasel, popping up on Summer's shoulder. He wrapped his paws around Summer's ear and began furiously grooming her hair.

"They are unique to Orcus, I hope," said Glorious. "They speak a great many lies, and even their truths mean harm for someone."

Summer sagged against him. Despite what he had said, she felt that she had failed—escaped *wrong*, somehow. "I'm sorry," she said. "I didn't know how to get away. And Grub was talking about torturing me and Zultan is… is…"

She trailed off. She didn't know how to explain Zultan.

The two goose-guards appeared behind them on the road. "No one on our backtrail—" began Ankh, and then, "Miss Summer!"

Ounk flew to them and slapped Summer on the back with her wing, hard enough to knock the wind out of her. "You got free of those villains! Well done!"

"It…I think I did it wrong…"

"Nothing doing," said Ounk. "You're here, aren't you?"

"There was an antelope woman," rumbled Glorious.

Both of the Imperial Geese stilled.

"One of them, here?" asked Ounk.

And then Ankh astonished Summer by spreading her wings out and curving one around Summer, as if she were a chick. "It is my fault," she said quietly. "I left you alone with that traitorous priestess. I knew better, but she was polite, and it is easier to fight swords than courtesy sometimes. But you've done well, in a situation you should never have been in. You've tangled with an antelope woman and walked away, and if there are echoes from this, I will stand the blame."

Summer felt tears slide down her cheeks, but she was encased in the goose-guard's wing like a warm blanket. Ankh was a grown-up, in a way Reginald wasn't, and if *Ankh* said that she'd done well…

Glorious nodded. When Ankh released her, he pressed his nose briefly against her forehead, and Summer felt better.

"I shouldn't have left," whispered the weasel, so that only she could hear. "I knew I shouldn't, no matter what it smelled like. I'd have bitten her so hard…"

Reginald reappeared and landed next to them, looking disgruntled. "She gave me the bag," he said. "Into the rushes and no mistake."

"Probably stopped to tie his cravat," muttered the weasel.

Reginald ignored him and focused on Summer. "But it doesn't signify, since you've come back! Ho!" He reached up and shook her hand so vigorously that he nearly fell over.

"The antelope will draw them back to us, I suspect," said Glorious.

"Oh, well. If she squeaks beef, we'll give them a bellyful!"

Everyone looked at him.

"What?"

"If she raises the alarm," translated Ounk.

"We will deal with it," said Ankh.

"That's what I said," grumbled Reginald, and Summer let out a gulping laugh, because she was back and she loved them all and this was so much better than going home.

"Let us get off the road," said Glorious. "We were moving fast to try and catch up to you, but we should not stay in plain sight now. Sleipnerians run faster than wolves, but they are not good in trees."

"And we must determine…," said Ankh.

"…which way we are going," finished Ounk.

"Oh no…" said Summer, sagging against the goose-guard. She'd almost forgotten, in the horror of the ride over the spider horse and the face of Zultan and the wildness of their escape. "The priestess sold us out—"

"We know," said Glorious grimly. "She will not do so again."

Summer had been moving toward him to mount and ride, but stopped, eyes wide.

He snorted. "No, I did not kill her. She made a fool's bargain and guilt has its teeth in her more deeply than any wolf could bite."

Summer exhaled. She knew that in church, they said you had to forgive people, but she did not feel terribly forgiving. Still, Cereus had been… well…

Weak, but not evil. She was scared. I wouldn't trust her again, but she had to live in that horrible rotten cactus room and she didn't dare tell anyone. That might make anybody do stupid things.

She put one leg over Glorious's back. The wash of fur over her hands helped drive out the memory of the spider-horse's bristles against her skin.

If this were really Narnia, I suppose Cereus would come to me in chains and confess and beg my pardon. But I really just don't want see her or think about her ever again.

"So we didn't get a wasp," she said mournfully. "And now we have to go find *another* wondrous thing." She did not know if she could handle much more of this—going from glory to glory, looking for the one that was dying, while dodging Zultan and Grub.

"Now, now!" said Reginald. "We're not so far aground as you think! The little feathered chaps took care of us on that score, you may be sure."

Summer blinked at him, not sure what he was saying.

Reginald clapped his wings together and the valet-flock landed, twittering. Two dove into the pack and came out again.

They were carrying a bottle. It looked almost like a perfume bottle, made of tinted glass…and it was buzzing.

"M'very best feather oil, too," said Reginald sadly. "Dumped it out all over the vicious little blighter, and then crammed it into the bottle while the rest of us stood around gawping."

"Speak for yourself," said Glorious, amused. "A deer I might bring down, but a wasp is better prey for smaller claws. They did a fine job, though, and I thank them for it." He nodded his head to the valet-birds. One took off its bowler and bowed to the wolf.

"You mean they caught a *wasp?*" said Summer.

"Oh, aye. Any time you wish, we'll tie a string to the nasty little thing and follow it clear to the back of beyond."

"Then we did it," said Summer. She felt slack with relief and had to grab for Glorious's fur as the wolf broke into a trot. "We *did* it. We can find the Queen-in-Chains."

Chapter Twenty-Eight

They stopped that evening deep in the scrubby woods, in a little fold in the ground.

"Their steeds will find it hard to get through this terrain," said Glorious. "Though the antelope woman will not. I will light no fire tonight. These trees are not tall enough to keep the smoke from giving us away."

"How do you keep from having a fire in your fireplace?" asked Ankh.

Glorious closed one eye and scratched his ear. "I just do," he said. "A bit like coughing or not coughing—" and then he unrolled into the cottage.

They sat in front of the cold fireplace and talked. Summer wasn't sure how much Glorious was aware of, when he was a house, but she addressed the mantelpiece, for lack of any better place.

Reginald and the geese told her what Glorious had not. "When the priestess locked herself in and wouldn't come out, I flew up to the top and got the Ladderback—he's the woodpecker's chief—and brought him down. He'd been suspicious of the mess, and they'd seen people coming and going on horses they didn't like."

"The Ladderback went with us when the priestess would not unlock the door," said Ankh.

"There are few locks that will stand to a determined woodpecker," said Ounk. "He cleared the space away around the hinges and we took the entire door down."

"And then Glorious—yow! Straight for her throat, he went!" Reginald made excited wing gestures and toppled over backwards. "It was bellows to mend with her at once! That guide of ours set up yelling but we knocked him down and sat on him. She spilled her guts right away, told us everything."

"She had a wolf on her chest," said the weasel. "Although I'd have bitten her like fire if she'd talked any slower!" Summer stroked his back and he sat up straighter, several inches worth of grand ferocity.

"Anyway, the poor guide was so upset, but the Ladderback was cool as a skua, even when we all tromped in that awful back room. Lord! I never want to see anything like that again. Pure nasty, from top to bottom."

"What will they do?" asked Summer. She didn't ever want to go back to the Great Pipes, but the market and the woodpeckers hadn't been responsible for what Cereus had done.

"The Ladderback will deal with it," said Ankh. "I suspect that he could not intervene in the ruling of the lower city without a very good reason, but he has one now."

"Seemed a solid chap," said Reginald cheerily. "Sure he'll work something out."

And I have enough to worry about with the Frog Tree, thought Summer. *Let this be someone else's problem.* She remembered the saint's book again—*Don't worry about things you cannot fix.*

She told them, in turn, about Zultan.

Reginald let out a low whistle. "A dog! Well, that's a facer, isn't it? Heroes, the lot of them, I've always heard."

Ounk rubbed the back of her long neck with the edge of her wing. "I did not know that dogs could go bad."

"Not the sort of thing you'd shout from the rooftops, is it?" said Reginald. "Doubt they'd want to advertise."

"But he's old, really old," Summer said. "Like he should have died a long time ago, but for some reason he hasn't."

"There's magic for that," said Reginald. "Not *good* magic, mind you."

"You can't make more life," said Ankh.

"Only take it from others," said Ounk.

"Or so I've heard."

"And I."

It was harder to talk about the antelope woman. "I know she was bad," said Summer, but the secret writing in the chamber under her heart read *Was she?* and *Do I know?* and *What if…?*

What if we'd welcomed her? What if she was sitting here next to us? What would she say?

She knew that Glorious had to know more about it than she did, and yet…

"Antelope are tricky," said Reginald. "Tricky and tricksy. There's stories, you know. They say it was an antelope woman who really ruled the Badlands Empire, you know, and whispered into the Stone Emperor's ear."

He looked at Summer expectantly, as if that was supposed to mean something. Summer shook her head.

"Better to stay far away from them," said Ounk.

"She brought you back to us," said Ankh firmly. "And that is good, even if she meant it for her own ends."

Lying in bed that night, Summer put her face in the pillow and cried for the horror that was over and the fact that she was safe again, but also for the antelope woman and chances lost, a chance that might have been different, or better, or wonderful.

The next morning, they set about making a compass out of a live wasp.

Summer and the valet-birds had to do most of the work. No one else had the hands for it. Summer popped the cork out of the bottle and jammed a narrow cloth tube over the end to catch the wasp as it crawled out. The valet-birds managed the small, fiddly work of tying the string around the segments of the wasp's hind leg—and more importantly, of muffling the long, wicked stinger with a cloud of cork and gauze and a metal cap hastily rolled together from a sardine can lid.

"Peace-bonding its hind end," said Reginald, amused. "That's a first!"

The wasp itself was as large as a mouse. When the birds nodded in unison to Summer and she let it go, it buzzed up into the air like a hummingbird, then hit the length of the string and dropped out of the sky. It swung for a moment, righted itself, then rose again.

When it was in front of her, Summer found that it was less creepy than she expected. Perhaps after the spider-horses, a merely *large* insect could not scare her.

It was strangely beautiful. Its abdomen was banded in black and scarlet, and its wings were an iridescent glory. It had a triangular face and enormous dark eyes. It looked more like a sculpture of lacquer and porcelain than like a living creature.

"Gorgeous little thing," said Reginald. "Make a good brooch, wouldn't it?"

"Pretty things are usually poisonous," said the weasel. "It's why they can afford to be pretty."

"That's a bit harsh," said the hoopoe. "Plenty of pretty birds, and most of us aren't poisonous. 'Cept the shrikethrushes, of course, and they're all a bit dicked in the nob, if you ask me."

"I didn't," said the weasel.

Summer was holding the bottle with the string tied to it. She was pretty sure that the wasp couldn't sting through the sardine can lid, but she held the bottle at arm's length anyway. The wasp was huge and she didn't want it to fly into her face.

Fortunately, it did not seem particularly interested in her, or indeed, in anything else. The wasp looked up at the sky, antennae moving, and then it oriented itself and began to fly determinedly toward the northwest. When it reached the end of the string, it hovered there.

Summer walked in a slow semi-circle, but the wasp stayed pointing northeast like the needle of a compass.

"That way," she said. "I think?"

"The Tower of Dogs is that way, if I'm not completely addle-pated," said Reginald. "Or what's left of it."

"A cursed place," said Ounk. She didn't say it as if she were afraid, Summer noticed, she just said it, as if commenting on the weather.

"Rarely visited," said Ankh, in the same tone. She hefted her spear. "Very well! Let us follow this—"

A dozen high-pitched shrieks cut her off.

The valet-bird flock rose up into the air, screaming an alarm. There was a crash, a thud, and Glorious let out a yelp almost as high-pitched as the birds.

"Ho!" shouted a strange voice, practically in Summer's ear. "Got him!"

Summer whipped around. The wasp tried to reorient itself and buzzed at her face. She dropped the bottle.

There were three men in the road, big burly fellows wearing rough armor that looked as if it were made of leather and shingles. At their feet, Glorious thrashed back and forth, pinned to the ground by some kind of net.

"No!" shouted Summer, running toward them. "Leave him alone!"

"Blood and feathers," cursed Reginald. *"House-hunters!"*

"Go away!" screamed Summer. She felt like she was running impossibly slowly, like in a nightmare where you can't move fast enough and your voice is a thin, feeble thing. "Go away! Leave him alone!"

"Here, now," said one of the hunters. "We're just doing our job—"

And then, almost to her own surprise, Summer actually reached them.

She hadn't thought this far ahead. She was half the size of the largest hunter. If she went for one, he would probably laugh, and then would undoubtedly do what grown-ups always did—grab you by the wrists and tell you to calm down and then it would all be over because there was really no getting past that.

Summer flung herself over Glorious instead. "You won't take him!" she said. "I won't let you."

Under her, Glorious growled, a long, drawn-out growl of fury and despair.

"Now get off, there's a good girl," said the shortest hunter. "This is hunter business. Just give us a few minutes and we'll be out of your hair in no time."

Summer wrapped her arms around Glorious as well as she could through the net and clung for dear life.

Two of the house-hunters carried long poles with nooses at the end. One sighed and started to lower the noose toward Summer.

A goose-guard's spear knocked it aside.

"I think not," said Ankh.

"You will touch neither the girl nor the wolf," said Ounk.

"We've been tracking this cottage for weeks," said the biggest hunter. "Thought we lost it after it flipped the cage. This is *our* prey."

"This wolf is no one's prey," said Ankh.

Why doesn't he speak up for himself? thought Summer. "Glorious, tell them!"

Glorious heaved under her and growled again.

"We've got permits," said the shortest hunter. "All legal and notarized. We're allowed to take houses over a certain size."

The weasel hissed into her ear: "He can't. The net's silver-plate. Silver steals their voices if they touch it."

"I thought silver killed them!" gasped Summer.

"You don't have a voice, you'll find yourself written out of life quick enough! Get the net off him!"

Summer grabbed for the edges of the net. There were little tear-drop shaped bits of metal on them, like fishing weights.

"None of that," said the nearest hunter. He stamped his foot down next to her fingers and glared down at her in a manner that suggested that he would just as soon step *on* her.

"Don't be ridiculous," said the biggest hunter. "This is just business." He addressed the geese. "You take the little girl so she doesn't get hurt and we'll take the cottage and we'll all be about our business."

The shortest hunter squatted down so that he was at eye-level with Summer, and smiled like someone who believed that he was good with children. "Here, now," he said. "The cottage will be up on the market at Delta this month. You tell your mommy and daddy and maybe they'll come and buy it for you, hey?"

Summer stared at him with profound disgust.

"It's all legal," said the biggest hunter again. "We've got permits."

Do you have a title on file at the Registrar of Deeds?

It came to her all at once.

"This house isn't for sale," she said. "He's mine."

The shortest hunter's smile slipped a bit.

"Don't go telling stories now," he said. "This cottage is unlicensed, and it's free for the taking."

"No, he isn't," said Summer. She gathered herself and glared into the hunter's eyes. "There's a title on file in Fen-town. You can go there and see for yourself."

The hunter's smile vanished entirely.

"You said this cottage was unlicensed!" hissed the middle hunter.

"It was!" he snapped. "I checked when we started tracking it!"

"Maybe then it was," said Summer, "but it's changed. We registered him in Fen-town."

The hunters looked at each other.

"We lost the trail near Fen-town," muttered the middle hunter.

"She poached our real-estate!" said the biggest hunter. "That's not allowed!"

"Private sale, wot?" said Reginald. "All nice and tidy and notarized. There were stamps. Big ones. In red ink."

The hunters wheeled to glare at this new addition to the discussion. Reginald waved at them and tried to look stern and legal, which didn't go very well.

The three men formed a huddle. Summer stealthily flipped up one of the weights and Glorious reached a paw through the gap. A violent shudder went through him.

There was a line scored in his fur where the silver had touched. She could see raw skin underneath.

"Don't understand…" she heard one hunter say.

"Should have double-checked…"

"*She* said it was free…"

"Told you not to trust one of them…"

"Yes, but she told us which way it had gone, didn't she? That was true enough!"

Summer's fingers stilled on the silver net.

Inside her heart, the innermost chamber was lined with frost. She felt as if she were writing a word in the frost with her fingertip, but she did not know what the word was, only that it was very cold.

"Tell me," she said, in a voice that sounded as if it belonged to someone much older, "was it an antelope woman who told you this?"

Two of the hunters stepped back and left the short one looking sullen. "She said it was free! And on this road!"

Summer sat up. She did not look at Glorious. She drew, ironically enough, on the memory of the antelope woman herself.

Derision. Grace. Sardonic amusement.

And she lifted her head and curled her lip and said "And you *believed* her. One of the daughters of chaos."

"She told us where the trail was!" said the shortest hunter, as much to his companions as to Summer. "A week ago, and we found it, didn't we? How was I to know?"

"Antelope women," said Summer, with as much scorn as she could muster, "are not to be trusted."

The other two hunters looked at each other over their leader's head, then at the goose-guards.

"Making trouble," said one of them gruffly. "Like they always do."

"But we've been tracking this cottage for weeks!" cried the leader.

"She lied to you," said Summer. "The way she lies to everyone."

She was a little surprised that her breath did not come out in a cloud of ice.

The two taller hunters took a step back. The goose-guards pressed forward, and then their spears came down in an X in front of Summer.

"We'll dispute it," muttered the shortest hunter. "You'll hear from our lawyers."

"Oh, very good," said Reginald. "M'father's got solicitors for that. Perhaps you've heard of him—the Lord Almondgrove, of the Almondgrove Hoopoes?"

The house hunters retreated another few steps. They locked their hands around their leader's arms and pulled him with them.

Summer rose to her feet and dug her fingers into the net.

"Take this with you," she said, still feeling strange and cold and clear-headed.

She could not throw the net over one of them the way she would have liked—it was shockingly heavy—but she heaved it into the road at their feet.

The tallest scooped up the net. The middle one mumbled something that sounded like, "Sorry to be a bother," and then they hauled their leader into the trees and away.

"I'll make sure they're gone," said Reginald, and took to the air.

Summer fell to her knees next to Glorious.

He gasped air as if he had been drowning. There were red lines across his legs and his muzzle.

"Talk," begged Summer. "Say something. Don't let them have taken your whole voice!"

"Alive," he gasped. "Alive—" and that was enough for Summer to bury her face in his ruff with a cry of relief.

Ankh—or maybe it was Ounk—spread her wings over both of them. Summer had not known that the goose's wings could cover a full-grown wolf, but they could. The goose stood guard, and the three of them sat in the dust and listened to Glorious breathe.

Chapter Twenty-Nine

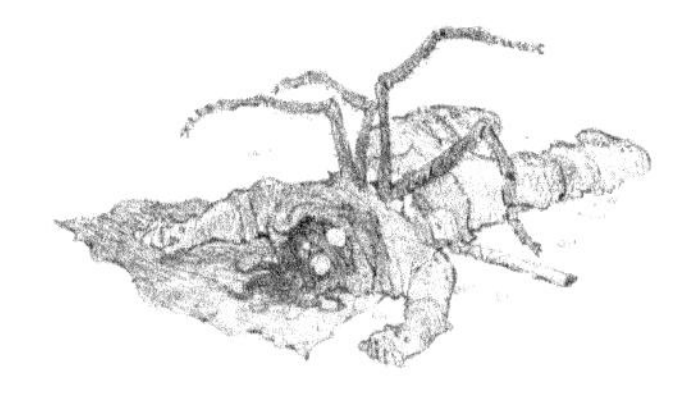

They found the wasp a little while later. It was a few feet from where Summer had flung it, crawling determinedly northeast with the bottle dragging behind it.

Summer felt as if she were standing a little bit behind herself. She picked up the bottle and set it to the northeast of the wasp. It climbed into the mouth of the bottle and she put the stopper in. It buzzed against the glass, still mindlessly pushing to the northeast.

Glorious was favoring his left hind leg, where three of the silver weights had wrapped around it. There was a burn across the joint that looked as if someone had stuck him with a hot poker. The valet-birds had dressed it as best they could.

"Later," said Glorious. His voice was still ragged. "We must move. If we can be found by one, we can be found by others."

So they moved. Summer didn't ride. They went low, under the scruffy trees, until Summer and the goose-guards had to bend down to fit. The sun rose high in the sky, but they moved through dappled shadows.

"She lied the whole time, didn't she?" she said abruptly.

"It is likely," said Glorious. Not needing to ask who, or about what. "She would have had to put the hunters on my trail some time ago."

"A week, they said," said Ounk.

I didn't trust her, said Summer to herself. *I didn't, I didn't, I knew I shouldn't!*

Her cheeks burned anyway. She felt embarrassed in front of herself.

So stupid, so gullible, so young…

I wouldn't have done anything differently! I still would have tried to escape!

But I could have left her once I was away…and she would have followed me, most likely, so what was the difference?

The difference was that she would have tried.

They rested for a little while in the shade of a rocky outcropping. There was a seep under a stone, enough to make a little pool no larger than Summer's cupped hands. By unspoken agreement, they let Glorious drink first.

The antelope woman lied, and the priestess lied. Who else is lying?

Summer leaned her head back against the stone. Perhaps everyone was lying. Perhaps there was nothing true in the world. What did she know for certain, anyway?

Perhaps the Forester had lied about the wasps. Perhaps the Queen-in-Chains was not responsible at all. Perhaps everyone had lied about the dogs and they were all exactly like Zultan. Perhaps there was some dark deception behind Reginald's foolish enthusiasm and the dignity of the goose-guards.

Perhaps Baba Yaga herself had been lying. How could she have been stupid enough to think that she would find her heart's desire here? How could her heart's desire be in another world where practically the first thing she saw was a dying tree?

Teeth gripped her hand and Summer's eyes flew open.

"Enough," said Glorious, releasing her fingers. "You're chewing your own wounds open now. They won't heal that way."

"How can you tell?" asked Summer. Her voice sounded as hoarse as his.

"Do you think I've never done the same, Summer-cub?" He shook himself. Hair flew in a blizzard, where the silver had loosened it. "I learned. You'll learn too."

He tested his hind leg and nodded. "Up on my back," he said. "We've gone far enough in stealth. Now we run."

In the end, they could not run far enough, or fast enough. Reginald went up on a short scouting flight and came down almost immediately.

"Sleipnerians," he gasped. "The hunters must have put them on our trail."

"Or they've been hanging back until now in hopes that the hunters would take out Glorious," said Ankh.

"Go to ground?" said the weasel.

Reginald shook his head. "They spotted me. The one with the crossbow shot at me—nowhere near, but I don't dare go up again. They know we're here."

The weasel let loose a long, chattering call, which sounded profane, and ended with, "You damn dandy, you've led them right to us!"

"Now see here—" began Reginald.

"No time, you two!" said Ounk. "Begging your pardon, Master Reginald," she added, somewhat perfunctorily.

"If we take to the air, we can lead them off—" began Ankh.

"No good. They know two of us are on foot," finished Ounk.

"I cannot outrun them on this leg," said Glorious. "But I can fight."

"A defensible position, then," said Ankh.

"And let us sell our lives dear," said Ounk.

It was all happening too fast. Summer wanted to say "Wait—stop—slow down!" But of course they couldn't. She wanted to say "I didn't agree to this!" and that should have mattered but it didn't, and the fact it didn't matter was even worse.

The valet-birds rushed in, twittering, and then zipped away to the left. Glorious veered after them. Summer ran alongside him, gripping his fur. He was half-dragging her along, and all she could do was keep her arm over her face to fend off whipping branches.

The goose-guards had it worse. Unable to fly for fear of arrows, their waddling gait was not suited to speed. But they could flatten their long necks down and get under the worst of the branches, and finally, all together, they scrambled and crawled and fell into the place that the flock had found.

There was a rock barely as tall as Summer and a line of dense bushes to one side. Other than that, it looked distressingly open.

"I have seen more defensible trees," muttered Glorious.

"Master Reginald and Miss Summer against the rock," said Ankh crisply.

"Now see here—" began Reginald.

"Glorious in the middle. We shall flank," said Ounk.

"I'm not an egg that you need to keep warm!"

"We must take the crossbowman first if we can," said Ankh. "Otherwise he will pick us off from a distance."

"A fine plan," said Glorious dryly. "How do you propose that we do this?"

"You know, I can fly right over the blighter's head!"

Summer wanted to ask if they were going to die, but it didn't seem particularly helpful, and she was afraid that she knew what the answer was going to be. She pulled the cheese-sword out of its sheath and stared at it. Could she stab somebody with it?

It's not that I don't think I'd want to, she thought glumly, *but if I stick somebody with it, can I push hard enough to make it go in?*

She'd never stabbed anyone before. It seemed difficult.

"Are you listening to me?" demanded Reginald, and then Summer heard the strange, multiplied sound of the spider-horses' hoofbeats.

They did not come from the front, as Summer had expected, but from the side. They ran along the line of bushes and as the first one began to turn the corner, the valet-birds surged toward it.

The Sleipneirian was not expecting a flock of tiny things pecking at its eyes. It stumbled, reared, and snapped at them. The horses behind had to halt their run, veering around them.

The pileup rather ruined the effect of the charge, but Grub made the best of it anyway. He spurred his steed around the embattled horse and halted.

"Surrender," he said. "Hand over the human and you will be spared."

Summer glanced back across the horses. There were six besides Grub's. She did not see Zultan or the antelope woman.

Feathers brushed her cheek as Reginald launched himself into the air.

The crossbowman jerked his weapon up and fired.

"Now!" shouted Ankh. "Before he reloads!"

"Surrend—" began Grub again, obviously caught flat-footed, and Glorious leapt.

He tore into the horse's neck as if it was a deer. Its front legs buckled and it went to its knees. Grub was thrown forward, over the saddle, but Glorious was already gone.

Ankh and Ounk looked at each other, shrugged, and waded into the fray.

Summer would not have thought that a bird could fight effectively with a spear held in a webbed foot. She had forgotten how often birds stood on one foot. The geese balanced like ballet dancers, striking with spear and beak and wing. The riders they hit with their wings did not get up again.

Reginald smashed into the crossbowman. There was no finesse to his method at all, he just flew directly into the man's face, battering with his wings and tearing with his claws. The man flung up his hands to defend himself and the crossbow dropped to the ground.

For a moment, everything was flailing legs and wings, spears and swords, the hiss of angry geese and Glorious growling.

And then there was a spider-horse coming right at Summer.

She threw her hands up in the air to protect her face and then she realized she was still holding the cheese-sword, so she lashed out with it wildly. It hit something and the shock travelled up her arm, which promptly went numb to the elbow.

The spider-horse screeched. So did Summer.

She looked up into the face of a rider and then something happened and he fell down and Glorious was there but so was *another* horse and Summer threw herself sideways without understanding why she was doing it and a sword much bigger than the cheese-sword slashed through the space where she had been.

She fell over backwards, which probably saved her life. The rider could not reach down to her. The spider-horse snapped at her but then the valet-flock zoomed between them. One exploded in a puff of feathers as the awful mandibles snatched it out of the air.

Summer screamed and crab-walked backward as fast as she could. She still had the cheese-sword—somehow—and she slashed it at the spider-horse, hitting one of the bristly legs right at the joint.

It cracked and the horse made a horrible chattering noise and then Glorious slammed into it from the side and knocked it back against the rock.

Summer scooted away, farther and farther, and then ran into something soft and solid.

It was Grub.

He lay motionless where the horse had thrown him…or almost motionless. His face was still and collapsed, like a Halloween mask with no one wearing it. But his back was heaving strangely, as if he were struggling to rise.

"No!" shouted Summer. "No! This is your fault!" She rolled to her knees and lifted the cheese-sword and slammed it down as hard as she could into her tormentor's back.

The first few inches slid in as if she were cutting butter, and then the blade struck something hard and skidded sideways.

The heaving motion grew far more pronounced. Before Summer's horrified eyes, Grub's clothes split open.

His skin was white and covered in thin ribbed lines. It swelled up like a monstrous balloon, and then it too split open. Something black and huge began to force its way out of Grub's skin.

The sound of the horses and the geese and the wolf behind her seemed to fade. All Summer could see was long, bristly legs poking out, and then pushing down Grub's skin the way that a human might push down a skirt that she was taking off.

It was dark, iridescent blue and black. It had wings like wet tissue paper. Its abdomen rose high in the air, but its head seemed to be stuck. It pushed against the deflated Grub, trying to get free.

"Wight-fly!" screamed Ankh somewhere behind her. *"Wight-fly!"*

Summer lifted the cheese-sword and hacked at the monster's wings.

They parted with a wet ripping sound. The Grub-fly made a high, terrible buzzing and jerked upright.

The old skin came with it. The Grub-fly scraped at its new face, trying to remove the old one that was blinding it. As the skin shredded, Summer caught glimpses of vast, segmented green eyes, shot through with white lines.

It buzzed, and in the buzzing Summer could almost hear a voice.

She thought that if she could make out words, she would probably go quite mad, so she screamed louder to block it out and slashed at the monster with the blade.

It caught the cheese-sword with one bristly, hooked leg, and flung it contemptuously aside.

Summer decided that this would be a good time to crawl away.

The Grub-fly tried to spread its wings and found them useless. It stamped after Summer instead, catching up and looming over her, and she looked up and thought, *I am going to die now.*

A spear sprouted out of the fly's right eye.

Ankh struck the Grub-fly with her wings outstretched and they rolled over in a tumble of feathers and hair, buzzing and hissing. Summer scrambled to her feet and looked around wildly.

The spider-horses had collapsed into strange piles of crooked-up legs. There were dead men strewn across the ground. She could not see Ounk. Glorious was standing with his head low and blood streaming over his face, looking at a last, tall figure, who stood gazing over the carnage.

Zultan.

She heard a wet, sickening noise, and turned.

Ankh had torn the Grub-fly open. It lay on its side, spasming, its legs moving like a mechanical toy winding down.

The goose-guard stood over it, swaying.

"There," she said. "There. That pays for all."

And then she too fell down, and did not move again.

Chapter Thirty

I've never seen a wight-fly so large," said Ounk. "Usually they grow in sheep, and once the lambs are weaned, they change. That was…"

She shook her head.

Summer could not believe that she was alive. She could not believe that Ankh was dead. It did not seem right that the entire battle, which had taken less than five minutes, was over.

The surviving goose-guard herded them away from the scene of the battle. Summer had to stop several times to be sick, and then, when there was nothing else in her at all, the valet-birds came and cleaned the snot and bile and tears off her face. There were barely half of them left.

"Still," said Reginald. "Five and a flock against seven on Sleipnerians. We gave 'em blood and thunder." He sighed. "Ankh most of all."

"Their mounts did them in," said Glorious, as the valet-birds cleaned his fur. One of his ears was badly gashed, and they were sewing it up with much chirping commentary. "If they had reacted as horses, they would have been far more dangerous, but spiders try to bite, not kick." He shook his mane and the valet flock took flight, scolding. "They protect the wrong places and leave their throats vulnerable. Ill-made creatures."

"I suspect that is why they tried so hard to remove you before the battle," said Ounk. She glanced over at Reginald. "And you, Master Reginald… you did not do badly. But if your father finds out—"

Reginald snorted. "With this great bloody gash on my face, he's deuced well going to!" The gash in question went across the top of his beak and up under one eye. Pale gray skin showed around it, and he was missing a tuft of feathers at the far end.

"Fop," muttered the weasel.

She had not seen him in the fight, but his fur was badly mussed. He groomed himself over and over, which only made his fur look worse.

"If we can move," said Ounk, "we should get away from here."

"I don't think Zultan has many more horses," croaked Summer. "There just…there weren't that many of them in the camp…"

Ounk paused. She looked incredibly weary, as if she was holding herself upright by will alone.

Nevertheless, she mustered half a smile and patted Summer's arm with her wing.

"It's not Zultan," she said gently. "It's the scavengers."

Summer thought she might be sick again.

"But…Ankh…"

"My sister is an Imperial Goose," said Ounk. "She would understand."

She held up a spear. The point was sticky with dried slime and caked with dirt. "I have her weapon. We shall give it to the last ones at Almondgrove, when we go home again."

She paused. "And I retrieved this as well." She held the cheese-sword out to Summer.

Summer stared at it as if it might attack. It was filthy and sticky and she hated it and wanted it back very badly, all at the same time.

"I will show you how to clean it," said Ounk. "But take it. If you had not cut off the wight-fly's wings with it, we would all likely be dead now."

Summer looked up at her, startled.

"They are nearly unstoppable in the air. It was soft from hatching, but still…that was too close. You did well."

"Not as well as Ankh," whispered Summer.

"No. Not as well as Ankh."

"My brave flock too," said Reginald sadly, as the valet-birds landed around him. There were many fewer than there had been. "Ah, lads…"

"Yes," said Ounk. "They, too."

Together, their numbers less, they stumbled away from the site of the battle.

When Glorious became a house that night, the door to the bedroom hung half off its hinges. The surviving valet-birds set about mending it.

There was a pool nearby—not large enough for bathing, but enough to drink. If they had more water, Summer would have scrubbed herself until her skin was raw. Instead she took off her T-shirt and soaked it and wiped at her face and arms over and over, until Ounk quietly took it away from her and said, "Enough."

"I want to go home," said Summer. "I don't think I can do this."

Ounk looked at her thoughtfully. "Do you wish to return to Almondgrove, then?"

Summer wished it very much. She wished it as hard as she had ever wished for anything.

She took out the acorn and stared into its carved eyes.

Ankh is already dead, she thought. *And if we don't fix this, why did we come at all? It won't bring her back, not going. It'll just mean that she's one more thing that's dead. Like the field of wheat and the Pipes and the giant turtle.*

"I wish to," she said slowly, "but I don't think we should."

Ounk nodded.

"Can't go back right now anyway," said Reginald. He peered at himself in a hand mirror provided by the valet-flock, tracing a feather down the cut in his face. "Not looking like this."

"It's not that bad," said Summer, painfully grateful to talk about something so inconsequential.

"No, no, my good looking days are over," said Reginald sadly, snapping the mirror closed. "Shan't be able to show my beak at the assembly."

"Miss Merope will probably find it dashing," said Summer.

"Do y'think?"

"Tell her you got it in a pitched battle," said Ounk.

Reginald puffed up his chest feathers. "Well, I might at that."

"Where do you think Zultan went?" asked Summer the next morning. She had expected to cry for half the night, but instead she had slept like the drugged dead. She felt sluggish and distant from herself, but alive.

The cheese-sword, scrubbed down with sand, hung at her side.

"Into a hole, if we're lucky," said Reginald.

Glorious tested his injured leg. "I don't know," he admitted. "He fled when the battle turned, and the wight-fly was…distracting. I would rather he were safely dead."

"If we were a larger force, I would say that some should go and look for him," said Ounk. "But there are not enough of us to split our forces, nor even to send back to Almondgrove for reinforcements."

"You could go, if you think it's best…" said Summer.

"No. We will go with you to the end," said Ounk, and then she paused, as if waiting for another voice to speak.

Summer watched the realization spread over the goose-guard's face, and then Ounk dropped her head an inch and said, quietly, *"I will go with you to the end."*

The land did not change a great deal. It was the sky that altered as they traveled, changing from blue to a strange, diffuse white, like clouds with no rain in them.

"We are reaching an edge of the world," said Glorious simply.

"I didn't think there was an edge here," said Summer. She tried to picture a map of Orcus in her head, the way that he had described it. "I thought there was a lot more…um…world in the way."

"There is," said Ounk, "but not straight through. There's a gap here and of course it has edges."

"Will we fall in?"

"No, no. There's nowhere to fall. No, it just gets very pale and murky and you don't know which way is sunward any longer. But it's not very big. Even a chick could find their way out again. There's not a hole or a cliff or anything. There's just nothing much *there."*

"Aren't there gaps in your world?" asked Reginald.

Summer had to stop and think about that. Did stuff like the Bermuda Triangle count?

"Not that everybody knows about," she said. "There's stories about places where things disappear. But there aren't edges that you can just walk up to like this."

The weasel peered at the sky and scowled. "I don't like it," he muttered.

When they camped that night, the sky was dark gray. If the sun came up, it did so on the other side of the whiteness.

Oddly enough, there were trees growing here. They were low, scruffy trees, much like the ones in the badlands that they had left behind, but instead of pines and mesquite, they had broad leaves to soak up every bit of the vague edge-light. It looked like a jungle of broadly spaced houseplants, but none were more than ten feet high, and most of them were darkly colored. They moved through leafy shadows and stripes lay over Glorious's fur like a tiger.

And then, quite suddenly, they emerged from the brush onto a hillside, and they saw their journey's end at last.

The palace of the Queen-of-Chains was made of paper.

It thrust up above the hillside like a pale fist. Summer's first thought was that it was made of newspaper somehow—*that makes no sense, there are no newspapers in Orcus, or if there are, I've never seen one*—because it was the pale, mottled gray of newsprint.

Then she saw the cloud surrounding it, millions of tiny black shapes swirling overhead, and their chained wasp strained at the leash and she knew.

It was a wasp nest.

"How…" Reginald stopped and swallowed. "How many wasps d'you think are in there?"

Glorious shook his head.

"Millions," said Ounk. She jammed the butt of her spear against the ground. "They flock as thick as starlings."

"A starling flock that size would be a god," said Glorious.

"Maybe it's a god of wasps," said Summer.

She felt strangely detached. Part of her, the part that cowered away from bees, that flailed in a panic at yellow jackets, said, *it is a hive and the things in there will sting you and sting you and sting you…*

Another part did not believe it. It was too large. Wasps did not make nests the size of cathedrals. A god of wasps would be easier to understand, somehow, and gods did not sting you.

The wasp on the string buzzed, straining toward the others. Summer untied it from the bottle with fingers that seemed to belong to someone else.

It flew away, still trailing the string behind it, and was lost in the cloud surrounding the nest.

They went a little closer, and then Ounk stopped.

"'Ware the edge," she said.

They had come to a gash in the earth. Their side of the chasm was higher, and so they had not seen it when they approached. The wasp side was perhaps twenty feet lower.

Glorious turned his head, looking both ways. "I could jump it," he said, "but I could not jump back."

Summer swallowed. On the other side, they would be trapped with the wasp nest.

That's stupid. Wasps can fly. They could get us no matter where we stood.

"There's a bridge," said Reginald.

Summer followed his pointing wing and laughed in disbelief.

The bridge had no handholds. It was a single piece of wood, though it looked more like an immense bark chip than anything else.

They approached it cautiously. You wanted to be cautious, because it seemed that if you breathed too hard, you might send it spinning into the depths.

"There's someone there," said the weasel.

"There wasn't—" Reginald began, and then "Oh, hang it, now there is."

A person…assembled itself…at the end of the bridge. They watched it grow from a low, crawling hump into something larger, and then it turned and looked at them.

Summer swallowed hard. She had met many people in Orcus and many of them were not human. *I am used to this. I am stronger than this. I can handle this.*

A thousand wasps crawled over one another, making a shape some eight feet tall. Sometimes it was roughly human shaped, but the number of arms changed as the wasps moved restlessly back and forth. Sometimes it was a bird or a wolf. Parts broke free and flew, buzzing, to join the main body.

Is there anything under there? Is it all just insects?

Wasps moved on the thing's head, pressing their banded abdomens together, so that suddenly the person had black eyes ringed with gold.

The eye wasps fanned their wings together, and the person seemed to blink.

I will not scream, Summer told herself conversationally. *I will not.*

The lower half of the face broke open and the person's tongue waved its antennae at her.

The voice, when it came, came from all parts of the body.

"Zzzzzzhhhy havvvve youuu commmmme?"

The jaw moved up and down, independent of the voice. That made it a little easier, somehow. She could think of it like a marionette. Marionettes were always a little creepy. *That's all this is. The wasps are moving it. It's not a real person. It's just a puppet.*

It spoke again, the same buzzing rhythm, the vowels more pauses in the buzz than sounds.

Ounk spoke, as formal as a herald bearing her monarch's wishes. "We have come to speak with the Queen-in-Chains."

The wasp puppet bobbed its head. It reached out an arm that got longer and longer (the other arm vanished as it did). The eyes separated and flew down to become fingers and splayed into a hand.

It pointed at Summer.

She knew that it said something but she could not hear it over the roaring in her ears.

What—no—not me—not alone—

It blinked again. The eyelid wings caught the hard blue light of the desert sky and for a moment they flashed turquoise.

…Oh.

She felt as if she had been struck a blow, and yet, she had been braced for it. Baba Yaga had sent her here alone. Her friends had come to see her this far.

The writing on the chamber under her heart said, *I knew it would come to this.*

Still, the blow was harder than she had expected. She took in a breath and could not seem to get it all the way to the bottom of her lungs.

Then she slid down from Glorious's back.

"Steady on," said Reginald. "If you go, we all go."

The wasp puppet shook its head in an exaggerated motion. Its neck grew longer as it did, and for a brief moment its head hovered independent of its body.

"Zzzzzonnnnly hhhhherrrrrr…"

"Do you wish us to fight?" asked Ounk, as calmly as if she were asking the time of day, and not *do you wish us to die?*

Glorious vibrated with a growl that could not be heard over the buzzing of the wasps.

"We came here to find the Queen," said Summer. "And they…they don't seem hostile. We should try to keep it that way."

"If you are trapped inside, we will probably not be able to reach you in time," said Ounk.

Glorious snorted. "If we ran now, with all our speed, they could have us all before we made a hundred yards. Let us not pretend that there is any more safety for Summer here than there."

Ounk scowled but did not disagree.

The great wolf turned and put his head on Summer's shoulder. "Go well, Summer-cub," he said. "And if we do not meet again in this life, let us meet in another with no regrets."

Summer leaned her cheek on Glorious's muzzle and said, very quietly, "I wish I were a wolf."

"If you were one of my cubs," said Glorious, just as quietly, "I would be glad to claim you."

He licked her forehead. She straightened her back.

"Dash it!" said Reginald. "Oh—blast! This shouldn't be happening!"

"But it is," said Summer. She swallowed. "It may be fine," she said. "I'll…I'll talk to the Queen and come back. If she's willing to meet with me, maybe that's a good sign."

"Blast!"

Ounk bowed to her as she passed.

The weasel squirmed furiously. "I'm coming with you," he growled. "Baba Yaga sent me with you, and I'm not leaving now. *They* can only sting me. She'll do something *nasty.*"

His weight made her pocket a tiny bit heavier, but Summer felt a very, very little bit lighter.

The wasp puppet did not object. It turned and walked across the bridge—though it couldn't really be said to walk. All the wasps flew forward at the same speed and so it moved, mostly upright, without any motion of legs or arms.

The bridge was sturdier than it looked.

Well, it would have to be!

It was definitely bark, though, a great slab of bark from some tree so large that it made the giant sequoias of Summer's world look like saplings. There were holes in it as big as Summer's two fists, and it occurred to her, about halfway across, that they were made by woodworms, and woodworms that size would be—

No. Don't think about that.

She had to watch where she stepped because of the holes, and that was good. It meant that she was not looking at the back of the wasp puppet.

On the far side she stopped and looked up and back at her friends.

They lined the canyon wall, looking at her. Ounk raised her spear in salute. The valet-flock swirled around Reginald like tiny, agitated planets around their star.

"Zzzz?" said the puppet, looking back at her.

"It's nothing," said Summer quietly. She turned back. "Please take me to the Queen-in-Chains."

Chapter Thirty-One

They toiled up the hillside for a long time. There was a path. *Zultan must come here. And presumably the Queen-in-Chains goes out sometimes too. She did…whatever it was…to the Tower of Dogs.*

Whatever she is.

It had occurred to Summer on some level that there was an excellent chance that the Queen was in fact a giant wasp queen. She couldn't remember if wasps had queens like bees.

The things they teach you in school are so useless! All that time on phonics and presidents and what I really need to know is whether or not wasps have queens!

Even if they didn't in her world, of course, there was no reason that wasps in Orcus had to behave the same way.

She kept following the wasp puppet. She was feeling some emotion that she could not put a name on, something powerful but strange. It was as if she had become so numb with terror that none of her regular emotions were any use, and only this new one was able to get through.

It allowed her to look up the path to the nest and see that the side was covered in a jagged tear that had been patched up, like a paper scar. And she could see, beside it, a perfectly ordinary little wooden door, and it was so normal and so out of place that she wanted to laugh hysterically or cry or sink down to her heels in the dust.

She did none of these things. She walked and the weasel rode with her, and the wasp puppet flew ahead of them like a stormcloud.

There was a second wasp puppet at the door of the hive.

She could look at it more easily now. The trick was to look at the eyes and pretend that they *were* eyes, not the striped bellies of insects.

And don't look at the mouth. The mouth is bad.

"Zzzzaaaarree youuu aaa hhhhherrroooo…"

"I'm sorry," said Summer. Her voice was shaking less than she expected. "Can you please say that again?"

"Zzzzarre youu aa hhhero…?"

"Ah. No," said Summer, thinking of the Forester. *You might become one, I suppose, but I would not wish it on you.* "No, I'm not a hero."

It broke apart.

She took a step back, knowing that if they came for her, there was no point in running. Her throat and her heart and the nerves along the backs of her arms said *we will try to run anyway,* and Summer, still in the grip of her strange new emotion, said *I know.* She found that she loved her heart and her nerves for their willingness to try to save her, even in the face of futility.

A thousand wasps landed on the door and pushed against it, their wings buzzing in unison.

"Zzzzen zzzeee Queen-inn-Chhhainzzz will zzzeee youu…"

Summer did not look at the wasps. She did not look at the door. She lifted her chin resolutely and stepped inside.

⁓

The Queen-in-Chains lived in a cathedral made of wax.

The floor crunched strangely underfoot. Summer looked down and saw that she was walking on…honey?

It was thin and red and had gone to crystals. Dust lay thickly over it. It felt like coarse sand beneath her feet.

In places, it had dripped from the ceiling and formed lumpy pillars and piles across the floor. One side of the floor rose up to meet the roof, giving the entire nest a tilted look. Summer felt as if she were standing at a slant.

Is…is the Queen even in here? Is anyone here?

Despite the constant hum of wings, the cathedral felt very still. It was a deliberate stillness, like a library, and it seemed to swallow up the sound. As if the idea of stillness was stronger than the motion of the wasps.

  Summer in Orcus

Summer looked around, then up. The ceiling was a fantastic construction of wax and paper and honey. Could the Queen be up there?

The floor moved.

There was a vast crackling sound as wax and crystalized honey broke apart, and the Queen-in-Chains turned her head.

She was a dragon.

Her body was a mass of lines and lumps and at first Summer could not make sense of it, and then she realized that under the wax lay chains: dozens, hundreds, chains as thick around as Summer's chest, chains as narrow as a strand of hair.

Summer stood rooted to the spot with dragonfear. Her tongue pressed against the roof of her mouth. In the back of her mind, in the chambers of her heart, she was a tiny animal in the undergrowth, and a predator moved overhead.

The dragon could move her head only a few inches. Metal wrapped her muzzle and wax and honey had sealed her eyes shut.

She opened her mouth an inch or two, setting the chains rattling, and said, "I cannot see you."

Summer drew in a deep, gagging breath, and then another. The dust was thick and she was not sure if she would choke on it first, or on the fear.

The dragon's voice was quiet and surprisingly high pitched, with a hiss of breath under it.

Wasps began to land on the dragon's closed eye. They picked at the crystalized honey and chewed away at the wax. Summer stood and breathed and her racing heart slowed while the wasps cleared the film from around the Queen's eyelids.

She can't get me. She's chained down. Someone's chained her down. Of course. She's the Queen-in-Chains. It must have been Zultan, he must keep her chained up here, but why would he, she's a dragon, she could burn everything, not just set little fires, he was afraid of a wolf *and he's got a* dragon—

"Why are you chained up?" croaked Summer.

"Ahhhhhh…" The Queen shivered. There were more crackles of wax and rattling chains. The wasps rose up for an instant in a buzzing cloud, then settled back down to their task of cleaning.

"Did…did Zultan do this?"

"Yesssss…" breathed the Queen and the hiss was louder now. Summer could smell the dragon's breath. It smelled of honey and sulfur and wax.

She had read all the fairy tales in the library. She knew how the stories went. It was utterly mad and she knew it was mad—*positively dicked in the nob*, Reginald would say—and she said it anyway.

"If I set you free, will you stop sending wasps to sting the wondrous things?"

The dragon screamed.

It was a shrill, childlike scream, backed by a dragon's lungs. Summer took a step back, horrified, and the sound struck the paper walls and wax and died away without echoes.

"No!" sobbed the dragon, thrashing as well as it could in the confines of the chain. "No, no, you can't! Don't touch them! Don't unlock them! *Don't touch me!*"

"I won't!" said Summer. "I won't if you don't want me to!"

This had not been in any fairy tale she had ever read.

"Odds and eggs," whispered the weasel in her pocket, "it's scared!"

He's right.

The dragon is frightened.

The dragon is frightened of…me?

It made no sense. It was like being told that a skyscraper feared a snail. The dragon was vast, impossible, ancient, built on the scale of whales and mountains. It would take a hero to slay one.

I would not wish that on you, the Forester had said, and Summer understood why at last. How monstrous a thing it must be, to be that hero. Like being the wasp that stung the Frog Tree to death. To be so small and to singlehandedly unmake a great and wondrous thing.

Summer was an eleven-year-old girl with her hair in tangles and her shoelaces untied. She felt tiny and fragile and…young.

"I'm not a hero," she said. She said it to reassure herself as much as the dragon, but the dragon quieted.

The wasps pulled away from the Queen's eye and she blinked.

The eye underneath was gigantic. It was easily as big as Glorious when he curled himself up.

It was hazel-brown with flecks of green, and it looked human, and that was impossibly wrong in that great draconic head, which should have had eyes like a lizard, eyes like—

—*the Forester*—

Memories crowded back. A story told around a fiery hedgehog. A woman with dragon's eyes in a human body. *How did I forget? How did I ever forget?*

"You're the one," said Summer. "You're the girl that took the dragon's body. You're a human, like me."

The eye rolled, and Summer learned what very few humans of her world would ever know, that the whites of a dragon's eyes are nearly gold and they glow like foxfire in the dark.

"How did you know?" cried the dragon, and this the wasps took up— *hhhhow hhhoww hhhhhow*—in a terrible sibilance from all directions, reflecting the terror of the Queen-in-Chains.

Wasps began to land on Summer's shoulders, their stingers poised above her skin. The weasel in her shirt pocket became utterly still, but she could feel his heart racing through the thin fabric.

"I met the dragon," said Summer. She didn't dare swat at the wasps, for fear that they would sting. She looked in the dragon's frightened human eye and determinedly did not look at the wasps.

If I don't look at them, I won't panic. If I don't panic, I'll be okay. She could feel the panic coiled in her chest, waiting to spring, but she jammed it down into the hidden room and wrote, *I WILL STAY CALM* across the walls.

"It's all right," she said. "I mean, she's all right. She isn't mad."

The dragon shuddered again. "Mad," she said hoarsely. "Mad! She should thank me. This body…this horrible body…you don't know. Oh god! Why did you wake me? I want to sleep. *Why won't they let me sleep?*"

And suddenly, like a bone snapping back into the socket, Summer understood.

She did not know why the Queen did not want to be unchained. She did not know how Zultan had gotten the chains on her in the first place. She did not know why the Queen couldn't sleep.

But she understood at last why, out of all the girls in the world, Baba Yaga had come to her back gate and sent her in search of her heart's desire.

She was not a hero. She could not snap a man's throat out like a wolf, nor soar through the air like a bird. But there was one thing that she could do well.

She sat down cross-legged on the floor of the cathedral, very carefully, so as not to startle the wasps on her shoulders.

"It will be all right," she said to the Queen-in-Chains. "What's wrong?"

"It's the dragon," said the Queen in Chains. "This terrible dragon. I was so small before. I lived in the city, in the temple city…I think it must have been far from here, I don't know. I was young. The things they did—no, I won't tell you!"

"It's all right," said Summer. "You don't have to." Her voice only shook a little when she said it, as she tried not to think of what the dragon might mean.

"A woman needed to get into the temple. I knew the side door. It was by the trash-heaps. I hid there most days. I could get her in. She offered me a gift. She wore a headdress but she had horns like a demon. She meant to kill the ones inside. What did I care? I took the gift. It was a wish tied up in cord and alligator skin. I wished to be a dragon."

Summer nodded. It would not have occurred to her to ask why someone would make a wish like that. Such wishes were entirely sensible, if you did not know what they would lead to.

"Then I was here," said the Queen-in-Chains. She made a hissing, keening noise, and Summer bit her lip, because she had not known until that moment that dragons could not cry. "In this body. Oh god! It was terrible. It wanted to kill and fight and burn and I was so small, I couldn't stop it. I burned everything around me. I burned the city. I smashed stones until I had ground half a mountain away and even a dragon would be exhausted. And I fell down and slept and when I woke up again I was hungry and I ate…I ate everything…cows…people…" She opened her mouth as far as the chains would let her and keened again.

"It's all right," said Summer, even though it wasn't and perhaps never would be again. Her part in this play wasn't to tell the truth, it was only to be soothing.

"If the dragon is very tired, I'm almost big enough to control it," said the Queen. "It doesn't think. It just kills and is hungry. I made it go fishing." She gave a hiccupping laugh. "If you dive very deep, it's easy to get tired. I crawled out on the beach. I slept. Sleep is good. But then you wake up. I don't want to wake up and burn the world. I just want to sleep for a thousand years. Forever if I can."

"That's why you're chained up," said Summer slowly, understanding. "So you don't get out and burn things."

The Queen nodded until the chains clanked together like bells. "I asked," she said. "I was exhausted and I wanted to sleep and the dogs found me. They didn't kill me. They thought I was a real dragon and I told them… you have to tell the dogs when they ask you…it's their eyes. And then they asked what they could do, and I said chain me up, don't let me do this again. And I slept and when I woke, I was chained down and the dragon couldn't break free."

She closed her eye and shuddered with remembered joy. "It was… *wonderful…*"

The cathedral was silent for a long time. The wasps on Summer's shoulders lifted off and settled along the dragon's spine. Summer felt her stomach unknot just a little.

"What happened next?" she asked finally.

"Zultan," said the Queen mournfully. "Zultan came. He unchained me. I begged him not to. He knew what would happen. But he said that if I took down the Tower, he would chain me up again and let me sleep. He fed me first. The body ate them. It wasn't me. I didn't want to!"

"I know," said Summer, as the Queen's voice rose to a wail. "I know you didn't."

"Once it wasn't hungry, I could follow him," said the Queen dully. "It wasn't far away. The Tower of Dogs. I tried not to. They'd helped me. The ones that ran, I didn't chase. I could do that much. I kept beating the body against the stones. I thought it might get tired. The Tower fell down instead. And then I was tired and I flew back to my chains. When I woke up, Zultan had chained me up again. He said I could stay chained until he needed me again." She shuddered.

"Why not kill him instead?" asked Summer. She was amazed at how calm her voice was, suggesting someone's death.

"Then there would be no one left to chain me," said the dragon. She shuddered. "I have to stay chained. It's the only way. The body doesn't really wake up, you know. It's mostly asleep now. But if they come off, it flies—it burns—I burn—"

She has trapped herself in a prison that will never grow old, the Forester had said.

"Where did the wasps come from?" asked Summer.

"They found me," said the Queen. "My friends. They needed a queen. They swarmed from another place…somewhere else…a narrow place between worlds. Oh, I don't understand it all! But they came and they built on top of the remains of my prison."

"They're poisoning things," said Summer, fighting to keep her voice steady. "Out in the world. Great things. Wondrous things."

The dragon shifted. Dust and wasps moved through spots of light on the floor.

"I know. I asked them to do it," said the Queen-in-Chains.

Chapter Thirty-Two

Summer swallowed several times. Her tongue felt dry. She wished that she had brought some water.

She thought about how thirsty she was very determinedly, so that she would not scream at the dragon. The dragon who was wretched and pitiable and who had been destroying the world.

When she thought that she could speak again without yelling, she licked her lips and said, "Why did you ask them to sting things?"

"Only big things," said the dragon. "Only magic. Only things that Zultan might want destroyed. If they're gone, he doesn't need me. When they're all gone, he'll let me sleep."

Summer counted to ten in her head. "They aren't just destroying dangerous things," she said. "They're stinging anything big and magic. There's a tree that makes frogs, and a giant turtle, and a cactus city."

"If the wasps don't do it, I will," said the dragon simply. "He'll make me. And my body will burn cities and eat the people, even the ones like I was, the little ones in trash-heaps and the ones who just want to get away, even the dogs who helped me. This way, some of them survive." She closed her eye again.

"If we stopped Zultan for you—" began Summer, with no idea how she would do such a thing, or if it was even possible to do so.

"If not him, then another," said the dragon. "Someone will come. Someone will find me and take off my chains."

"You could tell the wasps to keep them out," said Summer. Astonishingly, she found herself getting annoyed at the dragon's cowardice.

I shouldn't be. It must be terrible to have a body that goes mad and destroys things. Chaining herself up is responsible. She's doing the best she can do.

But the best she could do had her poisoning every wondrous thing, so she's not exactly blameless!

"It will be over soon," said the Queen. "When all the magic's gone, it'll be over. No one will need a dragon then. I can sleep. Really sleep. Not like this, where I keep waiting for the sound of a key in the lock." She shuddered.

Summer shifted her weight, and her jeans pulled a little, and she felt the objects in her pocket poke against her skin.

Waiting for the sound of a key in the lock…

She reached into her pocket and drew out the lock to the garden gate.

This is mad. This is stupid. *It's a little tiny lock. Zultan could probably snap it with his bare hands.*

"What is that?" asked the Queen.

"It's a lock," said Summer.

But it isn't about the lock, is it? This is about the Queen. The wasps could stop Zultan easily, I bet. And if not—well, we'll find a way to stop him. The important thing is that the Queen thinks she's safe.

"Where is the key?" whispered the Queen, and the wasps dropped from the ceiling and repeated the question with their wings…*whhhhhere isss isss isss the keyyy…*

"There is no key in this world," said Summer.

The chains shook as the Queen trembled.

"If you call back the wasps," said Summer, "I will lock your chains."

There was movement behind the Queen. Two great shapes formed out of the wasps, puppets nearly as large as the dragon. They looked like nothing Summer recognized. Things, perhaps, from a narrow space between worlds.

They blinked their great winged eyes and…nodded.

It had never occurred to Summer in her wildest dreams that perhaps the wasps themselves had no desire to destroy the wondrous things.

She said the wasps are her friends. Maybe they're doing this for their *friend. Can they think like that? If they're all together like this?*

Are they like the valet-flock somehow?

In her mind's eye she saw the chasm and the swirling and heard her friend say, "A flock of starlings that big would be a god."

The Queen-in-Chains closed her eyes. "Will I be able to sleep?"

Summer opened her mouth, not sure how to answer, and the wasps spoke.

"Yyyyessssssss…sssssleeeeep…"

Summer closed her mouth again.

The wasp puppets leaned down and stroked the dragon with hands made of insects. "Ssssssleeeep…" they said. "Ffffriennnnnd…ssssleeep…"

Summer held up the lock.

"Will it work?" whispered the dragon.

"Baba Yaga sent me," said Summer. And that was true, even if it did not answer the question.

She had learned, many years ago, that all you really needed was to sound comforting, when the other person wanted so very much to be comforted.

A wasp landed on her palm. It was very large, much larger than the one they had followed. It looked at her with ruby eyes. Its stinger was longer than her thumb.

Summer bowed her head to the wasp.

It reached out with two striped legs and plucked the padlock from her fingers.

The hive went quiet. The humming of wings stilled, as if they held their breath.

In the vast silence of the cathedral, Summer listened to the wasp fly almost silently over the dragon's back. It landed on the great mass of chains.

Another wasp joined it. Her angle was too low to see what they did, but she heard the sound of metal rasping metal, and then, very quietly…

Click.

The wasps led her out of the cathedral. She stumbled once on the uneven ground and they caught her held her upright, a grip made of hundreds of legs. Summer did not recoil. She, and they, were beyond that.

Had they done it? Had she and the wasps quieted the Queen-in-Chains?

The wasps released her halfway down the slope. She looked up at the wasp-puppet and it blinked at her once, slowly.

"Will it be all right?" she asked.

The wasp-puppet fell apart into a cloud that buzzed around her, and in the cloud she heard "zzzzall rrrrightzzzz…"

Mimicry? Or promise?

The cloud of wasps flew back to the paper nest. The light from the pale sky shone on their wings and turned them into ivory and scarlet and gold.

Summer thought, *I have done the best I can. I fixed it for now. I can't fix it forever. That's someone else's job, maybe.*

Don't worry about things you cannot fix.

She turned away and looked down the slope to the chasm.

There was a tall shape on the bridge, and her friends were nowhere in sight.

❧

Zultan's scarred face had gone very red. At first Summer thought that he must be flushed with rage, and then she realized that without his mask, his fragile skin had burned. The white hairs stood out against the scarlet like snow.

He did not look angry. He looked very calm, though he was swaying a little, but perhaps that was simply the motion of the bridge.

"What did you do with my friends?" demanded Summer, standing at the edge of the bridge.

"I did nothing," said Zultan. "They hared off chasing someone else without any help from me."

"The antelope woman," said Summer, almost inaudibly.

Even with his ruined ears, Zultan's hearing was better than human. He nodded.

"She hates you, you know," said Summer.

"Oh, I know." Zultan smiled. "She would not have given me this wretched half-immortality if she did not hate me. But I provide so many opportunities for mischief, she can't help herself. And it gave me a chance to catch up on my reading."

"You've got to stop using the Queen like this," said Summer savagely. "She'll stop killing everything if you stop bothering her!"

"Is that what she told you?" Zultan shook his head. "I haven't un-chained her for years. Not since I had her melt the stones around the last enclave of dogs. Though I suppose time is fleeting to a dragon."

"I promised her you wouldn't bother her any more," said Summer.

If it troubled him to be standing on a bridge in the middle of a chasm, with the wind hissing through his thinning fur, he showed no sign. "That was a rash promise," he said. "I have been thinking that the birds are getting

entirely too full of themselves. It may be time to finally unleash the queen again, and burn their foolish little roosts down around them."

He's trying to scare me, thought Summer, and then, *and succeeding, thank you very much!*

"You can't," said Summer. "The wasps will stop you. They didn't understand before, but they do now." She hoped very much that this was true.

Zultan gazed over her head at the wasp nest palace. "Hmm," he said.

One does not confront a murderer who has chased you across the world and expect them to say "Hmm," in quite that tone. Summer found, underneath all the terror and anger, that she was also rather nonplussed.

"Well, that's inconvenient," he said.

Summer didn't know what to do. Charge at him and try to knock him off the bridge? Ask him to move out of the way? Stall and hope that her friends came back?

He lowered his milky eyes. "So apparently you are my doom after all. I should probably have killed you when I had the chance, but one hates to do anything irrevocable without considering the options."

Summer had no idea what to say to that. "I wouldn't have been your doom if you hadn't chased me!"

Zultan shook his head. "It wasn't I who led you here," he said. "A wasp on a string! I could hardly believe it."

He was watching us. After Grub—after Ankh—he followed us. Him and the antelope woman.

"I'll take the blame for not killing you," said Zultan, "but chasing wasps was all your doing."

"They were poisoning things," said Summer. "Because of you!"

Zultan listened while she explained, with increasing fury, about the motives of the Queen-in-Chains.

"So it was your fault that so many wonderful things died! Your fault about the Frog Tree and the Great Pipes and the giant turtle!"

The old dog looked over her head to the wasp palace again. "Fascinating," he said. "I see now why a crone got involved. So many unintended consequences…"

Summer risked a look behind her, hoping that the wasps were still there, but they had retreated to the nest. Even the buzzing seemed muted.

Zultan shook himself. "And now here we are. My doom and I, meeting on a bridge. You without your wolf and your birds, and I without even a single guard or a mount to my name."

Summer took a step back from the bridge. He raised a hand. "Peace, my doom. I have very little strength left, I am afraid. The trouble with wight-liquor is that when you no longer have it, it takes back all the strength that it gave you."

Summer inhaled sharply and took another step back.

Zultan laughed softly. He took a step forward himself, and staggered. For a moment Summer thought he would fall, and she reflexively stepped forward, and then her brain got in control of her instincts and drove her back again. *What are you doing!?*

"Don't worry," he said. "I am not about to split my skin and turn on you. It does not take my people the same way. My flesh is riddled with wight-flukes, but they cannot grow in my flesh, so they die. Horrible, isn't it?"

"That seems like a very bad way to stay alive," said Summer.

"It is not the best. But I did finish a great many books, you know." He sighed. "It's a shame, really. If I had killed you before, I might have gotten through the last few. But then again, if I had killed you before, then I would not have known about the wasps poisoning the world. And perhaps Grub would have slipped his leash and killed me and tried to milk the last cursed drops out of my blood." He lifted his shoulders and let them drop again wearily.

There was a speck in the air far above. Summer glanced at it out of the corner of her eye. Did it have a hoopoe's crest?

Zultan took another few steps forward and went down to one knee against the end-post of the bridge. His breathing was ragged.

"The end is taking me quicker than I wished," he admitted. "Will you give a little comfort to a dying dog, my doom?"

Summer stared at him.

He reached out his hand. His blunt fingers flexed inside the black gloves.

"Take my hand," he said, "and promise that you'll never forgive me."

She did not want to. She knew that it was beyond foolish. She knew that it was mad.

She knew that Baba Yaga would have done it.

She took his hand.

"Never," she whispered. It was easy to promise. Her heart was full of the rotting shreds of the Great Pipes and the polished shell of the dead turtle and the smell of a wheat field decaying in the sun.

Zultan Houndbreaker's breath went out in a long sigh.

"Thank you, my doom," he said, and she believed that he truly meant it.

And then he grinned up at her with his broken teeth and his hand turned in hers and he grabbed her wrist.

"And now," he said, "I shall rectify my last mistake," and he yanked her toward the edge of the chasm.

Chapter Thirty-Three

Summer thrashed and tried to pull away. But he was not trying to throw her off the cliff, he was falling backwards and determined to take her with him.

He weighed less than she expected, less than Glorious, as if the wight-flukes had riddled his bones and left them hollow. Perhaps they had. For a moment, as she threw all her weight against him, they swayed, balanced, on the edge of the abyss.

She saw a brown blur of motion before she quite registered the feeling of something moving against her chest. The weasel exploded out of her pocket and launched himself down her arm.

He sank his teeth into Zultan's exposed wrist.

The dog did not cry out but his fingers spasmed. Summer wriggled away, bent her hand back at an angle that only a nearly-twelve-year-old girl could manage—and slipped free.

Zultan and the weasel went over the edge without a sound.

She staggered backward, tripped, and sat down hard.

No! No! *Weasel—!*

Something flashed past her, orange and black, not even bothering to fly, just to fall.

"Bloody eggshells!"

"Reginald!" screamed Summer, throwing herself flat against the ground. "*Reginald—!*"

Ounk slammed down next to her. In other circumstances, the landing might have been comical, since she didn't bother with her feet, just belly flopped onto the stone beside her. "Summer! Summer, are you hurt?"

"The weasel—Reginald—"

Goose and girl peered over the edge of the bridge.

Slowly, with labored wingbeats, the hoopoe flew back upward. His crest was flat against his head and his waistcoat was in tatters.

He landed beside them, took a deep breath, and said, *That was my last good cravat, you little devil!*"

The weasel crawled out of the folds of his neckcloth. His fur stood up in all directions like an angry cat. He stalked over to Summer, plunked himself down on her knee, and began to groom himself furiously.

"You're alive," said Summer. "You're alive!"

She picked him up and hugged him until he nipped her. "Yes, I am, but not if you don't quit squeezing! And what in the name of Baba Yaga's backside were you doing, taking his hand like that?"

"I thought he was dying," said Summer.

"Dying! Feh! A proper weasel-war-dance he did on you, and you went for it like a rabbit." He sniffed. "Could admire the artistry if I hadn't just been snatched out of the air by a feathered fop who doesn't trim his claws."

"Bacon-brained cravat-worrier!" said Reginald. "Anyway, you're welcome."

"Hmmph. Yes, well."

The weasel looked surly again, and Summer kissed him on top of his head, which made him scowl furiously through his whiskers.

"Where's Glorious?" she asked.

"A little way back on the canyon rim," said Ounk. "The antelope led us quite a chase, and then we found her sitting on a rock. He said we'd been played for fools and told us to come back to you on the instant. I only wish we'd made it sooner."

"And Zultan…"

"I wouldn't look," said Reginald. "It's…well, I wouldn't look. But he's stuck his spoon so far in the wall that no amount of magic would get it back out, if you take my meaning."

"No one ever takes your meaning," groused the weasel.

"Good," said Summer. "Good."

"And the Queen-in-Chains?" asked Ounk.

Summer looked over her shoulder. The wasp nest hummed, but very softly. A buzz like a lullaby, like something winding down.

"She's with friends now," said Summer. "Let's go find Glorious."

⌇

They heard the antelope and the wolf long before they saw them. A thin, atonal music pierced the air, and when they arrived, they found the antelope woman sitting cross-legged on a rock, playing the flute.

Glorious was standing, staring at her, with his fur erect and a low growl in his chest.

"Don't worry," said the antelope, lowering the flute. "It's not magic. It won't put you to sleep." She looked at Summer. "Hmm. I didn't expect you to survive Zultan, I admit."

"Zultan," said Reginald, "did not survive *her.*"

Summer's hands clenched into fists at her sides. Not for herself any longer—but for the Queen.

"It was you," she said. "It was you who gave her the wish. The woman with a headdress with horns. That was *you.*"

The antelope woman laughed. "You give me far too much credit," she said. "That was one of my grandmother's sisters. Or perhaps one of my great-grandmother's sisters. I'm not sure of the exact timing. But yes, it was an antelope. And she paid for that trick with her life, when the dragon burned the city down." She blew a few thoughtful notes on the flute. "Entirely worth it. Giving something that powerful to the utterly powerless always causes chaos. We will dance in her honor at the end of the world."

She put down the flute and scrambled to her feet. "Yours too, perhaps, child."

Summer's eyes narrowed. "Don't. Just…don't."

"Oh, that wasn't a lie," said the antelope woman. "We'll do a dance for all the ones we've used. It's the least we can do."

She laughed then, and as much as Summer hated her, she could not help but feel a stab of admiration for someone who would laugh so freely with a wolf growling at her feet.

"Can we tie her up?" asked Summer. "Take her to…to somewhere?"

Ounk shook her head slowly. "I don't think it's safe," she said. "For us, I mean."

Summer knew what she meant. Even if they weighted her down in as many chains as the Queen, if the antelope woman could talk, she would be impossibly dangerous. What authority in Orcus could they turn her over to?

She thought briefly of the practical thrush, the Prime Minister of the Dawn Chorus. Perhaps she could handle an antelope woman…but Summer did not think that they could find a way to get her there.

"Glorious?" asked Summer.

"I could tear out her throat," said Glorious.

"Go ahead," said the antelope cheerfully. "The taste of my blood will give you dreams like no wolf has ever had. If you think being a house is bad, imagine being a house haunted by my ghost."

"You're lying again," said Summer.

"Probably." The antelope woman lifted the flute to her lips. "Go home, innocent," she said. "This world is no place for you." She began to play again.

Summer wanted to say something. She wanted to think of some unbelievably scathing thing that would tear the antelope woman's heart the way her own was torn. She wanted to get the last word.

She turned and walked away. The thin, pulsing music of the flute chased her as she walked, and she was careful not to breathe in time with it. She did not want to give the antelope woman even that last small victory.

A little time later, there was hot breath on the back of her hand, and she stopped and put her leg over Glorious's back. The weasel grumbled in her pocket. They rode out of the edge lands with Reginald and the goose-guard overhead.

⚬

It seemed to go faster coming back than it had taken going.

"It's always the way," said Reginald. "You've done it once, you know all the shortcuts."

"Wolves say that your paws have already smoothed down the path," said Glorious.

"Also, we're going straight back to Almondgrove," said Summer, feeling like the practical one for once, "and I'm *not* getting kidnapped at the Great Pipes."

"Well, there's that, too."

They gave the Pipes a wide berth. They did stop at Arrowroot, a small town populated by birds and built on floating platforms in a marshy lake. Frogs sang from the cat-tails and hundreds of lanterns floated in the water. It was wonderful, but it was a small, person-sized wonder that the birds had built themselves. Summer was surprised at how cheering that was.

They stayed in Arrowroot for several days. Glorious left them at night, saying that he wanted to sit alone with moonlight on his eaves. Summer watched the lanterns in the evening and slept in a circular nest of blankets, and slowly her thoughts settled inside her.

Even so, she woke up on the third night with her heart pounding and the bluebottle buzz of the Grub-fly in her ears, and she thought, *I want to go home.*

The next morning, as they rode away from Arrowroot with the frogs singing madrigals in the marsh, she added, *At least for a little while.*

At Almondgrove Manor, they were ushered into Reginald's father's study—all of them, including Glorious—and they told the old hoopoe the story, all of them starting and stopping and stumbling over one another's words.

He wept a little for Ankh. When Summer told him about Zultan's face, he only bowed his head.

"They were a great people," he said sadly. "I wish you could have known one other than Zultan. But that would have to be in another world than this. Perhaps their time is over in Orcus."

In the end, he promised to speak to the Prime Minister about the wasp palace. "I'd set a guard," he said, "but I am afraid that would only call attention. Perhaps it is better that the place passes out of memory forever."

Summer woke again from nightmares that night, but this time it was Zultan's face she saw, and his broken teeth smiling down at her.

She expected there to be a funeral for Ankh—something lavish and elaborate, the way the ball had been.

Instead, the Lord Almondgrove and Ounk and Reginald met her in a far corner of the fields, while Glorious watched from the trees. "No offense meant, you know," said Reginald, "but we don't want to scare them off. It's bad manners."

"None taken," said the wolf.

They lit a very small fire and waited.

It did not take long. One by one, vultures appeared in the air, circling, and one by one they landed. They were very large, as large as the goose-guards, and their heads were dark gray, painted with thick charcoal lines. Their wings were unrelieved black.

One shuffled forward, hopping along on feet with claws like coffin-nails.

Ounk stepped forward to meet him. She held out the head of Ankh's spear.

"There is no body," she said.

The black vulture nodded.

He took three more hopping steps, with the spearhead tucked up against his body, and then he flew. The other vultures rose as well and began to spiral up into the air.

"We will leave a cow out for them tomorrow," said Lord Almondgrove. "They will come for anyone—rich or poor, small or great. They do not require payment. It is the bargain. But we can give more, so we will."

"If…if there was a body…" began Summer.

"They would take that instead."

She asked no more questions.

It was hard to leave Almondgrove. It was harder still to leave Ounk, who was taking up her duties again.

"I'm sorry," said Summer, burying her face in the goose-guard's feathers. "I'm sorry! If you hadn't…if she hadn't…"

"It isn't yours to apologize for," said Ounk. "My sister was an Imperial Goose. It is what we do." She draped her wing over Summer's shoulders. "When you are as close as eggs in a nest, you cannot be separated merely by death. I must simply speak for her as well as myself. That's all."

In the end, it was the same group that went back through Fen-town that had passed through before: Reginald and Glorious, Summer and the weasel, the flock of valet-birds twittering around them. Had it only been weeks? It felt like centuries.

For the first time in a long while, it occurred to Summer to worry about time passing.

It can't have been weeks in my world, thought Summer. *Orcus must be like Narnia, where only a little time passes. Otherwise…*

Don't worry about things you can't fix.

She rubbed her thumb over the acorn in her pocket. There was one last thing to be fixed, and then, perhaps, she could go home.

Summer was not entirely sure that they were on the right road until she saw the Wheystation ahead of them. It was dark inside, and there was a sign on the door saying, "Closed For The Season."

She left the cheese-sword on the front step. Her mother would never let her keep it, and while there were some things she might hide in her room, a sword was *not* among them.

They waited until nightfall to cross the desert. The scorpion stars came out and they went single-file across the sand.

Boarskin met them in the shadow of the tallest hill. She looked from Summer to the wolf to Reginald, and her eyebrows climbed up her forehead.

"You lived," she said. "And brought friends with you!"

Summer nodded. "We did it," she said. "At least, I think we did it. Is…" She swallowed, almost afraid to ask now that it came to the end. "Is the Frog Tree still there?"

Boarskin bowed her head. "Come with me."

They followed her. Glorious lifted his head once, looking around, and said, "I smell shapechanger."

"My sisters," said Boarskin. "Donkeyskin fears your teeth, and Bearskin stayed to guard her."

"And you do not?"

Boarskin laughed. "I no longer fear anyone's teeth," she said, and Glorious laughed as well.

When they reached the Frog Tree, though, there was no more laughter.

The leafless crown had cracked and fallen. Now there was only a trunk, taller than Summer, with a great jagged gash in it.

"Lightning struck a few weeks ago," said Boarskin quietly. "It might have survived even that, if it was healthy, but now…"

Summer slipped off the wolf's back and walked forward.

Black, charred wood edged the gash. Inside, Summer smelled the familiar rot of the wasp's poison. Tiny insects swirled around it, chewing at the tree's dead heart.

"No," she said, and she realized that she was weeping. "*No.*"

She dropped to her knees and put her arms over her head.

"Summer—" said Reginald, but Glorious said, "Wait."

"Too late," whispered Summer. "All this time, and it was too late. Ankh died and the people at the inn died and the valet-birds died, all so we could be too late?"

As soft as a breath, something touched her hair.

She lifted her head.

The Frog Tree's dryad lay curled on its side next to her. It could only just lift its hand, but it gave her the faintest, most tremulous of smiles, and pointed at her pocket.

Summer pulled out the acorn and offered it to the dryad with trembling fingers.

The dryad touched the earth between them. Summer could see through its flesh as if it were made of glass.

"Here?" said Summer. "Do you want me to plant it?"

It nodded.

She scrabbled at the dirt with her hands, terrified that she would not dig deep enough. Reginald came in beside her and said, very quietly, "'Scuse me, your Tree-ness, but I think I'm better at this," and raked at the dirt with his clawed feet.

The dryad smiled.

The smile was the last part of it to fade, but fade it did. By the time that the hole was three inches deep, there was only broken bark across the ground, in a pattern of light and shadow that looked a little like a face.

Summer dropped the acorn into the hole that Reginald dug. She started to pile earth over it, and paused.

The carved tadpole wiggled inside the hole and looked up and met Summer's eyes.

It blinked at her, two or three times, and then its wide, froggy face stretched into a smile. It curled up in the hole and closed its eyes and Summer pulled the dirt up over it like a blanket.

The seedling that came out of the dirt seemed to grow like a jerky stop-motion film. It put out two flat pads, like tadpole tails, and then grew taller. A line of buds swelled, then erupted into a spray of true leaves.

Summer dropped back on her heels. Reginald let out a startled laugh.

The first two leaves, the flat round ones, fell off and drifted to the ground.

Summer held her breath.

They shimmered against the earth, and then two tiny green frogs hopped away together into the leaves.

And then, Summer knew, she could finally go home.

Chapter Thirty-Four

I will water it," said Boarskin.

"Will it grow?" asked Summer. "More than it is?"

The shapechanger pushed her hood back. "The tree knew that it was dying, and it put all that was left into the seed, where the poison could not get to it. If any tree in the world will grow, it's that one."

"Better than it would have if there were still wasps poking it," said Reginald cheerfully.

The Frog Sapling had stopped growing visibly at about eighteen inches high. It sat there, looking green and absurd and alive, with the hulk of the dead trunk behind it.

"The rotten tree will fertilize the ground as well," said Boarskin. "Death feeds life and all that."

She hugged Summer tightly. "Thank you. I knew when I saw you— well. Thank you. When you come back again, I hope that it will be growing strong."

They left her with the Frog Tree, and they walked through the woods, past the Mouse Tree and the Horned Toad-Tree, until they came to a set of steps leading down into the ground.

"This is it," she said. "This is where I came in."

Summer stared at the dark entrance to the underground room. The stained glass shone purple along its sides.

She was tired. She had done what she set out to do, and now she was impossibly tired and she wanted to rest for a little while. Her heart was exhausted from looking on marvels.

The thought of her own bed nearly brought tears to her eyes. *I could sleep there. I could sleep and wake up and I'd be in a world where no one has tried to kill me.*

They never told you, in the stories, what a weight that was. In Narnia, you were attacked every few feet and you walked away from it and no one ever said anything more about it. If Peter woke in terror from nightmares about Fenris Ulf, it wasn't written down.

In her own bed, Summer thought, perhaps those nightmares would no longer be able to find her.

But if I go back…what happens? Does Baba Yaga make me forget?

No! I won't! I refuse!

"Go," said Glorious. "Back to your den to heal. We will meet again or we will not. But come back when you are not a cub, and if I am still alive, I will greet you as a wolf."

The weasel rubbed his furry head against her chin.

It was enough. It gave her strength to straighten her shoulders, and to hug Glorious one last time, and to only cry a little.

"Come back when you can," said Reginald. "We'll do the whole season—balls every night and parties and picnics. I'll take you up to Parliament Roost and they'll give you a medal. Two medals. Ten medals!"

"I'd like that," said Summer. The valet-flock twittered and swirled and tucked a few last strands of hair behind her ears.

And then she walked, with her back straight, into the hall of the stained glass saint.

The angels were not moving in their windows. The saint in purple sneakers stood at his initial position, holding the book.

Summer looked up at him, then looked away, and back again. Had she seen…?

Yes.

He winked down at her, under the eyes of the solemn-faced angel.

At the far end of the stained glass corridor was a door, and on the door was a familiar face.

"So you did it, eh?" said the skull. "She'll be pleased, I imagine."

"Did she send me here to stop the Queen-in-Chains?" asked Summer.

It is hard for a severed skull to shrug, but the wood grain around it rippled. "More or less, more or less. And to get your heart's desire, whatever

that was. And maybe to do something else entirely. She doesn't tell me anything. For all I know, you kicked a rock that had to be in exactly the right
place, and everything else was entirely incidental. Baba Yaga sees all the way
through time and chews off the bits she doesn't like."

The door swung open, and Summer stepped inside.

Baba Yaga's house was smaller and darker than she remembered. It still
smelt strongly of bleach, but the only light was from a single candle.

"Come in, child," said Baba Yaga. "You've done well. Better than I
expected."

Summer paused in the doorway. She could see the outline of the crone
in the rocking chair.

"What's wrong, child?"

"I don't want to forget!" blurted Summer. "And you're being kind and
that scares me!"

There was a long, long silence, and then Baba Yaga began to laugh.

It was not a cruel laugh, although it could have been easily. It sounded
like aged bourbon and owl feathers. It was the laugh of a woman enjoying
a joke that she has heard before, but not often. It rolled through the chick-
en-footed house and Summer was comforted, although she couldn't say
why.

"So you learned that much," said Baba Yaga finally, wiping at her eyes.
"That's good. I am much safer when I am wicked, you know." She beckoned. "You're safe enough for now. Next time we meet, you may not be, but
you've earned this one."

Summer came forward, her gaze on the single candle. She could see the
glitter of Baba Yaga's eyes behind it.

It was the frog candle. She had almost forgotten it.

It had burned perhaps two-thirds of the way down. The flame was
bright and strong.

"It didn't burn out," she said, surprised. "It's been days—weeks—I
thought—"

"No," said Baba Yaga. "You did it all quite quickly, all things considered. The frog lasts a season, but I'm not above fudging around with tapers
if it gets the job done."

She adjusted herself in the bone rocking chair. The runners creaked.
"Oh, I suppose it would make a better story if you arrived just as the wick

was falling into the wax. Raise the stakes, they always say. Raise the stakes! We must always have the fate of the world in the balance, never one person's happiness, and we must always arrive at the eleventh hour. No one wants the small stories any more. Bah."

"Did I save Orcus?" asked Summer.

"Orcus never needed saving. You saved the Queen and your friends and made things generally more pleasant for most of the inhabitants."

Summer felt a deep relief at this. She could not have dealt with saving the world. "I saved the Frog Tree," she said, standing up a little straighter.

"Yes. That alone was worth the price of admission."

She nodded. She felt triumph, but there was something complicated under it—sadness, maybe, and a sense of ill-use. "You sent me because I know what to do when someone cries and I tell them it will be okay. Because of my mother."

"Ah…" said Baba Yaga. "Yes. Quite a skill you have at it, too. A great and terrible magic, but not one that a dragon would think to guard against. Perhaps you should not have that skill at your age, but the world is unfair, and sometimes we must use that unfairness to our advantage." She rocked back and forth. "It would be a good day for the world if I could not find a child who knew terrible adult things. But I will be a great deal older before that day comes, I think."

The bone runners creaked on the floor. It seemed to be getting darker in the room, or perhaps Summer had been looking at the candle flame too long.

"I don't want to forget," said Summer. "If you're going to do the thing—the thing they do in books, you know, where you forget everything and it's all like a dream—I don't want that!"

"Are you sure?" Baba Yaga rocked a few times, and her motion made the candle flame flicker. "You want to go through life knowing that there was another world and you went there? And then you'll get a little older and you'll start to think you must have been mad. And if you tell anyone, *they'll* think you're mad. Forgetting's easier."

Summer wrung her hands in the hem of the blanket. The old woman's voice seemed to ring down a long corridor, as long as all the years she would live with no one to believe her.

"I don't want to forget my friends," she whispered.

Baba Yaga rocked in the chair.

"Well," she said, when the silence had grown nearly unbearable. "Well. What is it that you *do* want, then? Ask for what you want, child, or you won't get it."

Summer sat down on the floor. Her legs were trembling. She put her head in her hands. *Ask for what you want.* "I don't know. No, I do know. I want to go home for a little while. And then, maybe when I'm a little older—I—I think I want to go back to Orcus." She thought of her mother with anguish. Her mother was flawed and imperfect and sometimes frightening, but would Summer really be willing to leave her forever, to go to another world?

In the chambers of Summer's heart, there was a word written on the wall, and she was afraid that word was *YES*.

She looked up finally, and saw the firelight gleaming on Baba Yaga's teeth. They were very sharp, and she was grinning.

"Then I grant your heart's desire," said Baba Yaga. "It shall be so. Now blow out the candle and go home."

Summer blinked. "I can go back?"

"Oh, eventually. It'll be a few years, you understand. Things may look a little different."

"But not hundreds of years, like in Narnia, right? Where everyone has died of old age? That would be worse."

"I'm not a monster, child. Or I am, but not a completely unfeeling one." She waved her hand. "All will be well. Or well enough, anyway. With a bit of work."

"Is my mother very upset?" asked Summer.

"She hasn't noticed that you're gone." And when Summer gaped at her, "Oh, don't start. You look like a landed fish. It'd be a poor return for your service to have you go home to that. Your mother's half a madwoman already, and that much grief would push her over the edge completely. And you'd probably have to make up some story about being snatched by someone in a panel van, and the panel van industry has enough problems as it is."

"But I was gone for weeks!"

"Not while the candle burned," said Baba Yaga. "The grass doesn't grow under your feet while the wick is lit. At most she'll think that you've gotten too much sun recently and wonder why she didn't notice before." She waved her hand irritably. "Now get gone! I'm getting hungry."

Summer scrambled to her feet and blew out the candle.

The room was suddenly dark. The weasel moved worriedly in her pocket. She could hear Baba Yaga breathing, a deep sound like a hungry predator.

She found the door by the outline of light around it and pulled it open.

She was in the yard of the house next door.

"Shut me quick!" said the skull, and Summer slammed the door hastily. She could hear something padding around inside the house, something with nails that scratched on the boards like claws.

The house tilted forward on its chicken legs, and Summer stepped down into the alleyway. Then it rose up, up, high-stepping over the wall, and ran away down the alley. A car alarm went off as it stepped too close, and Summer wondered what the owner would think had set it off.

She went very slowly to the gate of her own house. It stood ajar.

Summer set her hand on the latch which no longer had a lock.

If I go in, all of this is over. And I'll be done.

But Baba Yaga said that I could go back. She said it was my heart's desire. Maybe…when I'm older. Maybe my mom will be ready then.

The thought hovered, unvoiced, that a day might come when the door to Orcus opened, and it would not matter who was ready or not.

The weasel climbed out of her pocket and looked around. "Is this where you live?"

Summer jumped. "I can't keep you," she said, horrified. "You're a weasel—my mom won't let me—but I don't want you to go—"

"Pffft!" said the weasel. "This place is lousy with mice and bugs and little birds. And trash cans." He licked his little white teeth. "If I can't find a way to live here, I don't deserve to call myself a weasel."

"You'll stay?" asked Summer.

"For a while at least." He scratched one ear, rapid fire. "I wouldn't object to the occasional egg, mind you."

"And…you'll talk to me? So I know I didn't dream it all?"

The weasel gave her a withering look. "If you suggest it was a dream, I shall bite you."

"Thank you," said Summer, and kissed the weasel on the top of his small brown head.

"Guh," said the weasel, and leapt off her palm. He went up the side of a tree like a squirrel and sat on a branch, glaring. "Now I have to groom *everything.*"

Summer laughed aloud. She felt suddenly very light.

She took off the blanket and folded it under her arm. She'd stash it under her bed later.

The back door opened. Her mother looked out. "Summer? Why's the gate open?"

"I don't know," said Summer. "I think the lock broke."

"You didn't see anyone, did you?"

"No."

Her mother frowned, and Summer could see the worry shadowing her eyes, but as long as she was worried about the lock, she wasn't going to notice the blanket. "You didn't go anywhere, did you?"

"No, mom," said Summer. She came up the back steps two at a time. "Nowhere at all."

⌒

"Well?" said the skull to Baba Yaga, when the crone had finished eating.

"Well, what?" She picked her teeth with a splinter of bone which belonged to a salesman. She did not like people who came around selling textbooks. If he had been more polite, he would have had a chance, but historically no one has ever escaped after trying to put the hard sell on Baba Yaga.

"Will she ever go back to Orcus?" asked the skull.

"Don't ask me the future," said Baba Yaga. "I'm a crone, not an oracle. You start poking about in the future and people start wanting things. For all I know, she'll get run over by a dump truck tomorrow."

The house slammed the shutters down in irritation. The floor tilted and the rocking chair skidded against the table.

"Settle down!" snapped Baba Yaga. She smacked the fireplace with her cane. "I can still trade you in, you know!"

The house stamped its feet. China rattled in the cupboards. Baba Yaga did not eat off china, but she kept a set in the house in case company came over.

"Fine," muttered Baba Yaga. "Yes. She'll get to go back some day. I promised her, didn't I? I keep my promises."

Mollified, the house sat back down.

"You fudged a bit," said the skull. "Her heart's desire was already granted, wasn't it?"

"To find out what she was capable of? To get out from under someone else's fear?" Baba Yaga worried at a bit of gristle with her toothpick. "Oh, perhaps. But it wasn't a *lie*, you know. Hearts are complicated. Hardly anybody wants just one thing."

"You're not going to do anything tricksy to her, are you?" asked the skull suspiciously. "Send her back when she's ninety years old or something?"

"No," said Baba Yaga. "I'm not an oracle, but I'm also not a monkey's paw. Not if you're polite. She'll go back soon enough. When she's a bit older. When it's a bit easier. When Orcus needs her again." She gave a jaw-cracking yawn. "Perhaps after I wake up from a nap."

She leaned back in the rocking chair and closed her eyes. She was always groggy after a big meal.

The house on bird feet rose up and tip-toed carefully away, to find a place where its master could wait, and sleep a little while longer.

Acknowledgments

S*ummer in Orcus* started as a place to put things.

I don't know how other writers do it, but I am constantly coming up with weird little tidbits that don't fit in what I'm currently working on. Images, vignettes, chunks of mini-story that don't fit any coherent narrative. Stuff like Regency birds in waistcoats, migrating houses, albatrosses going through the sun's shadow. Sometimes all I have is a single phrase—*Antelope women are not to be trusted* has been beating around my head for a decade now, and I have been going around trying to shove that phrase into various keyholes, hoping I'll find the story it unlocks.

These ideas pile up. Occasionally I'll rummage around and find one that goes into a story, but there's always so many more weird little tidbits than there is story to put them in. Eventually I started looking for a place to put a great many of them at once, and what with one things and another, that led me to Orcus.

It turned out, once I had Summer and a place to send her, that I had very strong opinions about portal fantasies. (I had always suspected this.) Narnia, mostly. I loved Narnia with a vast, hungry passion as a child and when I finally worked out that it was really about church, I felt betrayed as only children can feel betrayed. (I would shortly afterward seize on *Watership Down,* which was exactly what it was and not an allegory for anything else.) When I went back as an adult and re-read the Narnia books, there were seams and holes and lumpy bits, and I began to pick at them and brood.

They were also so short! I had remembered them being so much longer. Of course, now I sound like that apocryphal diner—"The food was terrible! And such small portions!" In my head, when I was a child, I had filled in so much space between the pages.

I wanted to write a story about a child who I could identify with. And I knew, as I was writing it, that it would be nearly impossible to sell to a children's book publisher because children are often impatient with slow meandering journeys, and very impatient with weakness.

"Why doesn't she stab the spider-horses?" demands nine-year-old me in my head.

"Because stabbing things is hard," I tell her wearily, from thirty years on, where I understand terror and freezing and that a knife is not a light-saber that cuts effortlessly through anything you point it at.

"*I* would have stabbed them," she mutters, and sulks back into my subconscious where she lives.

What could I tell her? That realistically, Edmund would probably wake up screaming at night from the vision of the Christmas squirrels turned to stone by the White Witch? That the smell of sugar and rose-water from Turkish delight would leave him slumped against doorframes outside of candy shops, trying to breathe? That Eustace is the only one who acts remotely like I would really act, and Coriakin the star is a dangerous tyrant and Aravis can do about a thousand times better than Shasta?

I wanted to write a story where someone acted at least a little like I would. I knew that meant that the climax could not be a battle scene. Summer was not going to become a hardened warrior in a few weeks. And we've had plenty of literary battle scenes already and I didn't feel the need to add another one. A scene where someone really listens and tries to reassure someone else…could I do that? Would that work? Would the readers feel cheated or baffled or lost?

It is in my nature to plow forward stubbornly while second-guessing myself at every turn. I plowed forward with *Summer in Orcus*, thinking that I would put it out as a serial and people could read for free and if they hated it, at least they wouldn't be out any money. This meant I'd take a total bath on book sales in the second half of 2016, but I could live on the royalties on the latest Hamster Princess book for a couple months, no problem. And then my patrons on Patreon said "No, we will give you money," and I said "But—" and then money happened and I wrung my hands and said "But what if you hate it?" and more money happened and this made the entire thing far more feasible, even if it did nothing for my nerves.

The best thing about my patrons was that they wanted everyone to read it. They didn't want a story just for them, they wanted to donate money to give a book to the world. And since the year that I am writing to you from was—well, let's say it was a very bad year for the world—because it was a serial, I could put out extra chapters on the worst days so that my readers could get a few minutes away from the news.

It's not often that you get a chance to help people with fiction in real-time. Even if it's just five minutes of respite, even if it's just a weird little story about hoopoes and wolves. So many of us right then felt like we were bailing the tide, like the world was breaking beyond any of our ability to fix. (I hope that when some of you read this, we are in a far happier future.) That my patrons had helped me be at a place, right at that moment, where I could do even this little tiny thing…that was a gift that can't be measured in dollar figures.

For them, and for you, I'm grateful.

T. Kingfisher
Pittsboro, NC
December 2016

Other Works

As *T. Kingfisher*

Nine Goblins (Goblinhome Book 1)
Toad Words & Other Stories
The Seventh Bride
Bryony & Roses
The Raven & the Reindeer

As *Ursula Vernon*

<u>From Sofawolf Press</u>

Black Dogs Duology
    House of Diamond
    Mountain of Iron

Digger Series
    Digger Omnibus Edition

It Made Sense At The Time

<u>*For kids*</u>

Dragonbreath Series
Hamster Princess Series
Castle Hangnail
Nurk: The Strange Surprising Adventures of a Somewhat Brave Shrew

<u>*Anthologies*</u>

Comics Squad: Recess!
Funny Girl
Best of Apex Magazine
The Long List

T. Kingfisher is a pen-name for the Hugo-Award winning author and illustrator Ursula Vernon.

Ms. Kingfisher lives in North Carolina with her husband, garden, and disobedient pets. Using Scrivener only for e-books, she chisels the bulk of her drafts into the walls of North Carolina's ancient & plentiful ziggurats. She is fond of wombats and sushi, but not in the same way.

You can find links to all these books, new releases, artwork, rambling blog posts, links to podcasts and more information about the author at www.tkingfisher.com

9 781936 689590